Praise for *Four Tales of Troubled Love*

"Matthew James Babcock is charming with a poetic bent…. Throughout all the stories there is a push and pull for what love really means. For all those beach readers or book clubs looking for their next read — this is it."

—J Bowen West, *The Times News*

Four Tales
of Troubled Love

Matthew James Babcock

Harvard Square Editions
New York
2019

Four Tales of Troubled Love,
by Matthew James Babcock

Copyright © 2019 Matthew James Babcock

None of the material contained herein may
be reproduced or stored without permission
of the author under International and
Pan-American
Copyright Conventions.

ISBN 978-1-941861-62-2
Printed in the United States of America

Published in the United States by
Harvard Square Editions
www.harvardsquareeditions.org

To my girls and boy
for all the love

and Jim, Eric, Quinn, and Jack
for taking the trouble

and the Four Epiphanic Dews
for all the tales

Contents

Help Phone Thirteen 5

Meer, Tarn, Water, Fell 103

Impressions 143

The Seal 213

Help Phone Thirteen

Reigning with foolish kings
And dying mid bells and wine
Ending with a desperate comic palaver
While before thee and after thee
Endures the eternal clown—
—the eternal clown—

—Stephen Crane

1

As AUGUST WANES and fades over the intersection of Seventeenth Street and Hitt Road, Dee McBride slouches in the passenger seat of his gray Dodge Stratus, chin sunk in his chest. The traffic light glares red. Cars barricade him on all sides. His wife, Reneé, sits in the driver's seat, arranging a fan of Sherwin-Williams sample strips like a poker addict fondling a flush.

"Shaker Sunrise," she says, plucking a paint-strip petal from the bouquet. "Kilmarnock. Dionysian Decadence."

"How about Pink or Yellow?" Dee says.

"Shut," she says, prodding an eyelash with her pinkie, "up."

In the back, Colette and Rae McBride, ages four and almost two, slump in child safety seats like drugged abductees strapped to lab tables. A bacchanal of cherry Icees and Chocodiles from MegaMart's Crazy Days Grand Opening in Ammon has thrown them into sugar comas. Magically, each girl keeps a catatonic grip on a jumbo Pretzel 'n' Cheese stick and a green cactus-shaped balloon. On leaving the store Reneé asked the clown working the crowd—he wore a Mexican bandido getup and a flashy gold name badge that said 'Doogins the Clown'—to give the sisters balloons of the same color so they wouldn't squabble. As he tied the balloons, Doogins gave Reneé a steady stare that made her feel as if he were reading secrets on the back wall of her skull, so she snatched the balloons and hurried away, girls in tow, trying to remember the facial features beneath the man's make up.

"Everything," Dee mutters.

Reneé inhales sharply through her nose. Her lips part and her hands clap together over the paint booklet in her lap. Dee clamps his jaw and rolls to his right, ashamed. Lately his brain has been venting through his mouth like a Freudian spring. He displays the hooded defense of his back and finishes his thought.

"Is wrong."

He stares out the window at the closest car, a poisonous purple Mercury Monarch stripped of its chrome trim. A pink bubble wobbles in the driver's dirty window and gets sucked into a teenage girl's pucker. The girl flaps mascara-caked lashes and looks away, working the gum in her jaw. She wears a flimsy red sweatshirt with a Highland High School shoulder patch. Black and blue dye streaks her blond hair. Her thumbs drum the steering wheel. Her earrings are little handcuffs.

"Including you," Dee says.

A haze of yellow chaff from the latest windstorm blurs the sky. Through this floating filter the evening light sends a final surge, bathing sour faces and cracked sidewalks and tilted strip mall signs in the red glare of a dying sun. For all Dee knows, he and Reneé could be driving on Mars. Dee doesn't look, but he knows his verbal barb has struck his wife by the way she huffs and fidgets in her seat. He releases a throaty sigh, turns from the Monarch girl, and reads a jumble of business signs that strike him as both mundane and apocalyptic, a reminder of how far he has sunk into the abyss of the average: *J. J. North's Family Chuckwagon. Soapy's Auto Wash. Teton Storage.*

Reneé says to the rearview mirror, "Could see somebody about that."

The volcanic light strikes her full in the face. She squints as if trying to digest a grapefruit whole. Then the bottom of the sun touches the high ridge of distant mountains and cools the world in slanting blue shadows. Her eyelashes flicker, and she sucks in her cheeks.

"Could be anger issues."

"Maybe I just need a second coat," Dee says. "Daddy Deluxe. Crystal Career. Husband Happy with Hormones."

Through the intersection, beyond the shopping plaza, waits Dee's new job, the one he loathes—without having worked a day, officially. Not a hundred yards away the tiny campus of Eastern Idaho Technical College squats like an abandoned bunker surrounded by stunted blue spruce and aimless willows. The brown clump of buildings resembles a penitentiary skewered with steel ladders and sprained black antennae. Aquamarine ducts arch like hamster tunnels from roof to roof. Dee sees them and imagines himself on his first day of class, scrabbling through cedar chips for food pellets, running himself to death on a squeaky wheel. He closes his eyes and sees concertina wire, searchlights, orangutan guards with M-16's in chrome-plated watchtowers. To eclipse the dystopian vision, he gazes beyond the Monarch girl's car to the MegaMart parking lot. A dogged cabaret of shoppers wanders through a maze of vehicles, lugging bowling balls, toilet plungers, and spools of steel cable.

"When do all these people work?" he says.

He shakes his head and lifts a copy of the Yellow Pages from the floor and opens it to the map section. The map shows the city of Idaho Falls and the town of Ammon sharing the border of Hitt Road, the street on which he and Reneé wait to move forward.

"You know that's two towns back there?" he says, as the light blinks green and Reneé eases them through the intersection.

"Where MegaMart is?"

"I'm driving," she says.

"Me crazy."

Reneé raises a hand and inclines her head away. "How about you stop talking and don't wake the girls?"

"How about you show me a scrap of decency once in a while?" Traffic jolts to a stop. Brake lights domino toward their front bumper. Dee grabs Reneé's arm.

"Watch it!"

"Ow," she says, wrenching out of his grip. "You're treating me like I'm two again. I'd appreciate it—"

Dee's eyelids lower half way. "Just showing you the weird place we moved to."

"Kinda figured that out."

A yellow Life Flight helicopter roars overhead like a huge hornet, rotors whopping. They gawk up through the windshield and watch starlings scatter from a wasted telephone pole.

"I'm just talking, Reneé," Dee says, sitting back. "Married people do. Breaks up the monotony."

Reneé blinks once. "Your point?"

"That MegaMart isn't even in Idaho Falls. It's in Ammon—"

"Really?"

"You should be more cognizant of your language," Dee says. He smirks out the window at a boy in a white hooded sweatshirt and baggy Lakers shorts. The boy dances at a strip mall entrance with a hand-held sign, a neon orange arrow that screams *Pizza Bomb Blastoff 2.99!*

"I hate it when I say something and people say 'Really' or 'That so?' or 'Did you?' like I'm lying."

"Really?"

Dee gives her a bored sideways look. "You know I hate going to MegaMart, so I'd appreciate it if—"

"I'd appreciate some help," Reneé says, glancing in her side mirror. "On the house."

"Why always the house?"

"We need the right paint for the girls' bedrooms."

Dee lifts his palms. "Way I see it," he says, "it's a toss-up between Aquablaze and Appalachian Cinnabar."

"Think it's a joke," she says. She taps the brakes. The car lurches. They inch forward in the endless train of vehicles, filtering through a four-way intersection. "It's me who—"

"Oo," he says, snatching the booklet of Sherwin-Williams samples from her lap. "Lookee, we have Siesta." He flips through the strips. "Moonlight Macaroon. Mazatlan. Saratoga Spring."

"*Lower your*—don't wake the girls!"

"We walk into their rooms," Dee says, fingering the cards with mock lust, "and thanks to the paint, we've got tasty *and* mysterious wedding reception cookies, your choice of drunk college students, dolphin petting, parasailing—"

Reneé swivels her head, looks in the back seat. "They're awake now."

"We walk in, see the paint, and"—he puts his hand to his mouth like a megaphone—"it's Bounding Boy coming through in the stretch!"

Like alien grubs Colette and Rae wriggle out of candied cocoons of sleep. Colette, the oldest, is all copper and curls. Damp tendrils of hair are glued to her cheeks. A spritz of nutmeg freckles dusts her pug nose and chubby chin. Rae is thinner and darker, a frail stalk of skinny joints and dainty doll teeth with a blond Dutch boy haircut. Her bangs brush the bridge of her nose, obscuring eyes of frosty crystal.

"Great," Reneé says. She smacks the wheel. "You're welcome to rock them to sleep."

Dee smiles toward the back seat. "Hi, babies."

"I'm not a baby," Colette says. "I'm a girl!"

"Daddy?" Rae chimes.

"Yes, baby?"

"I peed."

"Thank you, baby."

"Rae peed," Colette says, blinking out the window.

At the next intersection traffic thickens and the McBrides crawl to a halt. Battered trucks with rust-spotted paint jobs and hatchbacks with bald tires coil around an Arctic Circle. Greasy handprints smear the glass walls of the Play Place like avant-garde tributes to Vaseline. Dee and Reneé narrow their eyes, watching hordes of hyper children leap like mutant frogs through the terrarium of fire as parents plead mechanically into cell phones. Dee clears his throat and sits up. He blinks at a roadside placard on a wooden stake that wobbles in the wind—a bake sale to fight a teacher's cancer at Dewey Elementary—with the date of the sale two weeks ago.

"No clue what you're talking about," Reneé says, pulling through the intersection.

"Nothing new," Dee says.

"Just wish you'd help with the painting because it's me who—"

Dee cocks his body toward her. "Why are you so *freaked out* about paint?"

"Don't shout in front of—"

"It's trappings, externalities," Dee says. His hands spin like limp propellers on his wrists. "Not Alaskan Archipelago or Chaparral. It doesn't make *us* happier."

"It makes me feel clean," Reneé says. "Finished."

"Superficially."

"I'm superficial?"

"Sometimes," Dee coughs. "Maybe. So am I—I mean, everybody's—"

Reneé taps her sternum. "Real charmer, honey," she says. "All warm and fuzzy in here."

"Just saying it's easy to focus on paint and furniture and ignore life *at* home."

Reneé's face shrivels. "Stop talking to me like I'm one of your little students."

"Daddy," Colette calls.

Reneé releases a contralto sigh and turns on the radio. A throaty female news announcer strings together stories: US Airways bankrupt nearly a year after 9/11, The Danube cresting and over a hundred Europeans dead in floods, Charlton Heston's Alzheimer's.

Dee snaps off the radio, puts his hand over his heart. "Hey, sorry for wanting to talk about our marriage."

Reneé hunches her shoulders like a trapped cat. "What's there to talk about?"

"Daddy," Colette whines.

"Reneé, people talk all the time, especially married people who—"

"Nothing wrong with me. Maybe something wrong with

you. I'm fine."

"Mommy!"

"Would you take care of her?" Reneé says.

Dee lifts his chin and closes his eyes and expels a tortured breath and doesn't see the incandescent rafts of rosy clouds sloping across the deep and generous sky, the winking red lights that make the turbine towers on the drought-stricken hills look like a roller coaster frame.

"What honey?"

"Rae peed," Colette says, bouncing her balloon on its string.

"I peed," Rae echoes.

"So am I," Dee says.

Officially, Reneé isn't speaking to Dee. For the third time in two days they've driven from their house—a white gabled two-story fixer-upper in Thornton, twenty minutes away—to the Ammon MegaMart to return shoes Reneé bought for the girls. During this last trip Reneé accused Dee of 'hovering' while she tried to shop. He replied that her moods had more swing than Glenn Miller. At this, Reneé's whole body sagged, and she told him to do the best thing for all of them and die. Then she stalked out of toddler apparel and into kitchen wares, pushing Colette and Rae in an orange MegaCart.

Dee's bonehead *bon mot* fed him the usual dose of satisfaction salted with shame. But he wasn't surprised at his wife's death hex, her death fixation in general. The previous week, he returned home early from his orientation and training at EITC—where, in September, he'll start teaching communication and business writing—and walked in to catch

Reneé screeching threats at the girls. Looking sassy, sexy, and insane in her jeans and denim shirt, Reneé was slathering white primer on the ceiling with a telescoping roller brush and thundering that if Colette and Rae didn't give her some peace she'd drown them in the bathtub.

Only after their two little moppets were in the house did Dee begin to see that his wife's fits of depression and rage weren't temporary. Somehow, she had concealed it while they were dating, and now it seemed the overcrowded nest had hatched the monster egg in her belly. As ill-prepared and unschooled as Dee was in matters of mental health, when Reneé started morphing into Momzilla and kicking over Duplo skyscrapers and sending Colette and Rae scurrying away like panicked Japanese commuters, he could only sink in a mossy gutter of abandonment and dismay, the way he does now, as a margarine-colored bottle of St. John's Wort from MegaMart's homeopathics section rolls from his wife's purse and rattles against his foot like a can of magic beans.

"So what's the plan?" he says. He examines the bottle's label through bright swipes of oncoming headlights.

"For when?" she says, staring at the road. "What are you talking about?"

But Reneé isn't the only problem. Not long ago Dee's manic alter ego infiltrated the McBride home in full battle regalia. In fact, their move from New York to Idaho was the result of Dee's latest professional and personal crisis. After years of slaving as a marketing director for an obscure publishing house and enduring the comparisons Reneé's parents, Jillian and Harv, kept making between Dee's salary and the salaries of Reneé's siblings, he cracked.

When it comes to respect and reputation Dee still sees himself bucking some rough competition, even though he's the only adult keeping score. Reneé's oldest brother, Todd Slade, is a psychiatrist married to a Connecticut native named Heather, who is the first chair violinist in the symphony where they live in Durham, North Carolina. Todd and Heather's two girls and one boy—all bubbly, bright, and blond—are math and music whizzes and, Dee is convinced, will one day pilot the first kiddie space shuttle. Reneé's second oldest brother, Marc, is married with two children, drives a Lexus, and owns a quickly growing shipping company in Waukesha, Wisconsin. Reneé's older sister, Sadie, has three children and is married to a maxillofacial surgeon in Ithaca, New York, where they own two homes, one a three-story 'cabin' on Seneca Lake. Soon after marrying Reneé, Dee felt his grip on the bottom rung of success begin to slip. So one day he came home, yanked off his tie, plodded to the computer, and started making phone calls and firing emails around the country for a teaching job that related to his master's degree.

No place was too remote. New Mexico. Vladivostok. Jupiter.

Next morning, with Colette and Rae propped in front of a Sesame Street Sing-Along video, Reneé called her mother and reported how Dee was 'acting all weird.' By noon the next day Dee began receiving a torrent of faxes and emails at his office about job openings for teachers, all in the state of New York, all within driving distance of the Slade family high command, all from Jillian: *Here's one just in case. Just something I found. This looks good.*

Which pushed him to choose Idaho.

During his frantic job search he found an opening at a place called Eastern Idaho Technical College in Idaho Falls. *Perfect*, he chuckled as he clawed through the application packet, thrilled with the thought of chucking his junk in a Ryder truck and putting two thousand miles of sun-blasted American prairie between his family and the snobbish suburban baronetcy of Jillian and Harv Slade. *Won't find us in Idaho*, he laughed, firing off the application like a sweepstakes entry. As he watched his plan unfold he felt like a mad scientist juggling Erlenmeyer flasks of fizzy, luminous biohazard. *No place more podunk than Idaho*, he thought, twiddling his fingers. *That's the other side of the friggin' Rockies, man.*

To those around Dee, especially Reneé and her family, he had become the love puppet of some Satanic succubus. To his workmates, though, his actions proved completely rational when within the space of two months, he secured a phone interview and a beginning instructor's position in the communication department at EITC in Idaho Falls, Idaho. The envelope-opening ceremony drew looks of bottled fury from Reneé as she kneeled on the carpet and changed Rae's diaper, her double eye laser trained on her husband, her forearm raised to fend off Colette's red wiffle bat.

"Oh," she said. "Great."

"Isn't it?" he said, envelope aloft like an Oscar.

"When would we see my parents?"

Reneé pinned Rae's karate-kicking legs to the carpet and secured the tape tabs on her diaper. She blocked a home-run swing from Colette, disarmed her with superhero skill, and tossed the bat behind the couch.

"So, you'll do what?" she said. "Tell me again."

Dee's envelope sank.

"Teach."

At that moment Rae broke free and Colette chased her into a corner where they pummeled each other like cavemen. A trace of bleach-blond hair slipped over Reneé's forehead, covering her eyes. She swiped it aside and looked up at him, and he saw how beautiful and enraged she was, the hole in the hole in his heart.

"Teach what?" she said.

"*Teach*."

"Teach *what?*"

Now as August wanes and fades over the dusty homegrown city of Idaho Falls, Dee McBride sits in his car with his daughters and wife and wonders what the hell it was he missed. He glances sideways at Reneé and tucks the St. John's Wort bottle into her purse and watches the fading flames of late summer rake fingers of desire through her hair. His stomach wavers at the sight of her sundance eyes, flawless cheeks, fierce chin and jaw. Shrouded in the death of an Idaho sun, she looks like a teenager. Two kids—and she could be a high school cheerleader. Every time he looks at her he's reminded that her grandmother, Billie, was a Rockette. He catches her profile against the glare, and he hears Lloyd Cole and the Commotions singing 'Perfect Skin.' She is a perfect-looking woman who bore him two perfect-looking daughters, and their perfect lives are a thousand hopeful looks from happiness.

"What you want to do when we get home?" he says, hypnotized by the line of cars ahead.

"What's there to do?"

No torture more exquisite, Dee thinks, than being married to a sexy-looking woman who is not sexy. He's never shared his dilemma with anyone. In the eyes of others, complaining your gorgeous wife doesn't love you is like bitching that your Lamborghini doesn't have the right upholstery. He knows the response: You *have* her, so *shut up!*

"We could go out," he says.

"Who'd watch the kids?"

These are the moments of emotional shipwreck, when the beauty of Dee's daughters staggers him. Some days, he feels he's still trapped outside the maternity ward glass. His girls have surfaced from Reneé's gene pool but gene pools claim many drowning victims, he knows, and beautiful people become predatory actors and rehab-rebound pop singers and sleazy senators. Beautiful people change sexual partners as quickly as they change channels. They court the tabloid press and crave bouts of plastic surgery to the point of disfigurement. They consume tubs of cocaine and gin, pack the criminal courts of the country, and learn to fire a gun, slash a razor, and tie a dandy hangman's noose by the time they're eighteen. He wants none of this for his daughters, but he's worried that the Pissed-off Piper of Reneé will lead them down this mineshaft of vanities when she's grown tired of his presence.

For reasons even he can't trace Dee grew up with the notion that all children are loud, nasty, and should be poisoned like garage rats. So he wasn't prepared when Reneé bore him two shining stars. And they aren't just cute. They're rub-your-eyes-and-look-again cute. Campbell-Soup-kid cute. Two-hundred-thou-a-year-with-snooty-Giorgio-wearing-folks-and-a-photo-shoot-in-*Parents*-magazine cute. Occasionally he finds he can look past the physical splendor and see Colette and Rae as the key to the mystery, and when he's alone with them, he hugs them and makes moo-cow noises and goofy monkey faces as if to prove that Reneé *does* somehow love him. *We have them*, he thinks. To tussle and laugh with his daughters on the floor is to know he and Reneé have spooned and lovelocked under the covers beneath many a harvest moon. *So there must be something*, he rationalizes under a barrage of Reneé's mood bombs. *These cuties are the evidence.*

Then he doesn't sleep for days.

Part of the problem is that Dee is thirty-two but looks forty-five. Reneé is thirty and looks seventeen with her clothes on. He's the oldest kid from a Haight-Ashbury tribe. She's the silver-spoon baby from a New York suburb. He's balding, prone to periphrasis. She's a bleach-blond conversation stopper. In the passenger's seat he slouches like a temp worker in a tan fly fisherman's cap, army green T-shirt untucked, no belt, jeans and Asics cross-trainers. Her spine is a steel pole, and the billowy satin collar of her turquoise blouse flares like an Atlas moth between her breasts. In the driver's seat, where she loves to be as long as it suits her, she sports a black polyester jacket and flared pants, platform heels and a gold necklace, ready for her next press interview with her international coterie of fair-weather feminists.

Dee met Reneé in a photography class at Hobart College, where in the lab dark room they shared the private developments of some groping and straddle-kissing and semi-nude snapshots, the negatives of which were purportedly torched but mysteriously archived by the sentimental half of the marriage in a Reebok shoebox caked in lumpy gray dust under their bed.

Dee had no sexual partners before getting married. A few tender scrapes, but no partners.

Reneé can't say the same. During her senior year of high school and first two years of college, on the run from her parents' lockstep religious views, she couldn't get enough. She had two partners Dee knows about: Luke Fein, her brother's college swim team buddy; and the captain of the Penhurst High lacrosse team, Clint Fabbri. Dee suspects another one: Chris Benati, Reneé's senior prom date. Before leaving New York, despite Dee's protests, he and Reneé attended her high school reunion, at which Chris Benati—single, schnockered, and now an architect—buzzed around one suddenly flirtatious Reneé McBride. Benati called her 'Slade,' waved blurry photos of Reneé's drunken somersaults in her prom dress on his front lawn, and demanded that she dance 'The Electric Slide' with him for 'old time's sake.' All the while, Dee felt like stalking over and socking Benati in the mouth for changing his wife back into a Budweiser-swigging, twitterpated teenybopper. As he watched Reneé gambol like a groupie in heat around the swarthy architect, Dee crammed fistfuls of butter mints and smoked almonds in his mouth, and wondered why *he* could no longer plug his wife into a wall socket and change her into a horny can-can dancer.

On one of their many strained trips to MegaMart, Dee, without thinking, shared with Reneé his philosophy about sex.

"It's like a baby bottle," he said. "Puberty, it's full. You save some or guzzle it all and end up sucking an empty bottle the rest of your life."

Reneé locked steamy eyes on the highway. "Say that again," she said. "I'll drive us and the kids into the river."

After Rae was born, sex for the McBrides became a mere polishing of shoes, a quotidian filing of recipe cards. Dee has noted the changes childbirth has wrought on his wife's body. Veins decorate her calves like brush strokes in a child's watercolor. Her hips jut like bookends. Her breasts, once cocksure and firm, ride under her blouses with the heft of half-filled water balloons. Still, strangely, wonderfully, his desire for her has surged while hers has scuttled into a stalactite-barbed cave. When Rae was six months old, Reneé started demanding they leave the lights off. She would only let the conga commence after Dee gave her a prolonged massage, which would ring his passion buzzer and trigger her snores. To his knowledge, she's never come on to him, but merely *allowed* him to stroke the magic carpet and hope for a ride.

The one bit of background they share—that they were both sexually abused—they never discuss. Dee by a business associate of his father's named Toff Kramer, who traveled with a suitcase of *Hustler* issues, and Reneé by her Uncle Boz, who limped and chain-smoked and whose driveway sealing business brought him into the city. But when the conversation wanders close to the subject, Reneé shatters Dee's hope for an emotional breakthrough with long stares out the window and the suggestion that they get something to eat. In Dee's mind, a robust and adventurous round of Marvin Gaye's 'Sexual Healing' could soothe the scars of the past, but he fears the fallout from pushing Reneé from her perch on the precipice of every moment.

So instead of turning to her husband and children for

satisfaction, Reneé ranges beyond the tripwires of home life on search-and-destroy missions for volunteer work. Daily she scours the civic outback of local miseries for charitable deeds she might perform to salvage a trinket of redemption for herself. While she neglects her daughters and ignores Dee, with the punctuality of a Münich glockenspiel she delivers meals and laundry service to Evie Crouch, a cotton-headed, Alzheimer's-touched woman who lives next door in a swaybacked, creamsicle-colored rambler nested in malignant gray shrubs. Days after they moved in, Reneé called Dee at his office and asked if he could drive home to watch Colette and Rae while she walked over to give Evie lunch.

"Kinda busy," he said. "Starting the job soon."

"Looks like you'll never change!" she wailed into the phone. "Me, me, me, me!"

Before he could ask why she was training to sing opera she slammed the phone down.

Their most recent marital code three occurred when Reneé called him at his office to tell him that Cherelyn, her brother Marc's wife—to whom she hadn't spoken in five years—had been diagnosed with adenocarcinoma of the esophagus. Reneé wanted to fly out immediately to act as in-home help for Cherelyn, leaving the date of her return to be determined.

"She needs me in her time of need," Reneé said.

"Honey," he said. "With the girls, and classes starting, I don't know if that's feasible."

She refused to speak to him for two days.

In the interim he conscripted Colette and Rae into delivering make-up love notes to her, crayon sketches scribbled on pages from Barbie and My Little Pony coloring books. Reneé merely glared.

Now, Reneé's pilgrimages toward community rescue breed domestic chaos. Dee notices how she changes Rae's diapers and doesn't throw them away but leaves them to multiply like toxic stork bundles on the kitchen counter. He returns home daily to find the living room carpet littered with rank diaper landmines.

"Burn some extra calories," he says, reaping hard looks. "On the way to the garbage can."

Reneé leaves tangled stockings and dirty girlie undies in Gordian knots on the kitchen table between the butter and marmalade. The house is a hoarder's paradise, hillocks of moldy laundry in the hall, cereal spilling from tipped-over boxes, open drawers bristling with food-encrusted knives in reach of little fingers, ketchup-smeared newspapers and torn-out magazine articles and hasty to-do lists nooked and crannied between sofa cushions and appliances like abandoned alchemies. Reneé can never find her keys, blames Dee for making her so scatterbrained she can't concentrate. Once, Dee became so desperate he called Jillian and Harv to ask if Reneé had considered taking counseling.

To the sound of Jillian's indignant gasps in the background, Harv munched an English muffin.

"She has," Harv said with a deadpan flourish. "Since she married a damn fool teacher who gave up a good job to rope cows in a damn hayfield somewhere."

THREE PHONE MESSAGES blink on the McBride answering machine. One is from Jillian, concerning Cherelyn's throat cancer; the second, about marigold care and a proposed trip to the grocery store, is from Evie; and the third, astoundingly, is from Chris Benati in New York. Reneé listens to the messages. She plays Benati's message four times, a girlish glow on her face.

"Sweetie," Benati's voice croons, garbled with static. "It was so—great—seeing you, at the reunion. We oughta hook up, rehash. Cute kids by the way. Angels. Hey, and don't let me step on Dave's toes—Is it Dave? Don?—your, your guy?—I'd just hate to lose everything . . ."

A long bleep obliterates Benati's voice.

Dee stands in the doorway, a groggy daughter in each arm, MegaMart bags swinging like sandbags from his elbows.

Without speaking to him Reneé heats a plate of chicken, beans, and au gratin potatoes for Evie. She covers it with tinfoil and conveys it next door. When she returns Colette and Rae are sprawled in bed in their play clothes, Dee snores face down on the couch, and it's an hour and a half before she finishes talking to her mother on the phone about Cherelyn's prognosis.

The next day, after Dee leaves for an orientation meeting, Reneé calls Chris Benati at his architectural firm's office in New York and chirps a cheerful reply into his answering service.

TUESDAY. RENEÉ DRIVES COLETTE and Rae back to MegaMart with four pairs of polar bear Sleep-Tite pajamas riding shotgun in the passenger's seat, price tags attached. After speaking with her on the phone Dee drives home for lunch while she's away.

He pilots his orange VW bug north on Highway Twenty and breathes in at the sight of such beautiful and mundane surroundings. A spirit of spaciousness—the world's barn doors flung wide—flows from the dented granaries and white-faced cows and hunks of rotten fence post hanging like abandonment in ruined barbed wire fences. Dirt roads run forever in one direction. Roofless sheds of basalt rock stand empty, as do tree trunks charred and gutted by lightning. The clunky homes and trailer houses are what Reneé refers to as 'country kitsch.' Dee is secretly thrilled to think what Jillian and Harv Slade would do if they saw their daughter and granddaughters wading hip-deep through so much redneck junk culture. To them, it's kitsch. To him, it's a yummy chunk of Americana he's been missing. The raw backwoodsy reach of the land weaves perfectly into his agenda of claiming a new freedom for himself and his family.

At the Jefferson County line the sun-shocked fields and rickety fences give way to battlements of swaying poplars and cottonwoods. A black railroad bridge arches over the river. The shallow water flashes like liquid silver. Dee blinks away the glare and grinds the heel of his hand in his eye, catching glimpses of bony tree trunks in grotesque heaps, yellow willows that sprout like wild hair from rocky shoals. A kingfisher plummets from a dead branch, a train horn brays, and a fisherman in waders steps from a boat ramp into the shallows. On the other side Dee speeds past a small store built in log cabin fashion: 'Country Collectibles.' In front of the store five radial tires filled with dirt make beds for little cluster bombs of canary, fuchsia, and deep crimson flowers.

Dee cackles and lets fly with a buckaroo yawp: "Yee-freakin-haw!"

Snarls of sagebrush and billboards for roofers flit past. Road signs flash shantytown names that could pass for vaudeville acts: LaBelle, Menan, Lorenzo, Archer, Thornton. At the Thornton Texaco turnoff he passes a sign for the Blue Heron Bed & Breakfast and notes with concern that Jillian and Harv could deem its lodgings suitable for a visit. Past the old Thornton Merc & Café, which threatens to topple like Wild West scenery in a school play, two hound-faced flunkies in greasy blue coveralls tumble tractor tires into a shabby garage. He succumbs to an impulse, wheels right instead of left and, like one of the Beverly Hillbillies, bumps down the gravel road to 'Country Collectibles.'

As he drives he chews an invisible hay stalk, envisions himself in baggy Tom Sawyer dungarees, catfish rod bouncing over his shoulder. He laughs, yuk-yuk, and belts out off-key snatches of John Denver.

"Mountain Momma! Take me home!"

At home, he unrolls a bale of white twelve-inch wire fencing and strings it down both sides of the driveway. He steps back, hands on hips, inspects his work. The crappy fencing looks like an orgy of croquet wickets, a mangled chorus line of pipe cleaner dolls. To spite the Slade family and all the uppity New England decorum they stand for, he arranges three google-eyed flamingos, two lecherous lawn gnomes, and a daisy-spangled 'Well Wisher's Well' in attack formation on the grass.

On returning from MegaMart, Reneé stands in the driveway—as Colette and Rae do a rabid Maypole dance around her knees, hands gloved in melted Starlite Mint ice cream—and stares at the wooden monarch butterfly that hangs over the garage like a monstrous orange tumor.

ON THE LAST DAY of MegaMart's grand opening, a vicious downdraft drives the store's Crazy Days blimp into a nosedive through traffic on Hitt Road. The circus-colored blimp collides with a school bus of mentally-challenged fifth graders on their way to see the snow leopards and albino tigers at Tautphas Park Zoo. No one is injured, but the bus careens over the curb and causes two car crashes that total Mr. Icy's Sno Kone bicycle cart and Doogins the Clown's cotton candy mill. In Dee's class on the EITC campus, the incident sparks a mini-dialogue about The Hindenberg, Led Zeppelin's legacy, and the Montgolfier brothers—actually, more of a scattered monologue from Dee, as his students stare at him like landed trout while he distributes a passel of pink photocopied sheets and proceeds to shake their foundations with a pop quiz on Ferdinand de Saussure's 'Course in General Linguistics,' H. P. Grice's 'communicative presumption,' and floating signifiers.

After one o' clock, Reneé calls Dee at his office. "Hi," she says.

"What's going on?" he says. "How're the girls?"

"Fine—hey, I was thinking—"

"Good sign."

"Stop. I was wondering if you'd go with me to MegaMart this afternoon—"

"Reneé," Dee groans. "How many times we gonna do this?"

"You don't have class now."

"I'm busy," he says, looking around.

"With what?"

In the background Colette and Rae battle like samurai over some momentarily precious object.

"Things," he says. "I don't just stand in class and talk. There's a lot behind the scenes. I'm up to my armpits—"

Reneé's voice wavers into a puddle. "That's fine," she says like someone on a suicide hotline. "You need to work. But they are driving me up a wall!"

Dee's spine withers. Black spittle pools in his gut. "I'll be in the parking lot," he says.

At MegaMart early autumn breezes trouble the helium balloons and rainbow pennants strung between light posts. When the McBrides pull up, a cop car lingers near the smashed food carts and a popped bouncy castle. Red-vested employees haul away ruptured bags of fertilizer and use socket sets to fix the discombobulated bones of a swing set. Despite the destruction people crowd the sidewalks, slurping sodas, chomping corn dogs, and wrangling gangly ostrich marionettes. Shoppers stream through the wide entryway like pilgrims ransacking a shrine. Hot ticket items flank the doors: gas-powered trimmers, pallets of generic water-softening salt, lion-footed wicker patio furniture. Hundreds of red sale tickets spin like flags of revolution. Near the bike racks and American Fare soda machines, kids hound Doogins the Clown, who distributes balloon animals so quickly he appears to pull them ready-made from his floppy sleeves.

"Don't any of these people have jobs?" Dee says, entering the store with Reneé. He wrestles a cart from the holding pen and hoists the girls into it, Rae in the basket, Colette in the seat. Reneé takes command of the cart and pushes off with the girls, gliding across the waxed floor through cosmetics.

"Fifteen minutes," she says.

"Why am I here?" Dee demands.

"Just in case."

Colette thrusts her arms heavenward, a melodrama heroine swept downriver on a runaway barge. "Daddy!" she calls. "Save me!"

Rae opens her snaggle-toothed mouth and laughs, "Save Daddy!"

Dee's cart wobbles on one bad wheel. He blunders through the glittering aisles of snack chips, cut-priced lawnmowers, and pyramids of Rubbermaid tubs, desperate to leave, lost at every turn. The gumball-scented maze of septic pastels traps him in endless dead ends. Spastic kids capering like hobgoblins around his knees, hobbling grandmothers stonewalling him like crusty suffragettes—it all packs his lungs with claustrophobia. Walls of televisions squawk twelve different programs. Orange hatchet-shaped 'Hot Deal!' signs prick his sleeves. The scent of cucumber-lilac perfume and cholesterol-caked jalapeño corn dogs makes him gag. From every whitewashed ceiling beam swings a cherry or ultramarine poster on which sexy, slim people too young to be the parents of the multi-ethnic children with them champion the rejuvenating powers of plum passion body spray, Hawaiian shirts, or three fabulous notebooks for a dollar ninety-nine. Everything has a ninety-nine after it. This alone irks him.

He speeds past the checkout lines, cart plowing like a dogsled, head down to dodge the prostitute grins of the MegaMart 'Help Crew.' In the home and garden section, exasperated, fuming, he curses the unfinished work in his office.

He snatches a phone from a service kiosk.

The phone is lipstick red. A curly cord connects it to the kiosk. A sign above the phone blares in white block letters: HELP PHONE THIRTEEN. As Dee waits for someone to answer, he envisions himself as a rat trapped in a circular corridor, sniffing for a hidden door among the moldy shelves of non-stick frying pans and DVD players. He sees himself, like Robinson Crusoe, recounting in a raspy seafarer's voice how he came to be marooned in MegaMart, his beard eleven feet long, a maniac stare in his bloodshot eyes, his home a pup tent complete with fold-out lounge chair and beef jerky and Shasta Red Cream Soda and Pop Tarts warmed over a Coleman propane stove.

A female voice on the phone crackles like an Edison recording. "Can I help you?"

"Doubt it," Dee says. "I'm looking for office products. I got five minutes—"

"Really?" the voice says.

Dee pauses. "Really," he says. "Can you tell me where office products—"

"That really what you need?" the girl's voice persists, dabbling through a glacial creek.

Dee holds the phone from his head. He shakes it, examines it for defects, glances at the shoppers who continue to ignore him. *Some teenager*, he thinks.

"Hello?" he says. "Customer service?"

"Depends," the spearmint voice purrs. "What do you need?"

"No games," Dee says. "I'm in a hurry, and I need—"

"You don't have a clue what you need," the girl insists. Her voice jangles through Celtic ballads, a waterfall in the background.

"What's your name?" Dee demands. "Who's your supervisor?"

"I'm Help Phone Thirteen," she pipes.

"Never mind."

He slams the phone down, scoots past kitty litter and toasters, and cuts a beeline through a Death Star trench of amber spray-bottle cleansers to the customer service area: an oblong red counter near the checkout stalls. Outside the front entryway Doogins the Clown wrenches a balloon into a brontosaurus for a kid in hooded green sweatshirt and baggy gangbanger jeans who hops like an electrocuted lizard.

Dee urges the line forward with gruff throat clearing and asks to see the supervisor. A droopy sloth of a man wearing a pinstripe shirt under a MegaMart vest shuffles through a swinging door with the air of a spavined saloon keeper. The door and vest are the same jawbreaker red, so the man approaches like a head and pair of arms floating above black polyester pants with gold cowboy stitching. He smiles at Dee and smooths his shaggy brown mustache with a forefinger.

"Help you?" he says. His badge shows blocky white lettering similar to the kind on the help phone: MEGAMART HELP CREW. I'M KARL!

"Karl," Dee says, reading the badge. "Hate to tell you this, but somebody's screwing around on your phones."

Karl arches woolly eyebrows.

"Phones?"

"Customer service," Dee says. He twirls his finger like a lasso at the store's yammering wasteland.

Karl smiles. "Help phones," he says. "Bingo."

"Thirteen," Dee says. "Girl was giving me lip. Said I wanted office products, and she said I didn't know what I wanted and started goin' off—"

Karl scrutinizes Dee. "Girl?"

"Talking really weird," Dee says to the box of air in his hands. "She had this voice like—"

Karl puckers his lips. "Her name?"

"She was on thirteen." Dee looks up at Karl as if seeing him for the first time.

"They're numbered on the floor," Karl says. He jerks a thumb over his shoulder at the door behind him. "Two people in here do the answering, but—"

"Who's the girl on thirteen?"

Karl searches Dee's eyes as if looking for a fizzing circuit. Dee looks away.

"We've got two male employees back there now."

"Really?" Dee says, narrowing his eyes.

Karl places his palms on the counter and braces his elephant seal bulk on hyperextended elbows. "Ha, you know, I hate it when people say 'Really?' like—"

Dee waves his hand, erasing Karl's answer. He stares at a green Pop Rocks packet on the floor. "This was a girl. A woman—female. How long those guys been there?"

"Oh, two hours." The corners of Karl's eyes crinkle. "Maybe three. I was here seven sharp. When did this happen?"

"Just now," Dee exhales, backing away. "Thanks."

Karl pats his front and back pockets. "Wanna fill out a complaint card?" he says.

"No, no," Dee says, waving him off. "Thanks, Karl. That'll be fine. That's—fine."

Dee wanders woozily through the automatic doors. He totters through a mob of snickering kids, past a bloated man in roomy gold exercise pants on a motorized cart. He stands on the sidewalk, afraid he might topple from his disjointed legs. He squints at the glaring sea of cars and vans. From all directions people flood toward MegaMart's massive ark. A breeze shocks life into his lungs.

"What just happened?" he asks the world.

He reaches for handrails of air, a futile gesture that triggers an admission: he still feels lost in his new place of residence. He wonders what's taking Reneé so long. For the first time in a long time, he wishes she would hurry back and let him cling to the one sure fact of her body. He feels desperate to giggle with Colette and Rae, to loop his arm around his wife's hips and let her use her fingertips to trace tiny tattoos of assurance on his forearm the way she did when they were dating.

"What are we doing here?"

Shoppers swirl around the roaming island of his body. He moves to the soft drink machines and bounces like a prizefighter jostling knots from his shoulders, bobbing his head from side to side. A car horn toots. A mother shouts for her daughter not to get run over. But nothing chases the throbbing fear from Dee's bowels: that fiends are jamming his brain with a ham radio, that everything around him is a hologram. He wants to rake his fingers through the tapestry of air and reveal the smoking craters of a mythical world. He could be the well-dressed protagonist in a black-and-white B movie, on the verge of running amok in the MegaMart parking lot and tearing away the rubber faces from a race of bleeping androids. He fishes for an answer: a prankster with a cell phone behind one-way glass; a crossed connection; somebody thinking she was talking to a fellow worker and not a customer. He blows out a sigh.

"Hey," the clown says.

Dee spins and stares. Doogins the Clown stares back and gives a tentative wave. He wears classic white face paint, red foam-rubber nose, orange wig, and a rainbow Rastafarian cap. His jumbo sky-blue shirt puffs with good will. Sloppy ric-rac adorns his collar and cuffs, and white pom-pom buttons bumble down his shirt front. From the waist up, he's all clown. From the waist down, a regular guy in jeans and Adidas high-tops. A mess of balloons, like a gallon of rainbow worms, fills the yellow canvas bag on his shoulder. Doogins plunges his hand in the bag and produces an orange balloon. Whistling a Dixieland ditty, he stretches and snaps it back, applies it to his lips. He does a cheek-bulging Dizzy Gillespie and in two seconds a baby pterodactyl balloon perches in his palm. He hands it to Dee.

"For the kiddies," he says.

Dee jumps. "How do you know I have kids?"

"A hunch," Doogins says. His clown grin melts like cake icing. "Take it easy, man."

"Sorry, I—make it two."

"Two?"

"Balloons," Dee says, jabbing a peace sign at the bag. "The same. So they won't fight."

"Gotchya," Doogins says. He cracks his knuckles, double-claps, step-ball-changes, and twists a second orange pterodactyl out of the air. "Okey dokey, artichoky. There ya be."

Dee takes the balloons without looking. "Thanks," he says. He scans the parking lot for the approach of a disguised assassin.

"Things cool?" Doogins asks. "No offense, man, but you look kinda—"

"Sorry," Dee says, blinking. "I'm just—thanks for the balloons—I—do you work here?"

Doogins flashes the shaka sign. "Independently contracted."

"Really?" Dee chuckles. "Never thought of clowns as 'independently contracted.' Sounds bourgeois."

"Clown is all relative, man," Doogins says. He fans both hands out. "What we do? It's a social institution."

"Never thought of it that way," Dee says, looking around.

"Like that Stephen Sondheim song, you know?" Doogins says. He raises his arms to the arena of the planet. "Everybody needs us. But they wait till there's a crisis, and only *then*—"

"You know anything about the phones here?" Dee interrupts. He clamps a hand to his chin, finger over his upper lip.

"Phones?"

Dee points to the entrance. "Help phones."

Doogins apes Dee's finger-over-the-lip. "Why?"

"Don't know," Dee says, eyebrows pinched. "I asked for help on one—thirteen—and this girl comes on—"

Doogins peeks in his bag. "No girls working the phones now."

"Yeah, I asked Karl—"

Doogins bobs his head. "Karl's the man," he says. "Karl'll set you up. So what's the problem with the phone?"

"Nothing," Dee says. He wags his hand, as if dismissing the world. "I wanted office supplies, and this girl's on there mouthing off, telling me I don't know what I want and all kindsa crap."

"Mm," Doogins says, examining Dee.

Dee's jaw trembles. "Her voice—it was like—not human—"

Doogins folds his arms. "Like a recording?" he asks.

"Not a recording. Like the wind or—"

"Wind?" Doogins laughs.

"Awright, that's stupid. But it was—like the wind. And—other stuff."

"Probably not my place," Doogins says, assuming a confidential tone. "Sounds like you're stressed out."

Dee gives the clown a stern look. "Balloon animals and therapy on the side, huh?" he says.

Doogins steps back. "Just telling you what we do," he says. "If we can help, give us a call."

With a magician's flip of the wrist, Doogins produces a psychedelic business card that bears his Idaho Falls address and phone number.

Dee smirks and pockets the card. "We'll let you know."

"Don't underestimate it, man," Doogins says with a Cheech-and-Chong lilt. "Lotta people do."

"So, what do you guys do?" Dee says. "Jump out of a cake and saw inkblots in half? Party horns and Oedipal complexes all around?"

"Funny," Doogins says. "People don't—"

Dee tosses an invisible dart. "Pin the tail on the co-dependent donkey?"

"You got a pistol wit," Doogins says. "You'd be good with us if you could tame it."

"With you?" Dee laughs. "What's the clown gig pay

these days?"

"It's quality of life with us," Doogins says. He does a four-fingered kiddie wave and waggles his tongue at a passing mother and baby. The baby spits cottage-cheesy puke on the woman's shoulder. "Oopsie, sorry!" Doogins says, then to Dee, "What do you do?"

"Teach," Dee says. He jerks his head toward the EITC campus.

"Like I said," Doogins says. "Clown is all relative."

Dee leans back, eyebrows slanted. "Oo," he says. "That repartee go over big at little Johnny's party?"

"Sorry," Doogins says. He jabs a good-natured punch at Dee's shoulder. "That was bad. I apologize."

"Accepted," Dee says. "Besides, I got a wife and kids. We're barely making it now, and my wife thinks what I do is basically clowning around—"

Doogins shrugs. "I got kids."

"Really?"

"No offense," Doogins says, masking his exasperation. "I hate it when people say that, like I'm lying or—"

"Know what you mean," Dee says.

"Daughter's a freshman at ISU," Doogins says. "Information systems. Son's a sophomore at Skyline. Curve ball breaks a foot and a half." He whistles through his teeth and swings an invisible baseball bat.

"Guess I learned something," Dee says.

Doogins crosses his ankles and leans casually on his air-bat. Dee frowns, steps back, and searches for the wires holding him up.

"Most people don't know," Doogins says. He speaks like a

casual tour guide. "Thirteen of us serve Eastern Idaho, the greater Snake River plain. Regional chapter in the Rockies. Seriously, profit sharing, benefits. Conventions in Maui, Paris. *Le monde aime un bouffon*! Textbook drives for Nigeria, Haiti. Company car, too, if—"

"This part of the act?" Dee says, spotting Reneé as she emerges from MegaMart. Colette and Rae trundle behind, each carrying a teddy bear balloon and cinnamon churro.

"You hit the wall teaching," Doogins finishes, "check us out."

"I will," Dee says. "Hi, dear."

"Hi," Reneé says, visibly refreshed. "Who's this?"

"Daddy!" Colette shouts. She hops on one foot, strawberry curls ringing with sun. "A clown!"

"Clown!" Rae echoes. She juts out chipmunk teeth and peeps at Doogins through her bangs.

"Made you balloons," Dee says. He holds up the pterodactyls like big six shooters. "But you already have some."

"Sorry," Reneé says. "Keep the troops happy."

"Can never have too many balloons," Doogins says. He bobble-heads at the girls, dashes off a clumsy grapevine step and finishes with a Fred Astaire flourish. The girls squeal.

Dee takes each girl by the hand. "Gotta go," he says.

"Daddy!" Colette protests. Her body sags like a sack of jelly to the pavement. "I want the clown to come!"

"He's coming," Dee says. Like a cop removing a protestor, he starts to drag Colette by her arm. Rae clamps a bear hug around his knee. Burdened by girls he shuffles to the car through passing vehicles, a disgruntled gorilla besieged by clingy chimps.

With the girls strapped in their seats, Dee unloads. "I'm

glad to see you," he says to Reneé, snapping on his seatbelt.

"Really?" Reneé says. "What's the change—"

"I'm glad you came back," he says. "I was getting tired of—"

"Oh," she says and turns the ignition.

"I got on one of those help phones, and this girl answered. She started talking back to me, insulting me, saying I didn't know what I wanted."

Reneé pulls into traffic, looking for oncoming cars. "Somebody messing around," she says.

"Somebody," Dee echoes. He turns to look at the girls. "You guys have fun?"

"Yeah!"

"Good," Dee says. He swivels back to face the front. "Cause I've got a ton to do. Could you drop me off at the faculty turnout on your way—"

"I guess," Reneé sighs, rolling her eyes. "Why can't you just come home? You're done teaching. What do you do in your office all day?"

"Research," he says. "Grading, prep stuff. And I'll be home later now cause this trip has set me back."

Reneé adjusts her sunglasses. "So sorry your wife and kids are such a hassle."

"Didn't say you were."

"We are," she says, patting the dashboard. "Admit it."

"It's just hard to juggle what I'm doing with the kids—"

"Tell me about it."

"Drop me off here," Dee says. "I'll be home later."

Dee opens the door and steps out and a hopped-up, mud-spackled black Toyota truck with knobby tires roars through the campus drop-off zone. Oily smoke shoots from its chrome exhaust stacks. Dee gives his daughters a weary wave.

"Bye, Daddy," Colette sings.

"Bye-bye," Rae says, whirling her arms in dance aerobic circles.

In his office Dee rushes through his grading and preparation for the next day. Before heading home to Thornton, he drives back to MegaMart and parks outside and watches the workers change shifts. He lets the engine idle, sunglasses on, scrutinizing the red-vested employees as they file in and out, searching for the girl whose voice was like the wind.

At home he stalks through the door to find seated around the kitchen table, like poker buddies, three people vetting a booklet of Cloverdale paint samples. They are also discussing the esophagogastrectomy planned for Reneé's sister-in-law, Cherelyn. The people are Reneé, as effervescent as a puppy; Evie, medicated, in filmy maroon nightgown and mangy jack rabbit slippers; and in leather jacket and biker boots, looking like a stunted Lord of Flatbush, Chris Benati, who's flown in unannounced from New York.

5

"HE'S SLEEPING IN OUR HOUSE," Dee says, staring at the cobwebs undulating like filmy trapezes from the ceiling.

"Go to sleep," Reneé yawns. "He'll hear you."

"Creepy."

"What is?"

"Your stubby Italian prom date flies from New York, and sleeps in the same house as our girls—and us."

"So?"

"Creepy."

"Stop saying that. He's going back tomorrow. I think it's sweet."

"Sweet? You're killin' me, Reneé."

"Stop being dramatic."

"You want dramatic?" Dee's arms shoot toward the ceiling. His fist thumps his chest.

"Who is this guy in bed next to you? Who is he?"

"I don't have to listen to—"

"Has a decade gone by? Are those girls downstairs sharing our chromosomes?"

"He's leaving in the morning. Will you please shut up?"

"This is insane! We're married! I can't believe you don't see how this hurts me." He sits up and speaks to the dim contour of her body. "Okay—what if I brought an old flame home? Invited her to stay the night?"

Reneé lies flat in her coffin of stillness. "First off," she says, "he invited himself. Second, that would never happen because you don't have an old flame."

"Huh," he utters thickly. "I guess—I was saving myself for you."

"I married you, didn't I?"

"You married marriage."

"He says we should paint the girls' rooms Persian Pomegranate or Ragtime," Reneé says.

"Architects don't know paint," Dee says.

6

DEE MCBRIDE'S TEACHING stems from his master's thesis. At Columbia, while holding down a middle management position at a copy center, he wrote a cross-cultural Fichtean study and application: "Achieving Synthesis: Universality in Communication Modes and Modules." In it, he posits that all communication snags—political, social, professional, domestic, electronic, and/or interpersonal—can be described and resolved by what he outlines as a "TASC module." The acronym stands for Thesis, Antithesis, Synthesis, Communication. "In all modes of communication, especially conflicting ones," he writes in his preface, "there is a first position (thesis), a second position (antithesis), and the potential resolution originating from the two opposing positions (synthesis). This module applies universally to all communication scenarios and can be implemented *in theoria* or *in praxis* in order to bring about harmony from discord, clear communication from chaos."

The third week of class Dee assigns his students to use his TASC modules to explore the social branch of communication outlined in his thesis. The modules are printed goldenrod email attachments that show a large capital T in the center of the page, the left side labeled 'Thesis,' the right 'Antithesis,' and the bottom of the T reading 'Synthesis.'

"This week," Dee tells his students, "Your TASC task"—waits for deflated chuckles—"is to document all the communication hang-ups you experience in social situations."

"Document?"

Dee pivots toward the question and sees a camel-faced young man in an Orange Crush T-shirt staring back, his tongue glistening like something in a butcher's window.

"Write each claim, or thesis, you encounter in social settings on one side of the paper," Dee says, holding a TASC module aloft. "Put its opposite, or antithesis, on the other side. Leave the synthesis space blank for class."

Dee teaches Communications 100 in the octagonal rotunda of the Alexander D. Creek Building. The worn tracks in the feeble green carpet and cinderblock walls lacquered in sickly yellow paint lend his teaching space all the cozy charm of an asylum. The door to his room, number 519, is a wooden slab with a stainless steel lever instead of a doorknob. Through a rectangle of reinforced wire-mesh glass outsiders peep at the souls on lockdown in Dee's cell of learning. To bolster school spirit the department secretary has taped a photocopy of the school's 'Mission' and 'Vision' statements next to Dee's classroom. Dee hasn't taken the slightest interest in his school's mission or vision. If he has no vision himself, why should he give a flying fig about his school's?

In Room 519, five tiers rise toward the back wall, conveying the impression of Greek theater, apart from the glaring fact that *Oedipus* is interesting and Dee's classes aren't. Desks are made of shiny tubular steel with kidney-shaped desktops: pylon orange, putty beige, birthday-cake blue. Most days, Dee's students gaze down like dazed transients observing a nineteenth-century science experiment. A burned-out overhead projector on a rolling stand rusts in one corner. Moon-colored dust coats the fronds of a fake philodendron in a wicker basket. Dee's big desk sits center stage.

He lectures from behind a small wooden podium. With choreographed gravitas he strikes forceful poses and for dramatic effect lifts the podium from the desk and bangs it down with Jonathan Edwards thunder when students begin to drool.

The desk drawers contain three paper clips, an empty stapler, and a business card bearing the name and address of the previous teacher's therapist in bold cranberry letters on a mint background: *Teton View Mental Health, Dr. Wendee Sonderegger.* Two skinny windows in the wall let students watch Daryl Qualheim, the groundskeeper, putt around on a John Deere mower in frayed overalls and crumpled Cray's Feed 'n' Seed cap. Some days Dee's students cast looks of such earnest longing through the windows that, often in mid-lecture, he expects them to charge down in revolt and dump buckets of molten lead on his head. Despite his medieval moods of professional despair, he sees himself scaling a ladder of trumped-up hope, believing, however vainly, that he can reach the topmost turret and teach the princess in pink pantaloons how to spin lead into gold with the cabalistic formulas of good communication.

"As you come in," Dee announces to the shuffling herd on Monday morning, "do two things for me. One, try to forget it's eight o' clock. Two, turn in your completed social TASC modules."

As Dee stands at the door and collects homework in an Easter basket bearing a neon-yellow card that reads 'A Tiskit a TASC It,' the strenuous events from the recent past replay in his head to a circus calliope: cancer, architect boyfriend, clown, help phone thirteen, neighbor, wife, girls. He's already exhausted and can't shake the hornet's nest from his head. Clean-cut in shirt and tie, he stumbles in a wilderness, wondering if all teachers play the part of polished cruise directors while inwardly they are mad bag ladies pushing shopping carts to the same emotional junkyard.

"Thank you," he says, trying not to fall over. "Thank you."

As he forces a smile and gathers assignments, he notices two students making out in the back of the room. He's seen their love games before, but he's tried to ignore it in the hope that they might get infected or get a hotel. The male student, a fluffy-headed kid in denim jacket and jeans, looks no older than seventeen. His eyebrows and eyelashes are an unearthly blond. A wispy tuft of beard clings to his pimply chin. The girl, also in denim jacket, wears peacock blue eye shadow. A ponytail wrapped in a pink bandana spouts like a fountain from her head. It's too early in the term to know names, so Dee coughs. He clears his throat. Oblivious, the couple continues to moan quietly and work their jaws, arms and legs entwined in a grappling match of lust.

"Excuse me?" Dee calls. "Could we try not to become impregnated until the end of the term, please?"

The couple blushes and stares at Dee. The students entering class freeze then continue to flow.

"Thank you," Dee says, prying apart the air with his hands. "It's just—"

The guy jerks his head upward. "Screw you, dude," he says. His girlfriend giggles.

"I wanted to avoid that in class," Dee fires back. "Never mind—names?"

"Fender," the young man says. "Dallas."

"Fender?" Dee chortles.

The girl flaps Vampira lashes. "I'm Ali," she says.

"Alley?" Dee says. "Like where you get picked up?"

Ali's expression sours.

"Back off, dude," Dallas says.

Dee inclines forward, eyes wide. "I'm the teacher," he says. "I don't back off. Especially not from a guy whose name is half TV drama, half car part."

"What's yours?" Dallas returns. "Letter in the alphabet— and a burger for married women?"

Ali snorts. The rest of the class roars. Dee colors.

"All right," he covers. "Cool it. Let's get to work."

Later that day Dee gets a call from Roger Ferguson, dean of the college. A little after two, the division secretary ushers Dee into the dean's office where he finds his boss seated on a high-backed black leather chair, hunched forward with his face so close to his blue computer screen he appears to be trying for a tan. The dean's office rings with Spartan order. A militaristic rainbow of reference books and periodicals lines three of the four walls. An aquarium of angelfish bubbles on a gray file cabinet. From a portable stereo Rachmaninoff thrums reverently. On the dean's desk a white ceramic bust of Pascal gazes like a beheaded saint out the window, seeking the solution to the cross-currents in the wind. Dean Ferguson, a silver-haired, sober man of fifty-four rocks back in his chair and rises to greet Dee with a nutcracker handshake.

"Have a seat," he says.

Dee sits and examines the dean's sport coat fabric, which

reminds him of a gunny sack. Dean Ferguson wears a jubilant orange plaid tie, and his round belly surges over his rodeo belt buckle as if his pinstripe shirt might burst. In the window a bony quaking aspen flutters leaves of patchy yellow and bright green.

"Dee, we had some problems in your class today," says Dean Ferguson. "I just want to get your side."

Dee swallows. "Problems?"

"Take it easy," the Dean says, waving a hand. "I know students. There's been a report. I need to follow up."

"Okay," Dee says.

"Did you have words with some kids today?"

"Two students weren't showing proper respect, and I—"

The Dean creaks his chair closer. His kneecaps pop. "What were they doing?"

"Kissing," Dee says, sitting back, folding his arms. "Practically undressing in the class—"

"Couple of love birds, huh?" the Dean chuckles.

"Could say that."

"Go on."

Dee speaks to the carpet. "Well, I asked them to stop, and they—the male student, Fender, Dallas Fender—mouthed off, and I came back at him, and then it was over. Nothing big. But we had a spat."

Ferguson probes his tongue against the inside of his cheek. He blinks at the upper reaches of the ceiling then brings his fingertips together and leans forward. Over his shoulder, outside the window, a black-capped chickadee hops like an acrobat through the flickering aspen leaves.

"Tell me, how are you adjusting?" the Dean says.

Dee strokes his thighs with his palms. "Adjusting?"

"To us. We aren't New Yorkers. Go at a slower pace, isn't that right? How are you fitting in? Wife and kids happy?"

"Yeah, yeah," Dee says, whetting a fingernail with his thumbnail.

Dean Ferguson grins. He reaches back and scratches the base of his skull. "Little slice of culture shock, coming out here, I bet," he says. "Can be tough, can't it?"

"To be honest, Dean Ferguson," Dee says. "We're going through some things right now. Finishing our home—"

"Sure."

"—adjusting to the area, the kids and Reneé—"

"Uh huh."

"—she's been depressed since I've known her, and last week, I thought I was losing my mind—"

The Dean's eyebrows jump. "That's not good for teachers," he says.

"I know. It's just, last week, everything happened at once and—"

"Dee," the Dean says. He cups his elbow in his palm. He pats his cheek, making the pop of a champagne cork. "Want to know something up front? We haven't seen presentation as creative as yours since I've been here. We love your stuff, and we'd like to keep you."

"I'd like to be kept," Dee says.

"Base level, we can't have teachers running down their students. Can we leave it there?"

"I understand," Dee says, rising. "I'll watch it."

"Good," the Dean says. He strains into a bowlegged stance,

waddles to the door and heaves it open.

"Take those kids and that wife out. Stress can blindside you if you don't keep an eye on it."

"I will," Dee says. "Thank you, Dean Ferguson."

"You bet, Dee. Give me a holler."

Before going home Dee drives to MegaMart. The lavender light slants across the sullen playgrounds and 1-800-Collect billboards and scrap yards crowned in concertina wire. The purple glow of the landscape is dreamy, clarifying, full of poetry and redemption. But his sick heart swings like a clapperless bell. His girls appear in his mind with the angelic force of carvings on a cathedral. Classic, severe, empyreal. Reneé, Rae, Colette. He wants so desperately to love them—to be maddeningly, achingly, overwhelmingly in love with them. And to know they love him. But he and his tribe are little more than a family posing for a magazine ad. And how long before the ad gets canceled?

He enters MegaMart and passes Doogins the Clown, who has retained his red nose, orange wig, white face and blue eye paint. But he's traded the Rastafarian cap and floppy shirt for a fringed The Mamas and The Papas vest and giant pink foam-rubber cowboy hat. He leans against the bike rack, smoking.

Dee fights off the temptation to fly to help phone thirteen. Instead he breezes to the entertainment aisles past racks of sunglasses, strongholds of Wild Cherry Pepsi twelve-packs, and headless orange mannequins in skimpy red day-glo bikinis. In the music section he finds himself jailed in terraces of glitzy, cellophane-sheathed CD's. An anorexic-looking MegaMart employee, a girl in scarlet 'Help Crew' vest, stands in the aisle. She gawks at her reflection in the mirrored shelves of music. She wears stovepipe denim Capri pants and chunky vanilla platform sneakers. Two ponytails in peach-colored bands shoot like squiggly antennae from her head.

"Excuse me," Dee says. "Could you help me?"

The girl steps back as if avoiding a mugger. Her forehead puckers and she stretches a string of bubblegum from her pouty plum lips and spools it around her index finger. Her face sparkles with teeny stars of glitter.

"Yeah?" she says.

"I need a CD," Dee says. "Sondheim something or other. About clowns? Do you have it?"

"I don't know."

"You don't know?" Dee asks.

"The guy at the photo desk," she says. "This is his area."

"Where is he?" Dee says, rotating his head like prairie dog. "Can he help me?"

"Probably on break," she says. Then she pops her gum in her mouth and wanders away.

"Thanks for your help!" Dee calls.

With both hands he paws through the CDs. The plinky xylophone and watery saxophone from the intercom muzak, 'Islands in the Stream,' trickles like chemical irritant into his ears. After some frantic fumbling through the Broadway/Musicals section, he finds what he wants—a *Best of Stephen Sondheim* collection including a song about clowns—pays for it, and exits the store. On the way out he shoots the customer service counter a guarded glance and avoids the eyes of Doogins the Clown.

At the Jefferson County line he speeds across the river parallel to the railroad bridge. The new CD blares on the stereo. In the ruddy light black willows and cottonwoods rise from the riverbank like dark, fibrous lace. The strangeness of the past weeks and the stress from the move to Idaho have left him quarantined in time. His soul feeds on hollowness. The road rolls beneath his car like a honky-tonk treadmill, complete with Scott Joplin score and shooting-gallery scenery. When he makes eye contact with himself in the rearview mirror the monster sadness rises from the center of the earth to claim him.

"Beautiful wife," he says.

His car bounds over the bridge with a bump, and he is momentarily airborne in his seat, as Barbra Streisand launches into the last parabolic strains of 'Send in the Clowns.' Across the shallow river and rocky shoals the fading sun shoots bolts of fire through poplar and white pine, through tangled barbed wire and crooked telephone poles, leaves and ripples and dashes of electric gold.

"Cute kids."

The sorrow clamps talons in the turkey flesh of his shoulders. In vain he gulps back the pulsing sobs. His hands enter from another dimension, seize the steering wheel and guide his car to the shoulder. Out of traffic, he trembles in his seat, cries for twenty minutes like a lost girl. The throbs of weeping wash the oil slick of grief from his organs. Eventually the sadness empties itself, a rolling but pleasant rhythm through his frame. Rivers and lakes of clean misery. He glances around, hunched over the wheel, ashamed, as if one of his old schoolteachers might see him. He sniffs and wipes his nose with the back of his wrist. The last spasms work in and out, a soft whimper trailing away with the cowboy brake lights caravanning north on Highway Twenty.

"A good job."

He waits for an answer and hears nothing. So he shoves the stick into gear. Before pulling into traffic he stares across the river at the dusky fields where helpless next-door neighbors, innocent little girls, cancer-ridden sisters-in-law, bulldoggish architects, sexy heartless wives, and Jillian and Harv Slade—all in raffish clown robes—frolic in the renaissance of a western night, spinning out of their gang choreography a circus of small tragedies, singing a thousand songs of sorrow for no one.

7

ON LABOR DAY a warm air mass moves into the valley and settles for three days like a sleepy animal sunning itself before getting banished by a swift cold front. At the Thornton Texaco two landscapers for Green Genie, both named Dale, both in forest-green shirts and khaki cargo pants, pull their tank sprayer truck in to take a break from talking about working. Crew boss Dale, the shorter one, drove a frozen seafood van in Pittsburgh before moving west. He is so hairy he was once misdiagnosed with hypertrichosis. Crew member Dale, bony and bald, wears steel-toed work boots, lacks a right index finger (thanks to a wobbly tree chipper), and stoops from bending down to hear people. All day, news has dribbled through the dash radio: civil war in the Ivory Coast, Tropical Storm Hanna, the Swiss no longer neutral. But it's the passing of The Steelers' seven-time All-Pro center that has furry Dale moping as he drops his sunflower seeds, Big Hunk, and lemon-lime Gatorade on the counter. He scoops a hand in his pocket and drops a jangling trove of change on the counter.

"R-I-P, Iron Mike," he says. "Least we still got Arrowhead."

"Pentagon's patched up," bald Dale says, eyeing the cigarettes and chewing tobacco. "Show 'em they can't do it to us again."

The pale girl at the register has tinted brunette hair, splotchy freckles. Her lipstick is the color of tomato paste. She uses a fingertip to slide the coins into her cupped palm. Furry Dale seizes the Gatorade and twists off the lid, which makes a slurpy pop. His eyebrows scrunch together as he brings the bottle to the bristly hole in his beard where his lips should be.

"Chuck Heston, huh? Rough."

Bald Dale sets a PayDay and chocolate milk on the countertop. "What is?" Then to the cashier, "Skoal long cut mint."

"Alzheimer's."

The girl twists a coil of her dark hair around her finger and twirls to face them, grinning apologetically. "We're out of Skoal."

Bald Dale goes google-eyed at the girl then grimaces in exaggerated pain, tips his head back, eyes closed. He writhes as if stretched on a rack.

"It's a madhouse! A madhouse!"

Furry Dale laughs then with gravity brings his Gatorade to his face and peers into the lemon-lime translucence. "It's people!" he says. "Tell them, it's people!"

The Dales wheel their sprayer truck out of the parking lot and are nearly blindsided by a Dodge Stratus that comes screaming off the highway, spitting gravel from its rear tires like a stunt car. They holler "Whoa!" as the Stratus fishtails down the unfinished road to the south. At the gabled white ranch house with the pretentious Ionic columns on the porch the Stratus bumps up the driveway and stops, and Reneé jumps out and storms inside where with an animal grunt she dumps a heap of groceries on the kitchen table. Colette and Rae tear past her into the living room like wolverine kits, screaming and scrapping over which Happy Meal Barbie is the best. Colette, face maroon with anger, holds the Pop Sensation Barbie—the one they both want—above her head, too high for Rae. Rae howls. She hops like a dwarf trying to snatch a peach from a tree limb. She clenches her fists and stamps her pink Heely skate shoes on the un-sanded hardwood floor. With a shriek she launches Theresa Barbie across the room, where it strikes a potted Wandering Jew. The sisters pursue each other around the coffee table like Tom and Jerry on speed, cries shredding the air.

Reneé drives her fingers into her temples and sags into a chair. Her Columbia paint sample booklet flaps on the table, earmarked to Abalone, Embers of December, and Patagonia Thunder. She tries to block out the noise, but the ruckus in the next room pumps venom through her jaw muscles. She shoots to her feet and with both arms sweeps the groceries to the floor.

"Shut up! Now!"

Colette halts, trembling, and stares at her mother. Rae's face shrivels into a tortured, tearful mask. She bawls.

Grinding her molars Reneé marches over and snatches Colette's doll away. The girls yelp as Reneé stalks to the sink, grabs a butcher knife, and axes Pop Sensation Barbie to ham salad on a cutting board.

"Mom! That's mine!" Colette protests. She drops to the floor and writhes.

"Miiiiine!" Rae wails.

"Both of you! Shut up!"

Reneé grabs the paint booklet and flees the room. Both daughters wail hysterically and chase their mother upstairs, but she outruns them, ducks inside, and slams the door, locking herself in with the catalog colors of fantasy and escape.

8

FOR TWO NIGHTS, Dee squirms in bed. A flinty viper of suspicion coils around his body, feeding on his bankrupt brain. For days he's battled the notion that he must know something—however ridiculous—for certain. After classes he calls Reneé from work.

"Let's go," he says.

"Where?" she asks.

In the background, Colette and Rae screech and batter each other with sections of Tootie-Toot Train Tracks.

"MegaMart," he says. "I need a break."

"You want to go to MegaMart?"

"I always go," he says, cradling a casual tone in his chest. "Anything to return?"

"Two outfits I bought for the girls, but—"

"Pick me up after lunch," he says. "Bye."

At MegaMart the sun heats the pavement, but the air carries a blustery chill. Towering cumulus clouds crowd the sky above the hills, moving eastward over Palisades Reservoir and Grays Lake. The McBrides park near the front entrance and usher their girls inside, swinging them in a human chain of silly songs about sticky oatmeal and blue birds doing loop-de-loops and the quirky letter Q. Doogins the Clown sports a yellow chicken suit with English butler dickey and green polka-dot bow tie. He juggles big pink and blue eggs, and as the McBrides pass, his dickey flips up and rolls like a flapping window blind. Reneé snares a cart and propels the girls through archways of Fuji film and

KarmelKorn. Dee dispy-doodles like a speed walker straight for the home and garden section.

At the help phone thirteen kiosk he glances around like a man hoping to spot something grand in his last look at the world. He is rewarded with the sight of hangdog shoppers plodding through mopped aisles of cheap goods. He feels giddy and frantic among the kaleidoscopic racks of bagged fertilizer, garden hose, and sprinkler heads on clearance. Sure that no one suspects him of mischief, he picks up the phone. His head throbs. His voice cracks.

"I'd like some help in home and garden, please," he says. He scans the rafters, the one-way mirrors and service doorways.

"You're back," the voice hums like a cello string.

"I want to know what's going on," Dee says. "Now."

"First," the girl's voice purrs through a prelude of Icelandic waves. "Let's get this straight. I ask questions. You give answers. Capiche?"

Dee scours the store for a glimpse of his tormentor. "You on some Venetian exchange program?"

"Why the sarcasm?" the voice asks.

"Call it wit," Dee says. "When I find out who you are, your ass is grass."

"Threats," the voice says, taking notes. "I'll remember that."

Dee jabs the kiosk console with his finger. "Let's start with last time," he says.

"Shoot."

"You said I didn't know what I wanted."

"You don't."

"Where the hell do you get off—"

"Profanes," the voice says, releasing an explosion of larks. "Goes with threats. And you don't, by the way—know what you want. Evidenced, I think, in your recent slip into the gutters of unprofessionalism in class, your little confab with Dean Ferguson—"

Dee's mind spins like a hamster wheel. His eyes dart left and right, loose in their sockets. Mothers and children putter past monoliths of shrink-wrapped baby formula and toilet cleaner as if their batteries are running down. Then—voila!—the answer snaps in a socket in his brain. He breathes easier, no longer ready to pounce.

"—and you looked pretty stupid in front of Karl, the customer service guy, too. College instructors have a certain amount of respectability to maintain—"

"Zip it," Dee says.

"—a certain level of decorum—"

"We'll see."

"Call again," the girl's voice chimes, church organs and singing mice in the background.

"Why? You're no help," Dee quips and rams the phone down.

On Friday, the deadline for Dee's students' political TASC modules, he asks Dallas Fender and Ali to stay after class. They slouch in their desks like Jack and Diane, legs spread salaciously, emanating teen sex and idle time, perfumed with the scent of breakfast burritos and their parents' bank accounts. After the last student exits Dee slams the door and pivots to face them. He jams his finger into space, a ruffle of lilac political TASC modules cocked on his hip like an ostrich plume.

"Where do you and your little—floozie—get off trying to embarrass me in public!" he fumes. "How dare you make a fool of me! Especially with everything that's been going on with my family. New job! New place!"

He breaks off, panting, his throat lined with sandpaper. Dallas and Ali's expressions cloud then cool into watchful smiles.

Dee rips a check mark through the air with his index finger. "Far as I'm concerned," he spits, "this is stalking and harassment, and I haven't ruled out legal action. I trust your behavior will cease immediately. End of discussion!"

He stands back like a swordsman after a fencing match. TASC modules flutter to his feet.

Dallas slouches in his chair, arms folded across his chest. His tongue rolls a Denny's toothpick across his bottom lip. Ali sits forward, dimpled chin trembling. Tears leak from her eyes, not from guilt, but from the Calvinistic force of Dee's rhetorical slam dunk. She releases a whimper and stares at her teacher like a Pomeranian that's peed on a rug. With the brusque civility of a French gendarme, Dee excuses them from class, mission complete.

In thirty minutes, he's in Dean Ferguson's office and put on probation.

He decides to tell Reneé nothing about it.

Moments after receiving his sentence, Dee stands in the EITC parking lot, shoulders sagging, and watches a white Buick Skylark with baby blue rims cruise by and honk. Dallas and Ali wave from the front seat.

Dee drives to MegaMart in a blind rage. In the parking lot his car crashes through a blockade of carts and skids to a stop.

Doogins the Clown has changed into a ringmaster's tie and tails and holds a Chihuahua that wears a Francis Bacon ruff collar. Doogins waves weakly. The dog snarls and bares its teeth. Half-stumbling, half-running, Dee reaches the home and garden section. He picks up help phone thirteen.

"Who are you?" he hisses, cross-eyed with bloodlust.

"Probation," the voice says through a trucker's CB radio. "Slick. Some of your students aren't even on that."

Dee's jaw juts forward. "I swear, if you don't tell me—"

"You didn't even call first to see if they work here—"

"I'll find out, and even if I don't—"

"—or if your other students work here, or someone they know—"

Dee's temper rises to volcano force. "Who are—"

From the phone comes the sound of an ambulance siren. "Remember, think before—"

Dee bellows and seizes the phone cord. He heaves his body into a hard arc and like an Olympic hammer thrower whips the phone over his head. On the back swing he nearly removes the head of a girl with brown two-foot braids who's sailing a toy purple jumbo jet behind him. The girl's mother yelps and shields her daughter with her body. With a roar Dee shatters the phone against the kiosk. The blow topples a croquet set, sending a solar system of colored wooden balls spinning down the waxed aisles. Dee races to the front of the store.

He barges to the head of the line at the customer service counter and finds Karl standing like an orangutan waiting to be fed. With each word, Dee strikes the counter with his fist.

"Tell—me—what's—going—on!"

"Get security!" Karl calls to the back room as people scatter.

Before Karl can call the cops, Dee storms out into the blinding sunlight, shirt collar flapping, arms battering swarms of invisible bats. A portly redheaded woman lugging a boxed food mixer yips and skips out of his way.

"Hey, man!" Doogins calls, restraining the growling Chihuahua.

Back on campus Dee locks himself in his office. He rifles through a teetering pile of correcting and scoring and slops together Monday's presentation on electronic TASC modules. Halfway through, he rakes aside the mountain of papers and weeps into his hands.

"Un," he babbles. "Un. Sane."

Somehow the acknowledgement is sweet. The liberating confession swims, thick and syrupy, like healing balm into the basin of his burning skull. He feels pleasantly pure, changed and reborn. Having admitted his brain has turned to semolina, he can taste peace. He sits up, exhausted but newly calm, fixes his tie, runs a hand over his head. Whistling 'Send in the Clowns,' he rummages through his desk for his cell phone and calls home.

"Honey?" he says. "Late again, yep. Grading, committee work. Be home as soon as I can."

With his thumb, he ends the call. "None of which is true, by the way."

As he drives around the outskirts of Ammon, blue darkness douses the fringe of warm pink light above the hills. He counts the bulbs and streetlamps and electric signs that string beads of colored light from porch to gas station to strip mall. At ten minutes to closing, he wheels back to MegaMart and parks in a far corner of the lot and from the back seat produces a fishing cap, sunglasses, and navy blue windbreaker. With an air of stealth he dons them and re-enters the store.

In every quarter MegaMart is shutting down. Between the Cheetos and Hallmark cards, red-vested 'Help Crew' workers zigzag across the polished aisles like extras from Aldous Huxley's dreams. The muzak—'Up Where We Belong'—floats in the rafters among suspended kid's bikes and inflatable play forts. Destroyed, drained, shaking, Dee picks up help phone thirteen.

"Hello?" he wheezes.

"Hi," the voice says. A Siamese gong sounds.

"I know you're almost closed," Dee breathes.

"I never close."

Dee blinks at the ceiling. "Who are you?"

"Help Phone Thirteen."

"Then why won't you help me?" he pleads.

"You never asked."

"Help me," Dee heaves.

"With what?"

"Everything!"

The voice clucks its tongue, trips a game show applause track. "No good. I need specifics. Ain't no genie bottle waitin' to be rubbed."

Then, the loosening. In Dee's core blue glaciers quiver and crack. Arctic torrents muscle log jams and beaver dams aside, and moonlit waters pour into dry creek beds, flushing out mud and tree branches and dead rodents. He holds nothing back, rambles more than speaks, blubbering from the gravel pit of his soul. The voice answers—a girl's voice, then a man's, then a cartoon parakeet's—the noise in the background mimicking traffic on Broadway, the Lunar Lander's afterburners, Mets game cheers, the night wind under an owl's wings, its talons outstretched, the panicked dormouse scuttling under a heap of dry maple leaves.

"My wife," Dee breathes. "Reneé—"

"Beautiful," the voice interjects. "What about her?"

"She's interested in everything but me. Why isn't she interested in me? We've been married for years. The girls—"

"Try asking her that."

He puts a hand to his forehead. "She won't talk about it," he says. His neck tenses. "About anything important! About real!"

"Yeah," the voice says as if admitting something. "I'll have to get her in here—"

"She's, she's—"

"What?"

Dee grips the phone with both hands and speaks into the mouthpiece. "Preoccupied."

"You're preoccupied with her preoccupations."

"I love her so much," Dee says, surrendering. "I want to grab her and squeeze the juice out of her sometimes, but she doesn't send anything back. It's like hugging a cactus."

"She's been hurt," the voice intones from within a church bell.

"So have I," Dee says. A fit of weeping throttles him. He snuffles, wipes his nose with a windbreaker sleeve.

"That's why I'm here," the voice urges.

"What do I do?" Dee says. "We're the parents, and we're not fit to wipe our own butts."

"I'm Help Phone Thirteen. I don't give help I'm not asked for."

"I want help," Dee says, as if speaking with a jawful of ice cubes. "Help me with Reneé. Please."

"Tell her she's beautiful," the voice says, launching a flock of flamingoes into azure sky.

Somewhere in the store, a ponderous metal door slams. A breaker box clanks. Dee looks around and presses his body to the kiosk. His arms circle the smooth cylinder, his cheek and open mouth mashed against the cool metal, slurring his words.

"Thee knowth theeth boodifoh," he says. "Theeth gohjuth!"

"When's the last time you told her?" the voice says, tuning a tuba.

Dee peels his face away. "Don't know."

"So what's holding you back?"

Dee shivers. "Don't like stating the obvious, I guess."

"So you got it?"

"Beautiful," Dee repeats. "Tell her."

"What else? I gotta run."

"Thought you never closed," Dee says.

"Don't," the voice answers, gunning a dragster engine. "Just gotta go."

"There's, well," Dee says. The words flow like a hasty translation. "She's got this sister-in-law. Cherelyn, her brother Marc's wife? Who's got throat cancer? They don't know if—"

"Right, right."

"It's just—never going away. Those things drag on, even if there's a remission. I know it's sad, and I feel bad and everything.

But it's—possessing us—"

"Cancer's a biggie," the voice clatters, rapping at a manual typewriter. A cash register drawer chimes, followed by a loading dock buzzer.

Dee massages his eyelids. "It's all Reneé thinks about. What can we do? Anyone—she's on the phone for hours with her mother, and meanwhile, the kids need bathing and food. Our relationship takes a hit—"

"Sounding a teensy bit insensitive, aren't we?" the voice says, kicking away bagpipes. "Like the world centers on you."

"There's another sticking point for us."

"For you."

"Me."

"So would you like help?"

"Yes," Dee says. He licks his dry lips and glances around the store's million-dollar mausoleum. Lights flicker off. "I need help."

"Pick up your phone then."

Automatically, Dee answers his cell phone, which is attached to his belt, chirping a Mozart concerto. Jillian Slade, Reneé's mother, sings on the other end. Distant static warps her voice and makes it cut in and out.

"Dee!" she says. "Is that you? I was just saying—Cherelyn's cancer is gone. Er, remitting. The doctors are dumbfounded. It's a miracle."

"That's wonderful, Jillian," Dee says. He holds the two phones like mouse ears to his head.

"The procedures," Jillian bubbles. "The treatments must have taken."

"Amazing," Dee says.

"It is," Jillian says. "I've got to go. Just wanted to spread the good news. I called Reneé. She's waiting for you at home. How are you kids? Fine? We'll talk soon, okay? Bye-bye, now."

"Bye," Dee says. He punches the 'end call' button with his thumb.

He floats. Reels. Goes numb.

"How can you do this?" he rasps into the store phone.

"Thesis, antithesis, synthesis," the voice says. "I'm Help Phone Thirteen. Bye, now."

The jaunty voice slithers into the bell of a sleepy slide trombone. A dial tone buzzes in Dee's ear then fades into an orchestra of toucans and howler monkeys in a bubble bath. Using his cell phone, he calls Reneé, who confirms the report in a flattened tone, as if it's somehow old news. Dee listens and tells her he's coming home because he has something to tell her, which dampens her mood somewhat.

At home the girls are asleep, and Dee finds Reneé seated at the kitchen table in a sleek black turtleneck and jeans. She's floofed her hair like a magazine model. Shimmering triple-loop earrings swing from her ears. She droops her head in her hands under the kitchen light and stares at the paint booklet on the table. Dee enters and she lifts her head to greet him.

"How'd you hear about Cherelyn?" she says.

"Talked to your mom," he says. He remains in the doorway like a palace guard. "It's wonderful news."

"My mom called you?" she says. "When? You don't look happy."

Dee blinks. His shoulders squirm. "I have something to tell you," he says.

Reneé rises. "What?"

"You're beautiful," he says, weightless as a paratrooper.

"I'm—what?" she says. "What's that have to do—"

"I think you're beautiful," he repeats.

"Dee," she says, drifting closer.

Then with the other abandoned and destroyed spare parts of the world, his body drops into her arms.

"And I'm—not!" he wails. His voice sweeps down a tunnel of years. "I'm not!"

9

OCTOBER SETTLES IN THE VALLEY, silent and smoky. Frost scorches pumpkins and melts to a bright gloss that hardens to a glaze at twilight. The cold saps chlorophyll from aspen leaves, leaving them blotched and brittle. When the wind blows through they make the sound of cautious applause. Late in the day plowed fields send up spirals of shimmering vapor. A chill clings to split-rail fences black with rain. Aluminum sheds and mountainsides glisten. In the pastures along Highway Twenty Holstein cows puff plumes of steam, noses gummed with dew. Gutters overflow with a papery salad of colored leaves: russet, maple, butter, husk. Stars scatter grains of light above Dee's heavenward gaze. Reneé stares too—then at him. After work and dinner Dee slips his hands in his pockets and without speaking steps out on the back porch to gape upward. The girls toddle out and tug Reneé's pant legs.

"Hello," Rae squeaks.

Colette cups binocular hands around her eyes. "What are you looking at?" she says.

"Nothing," Dee says.

"Everything," Reneé says.

Midway through the month two cheerleaders from Mud Lake High School die in a drunk driving accident. EITC volunteers and high school students erect corn mazes and spook alleys in local fields and barns to raise a memorial fund. In Thornton the Ririe High School Pep Club commandeers a vacant four-story grain elevator and with a bed sheet and scarlet paint dubs it 'The Tower of Terror,' charging five dollars for admission.

On Halloween Dee and Reneé drive their girls to MegaMart's 'Trunk or Treat.' Dee dresses as a W. C. Fields-ish honeybee in black tights and Chuck Taylor high-tops. Reneé wears a green turtleneck and skirt, with a purple and yellow sunhat to make her the flower. Colette and Rae, in white sweat suits and ping-pong ball glasses, are grubs.

MegaMart stays open late, and the parking spaces swarm with parents in station wagons, teens in SUV's, and local merchants. A Q102 Classic Country Radio van blasts Roger Miller and Johnny Cash. There are tailgate displays for recycling, adopting animals, taxidermy, chemical dependency, and Meals on Wheels. A Toyota Supra drapes from its open hatchback a curtain of Hefty sacks dotted with construction-paper pumpkins. The banner that spans its raised hatch drips with vampire-blood lettering: Domestic Violence Outreach. Car bumpers balance buckets of candy corn, Dubble Bubble, and Idaho Spud bars. The fatty aroma of burgers and bratwurst wafts from barbecues. The glowing orange grills of portable heaters turn the asphalt into runways for little goons and gurus trolling for treats.

The McBrides wear mittens and ear muffs and wait in folding chairs behind their Stratus, old blankets bundling their knees. As each pint-sized Captain Bly or Nefertiti rustles near in gold lamé collars and magenta breeches, Dee and Reneé invite them to dip their fists into a tinfoil cornucopia of caramel, cherry chocolate, and nougat. The McBrides take turns leading Colette and Rae to the other cars—Dee humming for his wife and girls not to get stung, and Reneé answering, with a smirk, that her 'honey' shouldn't worry. After three candy rounds Dee shifts in his chair, thinking.

"Restroom," he tells Reneé. "I'll 'bee' two seconds."

"Buzz back," she says.

At MegaMart's entrance hay-bale igloos shelter gremlins handing out fluorescent orange coupon booklets. Doogins the Clown flaunts purple tights, a crushed ten-gallon hat and a fiberglass jack o' lantern sandwich sign on rainbow suspenders. A squawking green parrot hops from his head to his shoulders. A witch's cauldron of dry ice root beer bubbles at his side. As Dee enters the store he glances at Doogins, who makes brief eye contact with him then offers caramel apples to two pogo-sticking Jawas.

"Closing in five," Karl calls from the customer service counter.

"I'll be three," Dee says, hustling past bathtubs of Atomic Fireballs and Brach's circus peanuts.

In the home and garden section leaf blowers are on special. Dee picks up help phone thirteen.

"Hello?" he says.

"Hi," the voice says, tortured ghouls and creaking coffins in the background.

"What's with the scary soundtrack?" Dee says.

"Sorry," the voice says. "Spirit of the season." The Halloween sounds fizzle out. "How are things going?"

"Better," Dee says.

"Told ya."

Dee moves the phone to his other hand, cradles it against his jaw. "You did. But, Reneé, she's—I don't know—not happy. She moved out here with me and—"

"The big move," the voice commiserates, tooting a fife.

"Right."

"So whatcha gonna do?"

"Don't know," Dee ventures. "Thought I'd—ask you."

"Let me get this straight. You're asking for help?"

"Yes," Dee says. He searches the rafters, the aisles, the floor. "I'd like some help with my marriage."

"Awright," the voice says, flushed with mandolins and circular saws. "In two weeks—got it?—two weeks, leave work after lunch, drive over here, and at precisely 1:13 p.m.—not a second sooner or later, hear me?—I want you to enter the Hawaiian Vacation Getaway Sweepstakes at the customer service counter. Everything else will take care of itself."

"Everything?" Dee asks.

"What?"

Dee hooks a thumb in his belt and chews the inside of his lip. "Nothing. Just—everything's a lot."

"Everything's what I do. I'm Help Phone Thirteen."

The store lights waver to black. Dee hovers in a pod of darkness. A service light on the kiosk shrouds him in a cone of green radiance.

"Thanks," he says. "I can't tell you—"

"Better go," the voice says. "You may never get this chance again."

10

NOVEMBER SLEET RATTLES shocks of dried corn stalks. Bonfires gutter in dark fields. Cats scuttle into garages. A charcoal mist lingers over the valley for days, and on the banks of the Snake River, cattails freeze in scrims of bubbled ice that narrow the current to a winding black ribbon. Up and down Highway Twenty diesel rigs bellow and whine. Huge white tubes of industrial plastic stuffed with alfalfa lie like mammoth grubs in muddy stubble. At the Texaco station truckers stamp their feet, steamy breath ballooning from their beards.

Reneé lies in bed.

It's noon.

As if gripping a stiletto, she holds a single Benjamin Moore paint card in her fist: Montego Moonscape.

She's called Chris Benati three times.

Downstairs Colette and Rae kneel in pajamas and stare at the television like dazed lab rats. They are entering their third hour of Nickelodeon cartoons. In the kitchen sink the dishes from last night's spaghetti dinner molder in a crusty heap. A soggy landslide of clothes and bedding and bagged garbage barricades the laundry room door. The dining table overflows with orange rinds, bowls of Cheerios, splattered milk, crayons, and soggy coloring books.

Reneé lies in bed and stares at the ceiling like a slain saint. The clawed bats of depression have come swiftly this morning, hideous and unrelenting, with jeering fangs and jaundiced eyes. She fights for a taste of what's been happening over the past weeks—the good things, Dee's change, the way they talk to each other. But these bright spots sink in tar pits of more sinister thoughts. She sees the mocking faces of her high school boyfriends, Captain Hook hands corkscrewed into the bloody nubs of their wrists. Her skin feels the scabby talons of a family friend with a ratty mustache who reeked of tobacco and chili peppers. She recalls the way his moist palms leached poison into her young flesh, his beefy fingers typing a trashy horror novel down her thighs.

She shivers. Her body shrinks into a fetal curl, and she fights for air beneath the sinking ceiling of obsidian chandeliers that shatter in slow motion. Then daylight floods her eyes, washing away the muck of sadness until she's standing on a smooth beach. She doesn't recognize the village, but grass huts grow in clumps, carefree tourists stroll arm-in-arm, and plump natives hawk fruit-colored T-shirts from banana-leaf baskets on their hips. Reggae music ripples on the daiquiri breeze. She rents snorkel equipment, learns to sailboard, canoes the fragrant sea. All day, she's borne on balmy wind, the intoxicating odor of spindrift and coconut oil.

A peach kayak appears from nowhere. She climbs in and paddles to the breakers and plunges into the sea in her snorkel gear. At first, she's frightened. But her strokes grow more powerful as she knifes like a mermaid through the surf. She throws her head back and turns hundred-foot loops through shape-shifting screens of snapper and silvertail, shedding snorkel gear and flippers. Craving more freedom, she peels away her sherbet bikini, and in the mirror eye of a gray whale she sees the sea has returned her high school physique. No stretch marks, cellulite, deflated bust line. She's sixteen, and her skin snaps back. She admires her reflection. Spinning, primping, turning. She places a sprig of blossomy seaweed behind her ear. A convoy of loggerhead sea turtles swoops down like a fleet of submarines and she snags a passing flipper. On the back of the lead male she shrinks to the size of a shrimp and clings to its shell to avoid being bucked to the sea floor.

The turtles deposit her in a bed of florid coral. Fascinated, she retrieves a jagged piece and runs the lovely shard over her fingers. She dandles it across her wrist, lets it linger when it feels like the blade of a large kitchen knife. Should she leave her new world?   The frisky sea lions and genial groupers?   A cavernous longing floods her bowels and hardens her resolve to a razor edge. She toys with her choice, weighs the outcomes, presses it against her wrist. So much beauty, an ocean of weight: the purple sponges, the shimmering arcs of gold light and mobs of translucent orange jellyfish in the unwashed kitchen windows, the anemones of dirty laundry, buried treasure, buried life, the whale songs and stupid cartoons in the living room. Her throbbing two-hundred pound heart urges her to break the surface, to barrel roll through the sky like a killer whale, heaving pure sunshine into her lungs. *Still*, she thinks, *I'm so safe here. I want to stay where love is.* She rocks and weeps Pacific tears. *I don't want to go back up there.* A little squid curls a tentacle around her ankle. She presses the coral to her wrist, annoyed at the squid's touch, ready to part her flesh. But she is crying. She can't understand. Sea and tears flow from the same salt. *Why?* she pleads through the tempest. *Why am I so sad to leave everything I love?*

Then Dee stands in the doorway to the bedroom, brandishing a red MegaMart sweepstakes entry over his head.

"Like doing the hula?" he thunders like a game show host. He strides to her side and rests a hand on Rae, who is tugging at Reneé's leg. "Oo, let's put that away," he says, setting the knife on the dresser.

Reneé sniffs, sits on the bed. "What?"

"Crying?" Dee says. He sits so hard on the bed she bounces up. "No wife of mine cries! What's going on around here?"

She shutters her face with her hands. "I was, I thought—"

"You okay?" He loops his arm around her shoulder. "Reneé?"

"Fine," she says. She thumbs tears from her eyes, forces a smile. "Why are you home?"

"We," Dee says, "are going to Hawaii. I won a contest."

"When?"

"I entered something at the MegaMart—"

"No," she says, turning her streaked face to him. "When are we going to Hawaii?"

"Tomorrow," he says. His hand finds the back of her neck.

"Now," she says.

"What?"

"Let's go now."

11

OVER CHRISTMAS BREAK the McBrides send identical postcards home from the Grand Wailea on Maui. Evie builds Tinker Toy palaces and collects the mail and spends an hour every day on the phone convincing Jillian Slade not to fly out from New York, while in the background Harv roars about calling child protection services. For eight days the McBrides dine, snorkel, and fall off surfboards. They play shuffleboard with car dealers from Cincinnati, hold hands while spelunking, and island hop to watch Kilauea ooze smoking lobes of lava into the sea. They fish for skipjack tuna and sleep late. They doze in hammocks, read racy airport novels, drink piña coladas served in coconut half-shells garnished with chartreuse tissue-paper parasols.

As he strolls on the beach and traces the acrobatics of seagulls, Dee sees the sunrise creep into Reneé's eyes. Her laughter rings in his chest. She takes his hand freely and asks him to share his thoughts. She flirts in the way she walks, the way she lets him approach her. At first they resolve not to call the girls—for it to be just them. But by the second night Reneé breaks down, and they call Evie and blubber like babies at the end of the conversation with Colette and Rae, who hoot and giggle long-distance at their funny mommy and daddy.

On the last night they sit on the veranda and talk. Sunup to sundown. Breakfast, lunch, and dinner arrive on the balcony. Reneé talks about her parents, their aristocratic pretensions and control-freak obsessions. She even ventures into the sanctum of her high school and college relationships, which leaves Dee aghast because his wife is surrendering—outright offering—hurtful but helpful information. Paradoxically, he feels not crushed but loved more than ever under this new canopy of trust. For once, Dee listens. Their talk eventually ebbs to a whisper, and they find themselves sitting opposite one another, a rosy membrane of sun dividing two heaps of food-smeared dishes on the table. Reneé smiles, looks away. Dee feels brave, says what he's thinking.

"What came between us?" he asks.

"When?" she says.

"After Rae was born. We don't—chase each other like we used to. I miss it."

Reneé's eyes grow foggy. "Memories," she says.

Dee shifts to the seat next to her. "Yeah."

She wipes an eye, and he hands her a monogrammed napkin. "Hurts to remember," she says. "My way of dealing with the past is"—she gestures, like an umpire calling someone safe—"hate feelings."

Dee shifts a plate of cold teriyaki shish kabobs. "What about new feelings?" he says. "Cancel the old."

"Yeah," she says, lacing her fingers through his. "How long does that take?"

He helps her up. "Find out."

On the pool deck below somebody plays an old Don Ho number on an accordion. Dee and Reneé limp through a foxtrot. He dips her, and she laughs.

"Tell me," he says. "Why do you go to MegaMart so much? Is it a girl thing? I can't stand it. Help me. I'm a guy."

"Because," she says. She looks at him like a child about to get whipped. "It gives me something to do."

"Reneé."

"No, no," she says. "I need to say this. This is how messed up I am."

"You're *not* messed up."

She stiffens in his arms. "Know what else?" she says. Tears thicken in her eyes. "Sometimes? I get so cooped up with the girls, I buy the wrong clothes. I buy the wrong ones on purpose—"

"Hey—"

"So I can get out of the house, I buy the wrong ones on *purpose!*"

Out of the circle of measured steps the dance slows to an island of stillness, and husband and wife fold together in a standing embrace, their words washed away in the rolling hush of ocean breezes and the chatter of guests from Houston and Tokyo.

12

AT HOME RENEÉ AND DEE paint the girls' rooms Mango Tango. They rifle the MegaMart bargain bins and get hooked on Conway Twitty and Merle Haggard. They crank call Chris Benati's office in New York eight times.

FROM JANUARY TO APRIL Dee takes Reneé and the girls to MegaMart once a week. Doogins the Clown dresses as an Eskimo, a Botticellian cherub, a leprechaun, and an Italian mafia tulip armed with a violin case and air-powered Tommy gun that shoots Tootsie Rolls. Reneé shops for clothes. Dee splurges on sno cones and tater tots for the girls. At the suggestion of Help Phone Thirteen Dee enrolls Colette in preschool gymnastics. A competent, affordable pediatrician is found to treat Rae's wheezy breathing. When the transmission in the McBrides' Stratus goes kaputt, the voice on the phone tells Dee where a used minivan can be found at a steal of a price, two weeks before it's officially on the lot at Bonneville Auto. When Dee finagles an exchange—used Stratus for bargain van—Reneé congratulates him on his business savvy. While hunting for MegaMart sales, Reneé strays through the purses and makeup, leaving Dee with the girls. Convinced she won't see them, he leads his daughters to kiosk thirteen.

"Hi," Colette says into the receiver.

"Hello, little missy," the voice crackles through popcorn and candy wrappers.

"This is Rae," Dee says, hoisting Rae up.

"Hi," Rae barks into the mouthpiece. "I'm fine. Good. Bye."

"Cute," the voice says to Dee. "Have a good trip?"

"Yeah, when's the next one? We're thinking Bora Bora."

"Whoa, cowpoke," the voice says. "One per customer. Got a long list of people to serve."

"Really?" Dee says.

"I won't tell you how I hate it when people say that."

"Don't have to."

"Anything else coming up?" the voice says, sawing wood. "Anniversary? Birthday?"

"I'll let you know," Dee says before hanging up. "You've been a big help."

Then after midnight in early June, in the same way Yeats rises to go to Innisfree, Dee McBride rises from his bed with a scribbled note to himself in his hand and a fish hook of suspicion in his heart. Something tells him he's been duped, that it's all too good to be true. Without waking Reneé or the girls he pads downstairs and dons a denim jacket and black stocking hat. With a water-based magic marker from his daughters' coloring boxes he blackens his face. Before leaving, he tapes a note on the door: 'Back for breakfast.'

Through the darkness he buzzes down Highway Twenty. His senses trip on cosmic energy, as if he could never sleep again. Big rigs throttle past, rocketing to Montana. Inky clouds with fluorescent fringes rove above the gaunt cottonwoods and slumbering lumberyards, blotting out stars. He passes the 'Birthplace of Television' sign—maroon and gold, with Philo T.'s name on the screen of an old TV. A gigantic American flag flies over a used car lot, illuminated in a floodlight. At the loading bay in front of The Old Sugar Mill, whose painted façade mimics a European villa, propane tanks wait like fat white warheads. Distant windows and street lamps string droplets of light along the base of the snowy, moonlit hills.

Instead of entering the heart of Idaho Falls he veers off at

Hitt Road and slows to school-zone speed at the EITC complex. Driving his daytime route after hours is disorienting. He gazes through the eyes of a voyeuristic stranger at the little campus, which hunkers like a vacant bomb shelter in the night. A watery spotlight casts a yellow glow on the American, navy blue Idaho and white EITC flags. The EITC sign, a gold sun rising behind mountains—he notices this, as if for the first time—looks more like a wheel of Double Gloucester cheese impaled on a spearhead. At the traffic light he speeds west into the suburbs.

Using a map torn from the phone book, Dee sniffs out a side street called Shelby Drive, where he parks and cancels his headlights, surrounded in humble ramblers and brown duplexes and bungalows coated in flaky blue paint. He shines a pocket flashlight on a green Xeroxed flyer from a place called 'Clown World.' In his handwriting the paper reads: *2401 Shelby Drive, Doogins' home address.*

He eases the door open—it creaks, he grimaces, freezes—then he steps out and slinks down the street. Through thick blue shadows he sidles past tiny overgrown yards and crumbling driveways, past ruined chain-link fences and Mustangs and Celicas on flat tires with rusty rims. His menthol breath steams in the shallows of his lungs. In a way he doesn't want to spoil the mystery, doesn't want to know. But some hot broth in his veins urges him forward. He's come this far, so he might as well finish it. He finds 2401 Shelby Drive, a red brick cube with empty flowerboxes and scalloped awnings, and circles the house for ten minutes, trying to peek in a window. But the shades are drawn, so he retreats to his car, where he sleeps until dawn.

Before sunrise he snorts awake and rubs the sleep from his

eyes. For an hour he stakes out Doogins the Clown's home, yawning violently and kneading the kinks from his neck, ignoring Reneé's calls to his cell phone. After seven a man exits the little brick home, gets in a battered yellow Toyota truck, and drives away—with Dee tailing him. On Seventeenth Street the morning traffic swells, and Dee loses the tiny truck at Harvest Bread Company. Using an alternate route he speeds toward MegaMart, wiping the black from his face with Mega Kleen Kiddie Wipes from the back seat. He finds MegaMart open for business, but Doogins hasn't arrived.

He hustles inside, passing customers who, like medicated circus apes, pluck diapers and granola bars from the shelves. A skipping banjo and vibraphone version of 'Somebody's Baby' plays on the intercom. Near the back of the store he swings through the 'Employees Only' doors and saunters into the loading dock.

The storage area echoes like an airplane hangar. High ceilings, dusty lights, a vast perpetual humming. He scans the stadium-sized inventory then lifts a MegaMart 'Help Crew' vest from a nail. Whistling, he slips the vest on and checks the service entries and break rooms. The pallets of shrink-wrapped merchandise tower to the ceiling: bikes, bundt cake mixes, mac and cheese, double strollers, bacon-flavored dog biscuits. The mammoth cargo waits like something from a science fiction film, cells of killer cyber-hornets, alien embryos in hyper-sleep. Expressionless 'Help Crew' workers nod and pass, swapping gossip, bellyaching about management, pushing pallet jacks and loading dollies to their attack posts, deaf to the whine of generators and ventilations systems. Unable to spot anyone who resembles Doogins without makeup, Dee gives up, returns his vest to the nail, and heads to the home and garden section where sprinkler heads and gardening trowels have been dumped in shopping carts and tagged with red bargain stickers.

Looking around, he picks up help phone thirteen. To hear a funeral organ.

"It's not Doogins," the voice says, disappointed.

"I didn't think—"

"Exactly," the voice says.

"Wait," Dee says. "I was only—"

"Trust," the voice says. "Is the central pillar in any relationship. But you had to meddle."

"Please—I—"

"So it's gonna cost you."

"What do you mean?" Dee pleads.

"I'm Help Phone Thirteen," the voice says. In the background a cathedral bell tolls. "Get ready to bleed."

Then the phone goes dead.

Dee holds the phone away from his ear. He looks around like Matt Dillon in *Tex* after he gets shot. He shakes the phone once, expecting a dead gnome to drop out. Thunderstruck, he returns home.

Over steel cut oats and apricot danish he asks Reneé if she and the girls will accompany him to MegaMart.

"You were just there," she says.

"Got the wrong stuff," he says. "Accidentally."

"Well, in that case," she laughs.

With both of them tag-teaming, it still takes two hours to get the girls cleaned up and ready to ride, so by the time they arrive, it's almost lunch time, and as they walk through the MegaMart entrance, holding hands, they pass Doogins the Clown, who stands like a garden sculpture in violet tutu and scuba gear.

The store is a glittering Oz of sleep-deprived, muffin-stuffing, coffee-quaffing customers. Reneé takes Colette and Rae to look at swimsuits. Dee, whipped and apologetic, heads to home and garden.

To find help phone thirteen gone.

No kiosk. No phone. No help.

A terrifying emptiness gapes at him from the floor. Someone armed with a jackhammer has gouged a jagged crater in the tile. Colored wires and silver connectors sprout from the hole like tendons from a limbless socket. Dee races to customer service, spies Karl smiling through his mustache.

"Where's help phone thirteen?" Dee demands.

"I'll help you," Karl says.

"Where's the phone?" Dee begs. "It was here this morning."

"Remodeling," Karl says. "There are other—"

"I need thirteen," Dee says.

"Why?" Karl asks.

"I just do!" Dee cries. He staggers through the exit like a mugged tourist into oncoming crowds. Noting Dee's distracted demeanor, Doogins the Clown approaches. Soap bubbles froth from his snorkel.

"Find what you needed?" Doogins asks.

"For a while," Dee says, searching the parking lot for a savior.

"Huh?"

Then the payphone mounted on the wall near the vending machines rings.

"Better get it," Doogins says.

By force of habit Dee walks to the phone and answers.

"Hi," the voice says.

"It's you!" Dee exults. "Where did—what do I do?"

"Excuse me?" the voice says.

"What do I do?" Dee repeats, gulping tears. "They tore the phone down. I thought I lost you." The phone simmers in static. After a tense pause the voice speaks again.

"Um, I'd like help in electronics?" it ventures.

"Really?" Dee says.

"No, I'm lying," the voice spits back, spiced with sarcasm. "You know, I hate it when people say that."

"Yeah," Dee laughs. "You'd like help. That's a switch, huh? You really had me going there—"

"Look," the voice says. "I need some help in electronics, and if—"

Dee swoons. He holds the phone from his ear and stares at it then looks around at the haggard bustle of humans in the small northwestern city that has become his home. The armies of shopping simpletons, his brothers and sisters, advance and depart, as if burdened with the desire for real answers in plastic bags, and few of them receiving much of what they can use. What should he say? Then action gives way to reaction, and he summons the sweeping calm.

"You don't know what you need," he says to the voice on the other end.

"What? Who is this?"

"I'm Help Phone Thirteen," Dee says, tumid with authority.

"This says twelve."

"Twelve," Dee says. "Whatever."

"What do you mean I don't know what I need?" the voice demands.

"You don't," Dee says.

"Naw," the voice withers. "You're right. I don't know what the hell to do with my life. Everything's just so, so—"

"See?" Dee says, gaining confidence.

"No, I'm messed up," the voice says. "But who cares, right? You're a phone."

Near the end of Dee's conversation Reneé and the girls crowd around him, poke his ribs, and hug his legs. Smiling, he finishes the exchange and hangs up.

Reneé opens a MegaMart shopping bag. "Who you talking to?" she asks.

Like cheerful elves Colette and Rae cavort around her legs. They toast each other with cookies 'n' cream Moo Juice cartons and Sugar Shack raspberry-filled donuts.

"Communication department," Dee says. He shrugs. "Business."

"Why not use the cell phone?" Reneé says. She rummages in her bag. "Drive to campus."

Dee waves his hand. "Needed help now," he says.

"Like it?" she asks. She drapes a mint-green dress shirt over his chest. "Your size. On sale."

"Thanks," he says. He kisses her. "I love it."

"You can return it if you don't like it."

"Let's return it today."

"Stop."

"Three times—"

"Daddy!" Colette calls. She yanks his pant leg and sloshes brown liquid on his shoe. "Where'd the clown go?"

"Clown go!" Rae mimics, bunny-hopping in a circle.

Dee scans the entrance, the parking lot, the horizon. "Maybe helping someone," he says.

"Race you to the car!" Reneé cries, off with a head start.

"Or looking for a new job. Hey!"

"BET YOU'RE BREAKING THE BANK here in cow country," Harv Slade says to Dee. With a white plastic fork Harv picks at his MegaMart nachos like a beachcomber prodding a dead squid.

"Dad," Reneé says. "We have everything we need."

"Really?" Harv says.

The McBrides and Slades occupy two tables in the MegaMart food court. The Slades have flown out to see their daughter's refurbished house. Basically, they've come to snoop. Harv sits opposite Reneé in a pressed royal blue Polo shirt, tan slacks, and brown leather belt from the St. Andrew's pro shop. His silver hair and mustache are trimmed, and his Rolex glitters like gladiator armor. His stomach churns, and he still isn't convinced his daughter hasn't been brainwashed. *Idaho*, he says to himself. *Sounds like a disease you get from a damn tick.* He checks his daughter's eyes for any glint of insanity and scours a canine tooth with his tongue.

Reneé inclines her head toward her dad and gives him a look of mild dismay.

"Really."

Jillian has paid eighty-five dollars for a shampoo and set. In flamingo pantsuit and gold Nigerian jewelry, she sits facing Dee, trying desperately to save her monolith of cotton candy hair from the karate chops of her two whirligig granddaughters, who wriggle like piglets on her lap. Weary with fake laughter, she dodges a hail of kiddie haymakers. She swivels her face away and fights back with feckless, open-handed jabs. Dee watches, smiling steadily.

Through squeegee-cleaned windows August wanes and fades

over the Ammon Town Center shopping district. The rich
crimson glare warms the leased buildings and stalled cars,
accentuating the largo gestures of tired people and changing
the ordinary scene into a theater of radiance. With her
granddaughters in a straitjacket hug Jillian looks out and sees
the fiery western dusk, as Reneé and Harv continue to chat
about house paint colors. Her jaw slackens. Her lungs swell. The
light intensifies, filling grassy sidewalk cracks like smelted gold
poured into ingots, bathing the creased faces of mothers and
cranky children in tragic splendor. Then she's blindsided by a
Colette McBride uppercut and a Rae McBride sucker punch. She
yelps a weary S. O. S. and is ignored. As a last resort she pulls
faces, wheezes 'Old Mother Hubbard,' and launches a patty-
cake defense the girls parry easily and reduce to feeble hand-
jiving.

For its Crazy Days Anniversary Celebration, MegaMart stages
a fireworks show. The night settles on a parking lot of people
postponing the return home, and the sky blossoms with colored
flares. Pyrotechnic rain falls on windshields and upturned faces
and green plastic yard rakes on special for seventy-five percent
off. In the shoulder-to-shoulder crowd the Slades and McBrides
gape at the small-town sky. Dee covers his eyes with each
boom of crackling light, hoping to elude discovery. With his
daughters squeezing his knees and his wife's fingers tracing
rivulets of desire up and down his arm, he gazes at the symphony
of orange-violet and green-silver explosions. Exotic, sappy
names for the colors bloom in his mind: Dreamglow, Miracle
River, Trysting in Arcadia.

Right now isn't a good time to let Reneé and his in-laws see him get emotional. They'll only condescend and draw faulty conclusions. When he and Reneé are lying in bed he'll stare at the ceiling they painted and tell her about the times he bawled like a teenager in his car when no one saw him, about how the look on her face this night was the face of a life truly lived, how her declaration of contentment to her father was the greatest speech he's ever heard. Using simple language, he'll say that when he looked at the sky, he saw starbursts of imperial red and astral purple and golden ash, but he also saw embers stream to heaven like body and soul, bursting into a thousand new universes. He'll tell her how the fireworks spangled the night with rainbow coals, how he looked up and saw the lightning strikes of their generations, their children and children's children, streaking to earth like tiny meteors, some burning out, others blazing with a brightness more glorious with every second of their descent.

Troy Fawcett made his fortune in electronics as CEO of Global Tech, Inc. Then he retired early and moved to an obscure town. As his children have grown, he's found himself hungry for something bigger than success, which he's already achieved. So when the long evening comes sifting through the grasshopper hum on Shelby Drive, he finds himself scratching the itch of an inner restlessness. This urge to challenge himself in new and meaningful ways is fed by the sounds of suburban solace: children giggling, Big Wheels and bike chains, the clink of lawn sprinklers, the wispy wings of gossip, church bulletins, and steady weather.

His ex-wife, DuPree, has no idea how much he's worth because he never told her—not out of selfishness but reluctance. And a magnetic cloud of guilt. He simply doesn't want to know how much anymore. As often as he worries that DuPree might leave the Manhattan real-estate tycoon she abandoned him for and try to burrow back into his heart some day, he slumps in his recliner and stares at the elkhorn chandelier in his living room and thinks about how things could have been different between them.

When he first mentioned the idea of moving to Idaho, back when they were younger and still together, his family stood slackjawed around the kitchen table. One by one they strode over and gaped out the window at the murky L. A. skyline as if Martians had bombed the city. They still think he's crazy. Now, he craves only to be left in the company of his daily quest. To be lost forever in Podunkville, at his regular corner table in the Nowheresburg Diner. Friends from the old corporate machine—

the one he started—still call his house and try to coax him back into the gasoline-powered coliseum of concrete and steel. But he won't budge.

He's changed his phone number.

He's moved twice.

Mornings, his schedule is simple. After seven, sometimes as late as eight or nine, he pauses in the driveway to speak with his neighbor, Marjorie Jeffcoat, as she waters her French marigolds and gives him an update on her baby granddaughter who was born without a heart chamber. Then he heads to his office in the Teton Mall. Halfway down Seventeenth Street he turns his Toyota truck into Tautphas Park and strides with a duffle bag across the wet grass. He dodges the water sprinklers and enters the cinderblock men's rest room. Inside: a poofy blue shirt, orange wig, white makeup, and—depending on the theme for the day—other sundry props, gimmicks, and novelties he's scrounged up from the Salvation Army across from Scotty's Hamburgers on Northgate Mile. In the warped metal mirror over the sink he stares into his eyes, searching for any remote traces of sadness until a smile crinkles the corners of his mouth. He fiddles with his costume and thumbs away a smudge of red makeup, then he reads the graffiti on the walls and laughs. Sometimes he reads a scrawled message and lets his shoulders sag, thinking about the desperate soul who wrote it.

At the MegaMart in Ammon he uses a complimentary key to enter the store. At the customer service counter, without looking, he shoots a sideways gun motion at Karl, who grins behind his walrus mustache.

In the maze of the store he selects one of the many help

phones. Avoiding the eyes of security and staff and janitors, he unscrews the earpiece and inserts a tiny two-way radio speaker the size of a baby aspirin. He hides a similar device in the mouthpiece. As morning brightens the parking lot, he repeats the routine with the payphone receiver. Having prepped the phones, he stands like a man whistling and waiting for a cab. From his shirt pocket he produces a third shiny radio pill—this one crowned with itty bitty remote-controlled retractable hooks, like a tic's claws. He flips it idly from his thumb into the air and traps it on the back of his hand. He rehearses a sleight-of-hand sidearm motion with the teeny device, as if patting someone on the shoulder to attach it to the person's clothes. He drills the fluid flip-catch-and-attach routine until its liquid rhythm fills his arm. He gives a stealthy pat to the concealed weapon under his costume: a compressed-air pistol like a blowgun that shoots the attachable radio pills fifty feet. Then, slowly, moving nothing but his arm, he reaches down and whips a cell phone from his pocket. He flips it open, punches keys, listens, snaps it shut, twirls it, plunges it in his pocket, and stands motionless like a Buffalo Bill gunslinger.

He thinks of the others. Many of them he's never met. The majority he will never meet: the gossamer-haired former insurance rep who drives from his Florida bungalow, emerges from the restroom at Super China Buffet in red nose and ruffled jumpsuit, and starts cabbage-patching like a hip-hop snake-oil salesman in front of Bargain World. In Lewisburg, Pennsylvania, the former UN ambassador who paints a blue tear beneath his eye in the mirror of the Valu City employee break room. The retired rock music executives in the dark cowl and red-and-blue tights of mountebank and jack pudding who in an April hailstorm in front of Fuccillo Automall in Watertown, New York, hold umbrellas over customers and lead them around fake vomit on the sidewalk only to take their hands and goose them with joy buzzers. The British marquis who dons Groucho Marx glasses and lavendar trenchcoat at the Bayswater stop on the Underground, bangs his tambourine and cackles knock-knock jokes. Or a willowy Sacramento internet entrepreneur in false skinhead and giant sunglasses who produces a banana cream pie and rubber chicken from the folds of his papaya-colored robe and spooks snake charmers with ah-oo-gah blasts from a bicycle horn on the streets of New Delhi.

All of them, they smile and cut capers and mix with the locals. They stop arguments and start conversations. They wait in sunlight and shadow as the dusty earth rolls through an endless wind of receipts and pink slips and punch cards toward the next fantastic setback.

They take what they've recorded and make notes, tap it into databases, make calls, send emails. They watch thesis war with antithesis and pray for synthesis. They wish things were different and hope things never change.

After rehearsing his warm-up ritual, Troy pops his knuckles, jogs in place, cracks his neck. He assumes the goofiest stance he can then strikes a medley of poses: Heisman Trophy, *Discobolus*, Lurch from *The Addams Family*. Sometimes he opts for a cotton candy stand, sometimes jokes or optical illusions or toy balloons. Under his wig he's rigged a headset to a computer chip he developed for the FBI. The chip, when spoken through, warps the speaker's voice and makes a man sound like a woman and vice versa. The chip laces in a digitally-enhanced lexicon of sound effects from the wild, the media, the world of commerce. He triggers the entire program, which he wrote, from a palm-sized computer Velcroed to his wrist.

"What would you do," he mumbles sideways to the passing shoppers. "With the world wired to your soul?"

The mobs of customers descend on the store every day, bringing with them waves of despair and hope. And shame—because in a way, he's helped them mortgage their minds, fired their insatiable lust for overpriced high-tech gadgets. He and others like his former self have made and marketed the gizmos that bleep and jingle and store thousands of computer files in a space the size of a thumbnail, that save recipes for blueberry crumble and save the world from killer space candy and suck human souls into little electronic hand-held coffins. So shame, yes, because it's partly his fault. But hope, ultimately, because he knows it's not futile. They've lost their way, but only for a season. They've offered their zombie hearts to the chrome-plated god of consumerism and learned to look past the ones they should love. But everything he's done, he can undo, one laugh at a time.

There's really—really—one thing that keeps him going: wonder. In all the sun-drenched hours he's logged in front of so many malls and marts, he's witnessed some baffling events, many of them sights and sounds even he can't explain. But as his experiences have relaxed his existentialist grip on the plausible, he's found himself turning to mystery, to surrender, to the ring of chatting faces at the busy corner tables of belief. So each morning he sets up.

Then he waits.

And as the crowds arrive as relentlessly as dawn troopers, arms burdened with bags and crying kids and the crushing weight of ordinariness and mediocrity, he receives them.

As any true master would.

He sings.

Loudly at first. Then, as they march closer and push past him, a little more softly until his song is a rolling but barely audible whisper.

"Where are the clowns?" he sings to them, to himself. "Send in the clowns!"

Meer, Tarn, Water, Fell

Myself will to my darling be
Both law and impulse; and with me
The girl, in rock and plain,
In earth and heaven, in glade and bower,
Shall feel an overseeing power
To kindle or restrain

— Wordsworth

BEFORE BUMPING INTO HIS EX-WIFE in Grasmere of all places, Vincent Van Rooij, who hated poetry, unloaded his tour group in Windermere at The Brendan Chase, a twin-gabled Victorian town house with walls of packed gray slate, white bay windows, and a pugnacious grizzle-and-tan Border Terrier on the front step. Having locked the coach in Bowness-on-Windermere, opposite The Boatman's Café and a plot of pristine tennis courts, he hopped a shuttle to Dove Cottage with a mob of the gabby, headphone-wearing students. Along for the ride was the tour's director, Hemden Craig, whose degree in comparative literature and applied linguistics at UC Santa Barbara produced a dissertation on subtextual echoes of Norse folk mythology in William Wordsworth's *Guide to the Lakes* and Achim von Arnim's *Des Knaben Wunderhorn.*

"Hey, Vince!" Dr. Craig woofed, hustling down the narrow walk. A wedge of cheese and onion sandwich hung from his lips like a floppy tusk. He was trying to eat and walk and wriggle into his long navy blue raincoat. "Last one there's a flightless Dutchman!"

"You may expect me when I arrive!" Vincent called. He grimaced at the sodden sky and flipped the hood of his Elbobus jacket over his head. He drove his sledgehammer fists in his pockets and stomped off like a mutant from a monster movie. "No sooner!"

At the visitor's center the Americans clogged every doorway like goats in a cargo hold. In their brash pink sweatshirts and scruffy sandals they stepped on French toes, drew gruff sighs from Finns. Their bulging backpacks knocked Belgians off balance, and dapper South Africans and stolid Turks traveling in modest twos and threes smirked at their gum-smacking wisecracks.

Dr. Craig shoved sideways through the crush of loudmouth students and paused at each display like an orphan window shopping on Christmas Eve. His camelhair jacket, olive-green turtleneck, and gold corduroys gave him a Sigmund Freudish air as he hovered about the room. His mouth flopped open at the sight of the crabbed writing on the journal pages, the boyhood accoutrements from Hawkshead, the portraits of Lady Beaumont, Mary Wordsworth, and Coleridge by Reynolds, Gillies, and Northcote. He rocked on his heels, hands squirming in his pockets. The muffled throb of post-grunge and rap music droning from his students' headphones left his reverie unfazed. Clamped under his arm was a book from the gift shop: *The Wordsworths and the Daffodils*. The cover announced that The Wordsworth Trust had published it on April 15, 2002.

"The timing," he said.

Without planning it his tour had arrived on the centenary of the day the Wordsworths strolled around Ullswater and saw the daffodils that led to the poem—first draft in 1807, revised and expanded in 1815. He exhaled in wondrous disbelief and smiled at the kismet, the cosmic serendipity. Exactly two hundred years ago Wordsworth's devoted sister, Dorothy, preserved the seed of his most famous poem in her journal. By that time William had garnered himself a national reputation from 'Tintern Abbey' and a revised edition of *Lyrical Ballads*, all with the craggy core of *The Prelude* stashed in private notebooks.

"Unprecedented."

Dr. Craig swung around and spied Vincent, who, cyclops-footed and adrift, had wandered in and now wobbled amid the students like an obelisk in a marketplace of slaves. Dr. Craig wagged his Wordsworth book.

"Say, Vince," he said. He slapped his driver on the shoulder. "Whaddya think?"

Vincent stepped back and banged his head on a conical light fixture. He shut his eyes and pressed his lips together. The fixture pendulated behind his head. He exhaled and aimed a bored gaze at the illuminated glass case that held Wordsworth's ice skates.

"Poetry," he said. "Useless!"

"Whoa!" Dr. Craig said. "You're on a literary tour."

Vincent snorted. "I am driver *for* a tour."

"On the bus, we were talking—"

"Agh. Doing my job." Vincent narrowed one eye and shrugged. "If you want to say something, say it. Why must you say it with flowers?"

Dr. Craig blinked at his book, deflated. "Wordsworth showed that's the only way you *can* say it," he said. "He gave voice to the daffodils and wandered lonely as a cloud, and nobody's been the same since."

"Agh," Vincent said. "I will leave."

"Awright, buddy," Dr. Craig called after him. "Catch you at dinner."

Vincent lumbered outside, grumbling curses. *Stom! Zuig mijn ballen!* Like Poseidon he plowed through sluggish waves of Chinese senior citizens, sniffing the wet breeze for a Soproni or Torvasi Sör. Soiled clouds marred the sky. Chilly rain needled his red cheeks. He strode down the narrow walk as if dragging stone weights from his ankles, the mossy walls and dwellings of packed stone hemming him in. At a bus shelter a downward-looking Korean couple in Kelly green slickers forced him off the walk into the path of a rickety television repair truck. The horn beeped like a clown gag, and the little truck swerved. Vincent bounded back on the walkway and found himself facing the The Red Lion Inn. A huddle of oddball coaches waited in the inn's gravel parking lot: glossy peach, bold magenta, silver with swooping blue arrows. Italian, French, Spanish. A shuttle would take him back to Windermere, he told himself, as he hoofed across the road and shouldered into the Red Lion's tea room.

The Red Lion's cramped lobby swam in pleasant blue light. Swift-footed waiters zigzagged through the foyer like figures from a glockenspiel. The décor matched the rugged outdoor landscape: heavy oak chairs, pewter candlesticks, custard tablecloths. The refined clink of cups and saucers drew an arpeggio of sophistication through the chit-chat of white-haired men and women who sipped tea and tipped forward as if parsing apocryphal texts. Below the staircase a man in a tweed jacket and orange hiking gaiters spoke over the desk to a baggy-eyed Scotsman in a cherry vest and wrinkled gray apron. When Vincent entered, everyone turned to see his pro wrestler hulk pack the doorway. The way he lifted his Kris Kringle glasses from his nose and swabbed the lenses with his handkerchief—pausing to grind a fist in one eye—made him look like a big kid who was lost and crying.

Vincent's fellow drivers dubbed him 'Double Dutch' when the Frankie Smith hit reached The Hague and boogied eastward through the discotheques of Hanover and Gdansk. After that, any bus he drove became known as 'Double Dutch Bus.' At fifty-one years old, he weighed two hundred sixty pounds. His six-foot, five-inch frame was stooped from a lifetime of negotiating low doorways. His ruddy cheeks reinforced the image he hated—that of a pug-nosed, pudding-faced, Sasquatch-sized gnome with wisps of black hair forking across his moist forehead. To compensate he wore his Elbobus gear everywhere: battered Doc Martens, white shirt, dark blue windbreaker with the company's gold logo embroidered like griffin wings across his shoulders blades. This military look was intended to make anyone near him feel the tower power of an Egyptian pyramid, the ogre-sized oomph of the quadruple extra large.

As he stood in the doorway, blinking and polishing his glasses, two waiters swerved around him like tugboats avoiding a freighter. He sensed the evasive action and sighed. Whenever he entered a room, it was the same—people danced away as if avoiding a toppling redwood. When his ex-wife, Hilde Lamprecht, left him years ago, he had fled Hungary, surrendered his job as a supermarket manager, acquired a vocational license, and started driving for Elbobus, Inc. For the second time he had lived the aloof and functional life of a bachelor, a bland routine spiced with moments of peace and, occasionally, the cleansing outrage of solitude. His plan had been to forget he had forgotten her. But he never expelled the gutful of green bitterness he gulped down the day she walked out— which is why his head jangled with delusions when he saw her at a corner table at The Red Lion. Between the hot beats of his heart his past shrank to the size of a rare postage stamp, which he imagined himself licking with rueful relish and sticking on the charred postcard of payback he would now deliver.

His eyes narrowed, and his smile flattened. "So," he said.

He approached and teetered over her table like a menacing cliff until she was forced to sit back and acknowledge him. With one massive hand he indicated the opposite side of the table.

"Room for me?"

"It is you," she said, glancing up from her black appointment book. Her glacier-green eyes peeped at him through spectacles with fine gold rims.

"As you would expect," he said then blew his nose in his Swiss lace handkerchief. Before she could summon her reply he squeezed his mammoth hams in the other chair. The chair legs grated like pickaxe points across the floor.

Hilde Lamprecht, always business-like and unflappable, especially in matters of love, waited to speak and avoided eye contact. Over Eccles cakes and lemon tea, Vincent noted how time had scoured away the stark beauty of the woman who had tried to crush him like a cockroach on a spring afternoon in Budapest, but who would soon be crushed herself. How? Could he leg-sweep her to the ground? Stomp her glasses into gravel? He imagined taking her hand in feigned civility then increasing the pressure until the tendons in her wrist popped like the bones of a baby chick. He accepted a silver-stitched burgundy napkin from the waiter and flapped it open across his knee.

"This is business for you?" he said. His eyelids drooped when he saw that even while sitting he was the same height as the waiter. "Perhaps pleasure?"

"Working," she said. She blinked rapid-fire and shook her head, as if chasing static from her inner ear. "As always. The beginning of the season."

After a short wait she was sitting like a praying mantis and nibbling her Eccles cakes, her monogrammed napkin a shield in her pincer-like fingers. Every year of forty-eight showed in her gray-streaked chestnut hair, which framed the pale rectangle of her face. Her elusive eyes flitted from emotion to emotion: watchful, sedate, blazing, detached. She conveyed the image of an older copy of herself. A schoolteacher from a lost century. A former Nazi mistress awaiting her next call to devotion. She wore her travel director's pleated mint-green skirt, heels, and blouse. The name of her company was stitched over her breast pocket: SchoenReise. As they talked Vincent took secret pleasure in the way he had so coolly approached her. He was an iceberg steaming across a sea of twenty years to grind her to pulpy gore against a continental shelf. As they reminisced and ate with almost choreographed counterpoise his plan for revenge, fresh but unformed, swayed brightly in his heart like a pot of bloody tulips.

"Your work is—enjoyable?" he said. He imagined himself yanking her chair with a magician's flourish, and she, his fatuous assistant, sprawled on her rump.

"It is work. But, yes."

Vincent didn't hide the wedding band of Austrian gold on his finger but let it glimmer in the light when his hand hung like a backhoe scoop over the ceramic bowl of pink sweetener packets. Could he twist the ring off and fire it like a hot spike into her eye? Invite her to hike Orrest Head and ram it down her throat with a tree branch? He saw himself joggling her upside down by her ankles, as if shaking a child that had swallowed marbles. She would cough up the ring, and he would hurl it after her as her mannequin body tumbled down the soggy turf slopes of Orrest Head. He would yank the ring off and curse the wrinkles from her forehead. *So much for love!* With typhoon force he would rage in her face, bellow a world of agony to the wooded hollows. *So much for what you thought you did to me!* So much for converting from Lutheran to Catholic, for all the lies and romantic charades in Budapest, all the times—daily!—he cringed when she called him her cuddly Gartenzwerg. *So much for thinking you could kill this survivor!* His spit would coat her glasses with cobra venom. Then with his finger he would give her a savage poke, a saber thrust at parting, so later when she undressed she would find the bruise blooming below her collarbone, a reminder of the color of her soul, a purplish yellow sore that would never heal.

A good plan, he told himself, as they chatted. Epic poetry, in a way. And all on their anniversary.

Anniversaries, actually. April fifteenth: the day they wed, the day she fled, never saying why, just a few sheared-off words before she nestled a rusty stiletto of gall between his ribs and escaped down the gray manhole of the future, his last hope stuffed in the suitcase with the faulty latch she lugged at her side. What whetted the tang of his pleasure more was that she appeared to have no inkling that the day was significant. She had never shown signs of understanding anything important, he recalled, but he would awake her to the nature of the facts. With his napkin he brushed crumbs from his lips then stood, knocking his head against the amber cut-class chandelier above the table. He rocked forward, eyes closed, the chandelier swaying like a sparkly piñata.

"If you have the inclination," he said, opening his eyes.

Her eyes widened as she dabbed the corner of her mouth with her napkin. "Yes?"

"A pleasant trail leads to Orrest Head."

"For?"

"A walk and talk."

"I see."

"My group leaves shortly. When else would we see one another?"

"Of course."

"If you have the inclination."

"Yes."

In his pockets his fists hung like blunt weapons. She aimed a businesswoman's smile at the floor. Having secured her promise, he spun and ambled away with the ungainly ease of an armoire being pushed out of the room. She stared in a trance at the embroidered eggshell-blue cubes adorning her placemat. She clipped her purse closed and jerked her head in a stiff nod.

"Yes, I think," she said. "Yes, my little Gartenzwerg."

Down the road from the Red Lion, near Dove Cottage, Tilde Lambert, who loved poetry and who was studying to become a teacher to compensate for the lack of parental love in her life, abandoned the Japanese tour group she had been using as cover and plastered her body against the stone wall that bordered the street. She licked rain from her lips, aimed her hand down the road in revolver shape, and slaughtered a Cockney accent.

"Ello, Peetuh Wabbit."

She was three weeks into believing what she had read in her behavioral psychology class with Dr. Todd Fallon, about sexual promiscuity in unmarried girls being connected to a lack of fatherly presence and affection—hugs, in particular. She was minutes into trying to stay invisible, scanning the Red Lion's grounds for a glimpse of her birth mother. She was eighteen, traveling alone, and very much into a certain emo band, Soggy Puppy, who every Friday and Saturday night pumped shock waves through the bedrock beneath her hometown of Vestal, and whose pirated indie CD, *Teenage Hatchet Job*, swung in a black Velcro case from her hip like a pouch of pixie dust. Having not expected the teeth-gnashing pinch of a northern English spring, she shivered in her T-shirt, gray corduroys, and Teva sandals. Her toes looked like red sausages. She had dyed her hair black, which had camouflaged her in the herd of Japanese, but now she felt exposed, even a little childish, considering the conspicuous scene she was certainly making—her loose belongings bundled in her arms like those of a scatterbrained schoolgirl, her hair parted and secured in stumpy ponytails with mustard rubber bands. Her Razor scooter clattered to the pavement, and from her purple Land's End shoulder bag, which was strapped to her middle like a reserve chute, she pulled a gray windbreaker, which she threw on, and then hugged the wall and eyed the Red Lion's exit. She raised and lowered her sunglasses like a double agent in a sappy thriller and switched her accent to stereotypical Gestapo officer.

"Vell, vhat haff vee here?"

Fabiana, Tilde's adoptive mother, didn't know Tilde was traveling The Lake District, let alone that she was out of the country. As a legal adult Tilde wasn't afraid of what Fabiana would do. They had never lived on threats and recriminations, just love and getting by. But the unknown and unfinished had driven Tilde to chase this impulse, the same nagging fear of being sundered from her past that always sent her running. Fear had sent her bed-hopping through the benchwarmers on the Bearcats lacrosse team. Fear had pushed her to withdraw her life savings, buy an airline ticket, swing aboard a midnight Greyhound to JFK, and fly to Heathrow. The envelope she had discovered bore a German address she had never seen, but it was an address Fabiana had apparently kept for years. The envelope in her shoulder bag bore this address in loopy pink script. It was hard to believe she was in Great Britain only days after she had crammed the envelope in her bag and hurried out the door as if bearing the deed to the planet.

She sidled down the street. The letter throbbed against her body like a second heart. The way she was feeling—the inner heat, the sense of purpose—she wondered what would happen if the rain struck her insides: if the drops would dissolve in her blood or sizzle like spit on a hot griddle. She was a crusader, a pilgrim summoned through the brutal seasons to settle a musty treaty from a war fought over a patch of holy ground. She would pile stones and heal the dimensions. She would hug her dad.

"Don't blow it," she said. "When you meet her be nice."

Hilde Lamprecht looked more like a jade statuette gazing out the window than a German travel director and divorceé of twenty years. She re-arranged the articles in her purse, flustered but excited. She glanced into the oval walnut mirror that hung above the polished oak table in the entryway. On the table rested a box of Red Lion business cards and, underneath the box, three fancy doilies like white lily pads. With cautious glee she looked through the window at her ex-husband's familiar stone-footed saunter, his lumberjack bulk and cumbersome but gentle gestures. He stood across the road, hands in pockets, a giant slouching against a background of shaggy trees and a low stone wall. In his driver's uniform he looked the way she always thought he had, like a big cuddly gnome. A gust ran invisible fingers over his head, toying with his thin hair.

"So very long," she said. "So much time."

He had said Orrest Head, and Orrest Head it would be. She poked through the jumble of things in her purse, as if eye liner and saucy pink lipstick might click the button on the stopwatch in her chest. Time and space had duped them, but surely there could be some reconciliation, an exchange of best wishes if nothing more.

"Reunion, no," she said. "Just talk, of course. That is something."

Then a vision flashed on the screen behind her eyes, and she saw, like a prophecy, the drama as it would unfold on the blustery summit of Orrest Head: an exchange of mutual regard; perhaps handshakes; words of well wishing; inquiries about past years; modest congratulations on successes; perhaps a mutter of surprise at having met in such a beautiful corner of the earth; no apologies; no sentiments of love; but yes, ultimately, some agreement between them; a silent understanding that things are okay and that the earth is still turning in harmony with its music recitals and oil portraits of children and lap dogs and spring trips abroad. She reached for the arm of a young waiter who glided behind her.

"Orrest Head?" she said. "Vo—where is it?"

Three long-stemmed glasses wobbled and clinked on the waiter's tray. He presented a bullish Don Juan figure, greased licorice-black hair parted on the side. The waiter flung his arm in the direction of Windermere.

"Straight down," he said. "There's Ambleside, right? Then straight on opposite the tourist stop. Can't miss it."

"Bitte," she said, turning to the window. "Thank you."

She couldn't possibly know it, she told herself, but she felt in her core that some gatekeeper of goodness had arranged for the day's events to break free across open country as rocky and wildly green and revolutionary as this place of poets. But as she stepped across the gravel walk, followed by her driver and tour group, she held her jacket closed and promised herself to keep some things shut away. They would meet on Orrest Head, they would talk, and they would be reconciled. But she didn't want to haul wheelbarrows of muck and the sod of old bitterness from the graves of yesterday. She would not tell him he had a daughter.

She pressed her body against the wall and watched the spindly woman who had to be her birth mother leave the Red Lion Inn and board a SchoenReise bus that looked like a piece of orange candy on wheels. The dumpy bus driver and a clump of book-toting women followed their leader like a chain gang of ewes. As she slunk along the wall, away from the gabbling crew of Japanese men and women, Tilde realized it was the unknown that turned everyone to ghosts. All great poetry—everything Soggy Puppy ever sang about—centered on the two great destroyers: the unknown and unfinished. Following her mother, though, would write in the missing ending to her life. She would recover in that reunion the love she had lost. She would be the decree from the trumpet mouths of the invisible host.

A spluttering engine exploded her thoughts, and a gleaming silver wall of tinted windows halted in a cloud of carbon, inches from her nose. She read the words on the metallic banner of crimson and fuchsia that swooped across the side of the vibrating minibus: Giles's Lake District Supertours.

The stocky driver—presumably Giles—rolled down the window and grinned, revealing a mouthful of yellow pirate teeth. His thatch of gray hair grew low on his lined forehead, and his head had a hunchback way of hanging off-center, as if bolted loosely between his shoulders. In a chain-smoker's baritone he called to her over the chugging engine.

"Where y'off to?"

"Not sure," Tilde said. She pointed in the direction of Windermere. "That way—is?"

"American?"

"I'm a lot of things."

"Well," Giles chuckled. "Get in Miss A-Lotta-Things. If you're—"

Tilde dug in her bag. "How much?"

"Oh, I'm not chargin' ya!" he said, turning brusque. "Way I see it, you're not sure what you are or where you're going, I shouldn't profit from it, I don't think. C'mon, then. In! Home's where I'm headed. It'll be raining again soon."

Tilde clambered aboard. Inside the minibus smelled of pickled onions and cigarettes. The seats were upholstered in fat red and blue stripes, fuzzy from use. High cushiony headrests gave her the impression that she had boarded a space probe from a 1950's television show.

"Only one rule on this ride, dearie," Giles called as he signaled and pulled away from the curb.

"That is?"

"Stand up, you might be sitting down! Ha, hah!"

Giles tromped on the gas. The bus lurched away like a roller coaster off its track. Trees and shrouded green hills and plaster-faced cottages scrolled past the misty windows, and as she whizzed toward Windermere, warmth flooded her cheeks and tingling toes. She couldn't stop smiling. Adopted by fortune, she was speeding in Giles's magical mystery bus toward the last tour of her soul's reclamation. It was her first day in The Lakes, and she had become the letter carrier of ancient wonders, the classic bringer of truth.

Vincent stood on the street, eyes skyward, thumbs hooked in his belt. Behind the sluggish crawl of Japanese, he resembled a fuming Andre the Giant waylaid in a strike of midget wrestlers. With the speed of drugged cows the Japanese group unpacked itself from the shuttle bus and shuffled down the walk. The instant they moved clear, Vincent hoisted himself aboard. The shuttle tipped like a cargo ship in a swell. In the back he took three seats, his Santa Claus knees jutting to his ears. On the way to Windermere he watched red double decker busses rumble in the other direction toward Dove Cottage, upper and lower tiers crammed with camera-laden poetry junkies. He laughed in disgust and wondered how, after dealing with his ex-wife, he might rig dynamite to his torso and board one of those busses and bloom like the black flower of death.

Outside the tourist information stop on Orrest Drive noisy delivery vans and taxis plugged the narrow streets. Vincent bounded off his bus and spotted the Orrest Head trailhead near a pedestrian crossing: painted steel fence, white sign, paved loop slipping through manicured hedges, an uphill slant of stone cottages with old world beams and pointed roofs. From the bottom of the path he strove upward, heaving his head and shoulders forward like a draft horse plowing through crosswinds, heedless of the pending showers. The clouds broke apart, and white light splintered the shadows of trees, dappling the dirty cobbles under his feet. He would disgrace her, crush her to an atom of nothing. He would fling her from the heights to the depths because she forced him from his favorite beers in Budapest, because she chased him from his cushy job at ASDA Supermarkets, insisted that he convert to Catholicism, called him Gartenzwerg. His brontosaurus pace increased.

"I am no Gartenzwerg!" he roared at the sky.

A greenfinch shot from a hedge. A knobby-eared, silver-headed man in a baby blue rain mack emerged from one of the cottages, puffed his pipe, saw Vincent, and retreated indoors. The way Vincent walked made it clear: he was the harbinger of heaven and hell, the poet of poets, and with a swing of his titanium fist he would deliver his ex-wife a century's worth of reproof and wisdom.

He looked up, toying with his ring. The sky had sunk lower. The tree line at the top of the hill combed clouds into ragged tufts, as if unraveling soaked wool. Habitually, Vincent pulled his ring off and slipped it on again over the thick knuckle of his finger. He imagined how it would fly—a twenty-four karat zero, a golden circlet of maledictions—through the grainy light atop Orrest Head, a pure curse driving the precious pain she deserved into the pitiful ice-black crags of her prehistoric heart.

Tilde barged like an April squall into her apartment. She flung a mesh bag of field hockey gear on their threadbare plaid couch, leaving her keys jangling in the keyhole.

"What's the food situation?" she called. "Talk to me!"

There was no answer from her adoptive mother, Fabiana Lambert, who sometimes worked late as an assessment coordinator at Glenwood Elementary. Tilde barged into the kitchen, yanked open the fridge's fungus-colored door, rummaged inside for honey-smoked turkey and celery stalks. From the cupboard above the sink she snagged a loaf of wheat bread and scarfed a sloppy sandwich. A bottle of orange Gatorade washed the wad of bread and meat down her throat. She mined pulpy food fragments from her teeth with her tongue and surveyed the apartment, ashamed that she was still panting from her sprint up the stairs.

In the living room the television rested on a bamboo wicker stand, flanked by fake palm trees that drooped like assistants tired of keeping up an act. A pizza box lay open like a greasy board game on the caramel shag carpet between two calico bean bag chairs. Thoughtfully, she examined the way her hockey gear adorned the couch with the reckless appeal of a contemporary art project—dark green plaid Lady Bearcat skirt, sweater, shin guards, cleats, all bundled in a mesh beg pocked with snags. A title flashed in her head: 'Life, Game, Score, Loss.'

The Soggy Puppy show was minutes from kicking off at Java Joe's. She checked the Boris Badenov clock in the kitchen, saw the time, swore, ran to her room, burrowed in a welter of dirty clothes, and emerged in her orange-and-blue 'Out in the Rain' Soggy Puppy T-shirt, grey cords, Tevas, and sunglasses. She bolted to the bathroom and snapped her hair into her signature rubber-banded ponytails, then she barreled into the kitchen and stopped to flip through a pile of mail on the table.

"Where is that lottery check? Never seems to—"

Kmart fliers. Utility bills. The grainy blue and white faces of missing kids, all tossed aside. With both palms she swirled the papers around the table like a collage artist giving vent to directionless passion.

"Where's the keys? I need to drive The Beast!"

She tore through the apartment, checking the usual places. Between sofa cushions? Kotex box? Toilet tank? In Fabiana's bedroom she yanked open the nightstand drawer and dug through pay stubs and tax forms and manila folders. She shoveled out binders and diaries and bundled bank statements on the bed like a burglar hunting for jewelry until the bed was a ransacked flea market of mundane documents. She stood back, hands on hips, panting and looking around when her eyes fell on a manila folder that had flopped open, revealing a stack of envelopes and faxes paper-clipped together. The top envelope bore her name. She snatched up the envelope.

"Hey, whoa."

As she read the letter, confused exhilaration surged through her head. She scanned lines, swerved back and started over, searching for any shred of sense, flummoxed as to why someone would send her a fake letter and speak to her as if she were somebody's mother in Germany. The mysterious sender had addressed the letter to a location in Germany where she had never lived. With no postage. And her return address in the corner. Parallel to these bizarre fantasies about Tilde's supposed job as a German travel director were true-to-life anecdotes: her grades, her athletic feats and academic performance, all the truth mashed up with all the lies. Two faxed itineraries—work schedules—were paper clipped underneath the mess of mail: the top one for a SchoenReise travel director, listing dates, times, destinations and addresses for The Women's Historical Society of Port Adelaide. The travel director's schedule said 'Seniors Tour.' After puzzling over the letter twice Tilde still couldn't make sense of it. She checked the envelope's address and noticed that the person who had addressed the letter spelled her name with an 'H' instead of a 'T.'

"Mom?" she said. "Are you here?"

With the envelope balanced on her palms she stalked out of Fabiana's bedroom and across the carpeted kitchen, through the unwashed sliding doors, to the back balcony. The glowing red sun hung in the glazed sky, a glassblower's orb behind the gnarled trees along the Susquehanna Valley. Smudged economy cars packed the Vestal Shopping Plaza. She watched the toy-sized vehicles stream in and out of McDonald's, Circuit City, and Kohl's. The spider-web evolution of nature cocooned her, its sticky silk clinging to her cheeks, tickling her neck with a gentle thrill. She floated in the springy web, her gauzy soul reaching out to someone who was somewhere else on the slipstream of light circling the earth. She stared at the two white deck chairs on the balcony. She watched for a genie to pop out of the crusty mini barbecue grill. In broken rows haggard crocuses and tulips struggled from brick-red pots of damp soil. She pinched the opened letter between her thumb and finger and watched a nimble-footed squirrel tightrope across a telephone line through the bonfire of sundown into a thicket of thrashed poplars.

Then she dashed to her room and snatched up her scooter, piled a mess of essentials into a suitcase, and threw on her shoulder bag as if arming herself with a quiver of arrows. Here was the answer, the sudden vector, and she hadn't sought it out. Everything she had wanted to know was sealed in the envelope of the moment, if she was honest with herself, everything she had been afraid to uncover, but now prudence no longer reigned and she was armed to pursue what prudence had hidden from view.

Inside an hour she withdrew her savings from the Albank in the Vestal Plaza, dug her passport out of her bottom dresser drawer, and hopped a Greyhound to JFK.

Halfway to the Orrest Head overlook the path changed to a slippery switchback of moss-bearded stone and a staircase of rough granite blocks. A film of rain cloaked the sky, blustering over the treetops, shaking down a litter of twigs. Vincent trudged up the incline like a murderous footman.

At the entrance to the Orrest Howe estate he stopped and propped his fists on his hips, a furnace roaring in his belly. The scent of blood rimmed his nostrils. He blinked at the tiger lilies and pilewort that sprouted languets of yellow and orange flame through the hedges.

"Bah!" he said, swatting the air, and pushed on.

Where the trail changed from pavement to dirt a natural archway formed in the ragged trees, and he stopped to examine a little blue-gray home with a gently sloping roof. Someone, presumably the owner, had hung a sign on the door: Steve Hicks, Custom Ironworks. Around the Hicks place a Hephaestean tangle of scrap-iron sculptures lay scattered like old car parts. The blowtorch artist who lived there had twisted the lanky sculptures into unearthly poses—some erotic, others ascetic—and abandoned them among muddy irises and leaves. Vincent identified the warped figure of a fisherman, an impressionistic mare and foal, love-making fairies, and a skipping goat.

A padlock secured the house's screen door. The white shutters were bolted. At the far end of the property stood a crusty cement-mixing barrel, a shovel handle poking like a toothpick from its cog-lined craw. Next to the mixing barrel, waiting for a rider from a lost decade, was a filthy blue moped with a rainbow knot of bungee cords on its chrome rack. A plaster gnome acted as sentry, guarding the moped with his red cone cap, bulbous belly, and blue breeches. The jolly gnome's facial features were drawn to the center of his face. The gnome stood in a roly-poly kiba-dachi stance, fists cocked at the waist, ready to poke Vincent in the chops.

At the sight of the gnome Vincent's jaw seized. He grunted and stretched himself to full height, tottering like a polar bear on its hind legs. In five strides he was at the gnome's side, searching the soaked ground. A boulder as big as a toaster was embedded in the earth, fringed in dripping weeds. Vincent straddled the boulder, hooked his fingers under its edges and like a steam shovel ripped it from its socket of sloppy earth. In one great heave he raised the boulder high and with the shriek of a god crushed the happy figure to dust.

The Orrest Drive information center, a wood-and-concrete rotunda, sat fifty yards from the bus depot. It was gridlocked with tourists. Three English agents in blue sweaters and red and white paisley neckerchiefs served a jostling mob of twenty different nationalities. The agents stood behind a long curved table and like frantic blackjack dealers working with oversized cards pushed around a mess of maps and pamphlets stamped with the flags of France, Germany, Japan, China, and Italy. When her turn in line arrived Hilde Lamprecht stepped forward and caught the attention of a young auburn-haired agent who returned her glance with the pinched look of someone in need of potent drugs.

"Orrest Head?" Hilde asked the agent. "Where is it?"

"Behind you, love," the woman said, pointing out the window. "Nip across. Follow the signs."

"Behind?" Hilde asked.

"S'right, love. Straight across."

At the trail head Hilde stopped to remove her heeled shoes. From her shoulder bag she produced a pair of sea-green Adidas jogging shoes, which she laced on. She smiled at the generous universe and considered how this chance meeting would take place now that her group was staying in The Lakes, exactly when she had a brief window of leisure time. Eyeing the sky, she pulled out a royal blue raincoat with white stripes on the sleeves and wrapped it like a magic mantle around her narrow shoulders. She drew on the hood and tightened the drawstring. As she motored up the path she tried to imagine the conversation she would have with her big Gartenzwerg after so many years. And all on April fifteenth.

Tilde bounced in the back of Giles's twelve-seater minibus and spoke little. The soul-crunching verve of Soggy Puppy's 'Make or Break' jackhammered her Sony Discman, and she bobbed her head to the beat.

At Ambleside she plucked out her headphones because she realized that Giles, her savior and driver, was addressing her, rolling his head and glancing in the rearview mirror when he wanted to make a point. Giles had the body of a beer barrel, soda-bottle glasses, and his face was the color of tenderized steak.

"Where y'off to again, dearie?" he called.

"See that bus?" Tilde said. "Where that bus is going."

"Beg pardon, dear," Giles said. He hacked three times, failing to clear the plug of phlegm from his throat. "Sounds like a strange way to travel, I should think. Following busses, rambling about. A bit dodgy. Everything on the up and up?"

"Sure."

"Know where you are?"

"Tell me, Giles."

"The Lakes," he said, slipping into tour mode. "Over two thousand, three hundred, sixty-seven lakes up 'ere, and only one of them is called a lake."

Tilde gazed out the window. "No joke?"

"The rest are meers, tarns, or waters. 'Meer' from the German for 'large contained body of water,' generally not so grand—big, I should say—as your lakes. 'Tarn' from the Middle English *tarne*, around fourteenth century, from the Viking *tjorn*, for the depression, the bowl in the earth, that fills with rain in the crags and fells, you see. Fells are the hills so famous here in the district, from the Viking for mountain: *fjall*. You see, dearie, there were Vikings in these hills, many years ago."

"Hate to be raped and pillaged," Tilde said. "It's so pretty."

Giles braked hard so a crook-backed Punjabi man in a gold windbreaker could scurry across the road.

"Oh, aye," he said. "Vikings all around these parts. Evidenced in the Herdwick sheep. Unique breed of sheep, that is. Vikings brought 'em over, seventeen hundred years back, and they stayed. Sheep, not the Vikings. Bred only in this part of the country. That's the sheep, there, the Herdwick sheep."

"Herdwick," Tilde said. She nodded out the window at an animal grazing among rocks on the hillside, something like a lamb's head and legs snapped on a sheepdog's body. "Sounds like earwig."

"Aye, and there," Giles said, pointing out the window to his right, "is the smallest house in England, here in Ambleside. Called the Bridge House."

Tilde spied the Bridge House as they chugged past: a skinny-roofed guardhouse, slender enough for a single gingerbread man to stand inside. She put her headphones back in her ears.

"Hard to sleep there," she said.

"Aye," Giles said. "Plenty to see up here, what with the Wordsworths, Hellvellyn, and the likes of Beatrix Potter. D' ya know she hated children? Despised the little buggers."

"Uh uh," Tilde said.

"The author of Peter Rabbit, aye. Couldn't stand the nippers. Makes you wonder, it does."

"Dad probably never hugged her."

In minutes they were entering Windermere at the top of Orrest Drive. A cheerful orange SchoenReise bus loitered dutifully opposite the information center where half a dozen other shuttles were stuck together like assorted lozenges. Glossy red double-decker busses waited outside the bus depot, loaded with animated tourists, poised to deploy.

Giles turned his head and popped three neck bones. "That your bus?" he called.

"Aye," Tilde said. "I mean—yes." She slipped her music gear in her shoulder bag, slid forward, and clambered out with her scooter. "Thanks, Giles. You did me a big favor."

"My pleasure entirely, dearie. Ta rah, then. Take care, now."

Tilde waved to Giles, who buzzed toward town and tooted his horn like a train engineer delivering a jaunty farewell. She waited under the information center eaves and watched her willowy, boxy-hipped mother remove her heels, don jogging shoes and rain jacket, and vanish up the trail, after which Tilde, scooter on her shoulder like a little grenade launcher, loped across the road, stashed her scooter in the base of a thick green hedge, and pursued her from a distance.

One hundred yards below the summit he halted where the path became unclear. He scanned his options, panting in the drizzle, his neck and ears flushed. The swaying branches overhead slashed the wind into the sound of a waterfall. Straight ahead the path forked up an easy incline of tramped-down earth. The steeper route was a scramble of leafy rocks and treacherous black topsoil. To his right stretched a triangular horse pasture with a high fence. Two mares fed in the pasture, one speckled custard, the other smooth brown with a white-flecked rump. The horses lifted their heads and regarded him in unison.

Because the day had roused his lust for rage, he chose the harder route. Exhaustion forced him to push off his knees with his hands. His grunting and snarling spooked the horses and sent them trotting away to lower their noses into the Queen Anne's lace and wildflowers in a far corner of the pasture. He thrashed up the hill, and slid back like a dizzy grizzly bear, at times scrambling up the hardscrabble slope on his hands and knees. He emerged, face dirty and scratched, through a weathered trench of shrubbery and toppled rock walls where with one final swinging thrust of burning thighs and banged elbows he stood and howled atop Orrest Head.

He blinked at the surrounding landscape, lips slick with rain. He couldn't help feeling he was standing in the footprints of barbarians, breathing in the smoky mist of forgotten conquests. Under his sore feet centuries of merciless wind and rain had stripped away the sod. The exposed granite looked like some cruel weapon had grooved a giant's half-buried skull. Every sculpted stone evoked a bizarre archeology, the chaos of curved gray pits and gouges complex enough to comprise a language. Sparkling green scum pooled in the grotesque pockets of rock, and in places the naked stone looked as if titanic fingers had dipped into gray pudding for a taste.

Vincent slumped on a lookout bench that was stationed on a concrete pad. He gazed over the wooded valley—Morcambe

Bay, the sturdy gray turrets of Wray Castle above the trees. The steely expanse of Lake Windermere resembled a Viking blade pressed into the soft green earth. Boats clustered around Belle Isle like confetti sprinkled over the blade's haft. The lake's tip aimed north as if to skewer the village of Ambleside—and her. He doubted she had the gumption to join him at a place of such primitive and terrifying beauty, more primitive and terrifying now that his spinal cord had become the most devastating lightning rod the Lake District would ever know.

He rose and turned an ungainly pirouette, taking in the meandering stone walls and distant cottages and sloping green fields. Had he been the sort of person to do so he might have flung his arms out like a crucified god and inhaled the fire and rain in the air. His diesel-tank chest might have swelled as he admired the undulating farms, lone hamlets, and loose caravans of sheep. Instead he plunged his fists deeper in his pockets. He hunched his shoulders and listened to his spleen boil in the crucible of a stormy spring. Here he would act as arbiter of justice. Here he would hand out thunderbolts like playing cards. Torn webs of soaked haze skulked across the low peaks. He closed his eyes and let their immaterial hands of vapor pass through him, mingling with his cells. A mighty scroll of doomsday clouds, black and gravid with rain, was trundling toward him. He would have to hurry. She would have to hurry.

"Waiting for her," he said.

The thought filled his belly with sludge. Twenty years of divorce, and he was still waiting. He twisted the ring off his finger and pocketed it.

In Budapest his life had been steeped in easy dreams:

managerial job, flexible hours, a snug third-story apartment across the Chain Bridge in the castle district. He leaned against the waist-high pulpit of packed shale on which the travel board had inscribed the history of the lakes. The guide plate listed the names of peaks, including Scafell Pike as the 'highest mountain in England' at nine hundred seventy-eight meters. Too bad, he chuckled darkly, he hadn't chosen Scafell Pike as the trysting point. He might have enjoyed watching her cartwheel over the rocks to the bottom like a stupefied doll. His ring glowed in the heat of his palm, a hot shackle for branding a slave's ankle, a volcanic moon ready to scald the cosmos. On the tourist display someone had carved a quote from Alfred Wainwright: 'Orrest changed my life.'

"And mine," he said. "Wait to see."

The leaden lakes and lush hills, the brawny stone walls stitching a network of nerves across a pristine world of anguish and suffering—it all spoke to the same truth: no matter the place, no matter how enchanting things looked from another perspective, you ended up alone. Somewhere a sheep bleated like a crone. Another sheep blatted back in a bass register, a grandfatherly chortle. A flashy crow veered overhead and snapped a glance back at the haggard colossus standing alone on this pinnacle of wilderness.

On the ground two smooth stones caught his eye. They were shotput-sized, half-submerged in grassy earth. He stooped and scooped them up. With a stone in each hand, he held his arms out, face to the sky, and let the searing ache settle in his shoulders, imagining how he might clap the rocks like earmuffs on the sides of a human skull.

Maybe around 10 BCE. Maybe in the swell of a rejuvenating April rain, or maybe with some Romans camping at Aquincum on the future site of Buda, where Vincent Van Rooij would have been happy if his wife had allowed him to savor his balcony apartment, beer, and cake-walk manager's job. But Vandals conquer Aquincum. And over the next five hundred years, Slavs and Avars trudge in like surly security guards, flaming shopping carts loaded with malice, ultimately surrendering Buda and Pest to the Magyars in the latter half of the ninth century. In 1241— many squashed hearts, unwanted pregnancies, and abandoned children later—during the Tartar invasion of Hungary, Pest is destroyed. Then in 1247, King Béla IV rebuilds and repopulates Pest with the forerunners of many robust home-wrecking Germans. He fortifies Buda, inspiring it to become a pulsating community of love nests for those who stick around. As if consigned to a tragic chapter in history, Pest is sacked by the Turks in 1526, Buda in 1541. In 1686, three hundred years before Hilde Lamphrecht demolishes a grown man's hope with the sweep of her vacant gaze, an Austrian-led league of states expels the Turks, and the cities, like two aged and estranged lovers, languish in ruins. But in the eighteenth century, a breath of hope! With the Danube River dividing them, the two urban hubs blossom into cultural and economic meccas, culminating, in 1872, in their marriage as Budapest. But during World War II, after a fifty-day siege, the Soviets take Budapest on February 13, 1945, and then the military squelches an anti-Soviet uprising, which leaves the city maimed and hopeless in the aftermath.

Then on April fifteenth in the dawn of the twenty-first

century, a newly wed and freshly-Catholicized Vincent Van Rooij reclines on his third-story apartment balcony in jeans and stocking feet. He reads a *Nemzeti Sport* and sips a bottle of Gössler Dark. The sound of carefree voices and sleepy traffic floats up from the street below. Potted tulips adorn the balcony—shimmering chartreuse parrots, faded violet Darwins, and Duc van Tols as red as healthy arteries. His wife, Hilde, enters the ochre-tiled kitchen behind him. He drops the newspaper in his lap at her approach and smiles at her drawn expression. In her travel director's outfit she presses her hands together like a soprano about to split the air with her first note. Her waspish glance flits around the room, out the window, avoiding his eyes.

He tips his chair forward, the legs creaking like timbers. "You have something to say?"

"I must tell you of my upcoming tour," she said. "Three weeks."

"I will miss you, yes."

"There is the plumbing to see about."

"Of course."

"And I must tell you I am leaving."

"Three weeks, you said?"

"Here," she said. "No. I feel I must tell you I do not love you."

The groaning chair rocks back. Like a blind the newspaper covers his face and he gazes at the screaming black text.

"So I must leave, okay? All in the open, okay? I am packed and ready."

For two hours Vincent stays on the balcony, elbows and legs

dangling over the railing, like a gargoyle soaking in a tiny bathtub. He glares at the newspaper as if searching for the editorial that will refute what he has heard. He searches for delivery in the soccer scores, his stocking feet propped on the rococo railing. In that time, the decision to quit his job strikes like an ax cleaving his brain in two fresh halves. He renounces Catholicism, overlooking the gold ring on his finger. He gnaws the inside of his cheek, stares, clenches and unclenches his fists.

Then he seizes the thing closest to him—the tulips—two of which crash together in his hands. With a strangled bellow, he seizes the remaining pots and hurls them to the street below, where they explode in supernovas of soil and baked clay. The street erupts in shouts and car horns and barking dogs. He slumps back in his chair and sucks in ragged breaths, having conveyed his feelings on his anniversary the only way he could. With flowers.

A tide of graphite-colored fog swarmed Orrest Head, transforming him into the glowing nucleus in a cold electron cloud. A steady rain pummeled the ground, the sound of thousands of boots charging across a ravaged shore. He had descended into a stone-age trance, hypnotized in the singularity of his purpose. He shuddered and stared into the void of himself, an acolyte of the times, seeing but not comprehending the rippled face of Lake Windermere, the battered fells, the sturdy rock walls and miles of tree clusters and low peaks. Heedless of the icy downpour he stood in front of the wooden bench, his hands slung in his pockets.

Something stirred in the foliage. A ridiculous-looking woman in a blue rain jacket emerged and, like a walking broomstick, ascended the slick steps.

"Hallo!" she called, picking her way toward him. "Hallo, my Mister Gartenzwerg. I have something to say to you!"

"I must say something," he said. He felt the ring in his fist bend into an oval. "It is slippery. Do not fall."

She hustled up the trail, zipping on her windbreaker. Awkwardly she reached back and yanked the useless membrane-thin hood from the neck pouch and pulled it over her head and tightened the drawstrings. Cool rain soaked her hair and dribbled down her temples into the corners of her eyes. She had tailed her mother past Orrest Howe and Steve Hicks's Custom Ironworks, and now as she hiked past bench after bench she caught blurred glimpses of the fairy-tale village below, the lake and hills to the west, all obscured in mist and rain, as if a hand had smeared itself across a painting in haste. Flashes of furtive undergrowth made her blink: starry pilewort, thorny shrubs pocked with prim violet blossoms and brash berries the color of lipstick. Her sandals slipped like blunt ice skates on the grimy stones. Gritty mud oozed between her toes.

At the horse pasture she caught her breath. Just in time she wheeled around to watch her mother's agile stick figure clear the summit's final ridge, vanishing through the tossed thicket of trees. In the pasture three horses—a chalky stallion in an emerald tarp and the two mares—munched long stalks of waterlogged grass. Tilde nickered and tossed them a branch, and they pivoted their dopey heads toward her like calm machinery, eyed her soberly, and returned to their placid meal. Then as if choreographed all three tossed their heads and shook rain from their manes. Where the forest gave way to the stony pedestal of Orrest Head, she hung back, undiscovered, watching the two adults in their face-to-face encounter, listening to the rain rattle the trees, waiting for the right time to charge.

The man, a small giant, appeared to be a bus driver in full uniform. He stood hunched over in sheets of rain, arms hanging to his sides, as if lugging invisible dumbbells. Then one hand swung upward and he held what looked like a gold wedding band to her birth mother's face. The rain had rubbed his face to the color of fresh raspberries. Thin black hair plastered his head. The primeval landscape gave him the appearance of a shivering Neanderthal, a psychotic Polyphemus carved from the mountainside by a meteor. He shouted something, and her birth mother clasped her hands at her throat, stared at him and trembled.

Unable to restrain herself Tilde broke through the barricade of trees and commando-crawled slipshod up the steps.

"Mom!" she cried. "I mean, are you my mom? I think you could be my mom!"

In a private ceremony Vincent Van Rooij kneels on a ruby rug fringed with shiny tassels and takes his first communion at St. Peter's in the tiny German village of Neunkirchen, the village in which Hilde's mother, Greta, grew up and worked in the family bakery. The priest has a head like a brass bedpost and his hands shake. Vincent listens to the words of the ceremony, his lips wispy with wine and wafer, his soul devouring the gold-lipped kiss of the chalice, the hearty crust of eternal union. Later they are married at St. Peter's and drive together to dine on wienerschnitzel in Mosbach Neckar-elz, where Hilde attended the Augusta-Pattberg Gymnasium. Then their jobs require them to move to Hungary.

Buda on one side of the river, Pest on the other.

On a Thursday, April fifteenth, on their way from Eusemere to Grasmere, Dorothy and William Wordsworth, aged thirty and thirty-two, skirt the foot of Ullswater, not far from Pooley Bridge, about seven and a half miles from Patterdale. They plan to stay at Dobson's Inn to dine on ham, veal cutlets, and potatoes, before setting off the next day, Good Friday, for Dove Cottage along Kirkstone Pass. Years later Vincent Van Rooij, the biggest expatriate bus driver the Netherlands ever birthed, passes through the area, oblivious to and even scornful of the event, bent on delivering a juggernaut of revenge. On the seventeenth of April Dorothy's journal erupts with sketches of the furious wind that pummeled her and her brother on their walk, forcing them to rest in a boat house, under a furze bush across from Mr. Clarkson's, and again in Water Millock Lane. On this day her prose blooms with fecund passages about the green and black hawthorns, cantankerous cows, scentless violets, strawberries, wood sorrel, anemone, the starry pilewort, and, ultimately, the colony of crusading daffodils whose seeds sailed across the lake like a fleet of microscopic Norse *snekkja* and took root on the other side. In her sentences the daffodils brush immortality. They trumpet silent splendor and sway in sunburst euphony. Before writing his poem, Wordsworth borrows a horse at Middleham, which helps him finish autumn wedding plans with Mary Hutchinson. A long-time despiser of poetry—mostly because he believes his life contains none—Vincent Van Rooij drives his bus of Americans to their lodgings and sees everything through the film of blood coating his corneas. With the Peace of Amiens, William and Dorothy travel to France to meet William's nine-year old daughter, Caroline, and to settle parental arrangements with Annette Vallon, whom Wordsworth loved ten years earlier before war divided them. On April fifteenth, gems of rain glitter like evanescent poetic sentiments on the wedding band Vincent Van Rooij holds to his ex-wife's baffled face as he prepares to ram it up her nose and into her brain.

"You see my ring!" he shouts, sweeping the question like a scythe.

"Yes, my little mister," she says. She squints and smiles, licking away raindrops. "You have kept it all these years. I must know—"

"Know what!" he roars. His body convulses, goaded by electrodes of fury. He rocks like a great orator, shaking the ring as if damning a counterfeit coin.

She steps back. "I have felt today we could—"

"Feel?" he shouts. "Such a woman! Even now, you do not understand!"

He spreads his arms, ring in one hand, the other cocked like a catapult. For a moment he looks as if he might smash her between two great cymbals.

"I think this of you! It is what you did to me!"

"Hey!" a voice calls through the din of rain.

His arms sink.

"Mom!"

Priest and priestess of a prehistoric order, they turn to see a young woman burst from the woods. The girl flings aside her shoulder bag and bounds like a wild lamb up the hill.

She watches and waits to charge through the screen of swashbuckling branches and tumbling rain. She tries to remember as far back as she can. At sixteen months, she walks. At two years, talks. In first grade she wins Mrs. Burnham's scrapbooking award and garners a reputation for spelling bees and haiku and God's-Eye Weaving. At Woodrow Wilson Elementary, Zagg Doyle, the P. E. teacher's son, kisses her on the cheek behind the lilac bushes at recess while the noise of tetherball and four-square games flutters like true delight in her ears. By the time she has her first period, she is playing the guitar and already driving boys wild in the school talent shows. As a freshman she quits piano lessons three times, starts skateboarding as a senior. As a university student, she enrolls early during the summer term and bops around the SUNY schools—from Plattsburgh to Cortland—finally landing back with Fabiana in Vestal for classes down the parkway. She reads poetry and flirts with psychology and secondary education and photojournalism. When Fabiana's gone, she smuggles a different guy home every month, and then one abortion, two homoerotic relationships, and three pain killer and gin cocktails later she's putting in forty-eight hours of screaming and kicking her feet against her bedroom walls, and after that a six-month spate of psychotherapy with Dr. Todd Fallon, rambling nonstop about dads and hugs.

Then in April she makes the discovery she wasn't looking for and takes a bus and a plane and a train and hitchhikes and barges through the primitive trees on Orrest Head above Lake Windermere, calling for her mom, wondering if the man yelling at her mom is her dad, howling pain and happiness from the same heart with her arms flung out to gather the storms of the world. On impact she is accepted like a cannonball shot into two mattresses—arms fight and fold her in—and she swoons at the torrents that thunder from the swollen tarns over the craggy fells, the fervid bleating of the Herdwick sheep, the fall and rise of Budapest, the honey-and-chainsaw lyrics of Soggy Puppy, and the slaughter and upheaval of so many torch-wielding Viking civilizations that invade from both ends on a timeline that includes the flaming drop of poetry that is her life and the letter William Wordsworth penned to Sir George Beaumont in which he declared the world's greatest poets to be teachers, wishing, he wrote, to be considered a teacher or nothing at all.

At the bottom of the Orrest Head trail Tilde Lambert pulls her scooter from the hedge and blunders into a gang of college students waiting at the crosswalk. Momentarily she is lost in a happy huddle of strangers who spit and chatter and fold umbrellas and with cavalier flair swing slickers of brash cherry and aquamarine over their shoulders. A cheery Dr. Hemden Craig, chin in the air, marches past like Jemima Puddleduck. He is leading his troop of intellectual ducklings to the Brendan Chase for dinner with their bus driver and, later, the newest *Star Wars* movie at the Royalty Cinema in Bowness-on-Windermere.

"You American?" an Italian-looking guy in a sideways

Yankees cap says.

"Sorta," Tilde says. Across the street she unfolds her scooter, as if whipping open a big butterfly knife.

"We're going to a movie," the Yankees cap guy says. "Wanna come?"

A girl behind the boy snorts a laugh. The girl's salon-tanned skin is the color of butterscotch pudding. Blue dye streaks her bleached ponytail. "I wandered lonely as a clone," she says, making droid bleeps.

"Too much with us, the world is," another girl croaks.

"Maybe we'll see you!" Tilde says, pushing off.

She rolls over the narrow walk, face radiant with rain, heading toward the lot where the touring coaches are parked. Past a Gothic-looking bank, she shoots down a hill, gaining speed. The shoulder-to-shoulder bakeries and pottery shops zip past. She hip checks a rack of hand-woven baskets and draws snarls from a three-legged terrier, her wheels clacking over the cracks, her wet hood slapping her shoulders like a cape worn by a common crusader, and only when she waves back at her new friends does she feel the oversized ring of gold, a hoop heavy with promises, twirling an unbreakable embrace around her thumb.

Impressions

Impressions light
are always lightly ready to take flight

—Chaucer

AFTER THE FUNERAL Allan Douglas sat on the back deck of his late father-in-law's cabin. With one hand he trapped a tomato-red Top Crest writing pad on his knee. He held a pencil in his other hand, as if aiming a small anti-aircraft gun at the sky. As a younger man he had found Jesus in Toronto. Over twenty years after that golden episode he married a beautiful and much younger woman, Mandie Hendershot, whose family remained shackled to a battery of bizarre if not blasphemous superstitions. The love Allan felt for Mandy—soaring, adventurous, youthful—didn't extend to her family, who on their best days reminded him of lobotomized pretenders to some imaginary throne. From his overlook above the glassy green waters of Skaneateles Lake he worked a quiet storm of words on his lips, waiting for the elemental wine of expression to soak his tongue. Mandie and her family were clustered on the shore for their latest paganistic farce while he stayed as impassive as a stone carving and tuned his soul to the voice of God, the breath of spirit that would help him write a letter to Mandie's older sister, Rory, about the way she beat her children.

"Lord," he breathed.

His shoulder muscles slackened. He calmed his churning thoughts until his pulse flowed like an underground river. Cicadas sawed the silence in towering maple and ash trees, and spider web filaments floated through shafts of sun. Over the surface of the lake funnels of seagulls spun and came apart. From the work site of the California bigshot's quadruple-decker mansion came the whine of power drills and syncopated hammer strikes. Though the day was warm Allan wore a lightweight gray jacket, a two-inch Harriet Tubman souvenir button pinned to the front. On a patio table at his elbow, ice cubes jostled in a silver insulated mug of unsweetened tea. He ran a hand over his jaw, clawed his fingers through his hair. He inhaled through his nose and blew air through a weary kiss. His pencil pecked the pad.

On the rocky shore the Hendershot clan toddled toward the boathouse like jesters in exile. Bonnimarie, Doc Hendershot's widow, inched over the treacherous terrain in brassy hairdo, egg-beater earrings, and melodramatic black lace. Craig was the oldest son, a studio guitarist with a wolfish out-of-date mullet. He scratched his elbows and futzed with his salmon short-sleeve shirt and skinny black leather tie, both of which looked borrowed from the mall for the occasion. Mandie followed cheerfully with Rebecca Ruth. Little Rebecca rode in her mother's arms like a kiddie celebrity in a cabriolet, grinning and clapping her hands and gazing about with wonder, her pale blue eyes as luminescent as moons. With a cavewoman stoop, Rory trooped ahead in a canary blazer and fruit-salad skirt, dragging her daughters, Trystan and Autumn Teal, who wore, inexplicably, matching 'Annie' outfits. Manny Jr., married to his accounting firm, was the caboose. He leaned back as he walked, hands in pockets, as blond and sinewy as a J-Crew model. He wore a white Oxford shirt and purple paisley tie, tan slacks and glossy penny loafers the color of maple syrup. He gazed across the water as if expecting a message from the far shore.

Craig swung a plastic Wonder bag of stale bread chunks in his fist: hot dog buns, leftover blueberry waffles, petrified pancakes. They had buried the old doctor with military honors at Lake View Cemetery in the village. In memory of Herman 'Manny'

Hendershot, Mandie's family was staging the annual ritual, the 'casting of the bread' upon the 'many waters,' as Manny had done with them over the last twenty-five summers. The late Doctor Hendershot had always struck Allan as a godless secularist, and even though he had passed on, Allan could barely restrain the urge to rain fistfuls of garbage on the chain-gang of pantheist mockery leading his wife and innocent daughter along the shore like drones in a cult sacrifice.

Halfway to the dock the Hendershots were proceeding in all solemnity when Rory's gangly blond girl, Trystan, giggled. A twitch shot through Rory's arm and she struck Trystan with a vicious backhand. Trystan bugged her eyes and tottered back a step, shame shriveling her face. Autumn Teal, the darker curly-haired one, took her older sister's hand. Rory slapped at the handclasp and severed the link. Allan wagged his head in disgust.

"Almighty."

His pencil drilled the page, poised to scratch the first line, when he noticed the paper bore the imprint of a previous message. Someone had written a note then torn off the top sheet. The impressions rippled like an elegant code across a ghost map. Allan forgot the Hendershots and studied the cabalistic text. He felt a throb of voyeuristic guilt, then a secret thrill, knowing he might have stumbled on someone's private thoughts. His imagination clicked like a roulette wheel. He could keep the letter, destroy it, copy the contents and return it—it didn't matter. The lines could expose a broken confidence, unclaimed inheritance, or family scandal, something from the no-longer-secret vaults of the Hendershot saga. His fingertips brushed the paper.

As if making a charcoal rubbing he angled the pencil point and shaded over the first lines of the old message. The words, written in slashing cursive, stood out like a flashlight slicing through smoke.

The message was from Mandie. It began, *Dear Allan.*

At the end of the dock a faded American flag on a tilted aluminum pole dabbed the sky. The Hendershots gathered beneath it in a half circle. A Nautica sport boat buzzed past, towing a female wake-boarder in a cherry life vest. The woman swung her arm over her head like a rodeo queen and whooped. Waves lapped the shore and slopped over the dock. Manny Jr. hop-skipped away from the water and with a hand smoothed his hair. From her post in the family crescent Mandie glanced up and sneaked Allan a toothy grin. Rebecca Ruth wore a burgundy tea dress, white stockings, and black shoes with shiny buckles. Like a ventriloquist, Mandie manipulated Rebecca Ruth's arms, making her wave to her daddy.

Allan replied with a firm-lipped smile. He raised a thumb and two fingers, his forearm on the armrest.

"Hello, ladies. Love you."

He scanned the penciled-over lines: *It hurts me to have to tell you this way, at this moment, but there's something about me you don't know.*

* * *

Copper light stains the empty beach. The bottle washes ashore and anchors itself in sand. Two wheezing lilac and orange Vandura Campwagons arrive and deploy a troop of bloodshot-eyed staffers who in floppy powder-blue smocks, white Bermuda shorts, and tangerine neckerchiefs resemble big black Von Trapp children. They bag trash and bundle hammocks. Their headphones leak Bruce Springsteen and Bon Jovi. They smoke and gossip and sweep the bungalows free of clutter from the rum-soaked clam bake and corporate karaoke the night before. Two of the women find a frilly red bra under a cabbage palm. Laughing, they pass it back and forth and drape it over their breasts and pose until one woman snatches it from the other and darts away through a lush eruption of chocolate mimosas in pink clay urns.

Four of the men huddle on the beach, oblivious to the bottle at their feet. Their talk becomes aggressive, and though they are really in agreement, they jab their fingers in their open hands, tap their watch faces, and hurl angry gestures at the beachfront casinos and hotels to the north.

With the chalets tidied and swept and re-stocked with brand-name water bottles and coconut-scented soaps, the crews depart. Soon pelicans and parasailers adorn the noon sky. At dangerously low altitudes jets for KLM and Qantas and Delta sweep in and roost at the airport. A rugged trawler crawls along the blue horizon. A black-naped tern lands near the bottle and pecks the glass, *tink-tink*. The tern flaps away, and a yellow fiddler crab fails twice to scale the bottle but after an hour finally clamps a choke-hold on the neck and like a window washer ogling a bikini ad on a billboard stares at the note inside. In the sizzling heat the crab enters a phase of stillness then slips, dangles by its claw, drops to the sand, and sidles away.

In the afternoon a pod of baby blue shuttle busses bumbles into the sandy parking lot. A chunky boy with scabby knees jumps from the first bus that creaks to a stop. His Belzer Middle School T-shirt is cut into a saggy 'wife beater,' giving the world a good view of his fat rolls and boy boobs through the arm holes. His Lakers shorts droop to his ankles like clown pants. He dumps his maroon and white 'Bruin Pride!' duffle bag at his mother's feet and sprints to the water.

"Bertram!" she shouts, dragging their luggage toward a flamingo-pink bungalow. "I need your help!"

The boy halts on tiptoes at the ocean's edge. The foamy swell surges out and in, bathing his ankles in tropical luxury. He snatches an iridescent shard of sea shell and skips it into the waves.

"Cool!"

He scans the sprawling strand for another fantastic object, spots the bottle and plucks it from the sand. He flips it into the air, end-over-end, and catches it like a juggler. The fact that it is a beer bottle plugged with a champagne cork means nothing to him, but he brings it close to his face and blinks at the wrinkled note entombed in the clear chamber. He gawks around and spies a black ridge of volcanic rock arching out of the sand like the half-buried spine of a barbecued dinosaur. He raises the bottle over his head.

"Bertram!" his mother calls. "Put that down! Last thing I want is for you to cut yourself!"

"I was putting it down!"

He glances at his mother, drops the bottle and with sagging shoulders sulks back to the bungalow. Hand shading her eyes, his mother tracks his return with a beady, military stare. Her billowy burnt orange blouse and purple beach skirt make her look like a hippo crammed into a tutu. Before her son can reach her, she pivots and starts back, her small heels leaving divots in the sand. Self-consciously she flips her skirt out, trying to cover her elephantine buttocks, which rises and falls like a large double bellows.

"I don't trust the hospitals down here," she says. "Nobody does."

In the evening the sun simmers in a broth of red haze. Dusk devastates the sky with erratic purples and lofty pinks and hot swabbings of orange. The staff serves seared tilapia and mango margaritas. Through the lull of jets and the lisp of the sea, hidden speakers feed easygoing studio music into the breeze: spiced riffs of reggae, mento, and cool calypso. From a laughing crowd of motivational speakers a pink and white Mikasa volleyball bounces down the beach and strikes the bottle, nudging it into the placid surf. A pale, big-boned girl with tight auburn ponytails and a Band-Aid on her forehead races from a quincunx of bamboo torches and rescues the volleyball from the undertow. She bear hugs the ball, belly distended, knees locked, and squints at the waterborne bottle. Her chapped lips part to reveal a rack of tightened braces. The bottle spins and bobs in sea foam, too far away for her to reach, a line of its text flashing in the firelight: *I can't wait anymore I need help now.*

* * *

The day before the interment Allan lunched with Mandie at the Bluewater Grill, one of the pier restaurants overlooking the lake. Bonnimarie shepherded Rebecca Ruth around the park at the lake's north end, sending her after portly geese and skittish squirrels, cheering for her when she scaled the gazebo steps or pitched pennies into the circular blue fountain. Over popcorn shrimp and strawberry daiquiris Mandie and Allan quarreled because Mandie wanted him to join the family burial rite.

"For daddy," she said, sliding her hand across the table top of beige snowflake designs. "For me?" Allan folded his napkin and fired it at the table, head shaking.

"Can't."

But she clasped his hand so close to her breast that the woody ginger scent of her perfume teased a strand of a smile across his face. On Genesee Street, strolling along like a seventh-grader with a first crush, he squeezed her hand and explained.

"I'm squashed in those traditions. Your traditions. You're forcing me against my beliefs."

"My husband, the martyr."

She stood back and pouted in her candy-apple dress, gleaming high heels planted on the cracked sidewalk. Her bouncy mane of curls blazed like a bonfire in the June twilight. All around, the traffic and pedestrians slowed to the speed of a mural in a museum of ordinary nights, the illustrated history of all endangered loves. A pause claimed the air, something they both felt, so that eventually she surrendered to his patient persistence, and they walked hand-in-hand past the Sherwood Inn and Judge Ben Wiles, the old paddleboat moored at the pier. Like a small ark The Judge Ben was unloading its cargo of snowy-headed souls. Wedges of bothered mallards and seagulls waddled away from the crowds. Allan watched the ritzy elderly couples disembarking from the upper decks to the green lawns spotted with droppings and goose down and saw in them a living hieroglyphic, a prophecy of a parallel descent he would soon have to make. He shook the sense of doom loose with a smile.

"Beautiful," he said.

"What?"

"The evening. You."

At the edge of the park rowdy kids with a monster bouquet of balloons stampeded through the ivy-covered archway, scattering crows and pink mimeographed fliers for the boat show. Allan and Mandie, though startled, walked on without speaking.

* * *

After his wedding Allan staggered into a miry depression. Every morning manacled him to the ocean floor of his emotions. This troubled him, when he considered how he and Mandie had met, how God had overseen their union. Soon, though, he linked his bouts of black sadness to the lockstep ways of the Hendershots. They ate the same things. They discussed the same things. Their brains stayed hardwired to one channel of verbal static. Associating with them was like being quarantined in a dining room with no chairs while a butler stood at a polished Steinway and banged his finger on middle C. In all the dinner conversations Allan shared with the Hendershots no one strayed from the holy trinity of topics: weather, food, and health problems. For twenty-five years, up to his seventy-second birthday, Manny Hendershot jogged the same two and a half miles from his house to the country club, dressed in the same gray sweat pants and Boston College sweatshirt. Even as Allan watched the Hendershots' post-funeral tribute from the back deck, he wondered if the doctor's heart had failed not from age but because Bonnimarie had served him a spinach and egg-white omelet one morning instead of his usual coffee and toast with marmalade—'just for a change,' she might have said—and that the shockwaves of foreign matter through his system had sent his organs into emergency shutdown.

In the beginning Allan tried patience and understanding. In all social settings with the Hendershots he nursed a low profile, simply spooned his gazpacho and savored his lime sorbet. Before long, however, their droning exchanges about a cold front over Lake Ontario, the temperature of the creamed beef, or a Navy buddy's gall stones drove him to introduce topics about art, religion, politics, or psychology—only to find himself shunned by glazed stares across the candlelit tureen or, worse, outright ignored. In the first five years of his marriage to Mandie—the oldest and, Allen felt, only humane member of the Hendershot clan—he sensed that their method of welcoming spouses into the family was like passing a rolling pin over an unbaked gingerbread man. With the mindless grind of a medieval torture crew, they rolled away every grain of character until the new groom was flattened to a skin of tasteless dough.

There was a comical side to the tragedy. But from the start he sensed a cloaked dysfunction, too. A hunchbacked demon handcuffed in the Hendershot cellar was ready to howl, break loose, and claw the stuffing out of the living room furniture. He saw it in the way Rory battered her children. His letter to Rory would be his most decisive move toward peeling off the family blindfold of narcissism, a way to defuse the buried bombs of hostility. The letter would also reclaim, if only to a small degree, his identity and destiny. But he struggled with doubts—timing, appropriateness, and, ultimately, Mandie's reaction. He had meditated with devotion, though, considered and observed, and he felt confident that a subtle sureness would prod him in the right direction, loosen his tongue and hands, if God wanted him to write Rory a letter. If only for the sake of the children.

Within a year of meeting his sister-in-law Allan could see Rory battled domestic rage. The passage of five years confirmed his suspicions, as with greater frequency—on an overnighter to their Minneapolis home, at the Hendershot time-share on Marco Island, or turning into the organics aisle on a group trip to the farmer's market—he started to catch Rory knocking her daughters around like a garbage man kicking two trash cans. His rank in the family, however, kept him in the wings, away from the contested zones of the obvious.

Of all virtues God wished to nurture in women and men, Allan felt—and his experiences had proven him right—the ability to wait was supreme. To wait was God's way. Too many times he had seen people in his own family and elsewhere act rashly and live out sorry lives of regret because of foolhardy urges. As a Navy pilot he had waited until the last minute before ejecting from his F-8 Crusader over the Gulf of Tonkin. He had waited until he was forty-nine to marry, waited with Mandie five years before having a child. He had waited to embrace his spiritual path. Waited to welcome the signs of its origins. Waited a year before phoning the woman who on Yonge Street in downtown Toronto stepped out of a Little Pigs Shuttle Bus and caught him staring at her. For all his patience God had blessed him in good time. He would wait now. And God would reward him in time.

He rolled the pencil between his fingers, considering how he could write the letter now and give it to Rory later. Rory dragged her daughters from the dock across the beach, fingernails sunk like talons in their wrists.

"Or," he sighed. He flipped through the pad to a section of clean pages. "Give it to her now."

Having married late into the glorious Hendershot bloodline, Allan didn't want to taint Mandie's relationship with her family by meddling in their ways, as perverse and sacrilegious and cruel as they were. Writing a letter to Rory could stir up a buzzing hill of ants. Early on he had been careful not to come across as the do-gooder, the spiritualized Jesus freak in the fringed white jacket, banging heads and Bibles and slinging millstones around the neck of every malcontent who spanked a cranky baby.

Then Mandie gave birth to Rebecca Ruth. Hand-clapping, cheek-smacking Becky Boo. Blond noodly curls. Pink-lipped smile. Hendershot eyes of rainy crystal so dangerous and deep you could sink to the bottom and never breathe again. From the first whiff of her almondy skin he loved his daughter with a love deeper and clearer than the glacial lake in front of him. But even at fourteen months Rebecca Ruth was acting violent. She would kick and bite and scream like a wolverine. She head-butted and slapped him whenever he held her. Allan had imagined a hundred plausible reasons for his daughter's kickboxing sprees, but he suspected she was aping Auntie Rory. So when Doc Hendershot died of heart failure, Allan's heart flip-flopped into the arena of bold but cautious deeds. His nieces were suffering. Even his daughter was in danger, and God had bequeathed him new eyes to see the errors of those who stirred the blood and tears of the young in the dust of the earth and looked away.

"When's the question," he said. He flipped back to the front pages and shaded over more lines. His fingertips rested on the impressions as if he were reading Braille. "How exactly."

Rory's outbursts had grown more volatile, more frequent. The weekend of the funeral—surrounded by strangers and the ribbon-spangled pageantry of the wake, the frilled dishes of assorted nuts, pastel mints, and blunt fruit cakes sheathed in thick white icing—Allan witnessed a few 'episodes,' as Mandie decorously referred to them. In the Rochester airport, when Allan and Mandie arrived with Rebecca Ruth, Rory attacked Autumn Teal for blocking the way of a withered Catholic priest who was zipping past the luggage carousel in a battery-powered cart. The skeletal priest was forced to overcorrect, and the cart's basket dumped its payload of roly-poly pink elephant toys on the floor. Rory shrieked. Her face became a bloodless mask, and she yanked Autumn's arm and spanked her thighs with such energy that a chattering crew of retirees in floppy Jamaican flag T-shirts stopped and gawked. At the Sign of the Dove Chapel, at the funeral's close, Trystan trod on the toes of Windy Ehrenreich, the minister. Rory seized Trystan's shoulders and shook her until her head and giant bow bobbled like loose toy parts and the emerald carpet became splattered with cookie crumbs, miniature chocolate éclairs, and white florets of cake frosting. Rather than intervening—how could they?—the guests sighed in concert and returned to purring streamlined condolences to one another over plastic cups of glittering mineral water.

After the fiasco Allan found himself standing on loose floorboards under the Sign of the Dove's Shaker-style exit, face-to-face with Trystan. They were backed against a mammoth clay urn that spouted tiger lilies and cattails. Obscure family members and well-wishers, faces earthward, filed across the gravel parking lot toward a phalanx of black Benzes and silver BMWs. Looking down and smiling, Allan noticed that all traces of shame from the recent ruckus had been burned away from Trystan's face. Instead she projected a tomboyish in-your-face, hip-cocked, freckle-faced moxie. She was a princess who had sparked and sidestepped a playground rumble, a leggy gang-banging Shirley Temple in white shoes, lacy ankle socks, and lemon chiffon knee-length party dress. The enormous bow in her hair drooped over one eye. She squinted her other eye and jutted her jaw out like Popeye.

"Know what this is?" she asked, raising her fist. The other fist she punched pugnaciously into her hip.

"Munchkin uppercut?" Allan ventured.

"The size of your heart."

Only later, as he and Mandie drove in bumper-to-bumper wordlessness past Doug's Fish Fry through the village, did Allan realize his niece was only repeating some anatomical trivia she had picked up and not using coded sign language to scream for help.

As he and Mandie and Rebecca Ruth eased through the traffic light at the center of the busy village, Allan fumbled in the jockey box for a map. Out tumbled a Corona bottle containing a scrolled message, its neck plugged with a sun-cooked champagne cork.

He caught it before it hit the floor then pinched the cork as if to pluck it out and read the message. Frantic, Mandie slapped at his hands. Their car swerved dangerously in the tight traffic.

"Stop, stop it!" she cried, snatching the bottle away.

"Hey, hey!" Allan covered his head like a prizefighter.

"What say we finally open this thing? Find out who it's from. Have a whirl."

"Uh uh," she insisted. She stuffed the bottle between her thighs. "Open the bottle, our love dies. Keep it closed, love thrives. I can't believe you don't remember! We promised—not until we're old and gray."

"I'm old and gray today."

Mandie rocked her head back and laughed. She swung left at the fire station, pointed and said "Oo!" at the vintage fire engine in the show room, and sped them south through the undulating farms and wineries and boat rental shops toward Mandana. Allan traveled in a dreamy half-state, riding his thoughts out of body, marveling at the resilient miracle of his wife. He gazed out the window, envisioning the scene they had left behind—the boat festival and its jumble of colored banners, like a waterborne carnival, the candlelit paper lanterns floating on the darkened water, the feisty terriers harassing geese, the million-dollar mansions, the red barns and tidy farms like unframed oil paintings, the hand-made scarves and candied fruit slices and remote-controlled airplanes as big as albatrosses in the shop windows. It was like something from a prophecy left on his doorstep, something vivid and subdued after a long spell of solitude, the lucid green glow of the lake, the surging laughter of children, the couples strolling and talking affectionately of the past as if waiting for the last boat to pull in and take them to the next world.

* * *

The two-story brick building was at one time the residence of a diplomat. After that, a free children's museum of natural history and then a bar called Tapsy's. The summer after the plumbing burst, volunteers in ragged jeans and bandanas marched in with paint rollers and cups of spackle and transformed it into the main revival hall for The Continental Crusade for Christ. It was this crumbling, patched-together version of the structure that Allan encountered when he passed by with a gyro and a Coke after a claustrophobic training meeting. His information systems group, Visicom, Inc., had organized a week-long retreat for employees in Toronto, specifically for the purpose of scoping out global competition. The group's director, Phil Lillibridge, had devoted an entire afternoon of slapdash overhead slides and rabid debates to why 'this fruit thing'—Apple Computers—was going to tank by year's end. Phil, in a long-sleeved dress shirt of blue and orange circuit-board plaid and a beige square-bottom knit tie, had testified with abolitionist fervor. Lips rimmed with spittle, he had gesticulated like a bald scarecrow lifted in a tornado, his voice grinding to gravel, his face turning a deeper shade of puce with each declamation.

Allan endured it with stone-faced stoicism then escaped for a stroll. Everywhere he walked weekend traffic clogged the streets. The sky was an eruption of stars, and long liquid clouds of inky blue slid over the tops of buildings and beer billboards and blinking radio antennae. Two blocks from the Ramada Inn, where his group was staying, he passed the Continental Crusade for Christ and stopped to listen to the bustle. The kick-butt thump of drums and the ragamuffin wail of an electric guitar drew him to the doorway. Close up, the building resembled a ruined mansion: red brick exterior, butter-yellow flowerboxes jutting from windows, pink zinnias and red impatiens shriveling in the dusky light. A fence topped with blunt spikes— the kind Allan imagined surrounded all haunted houses— enclosed the property. Some windows were barred, others covered with spray-painted plywood. A year was etched in the massive gray cornerstone: 1903. Chipped Doric columns rose on both sides of the ponderous oak front door, and a weathered escutcheon, a dove-shaped book floating over a torch, adorned a keystone above the columns. A spray-painted bedsheet drooped like a lost parachute over the entrance, obscuring the faded remains of a swooping 'Tapsy's' logo. The sheet said, 'Revival!'

"Be good for some people I know," Allan said. "Revive the unrevivable." A comical car horn bleated behind him. He stepped forward to avoid a chuckling couple in mismatched army jackets that was hurrying down the walk.

The Crusade's building was sandwiched between a porn shop, Adult World, and a trashy pizza parlor, Fat Louie's. Seduced neither by saucy sex nor unbridled mozzarella, Allan found himself mesmerized by the jubilant rock hymns that pulsed through the Crusade's crypt-like arch. Warm soupy light poured from the entrance and bathed the broken front steps in a golden glow. Without knowing what he was doing or why he was doing it, Allan pushed through the creaky gate. He strode up the walk, skipped up the steps, and stood at the threshold. He gazed inside at the band and dancing people. Then he wiped his face with a napkin, dumped his Coke cup and gyro paper in a trash can, and walked in.

Immediately he found himself adrift and anonymous in the

rumpus of music, dreamy lights, and gamboling bodies. The large room resembled a ransacked warehouse. Ghost footprints tracked through sheetrock dust across the beige and maroon floor tiles. High gravity seemed to have warped whole sections of the floor, while others appeared ready to burst from the pressure of underground geysers. Light bulbs swung from bare wires like incandescent fruit. The guts of the heating and cooling systems showed through rotten ceiling panels: pipes bandaged with rags, foil flaking from cracked ducts. In a few places entire girders were visible. Green picnic benches herringboned toward the stage, forming a central aisle.

Nobody was sitting. The band surged at peak intensity. Allan plugged his ears with his fingers. Some people wore business suits and dresses. Others worshipped in faded fatigues and blankets and filthy sweat suits, shimmying and bounding like dizzy frogs. At the command of some unseen choreographer they flailed their hands, closed their eyes in rapt ecstasy, shouted praises and hallelujahs. A haggard man with a Canadian flag bandana on his head danced on a bench like a leprechaun capering across a hillside of gold. He wagged his salt and pepper beard, clicked his heels, and threw his body into electric contortions, as nimble as a gymnast.

The bald drummer wore a black ruffled shirt under a lemon tuxedo jacket that had wide sequined lapels. The bassist, in orange Chuck Taylor high-tops, was a gaunt black man graying at the temples. A short spectacled guitarist in Hawaiian shorts and green bowling shirt kept steadying his oily rockabilly quiff and doing 'The Bump' against a wheelchair that supported a blind Chinese saxophonist in Roy Orbison sunglasses. The lead vocalist, also the pastor, clapped and leaped like a lunatic in his white T-shirt, jeans, and robe of liquid scarlet and silver lamé. He looked over fifty, but had the sprightly gait of a mountain goat. A hint of mustache and goatee graced his face, and white skunk-stripes streaked his hair and frizzy ponytail.

At Allan's elbow a black woman in a blackberry head wrap and zipper-crazy denim dress boogied and slapped her hands together. She shouted praises to the ceiling, eyes closed, head lolling back. A large button pinned to the woman's mammoth bust jiggled so violently the caption was hard to read: *Harriet Tubman Home. Auburn, New York. A. M. E. Zion Church, Founded 1796.* The button showed a black and white image of Harriet—stern, androgynous, a white cloth knotted at her throat. On stage the preacher spun a three-sixty and whipped the crowd into a frenzy.

"The Lord!" he shouted. "He is mighty! He is holy!"

His curiosity satisfied, Allan turned for the exit. On his way he stopped at a card table and plucked a powdered doughnut from a box next to piles of fuchsia and lime-green gospel tracts. He poured himself a Dixie cup of cherry Kool-Aid and surveyed the walls, smiling and shaking his head at the antics of the crowd. The walls bore a motley zodiac of Jesus pictures: pencil portraits, crayon impressionism, hasty watercolors, quilted scenes. From the scarred walls the many faces of Jesus gazed—some grim, others with blissful looks of bemused detachment—at the rapturous hullabaloo raised by Toronto's Christian crusaders.

In one smeared finger painting of brilliant red, yellow, and blue Jesus kneeled on a rock precipice. A dove like a watery trace of cloud perched on the wooden cross that angled across the bleary Jesus's shoulder. A severe pen and ink sketch in a silver frame showed a starved Jesus with his arms spread-eagled, his head bleeding under a spidery chaplet of thorns. A Picasso imitation depicted a muscular Jesus chasing children across a putting green of sportive lambs, and a sloppy Jackson Pollack spinoff of popsicle sticks and glue and glitter on paper plates put Jesus in a wine-red robe, his sandaled foot on the earth, his pale right arm raising a guitar of lightning.

In all, Allan noted Good Shepherd Jesus, Byzantine Jesus, Day-Glo Doodle Jesus, Black Slamdunking Jesus, Needlepoint Jesus, Heart of Fire Jesus, Jesus on a Harley-Davidson, Paint-By-Numbers Jesus, Garbage Mosaic Jesus, Sacred Goblet Jesus, Pink Pipe Cleaner Jesus, Elmer's Glue and Macaroni and Kidney Bean Jesus, Polaroid of My Kid Brother as Jesus, Hook-and-Eye Potholder Jesus, 'Have a Nice Day' Jesus, and Jesus Rolling the Earth Together Like a Scroll. Allan chuckled at the chintzy clutter, its veneer of cheap awe. But he felt a strange respect for the rambunctious gallery of vivid dreams, so raw and authentic and misguided. So many pictures—sad, peaceful, warrior, promised one. How could they all mean the same thing?

On the opposite wall hung a second exhibit. He scanned those images fleetingly and like a bird of prey downing a mouse bolted the last bite of powdered donut. As his thoughts were swinging between Tandoori and Thai for dinner his eyes landed on the picture at the bottom of the second display. The cup slipped from his fingers. Cherry-flavored blood splattered his shoes and the dusty tile. The black woman in the head wrap jumped back.

"Watch it!" she said.

The last Jesus picture hovered in fluorescent emerald light.

Pearl flames from a shelf of melted birthday candles tickled the picture's lower border. Allan's shocked movements triggered a change in the skunk-headed pastor, who sank to his knees and arched his back as if pole-axed with ecstasy between his shoulder blades. The band tripled its tempo. The crowd bounded like kangaroos.

"Holy!" the preacher bawled. "He is holy!"

The sight of the glowing Jesus picture entered Allan like the scent of wild mint. The maelstrom of music and emotion shot him from Toronto to the cockpit of his F-8 Crusader, over the Gulf of Tonkin, where before ejecting in an apocalyptic thunderstorm he had seen this very image of Jesus—eerily regal and green and glowing—in the tortured clouds. As a fighter pilot he had heard stories of this kind, always ludicrous and overblown, always told by someone three days from divorce, bankruptcy, or suicide. In Saigon, on furlough, he had passed a bamboo-and-sheet metal shrine where someone had spotted the face of Jesus in the grease stains on a pizza box. For weeks local Christians had lit candles, set up vigils, and sat on handmade blankets, strumming guitars. Allan's flight buddy, Marcus North, claimed he had seen the face of Jesus in the moonlit sea, which, North insisted, helped him drop safely on a carrier when his landing gear failed. Later, spotters reported that North had seen a concentration of bioluminescent algae.

But now, the same Stormy Sky Jesus from Allan's past stared at him from a ramshackle shrine made by born-again bombers. The serene image was mounted on fuzzy black felt, similar in style to the cheap posters offered as prizes in ring toss booths at county fairs. The figure's long face had geometric cheekbones that plunged to an arrowhead chin. The divine eyes telescoped like corridors, slanting to the razor ridge of the chrome nose. The hair scrolled over the shoulders in cumulus curls.

Allan's feet slid over the chalky tile on invisible guide rails. He shouldered through the hyped-up crowd, and the band's cataclysm fell mute, as if someone had wrapped a pillow around his head. As he neared the green Jesus's face, a hand cupped cosmic fire in his chest. A gem of bleeding ice squeezed from his heart. Tears steamed on his cheeks. He couldn't resist, didn't want to resist, felt like mounting the stage, grabbing the microphone, and shouting to the caravan of God goons that he was crying like he had never cried before. He wanted to cry until every drop of the Atlantic escaped his veins and roared into the Gulf of Tonkin, where his crippled fighter fluttered in time, a plastic model strung on fishing line from the ceiling of the universe, with Jesus's face sailing through the broken sky on a token moon. The sweet fist of pain in his chest tightened its rosebud tourniquet, crushing the seedling of his heart, flooding his flesh with supercharged sap.

He brushed his fingers across the picture's fuzzy surface. An electric black light made the face of Jesus more luminous. Allan slumped to his knees and swiped the tide of tears from his cheeks with the backs of both hands. The ice-vise pressed his heart into a ruby of flame. Every cell in his tissues rose to the cracked ceiling of the world from which his unhinged soul swung in the cradle of creation. Years back, in the womb of the exploding sky, after seeing this same heavenly face—after swearing to himself he had seen it—he had waited until the last second to eject from his fighter because at that moment death had seemed the greatest of desires. Then he had snapped to his senses and launched himself into the frigid tempest, only to land, years later, in a strange building where he wept at the blazing face of his past, his reason strapped to a skywriting rocket, his lungs a lashing sea of sacred anguish.

A hand touched his shoulder.

The black woman with the Harriet Tubman pin was gazing down. Like a guilty child, he gathered himself and stood, daubing at his cheeks with his cuffs.

"Sorry," he blubbered. "I'm—I didn't know—"

The woman took his hand. "Feels good, don't it?"

"Sorry," Allan said. He scanned the room for an escape. "I didn't realize—"

"No apologies," the woman said. Her eyelashes looked like spiders. Her round cheeks and nose and plump lips were squished in the center of her face. She patted the back of his hand and released it, slip-sliding toward the crowd. "No apologies necessary. Feels right, don't it?"

In the Nussbaum Convention Room at the Ramada Inn a brace of diehard Visicom researchers and sub-directors rallied to hear the final word of the day. Chairs with tan metal frames and watermelon cushions lined the room, as if waiting to launch a group of naïve recruits on a one-way mission to their cubicles in the Baby Boom Galaxy. A plain wooden lectern waited at the front for the next believer. On a table draped in a tasseled crème cloth sat a row of plastic drinking glasses, carafes of ice water, bowls of lemon wedges, black dishes of Andes mints. An overhead projector on a rolling stand held the presentation's title on the screen: 'Charting Course with the Elite: Projections,

Evaluations, and Recommendations.' Men in navy sport coats and women in business skirts and pant suits of taupe and mouse gray—all flashing orange nametags on their lapels—shuffled down the aisle. They jingled glasses of ice water and crammed manila folders and yellow notepads under their arms.

Gary Mummert, the speaker, buttoned his camel-hair blazer and approached the lectern. He wore an eye patch under his glasses. The projector glare blinded his good eye, and he banged his knee on the table. Laughter bubbled from the ranks.

"Sorry," Gary said, touching his eye patch. "Doctor says a few days. You're all so dazzling to behold, it's too much."

Gary licked his lips, nudged his glasses higher on his nose, and flipped his notes to the first page. At the last minute Allan hustled into the room, glanced an apology at Gary, and took a seat at the back.

"Evening," Gary began. "I'm sure you're glad this is the last—well, frankly I'm surprised to see anyone here, especially with the buffet still on. Fact, I'm calling dibs on the kebabs. So don't everybody hog 'em when this is over."

A pie chart sliced into seven wedges flipped onto the screen. The wedges in the pie, all shades of charcoal and gray and white, bore percentages.

Allan puzzled over the pie chart and struggled to concentrate. He took out a pen and pad and started jotting snatches of Gary's speech. He gouged each phrase into the meat of the paper with a force that frightened him. He kissed the air and exhaled.

"Easy," he said to himself. "Light and breezy."

Once Gary was blushing in a flutter of bored applause, Allan looked down and saw how he had carved his notes into the paper. His veins hummed with the energy of tidal waves, the boundless barking of seagulls. Something ponderous moved through him with the ocean-liner heft of glaciers. He wanted to sprint around the equator and feed on the milk of comets. As his associates filed out of the room, he tried to still his racehorse breathing and silence the waterfall roar in his heart. He thumbed through his notepad and saw that he had knifed his words so forcefully into the paper that they were legible three pages deep.

Hurts to put it like this. Better now than later. Should come clean, that's the best thing from my position. And not wait. There's something you should know.

* * *

He considered himself, as Paul wrote, 'one born out of due time.' He was trying to maintain a degree of outward respectability, for Mandie's sake, but he was also sending a message that he was his own man, the Son of Man's man. So in defiance of The Hendershots' overdressed sham he wore running shoes and ankle socks and faded Levi's jeans. Tiny blood vessels reddened his cheeks. Dippity-Do shellacked his wiry hair. In his lawn chair on the cabin deck he appeared to be exactly what he was: an older man clinging to youth the way a rock climber hugs a crag. He knew he looked the way Mandie always described him: paunch in the belly, sloped forehead, matted eyebrows, boxer's nose and chin. Once, over lobster and asparagus, she remarked how he would have made a good fifth face on Mt. Rushmore. Though pained, he had laughed and daubed butter from his chin with a napkin. But he never exorcized the image from his mind. Even now he felt time jackhammering his profile into a granite cliff—and breaking the jackhammer.

He raised his pencil and held it at eye level. He squinted and sighted down the shaft so that the huge out-of-focus point harpooned the sanctimonious quorum of Hendershots on the dock. He imagined skewering them with a sudden thrust, shish-kabobbing them like roaches to a bed of Styrofoam.

"How should I put it? How could anyone put it?"

Why had Mandie started a letter then slipped into a changing room of second thoughts? Most likely, the torn-away letter was one of her infamous practical jokes meant to keep his 'blood pressure down.' Or a jab of good-natured revenge for his refusal to join the family rite. Whatever the reason, one thing was certain: Rory's behavior was no joke, and neither was Rebecca Ruth's.

He inhaled the punky musk of forest-floor rot. He let his breath slip between his slack lips and listened, waiting for a summons of hummingbird wings, a theophany of woodpeckers. To banish the mental image of his face on Mt. Rushmore, he sat up in his chair, aping the Lincoln Monument, focusing his power on his spiritual ears. He emptied his mind of cares, offering his spine as a conductor for celestial voltage. He would wait a thousand years—or an instant—before writing a line to Rory. Before sipping tea, scratching his elbow, before tugging the zipper on his jacket or clicking a fingernail against the Harriet Tubman button on his chest, before writing the will of God, he would wait ten thousand millennia to hear heaven's memo.

On the dock the lame hoop of Hendershots centered on Craig. Manny Jr. folded his arms over his bulky pecs. He examined the swaying trees and patted his helmet of moussed blond hair. Mandie hoisted Rebecca Ruth on her hip and pecked a kiss on her cheek. Bonnimarie lifted a periwinkle handkerchief to her mouth and stifled a cry. As she did, her heel caught on a warped board and she staggered, but Craig was there to steady her. With bowed head he mumbled a homegrown chant. Then he dipped a hand into the Wonder Bread bag and drew out a clawful of crusts and moldy dinner rolls.

Autumn Teal strayed from her mother, squatted down, and pointed at a carp whose scaly head broke the lake surface then sank below an ellipsis of bubbles. Tiger-eyed Rory took three strides and cracked her knuckles against her daughter's skull. Autumn's eyes flashed wide. She released a wounded howl and stomped back to her mother.

"God above," Allan said.

On the far side of the lake an orange sea plane buzzed down and coasted clumsily across the water like a plump mosquito. As a backdrop to the plane the east shore rose like a ruined cathedral wall. Thick trees cascaded over cliffs of flaking stone. Trunks twisted from the bare rock face, knotted branches flinging tortured gestures at the sky. Higher up, the trees cleared away in jigsawed plots for luxury log cabins and clapboard homes, tidy farms and dull silos. Candy-colored pontoon boats and sailboards dotted the lake. From somewhere a Jet Ski gargled, unable to drown out a stereo playing Andy Griffith. A sloop raised a hot pink seahorse sail that billowed in the uncertain breeze. Unaware of the drama on the Hendershot dock, a couple and two Brittany spaniels paddled past in red and blue fiberglass canoes. They half-raised their paddles, but on seeing the

Hendershots' catatonic assembly lowered their paddles and rowed on.

At that moment a swell of wind blundered through the woods, jostling limbs and tossing leaves across the lake. The Hendershots clutched their hairdos. Craig's leather tie flickered like a black tongue. A google-eyed lumberjack windmill on a stump in the myrtle went into a spasm of chopping, battering a stack of tiny painted logs with its little axe.

Allan sat up, listening, ready. Something small but resonant, like the cry of a bee, sang in his core. His sternum hummed like a tuning fork. The hairs on his arm prickled.

On the adjacent cabin's dock, Fran Powers, the Hendershots' summertime neighbor of thirty years, worked in a chartreuse Speedo and dangly orange life preserver, his rickety arms and legs as thin as the boom in his sailboard rigging. He steadied the board mast until the wind died. A broad-rimmed maroon sunhat slanted across his head, and dark migraine goggles masked everything but the nub of his nose and his muskrat's mustache. Powers, ropes looped in hand, looked up and waved at The Hendershot dock. When no one waved back he removed his hat and bowed his head, revealing the crew cut he had worn since his days at Fayetteville High School, every hair that was once oil-slick black now Icelandic white.

Allan looked from Fran Powers to the pad on his knee. The pad's message was completely shaded over in pencil: *I've kept a terrible secret, and I can't go on without coming clean. Perhaps it's your belief, your influence on me. Please don't be angry, but this letter is the only way I could think of telling you.*

* * *

A quartet of brown boobies paddles around the bottle, having adopted it as one of their flock. Miles from land, they circle the bottle in the rolling ocean, murmuring and clucking. They duck their hooded heads under water, scouting the flawless green sea for anchovies. The sun sizzles in the cloudless sky.

From the womb of the sea the metallic groan of diesel engines unleashes a gush of bubbles. With a dinosaur gasp the submarine surfaces, bobbing and bucking. Boobies flap and squawk into the air. The bottle clinks off the blue fiberglass hull of the sub and wobbles away.

The sub hatch pops open, releasing a burp of sour air. A brown shiny arm snakes out, wagging a Dutch five-seven handgun. The gunman, also the pilot, is shirtless. He shakes his ragged curls and grimaces at the painfully bright sky. His teeth are the color of canned corn. Down in the hold, a portable stereo plays the guitar bridge from 'Escape (The Piña Colada Song).'

"Date prisa!" the pilot shouts. He motions with his arm. "Cágate aquí!"

A second sinewy man hoists himself through the hatch. His head is shaved, and a toxic orange number thirty-three decal hangs like a torn scab from his greasy green sleeveless shirt. He yanks down his Manchester United shorts, hangs his haunches over the side, and waits, the expression on his face a mixture of shame and bliss.

"Qué comiste? Híjole!"

Moments later, with the men inside, the hatch claps shut,

the engines bellow, and the boiling ocean seals over the sub as if performing a miraculous healing. Like a transparent buoy the bottle spins in a confusion of foamy whirlpools. Its note flashes snippets of its message at the castaway sun. *Someone. Please.*

* * *

He waited because everyone was waiting. The annual boat show had gridlocked the village. Mountain bikers slalomed around top-heavy campers and cane-wielding retirees. Rogue German shepherds galloped through the parking lot of the hardware store. Peevish children with cherry sno-cone faces howled and flopped on sidewalks. Testy weekenders jammed the checkout lanes at the Skaneateles P&C, arms overloaded with charcoal briquettes, ground turkey, and chocolate licorice. Shopping carts clanged. Registers chattered nonstop. At the end of his line Allan bounced Rebecca Ruth in his arms and browsed through a rotating postcard stand. Behind him a stout woman in mulberry stretch-knit pants backed into a pyramid of watermelons and sent them thudding to the floor. Black seeds and shards of pink pulp splattered on the waxed tile. Allan inched forward in line with nothing but his daughter in his arms. A stock boy with a diamond stud earring and two-tone hairstyle kneeled and sopped up the mess with a bucket and checkerboard cloth.

"Da-da!" Rebecca crowed. She gyrated her lower half. "Dada, down!"

Allan set her on her feet and guided her forward with his leg. Annoyed with Rebecca's restiveness and unable to find the postcard he wanted, he spun the stand, closed his eyes, and grabbed one from the whirling pictures—sailboats, gazebos, Old Stone Mill, Millard Fillmore site, snatch! The stand twirled and squeaked like a spinning Christmas tree of chrome. He stood looking at the postcard in his hand.

"Da-da!" Rebecca cried. She hopped on one leg, arms raised. "Up!"

Allan's arm stiffened in a cast of frosty flame. The black and white snapshot on the postcard showed a two-story farmhouse with a porch. Rounded evergreens flanked the house on both sides. A telephone pylon jutted skyward above the roof. Allan gnawed his lower lip. Why did this house look so familiar? He felt like an orphan viewing the childhood home he was too young to remember. On the other side the card read: *Harriet Tubman Home.*

A xylophone note chimed in his chest and started ticking seconds like a stopwatch. His breathing rose to a strolling rhythm, stepping in time with a roomful of raucous heartbeats from a down-and-out Canadian revival hall, so many years ago. A sense of urgency charged his bones. How could he visit this place? And why?

"You in line?" a red-headed mailman with smudged glasses asked him.

"Waiting. Go ahead."

He searched the store for someone to save him from his crazy thoughts. He squinted at the card again and said "Harriet Tubman." As he mouthed the words, Rebecca Ruth squirmed like a collared wildcat. She shrieked and jabbed a chubby forefinger at the postcard's photo.

"What is it, sweetie?"

Allan studied the immortal shine in his daughter's saline eyes—the classic vacant stare of the Hendershots. She giggled and chirped and clapped her hands. She pointed at the postcard, the simple but mysterious white house from history that Allan himself had become, windows open, curtains billowing, fireplace swept of cinders, oak bookcases stacked with gold-trimmed classics, guests soon to arrive in snappy hansom cabs.

"Da-dah!" Rebecca Ruth chanted. She pointed at the picture. "Ab-bah!"

A woman in savage monarch butterfly sunglasses shoved past Allan, shattering his reverie. The woman's highlighted hair glowed like Easter candy. She lugged bottled water, lighter fluid, beef jerky, and Cheerios.

"Beautiful granddaughter," she said, flashing gray teeth. Allan winced.

"Daughter," he said.

"So sweet," the woman said and scurried ahead.

Then Mandie arrived with two teetering packs of decorative peach napkins in her arms. Sunglasses drooped low on her nose. "Ready?" she said. "Which line's the fastest?"

"Fastest isn't always best," Allan said.

"What?" Mandie said, sizing him up. "Let's go. We're late."

Allan raised the postcard to her face. "Seen Harriet Tubman's home? In Auburn?"

Mandie jerked her head toward the checkout. "Talk about it in the car."

"I need to go here," Allan said, closing his eyes. "It's—"

"Fine. On the way home, we—"

"Today."

Mandie's eyebrows jumped. "Today?"

"I'm supposed to see this house."

"Babe," she said, rattling the napkins. "We're—there are a million things to do! You know I can't do it with her around. She's—"

"I'll take her. It'll be fun."

Mandie stood like a lumberjack with her feet on two logs drifting apart. She rammed both magazines of napkins under an arm, whipped her sunglasses off, and probed a canine tooth with her tongue. She studied his baby-faced smile.

"I'm tempted," she began, brandishing her sunglasses, "to say death means nothing to you. We come all the way for the funeral—my *father's* funeral—and the first thing you want to do is gallivant off with our daughter to some tub lady's house!"

"Tubman," he said. "She was an escaped slave. Abolitionist."

"So?"

"We're all escaping slavery of one kind or another—"

She pressed the heel of her hand to her eye. "Just—don't. Today, for once. You're already freakin' me out. It's hard enough with dad dying, now—"

"There are more important things than death."

"Like?"

"Life." He swept Rebecca Ruth into his arms, bounced her and tickled her tubby tummy and made her laugh.

Mandie sighed. She shoved her sunglasses onto her face.

"Again," she said, paddling air toward herself. "Why do you have to go?"

"I'm supposed to."

"Supposed, who's—"

"God wants me to go," he said. He tensed his body as if expecting a blow. Then, seeing she wasn't fazed, he regrouped. "He's waited until now to tell me."

Mandie massaged her temple. "God? To a slavemaster's house?"

"Former slave. Activist."

"Whatever."

Without warning Rebecca surged to life and pummeled Allan's droopy cheeks with a flurry of flat-handed slaps. With each strike she yelped with delight and grinned like a possessed imp going for a knockout. Allan did his best to rope-a-dope the pygmy haymakers, but splotches bloomed like bloody flowers on his face. He ducked and dodged and parried with his arm.

"Why does she do that?" he said.

"To humble you?" Mandie offered.

"Could be a violent streak from your side."

"No clue."

In one desperate lunge he wrapped his wiggly whirligig girl in a body hug. She scowled and moaned and kicked her feet.

"Does she do this with you?" he asked.

"Looks like you've got the magic touch. Hey, how am I going to get back?"

"Cell phone? Hendershot ladies in the vicinity?"

"My man leaves me hanging after the funeral," she said, gaping around. "Whoduh thunk?"

"Least I didn't at the altar."

He shifted his spastic daughter in his arms and set her on her feet then leaned toward Mandie and kissed her cheek with a juicy smack. Rebecca Ruth, mimicking her father, smooched her mom's hand. Mandie laughed and tweaked Rebecca's nose.

"You are so cute!"

"Genetic," Allan said, shrugging. "So can we go? Me and Becky Boo?"

"If the history lesson's over."

Allan turned sideways and shouldered through the aisle, towing Rebecca by the hand. "Every day's history," he said.

Mandie stuffed the napkins under her other arm and yanked her purse open as they moved away. "Just hope we're not," she said.

"What?" Allan called. He twirled Ben Vereen-style and swooped Rebecca Ruth, his dwarf dance partner, into his arms. Together they fox trotted around the dog food and Rug Doctors, past the gumball machines and purified water, through the automatic doors. On the way out he tossed his daughter on his shoulder like a farmer hoisting a gunny sack of grain. She hooted and expelled a loud hiccup.

"History!" Mandie laughed. She waved to them over the magazines and gum. "You're so weird!"

She stepped aside to allow a silver-haired woman carrying a jittery Yorkshire terrier and box of doggie treats to go ahead. The terrier sported a lemon-lime bowtie and miniature orange cardigan that bore the embroidered name 'Bobo Simpkins.'

"But I love you," Mandie said, rooting in her purse for change.

The woman and terrier stared back at her. Mandie looked up.

"Not you," she said. "Them. Though I'm sure you're a wonderful person. And dog."

* * *

Craig Hendershot raised a fist of bread chunks above his head, offering them to the gods of summer sky. Crumbs caught like dandruff in his bushy hair. Bonnimarie stepped close, brushed away the crumbs, then glided back and bowed her head with the rest of the family.

Rory, chin tucked to her breastbone, clinched her struggling Autumn Teal in a one-arm headlock. She clamped a ferocious grip on Trystan's bicep.

Mandie, eyes averted, hugged Rebecca Ruth like a mother panda and rotated her body back and forth in rhythmic half-turns. A mile from the dock, a bald man in an orange and black wet suit barreled by on a wave runner.

Allan read: *I'm ashamed at how long it's taken me to come clean. And this isn't a plea for pity because what I've done is almost unforgivable, for me, for a mother especially.*

* * *

Halfway through their anniversary cruise their ship, the Norwegian Sea, docked at Roatan for an onshore excursion. As the massive ship nosed into port Allan stood at the cabin porthole and watched the merciless sun scour a grungy haze from the scrubby green hills. On the pier a troupe of natives in floppy parrot costumes jiggled their hips in front of a trio of bongo players and a red bucket marked 'Tips.'

Allan stared out the grimy porthole, hands in the pockets of his white tennis shorts. Battered vehicles loitered around the pier like depressed predators—VW bug taxis, a red and white

Corvair Greenbrier van, rust-cankered Toyota trucks, and a school bus splashed with a mural of children linking arms around the world. Native kids in tattered denim shorts and Yankees jerseys sprang from the dock into the dark green water and thrashed around in ecstasy, grins as white as the clouds in the humid sky.

Mandie entered the cabin, and Allan turned. She wore a white tank top, which showcased her freckled shoulders and firm bust. A red-and-white pineapple sarong was wrapped around her curvaceous hips. Miniature pineapples, one red, one white, dangled from her earlobes. She flashed her signature gap-toothed grin and seized his hand.

"Everybody's getting off!" she said. "There's scuba diving!"

On shore they lunched at the Sea Breeze Inn, overlooking the sapphire sprawl of Roatan Bay. Under a canopy of thatched banana-leaf, they ate jumbo shrimp salad and drank margaritas while sluggish hawkers paraded past, offering chintzy watches and cameras, day-glo wind sock octopi, and dripping mango halves sliced with machetes.

After lunch the scuba instructor, a swaggering mossy-headed man in lifeguard trunks, emerged from a Quonset hut opposite the inn. He knuckled sleep from his eyes as he approached.

"Chicago Ted," he said, introducing himself.

With the brusque energy and urban accent of a football coach Ted marshaled everyone into groups. Mandie pleaded with Allan to join her, but he was unwilling to bare his fuzzy fishbelly-white torso to the tropical sun, particularly in the company of so many men twenty years younger.

Instead he rented a rainbow Sunfish catamaran and while

Mandie's group paddled out to search for loggerhead sea turtles, Allan buzzed around the bay in tight figure eights, carving the symbol for infinity into the jeweled water. Eventually he beached his craft, flopped on the boat's springy blue trampoline and slipped his wide-brimmed sunhat over his eyes.

He dreamed he stood on a wintry prairie. The boundless white wasteland, cold but not searing to his bare feet, spread in all directions like an unmapped tundra. No animals, no plants. A pulsing opal light trimmed the symmetrical hills. He wore a roomy cotton suit, like a traditional karate gi, with a rope cinched around his waist. Soon he spotted a thread of blood that trickled over the ground and meandered out of sight, and he followed like a prospector hungering for water. Dreaming within the dream, he traced the dribble of blood across the sleeping forms of his parents, over the bodies of Manny and Bonnimarie Hendershot, Mandie—scoring her abdomen neatly like an equator—and, ultimately, across the bodies of Rory and her daughters. The dream's forms and phrases wobbled like bubbles of salt water then shot forward with the urgency of city traffic, whining with whale songs in his toes. At the end particles of the dream crumbled to sediment in yellow darkness, where his sun-charred hands scrabbled after folklore treasure. He was losing something precious, something he might never feel again, and he yearned to weep, to know more, to stay forever in the weedy grottos of joyful pain. Abandoned in bittersweet daylight, he battered his clown fists at the black vaudeville curtain that fluttered over him like a collapsed tent. Then he was leading everyone by the hand in a game of Red Rover, plodding with Mandie and her family toward the northern

lights with the weary stride of a pilgrim. They followed the red
line to where it crossed foaming rivers of cream, kaleidoscopic
streams, and ruined stone viaducts. At a roaring waterfall they
gawked at two pierced feet that were suspended in a dead tree
and dripping diamonds of blood.

Allan gasped and shot into a sitting position. He flailed at
the catamaran sail and flung it from his face. A goblet of flame
floated in the center of the South Atlantic sun. His stubbly face
was salty and sunburned, his throat crackling and dry. His head
throbbed.

He blinked at Mandie, who was emerging from the sea. Like a
transformed mermaid she strode through the dissolving veil of
the dream, spangled in sunlight and salt spray. Her bug-eyed scuba
mask and snorkel rode her head like a rubbery turban. Allan let
his eyes rove over her body, noting the dainty impressions her
feet made in the sand. She grinned and broke into a jog.

She clutched a net bag—the spoils from her dive. The sight
of her young physique in a red bikini drove a trident of desire
through his loins, coated in a bitter syrup of age. He was happy
he'd waited for her, and he was happy she'd waited for him.
But he would always be older than his wife.

"Hey, sleepy head," she said, flouncing down beside him on
the trampoline. She kissed him, and his shame fled.

"Prayed for a sea goddess and got one," he said. "Lookie
there."

"Mussels!" She dumped her clattering treasures on the sand.
"Clams, and—check it out! Note in a bottle!"

"Dare we open it?" he asked. He took the crusty Corona
bottle and twirled it in his fingers. As if peering into a telescope,

he angled it into the glare in the sky. A tan paper scroll was entombed inside, brittle and sun-damaged but intact. A Bollinger champagne cork plugged the neck. Allan pinched the cork and pulled, but Mandie slapped his hand and snatched the bottle away.

"No way! Spoil the mystery. Break the magic."

"Meaning?"

"If we open it and read the note," she reasoned, "we'll feel obligated to help whoever wrote it. In fact, let's never open it. Till we're old and gray. As long as we keep it closed, our love thrives. If we open it, love dies. Swear!"

He covered her hand with his, flapped his other hand melodramatically over his heart and rolled his eyes at heaven. "I swear."

She smiled and kissed him again, letting her face linger inches from his sober expression. She cocked her head to the side.

"You okay?"

"Fine."

A hundred yards off Chicago Ted's divers were migrating to shore. They dragged their sodden pear-shaped bodies out of the surf like rejects from the annals of evolution. One man, a stocky Japanese day trader in jumbo pink swim trunks, collapsed in the sand on his rear end. His wife, a plump woman in a see-through navy blue wrap and bent sombrero, gave him a kick. The disgruntled man hoisted himself to his feet and plodded after her.

"Who's in there?" Mandie probed. She peeped down the tunnels of Allan's pupils, smiling flirtatiously, head jittering from side to side. He rubbed his eyes.

"This isn't the time," he said. "But, Rory? Your sister? I

know it's not my place, but she's—doesn't she seem strict, violent—toward her kids?"

Mandie's smile melted. She turned to watch Chicago Ted's gaggle of Cousteau wannabes trudge up the beach. They squeezed water from their shorts and squinted at the sun like children regarding a cruel parent. The women minced across the sand, on the lookout for sea urchin quills and razor clams. The T-shirts on the men clung to their padded bellies like wet membranes. The logo on an older man's shirt proclaimed 'Retirement Is For Wimps!' The shaved legs of the women gleamed next to the simian legs of the men, whose hairy shins were coated in sand that glowed like gold dust. Allan examined Mandie's cool reaction.

"Babe, look," he said. "It's not—my place. Like I said. And I'm—sorry—"

Her bottom lip protruded. She examined her pedicure. "No, I know."

"That kind of thing carries over," he said. "In my weaker moments, I wonder if you—if I, we—when we have kids—if!—if, we have kids—would—"

She looked at the bay. "Never."

Allan nodded. "Yeah."

"So kids, huh?" she said, brightening. Her fingers tangled in his. "Got the daddy bug?"

"No," he insisted. "Yes, I mean—when you're ready. It's probably best to wait."

Together they monitored Chicago Ted's legion of sea-pickled swimmers as they slogged closer. A limping woman in a wet suit caught up with her husband and slugged his shoulder.

"What do you think of the name Rebecca Ruth?" she asked.

"Pretty," he said. "It's—why?"

She looked at the horizon. Her face relaxed in a bountiful smile. He turned his head and watched her gaze assume a placid mistiness, each iris a seed of light.

"Just came to me," she said.

Chicago Ted loped up to their catamaran, close enough to showcase the steel-blue stubble glazing his shipwreck jaw, the flossy body hairs on his tanned skin. Allan applied a self-conscious hand to his belly paunch. He noted Ted's surf bum abs and collarbones, his triathlete calves. From a net bag Ted produced an apple-red crab. The crab, like a mechanical toy, brandished its claws and worked its legs. Ted held his trophy high, a cologne model grin splitting his face.

"Gonna eat good tonight," he said.

* * *

From the campground on the east shore a bugle starts reveille. The melody is bright and stirring then nosedives into a drunken drawl. The Hendershots cast annoyed glances across the lake then turn to Craig, who lowers his head and mouths a mystical mantra. The others stand like devout mannequins, heads bowed. In the trees a catbird screech slashes the ceremonial quiet. Bowlegged and bent, Fran Powers watches in heavy thought at the edge of his dock, gazing across the water.

And it hurts, Allan. It hurts so much to have to tell you this way. I can only pray for forgiveness, for the hurt I've caused. I only hope I can undo what I've done.

* * *

At forty-eight, he assumed the directorship of Visicom's northeast region. Three weeks after office staffers unpacked his boxes in his penthouse suite, he scheduled a two-week trip to Toronto and asked his secretary to book him at the King Edward Hotel. He went on business reconnaissance, but he also went to see if The Continental Crusade for Christ had changed in over twenty years.

On the plane he sat next to a Willy Wonka look-alike named Nigel, an EMI recording executive in an open-necked pistachio shirt and purple velvet suit coat. With Nigel he drank Bloody Marys and dozed to Liszt. At the King Edward he downed two martinis and a bowl of gourmet nuts from a shin-high walnut table. Monday, he opted for a rental car and drove to appointments and board meetings, noting how the city had changed—the packed sidewalks, the Las Vegas flare, monstrous malls and huge office buildings.

On Friday he didn't book any meetings but spent the day jetting around in search of the makeshift brick church that had changed his life. The years had wiped the tablets of his memory clean, though, and no matter how hard he tried to resurrect the scene, he couldn't remember the street, the location—concluded, perhaps, that he had imagined everything. Judging by the blank stares he received, he gathered that the Ramada Inn where he had stayed no longer existed. Nobody at the gas stations where he stopped to ask had heard of The Continental Crusade for Christ.

Late in the afternoon he surrendered and drove down Yonge Street and stopped at Sam's Records for the Mahalia Jackson box set. In the failing light he sat in Trinity Square, drank an Orange Julius, harassed pigeons, and by the time he grew hungry the evening sky had turned a fresh cobalt blue streaked with clouds smoldering like campfire coals. Night-time crowds strapped in leather skirts and flashy gold chains ascended from their subterranean mazes. In all directions people strutted like the relatives of royalty up and down the streaming sidewalks, dodging taxis and economy cars. In a restaurant called The Senator he sat at a pitted ebony bar and ate steak and jumbo shrimp, watching the fur-wrapped, tuxedo-pressed couples scurry into the Pantages Theatre for *Phantom of the Opera*.

After dinner he wandered over to the Eaton Centre where delivery vans blared, limousines rumbled, and quick stiletto heels clicked down wide sidewalks. The Eaton Centre's mirrored façade reflected a rainbow of neon madness. Everywhere he looked an urban facelift project was in full swing. Five spindly construction cranes towered against the night sky like conquering creatures from a science fiction movie. Rugged scaffolding and flapping canvas masked many of the buildings. Along the curb a street crew of four men tidied the gutters. Three in reflective yellow jumpsuits pushed wide brooms, and the other piloted a puttering cart with a swirling orange light. A triangle of orange pylons steered pedestrians clear of mishap.

On the corner nearest the pylons a man sat playing the drums. Allan watched the drummer and found he could follow the steady rockabilly rhythm above the thrum of city noise. The drummer was skinny and sunburned. A green bandana at the base of his skull bound his ponytail. He smoked a cigarette and kept a pack rolled in the right sleeve of his oil-smeared T-shirt. It looked like bear claws had raked the thighs of his jeans, and he wore calf-length black Doc Martens. Next to the biker hippie's drums two idle trap sets waited, duct-taped and battered. An open Paisley cymbal case on the ground contained an international mix of coins and dingy bills. A limp slab of packing cardboard served as a marquee: YOU PLAY the DRUMS! DOLLAR/MINUTE! A smile creased Allan's face.

He walked over, dropped a dollar in the cymbal case, and manned one of the sets. The ponytail drummer jerked his head upward and played on with greater gusto, twirling his sticks like miniature batons.

"Thanks, dude!" he called. "Rock on!"

Allan tried a polka beat, disco, a waltz. He laughed at his club-footed lack of skill. His terrible rhythm drew a crowd. Then a brass wind-up alarm clock clanged at the base of the hippie's kick drum. Allan walked over, dropped ten dollars in the cymbal case, sat back down, and with the heart of Shelia E. and hands of Gerald Ford unleashed the crappiest bossa nova in the history of Toronto street music. A Japanese man in a black Armani suit stopped to watch with his girlfriend, a pixie of a woman in a pearl necklace, form-fitting cocoa evening gown, and glossy black gloves. The couple grinned and tapped their toes and snapped their fingers. Impulsively, the Japanese man ponied up his dollar, took control of the third set, and pounded out 'We're Not Gonna Take It!' When the timer sounded the couple exploded in laughter and stumbled away, arm in arm. A big crowd burdened with handbags and backpacks lingered around the unlikely drum concert, blocking the sidewalk. The thrum of the urban night had inspired Allan, and he let loose with an offbeat, crippled medley of 'This Little Light of Mine' and 'Joy to the World.'

"Jeremiah was a bullfrog!" he bawled. "Was a good friend of mine!"

Behind him a screech of tires vaporized his ecstasy. Out of the whizzing Yonge Street traffic, a white shuttle bus jolted to a halt and bumped up on the curb. The crowd scattered and Allan lurched through his drum kit, knocking the high hat to the pavement with a crash. The hippie drummer played straight through the fiasco, switching from swing to samba.

Allan whirled and gaped at the runaway vehicle that had nearly squashed him. The van rocked on its shocks, and its side bore a magnetic-backed banner: *Little Pigs Shuttle Service.* A filigreed subtitle curled in pale blue underneath: *Wee We? Oui! . . . All the Way Home.* The driver, a bushy-bearded man in a florid Sikh turban and baggy overalls, stepped out and opened the sliding door. He hefted two overstuffed ruby suitcases to the sidewalk. Gallantly he offered his hand to the owner of the luggage, a woman with a molten mane of auburn curls, gap-toothed smile, and a long milky coat. She accepted the man's hand, cool and aloof, and stepped out, vetting the scene. She chewed her bottom lip and tapped her foot. Her hula hips swayed to the drum beat. She made eye contact with Allan. Stung, he looked away.

"Do I need to call the cops?" she said.

"Excuse me?" Allan said, raising his eyebrows. He angled his shoulders towards her. The crowd frittered away.

"Because I have a stalker?" she said.

The woman popped her purse open and gave the driver his tip. The driver jammed the bills in his pocket, jumped back into his seat, and shot the little bus into the electric river of traffic. A fresh wave of couples thronged the sidewalk, elbows linked, shouldering between Allan and the stunning redheaded woman in the white coat. Jaywalkers ferried like fugitive souls across the steamy street. Allan stepped closer to the woman and grinned, but he had to shout to be heard.

"Stalker?" he said. "I'll fend him off with karate or something."

He battered the air with a comic series of buzzsaw chops and Billy Jack elbows then shoved his hands in his pockets.

"I mean you," she said. "Is it nine-one-one in Canada, or what?"

"I'm a street musician," Allan said, waving his drumsticks in a peace sign. "Self-taught."

She cocked her head and applied a flexible forefinger to her temple. "Teach yourself any manners? How about some help with these, Drummer Boy?"

"Sure."

He moved the heavy suitcases away from the curb, straightened his jacket. "Listen," he said, "I've got some connections in Toronto—"

"Bet you have." She pointed an invisible whip. "Back, hombre."

Allan's hands flew up. "Nothing—like that. I could get you where you're going."

"I'm meeting someone," she said. She swiveled her head, scanning the busy street.

"I've met someone." He extended his hand. "Allan Douglas."

Behind them a taxi squealed to a stop. A black man with a bleached Mohawk and chain-spangled boots slammed his fist on the hood, swore at the driver, and jogged to the sidewalk.

"Smooth as a country road," she said, arms folded. "Besides, you could be lying."

"No way to prove I'm me?"

"Just ethics," she said. "If you're self-taught, bang me out some Beatles or Journey."

"You got it," he said and started righting the drum kit like a vaudeville stagehand.

The hippie drummer's beat had evolved into a blues shuffle. When Allan sat to play, the drummer tapped his wristwatch and jerked a sideways nod toward the cymbal case. Allan plied his wallet open and tossed in a five-dollar bill. The woman stood watching, her snowy coat open, her hand planted on her hip. The wrinkle of a smile eased across her face. Allan noted her budding amusement and whetted his drumsticks like a comic chef with two carving knives. At this, she threw her head back and laughed out loud, and Allan caught the full view of her statuesque figure, the beautiful accident of her toothy grin, the flash of purple summer in her eyes. His wrists turned to rubber, and he felt himself fighting for air in the face of what he knew: He could never be happy without her. For his finale he raised his sticks in a cross over his head and launched into a solo that halted the bustling crowd.

"Jeremiah was a bullfrog!" he bellowed, punishing the snare.

"Dude!" the hippie drummer shouted. "Easy on the skins!"

Allan lightened up but kept playing, bobbing his head, channeling the spirit of Gene Krupa, puckering his lips, grooving the souls of Earth, Wind, and Fire through his shoulders. He played with a galactic lack of rhythm, eyes closed, head back. Occasionally his clacking sticks struck the drumheads. Only when he reached the part about loving Jeremiah's 'ladies' and helping him 'drink his wine' did he open his eyes to see that the woman had commandeered the third drum set and with even more misguided energy was rocking out to her own 'Joy to the World.'

"In the deep blue sea!" they sang. "Joy to you and me!"

"She with you?" the hippie shouted.

"Maybe," Allan said, firing off a fiddlyump and rimshot.

"You know where the money goes," the hippie replied.

Allan hook-shotted another fiver in the cymbal case, and when their time was up, he and the woman both finished with an Emerson, Lake, and Palmer-slash-Neil Peart cymbal crescendo. The crowd cheered then faded into horns and headlights.

"Pretty good," she laughed, stepping out of the drums. "Now I'm self-taught."

A gloss of sweat glowed on her skin, and Allan saw in her array of wonderful traits everything he lacked—youth, beauty, energy, fearlessness. Looking at her on the busy urban sidewalk was like gazing down the parabolic tunnel of time, with every turn a truth-telling mirror. She was and would always be everything he wasn't, and the only way he could savor her goodness was to be with her.

"I'm serious about that help," he offered.

"I am meeting someone," she said, holding out a yellow

business card. "I'm Mandie."

"Thanks," he said. The card said she worked for a travel agency in New York. "I will."

"Will what?"

"Call you."

"Did I say you could call me?"

"Why'd you give me your card?"

"So you could call me."

"I will."

On the return flight the business card throbbed in his shirt pocket like a yellow songbird. He waited a year before calling—lunch time, in his office—and as he waited for her to pick up the phone, he tipped back in his roomy black leather recliner, wondering if she would remember him.

The longer the phone rang, the more he panicked. The longer he waited, the more he felt he should yank the phone from the wall and hurl it out the window with the rest of his foolish ambitions. On the blustery bay sailboats floated like discarded playthings. Feathery cirrus clouds fanned over the low, gulch-veined mountains. A red hang glider and pink hot-air balloon crossed like an accidental valentine in the faded sky. On the glittering face of the insurance building across the avenue a three-man crew in blue bandanas, aviator sunglasses, and olive-drab coveralls washed the windows. In the swipes of their squeegees, cryptic messages appeared and vanished before he could read them. The dial tone droned, and the ponderous world swung on a faulty pendulum. Then she picked up.

"Global Travel," she said. "Mandie Hendershot."

"This is Allan Douglas," he began. "From that time in

Toronto. On the street. I don't know if you remember—"

"What took you so long?"

They married the next month in a private ceremony.

"After all," she said—Max, his favorite driver, was whisking them from the city offices, and they were holding the marriage license between them in the back seat like runaways guarding a treasure map. "Why wait?"

* * *

Craig Hendershot finishes the recitation and lowers his hand and shakes his unruly hair as if to clear his head. Still clutching bread fragments, he gives his family a tired smile and offers the open bag to the others. Everyone, except for the small girls, dips a hand in the bag and draws out a clump of wasted bread.

On his dock Fran Powers stands with an open bag of Home Pride cracked wheat from his cabin pantry. With gravitas, he produces a hardened heel slice and, after examining it, takes a bite and chews slowly, then extends the bitten piece toward the Hendershot dock as an offering. He drops it in the water and a mother mallard and her ducklings savage it to soggy bits.

Allan massages his eyelids. He swallows and opens his eyes: *I told myself I would never do something like this. Me! The mother of this beautiful human being, so innocent, so helpless!*

* * *

He drove down Route Twenty from Skaneateles to Auburn while Rebecca Ruth, strapped in her safety seat, kicked her legs and paddled her hands in the air. The CD 'Wee Sing Silly Songs!'

played over and over on the stereo, so by the time they reached South Street, Old MacDonald's menagerie had oink-oinked and cluck-clucked and moo-mooed to the point of splitting Allan's skull.

On South Street he swung left through steady traffic past the golden, clock-towered Phoenix building and defunct Auburn Theater. Outside the tree-shrouded Seward Mansion a woman in a silky brown jogging suit and headphones bounded down the sidewalk, boxing the air. South Street, at first lined with fluted architecture and classy streetlamps that resembled green birthday candles, soon gave way to droopy maples, sagging electrical wires, and sunken homes, until it brought Allen past an armory and exiled pizzeria to two pillars that marked the Tubman site. Harriet's stern countenance glared at Allan and his daughter as they rolled through the entrance. In the parking lot Allan lifted Rebecca Ruth out and tried to strap her in her stroller, but she wheeled her legs and arched her back so vehemently he was forced to set her on her feet. She hustled off, pigeon-toed, toward the visitor's center.

"Walk myself!" she called.

Bloated white clouds stocked the hot blue sky. A pasty humidity clung to Allan's neck and arms. As he huffed after his daughter, he daubed his forehead with the back of his wrist. He reached the visitor's center in time to scoop Rebecca away from a man and woman in freshly laundered tennis clothing, who, embroiled in discussion, were hurrying out.

"So sorry! We're sorry! She's adorable!"

"You're fine," Allan said, waving his hand. "Look out, kiddo! Wait for daddy!"

Inside he paused in a spacious tiled room of metal folding chairs. Glass cases housed Tubman memorabilia: faded news clippings, yellowed photographs, a corroded pair of ankle manacles. Allan walked reverently around the room, yanking his froggy daughter away from everything, wishing he could hog tie her. He peered with narrow-eyed interest at each framed portrait and document as if the displays might speak.

"Hello, folks!"

A black woman angled her stride around the cash register. She waved her arm like a stage director struck with inspiration. Her head was overloaded with coils of glistening, decorative braids.

"I'm Christine. Follow me?"

Christine ushered Allan and Rebecca Ruth into an anteroom. A frowzy man and woman in olive T-shirts and a teenage boy in a forearm cast turned and looked at them as they entered. A green and red skateboard with dirty yellow wheels waited under the boy's chair. As Allan followed Christine, he examined the teeny threads of blue, red, and gold twisting through her slinky braids. Around the middle of her orange T-shirt a jubilant band of black men and women pranced like petroglyphs, whooping and shuffling, their bodies bent in high ecstasy. Christine gave a monotone introduction and started a video on a rolling TV stand. Allan excused himself two minutes into the video when Rebecca Ruth started whining, thrashing about, and kicking the metal chair in front of them.

"Sorry," he said. "Really."

Outside the center the small party regrouped. They walked down a paved path toward the Tubman home, and Christine listed her job's drudgeries.

"Inventory this week," she said, shaking her head. "Whoopee. Get those bi-monthlies in."

Near the Tubman home Rebecca Ruth wriggled like an escape artist fighting her way out of a straitjacket. With his daughter in a submission hold, Allan, beet-faced and sweating, silently asked God why he had felt so impressed to visit the site, but he got no answer. The house itself wasn't what he expected; in fact, in comparison to the epic swarm of emotions that prompted him to make the trip, it was a colossal disappointment, a simple two-story white house circled in sickly trees, scroungy flowerbeds, and a spacious uncut lawn. Three portable canopies of folding tables and chairs, reminiscent of an outdoor revival, remained on the grounds from a recent fundraiser.

At the house's threshold Rebecca Ruth yelped and writhed until Allan put her down. She scampered down the steps and fell on the pavement, skinning the palms of her hands. She sat up and examined her hands, wide-eyed and trembling. Her bottom lip popped out, and she tipped her head back and bawled.

Spouting apologies to the group, Allan skipped down the steps and scooped her up. The skater boy's father lifted his denim Harry's Tire cap and chuckled through the brown mess of his mustache.

"That's how they are," he said. "That's how they come."

"They are a handful," Christine offered. "Got two myself. Cute granddaughter."

"Daughter," Allan said.

"Ah," Christine said.

Christine led them through the first floor of the home and, in passing, mentioned tidbits about the home's structure, its present owners and reconstruction history. All the while Allan was struck by the simple interior, the lack of ostentation. At a mullioned window, the group gathered around an old White model sewing machine.

"How much did it sell for?" the skater's dad asked.

"Don't know," Christine said, frowning. "We'll get the shuttle, just outside."

The driver, a stocky black man with a trim mustache, announced himself as the Reverend Paul Carter. Allan moved through the shuttle like a gimpy mother chimp, grabbing the headrests of the seats on his way to the back where—and he smiled and counted it a blessing when he saw it—he found a safety seat mounted on the last row. Smiling and chuckling like a melodrama villain, he strapped Rebecca Ruth in, despite her karate chops and roundhouse kicks.

The shuttle trundled past the colonial-style houses of Auburn, and Reverend Carter spoke a clipped narrative through the intercom in an easygoing baritone that, to Allan, sounded like a hypnotist giving a quarterback's snap count. They paused for construction crews at the dilapidated A. M. E. Zion church. They passed the Seward Mansion, where on long tables a women's social club enjoyed tea and lemon meringue pie and a book discussion. At Fort Hill cemetery, the shuttle stopped, and Allan and the others disembarked.

"This is where Mrs. Tubman is buried," Reverend Carter said. "Little known fact. It was once an ancient Native American burial ground."

At the grave site, they snapped pictures of the bouquets and urns and flamboyant flags of all nations. Rebecca Ruth broke from Allan's side and sprinted like a pink and yellow flash to the headstone, where she snatched up a red carnation and Nigerian flag.

"Yeah!" she called. "I win!"

Allan lumbered after her. "Sweetie, put that down!"

Heedless, she galloped off like a Lilliputian standard bearer in hysterics, at every bush and obelisk shrieking and eluding her aged father with ease.

Aboard the shuttle Allan clutched at his heart and wondered why he had dragged his daughter to this obscure site. Despite the tour's historical appeal, he felt they had wasted a day. At the visitor's center Christine stood waving in the parking lot, and on catching sight of her, Allan felt a flood of doubts assail him: perhaps God wasn't invested in his puny life but had brought him on this trip to wave goodbye. He shook his head, rattling the dried pea of pessimism in his skull.

"Thank you," Reverend Carter purred over the intercom, "for joining us on this little jaunt through the pages of his- and her-story. Harriet had several bounties on her head. But she said days before anyone tried to take her fugitives from her, God would warn her in a dream, and she would move them to a new location. Driving through twenty-first century Auburn, you get a taste of the profoundly spiritual person Harriet was—who, even as a teenage girl, recorded in her journal how the Spirit of God would send her into blackout fits and, while she was suspended, tell her what to do and when to go. She wrote that she would wait—she wouldn't do anything or go anywhere—until God spoke to her spirit, telling her when and where to go."

"She'd what?" Allan called out, perking up. He was waddling

down the aisle with Rebecca Ruth crammed under his arm like a fullback protecting the ball.

Reverend Carter returned Allan's look and put the microphone to his mouth. "Wait," he said.

The skateboarder and his knobby parents filed off, and Allan followed on stepping stones of light. The boy, arm cast cradled to his chest, dropped his skateboard to the pavement and performed a perfect running mount.

"Wait," Allan echoed to the humid afternoon. "Thank you! Thank you all!"

"Something to remind you of your stay," Christine said. She opened a blue plastic sack of commemorative buttons and handed him one.

* * *

I've been hitting her, our daughter. I don't know where this—rage— comes from. I need help. I never should have waited this long.

* * *

He waited and fought the impulse to eject because of what he thought he had seen in the sky. The Crusader bucked and whined, tossed like a sardine can. Gashes of violet lightning shredded the night sky, whiting out his vision. He was jolted and jarred in the eye of destruction, but at its outer limits the calm universe rolled slowly like an old American hymn. The altimeter showed him catapulting through a clash of air cells, up a thousand feet, down a thousand. He couldn't gauge his airspeed. But he knew his power was failing and he was plummeting into the gulf. He tried not to think of it: his jet skipping like a cheap model across the choppy waves, scattering ailerons and smoking turbines along with his bones and charred hide. He reached to his thigh where he had strapped a tape recorder his buddy, Marcus North, had given him, and recalled North's offhand words: "Trouble comes, Baby San, hit play."

He punched the button, and Marilyn Sellars's mellow 'One Day at a Time, Sweet Jesus' soared through the cockpit.

"Baby san!" North's voice crackled through his headset. "Get out! Uncle Sam'll make you a new ride!"

Allan barely recognized the nickname his squad leader had given him. The other pilots always joked about how young he looked: like someone's prom date. But in the gravity of death, he felt like a toothless grandfather hurtling through a black hole in a rocket-powered casket.

"Baby san! Baby san!"

A bomb of lightning exploded off the nose cone, and the radio fizzed out. The rapacious sky flowered in blue-white bursts, a spinning vortex of cloud blossoms, crackling with fringes of midnight, buzzing in his ears. Then the cosmos swallowed him whole, and his plane corkscrewed through flashing rain to the center of the world. As he dropped, he barked out a prayer— not to anyone in particular—just a prayer, to live. He was looking through the streaked cockpit and felt his mind lock when he saw, like a floating idol etched into a stormy shrine, the glowing face of Jesus. The long tortured visage pulsed and wavered, green and unmistakable, lightning thorns laureling the head. Tempests of hair and beard curled into the wild fabric of the weather, part of the storm, but also its source, each eye a hurricane of love.

He shrieked and clawed at the cockpit—to banish the illusion then to get a better view. But it was gone, and his jet moaned and lurched downward, whinnying as if to chuck its tired guts into the sea. Millions of tiny white chevrons—peaked waves in the gulf—hurtled toward him to smash his soul to bits of burning steel. With Sellars's voice stringing a ladder to heaven, he yanked the ejection handle and shot himself across the dark howl of creation.

"Jesus, don't let me—"

The force blasted him into the vacuum of his eyes. His mind floated like a mote of dust in the harmless quiet. Despite the savagery of the storm, he watched himself sail through chambers of moon torches into a polished corridor of constellations. The emerald-eyed sky savior marked his descent, one hand cupped to catch the dandelion spore of his body, the other raised to fan the beautiful illusion of his flight. Feathery serpents waved flaming tails and hissed hot gas. His fledgling bones snared the lovely power in the air currents, and his silky soul flapped open, stitches straining. Pennants of St. Elmo's fire trailed from his shoulders and made him swoon and laugh. A shuddering shriek of lightning lit up the world, and he glanced down between his dangling boots to see his plane splash like a smoking plaything into the sea. Then the salty wind was dropping him into the lapping waves, cradling him in the cold tub of his tears. Chilly tongues licked his burned face awake in time for him to hear the scream of engines, the wop-wop of rotor blades, the Jolly Green Giant rescue chopper battering the sky.

A harness flopped into the water. Dazed, he floundered

toward it, muscled himself in, and felt his heart slip from the pockets of his body as he was hoisted to heaven. A crewman swung him through the entry port, and the helicopter dipped its nose and beat a path toward the misty coastline of exploding jungle.

"Why the hell didn't you bail out sooner?" the crewman demanded.

"Saw something," Allan gasped, flat on his back. "Waiting."

"Jesus!"

"Exactly," Allan said.

* * *

The Hendershots dump handfuls of bread into the lake and like jaded ballet extras stand and watch the pieces bloat and disintegrate. Craig wipes his hands on his trousers and looks north. Manny Jr. runs a hand over his boy-band haircut, folds his arms, drops his head. Bonnimarie trembles and sniffs, and Mandie squeezes Rebecca Ruth to her breast and moves to comfort her mother. Autumn Teal kicks Trystan, and Rory kicks Autumn Teal.

Fran Powers monitors the bread hunks that float to his dock. He lowers his sunhat over his chest and watches sleepy rock bass bubble to the surface and nip at the bread.

Allan sits with his jaw locked. A bulb of bewildered fury clogs his throat. His eyes zigzag over the letter's switchback madness: *Please don't be angry. I don't want us to split up. I want the best for our girl. She is so sweet to me, and she doesn't deserve this . . . anger, abuse. I don't know if there is a God. I know you say there is. If there is, then I hope he can understand what a woman goes through. If you can find it in your heart to look into mine and see I'm not an evil witch, then I have hope for us. We've had enough secrets, and it's led only to pain and suffering. I'll understand if you don't want to see me again—but I believe in you, and I believe we can work this out, if we stay true to each other. I'll be waiting to hear what you have to say.*

Love, your wife.

His trembling hand snaps the pencil. He crushes the letter and hurls it into the myrtle. Is this why Mandie wanted him to join the family circus? As a cover up? Mocked by silence, he bats his mug of tea into the thicket below the deck. All these years—a lifetime!—he waits, and God betrays him. His wife betrays him, tries to hide her betrayal, and all as a reward for years of patient devotion, all his energy and love given freely only so God can turn a perverse bait-and-switch and play him like a stupid smiley-faced puppet.

He watches the Hendershots through a smoke of tears. They adjourn their dockside desecration and in two columns ascend the path, dazed and filmy-eyed, and with them a vision of the chain of Allan's generations, as well as the answer for where Rebecca Ruth learned to hit with hands meant for playing and praying. He shudders and gags on a sob. Sickened to his core he rises and flattens the deck chair with a kick. Before anyone can reach him, he retreats into the cabin, slamming the screen door behind.

On the neighboring dock Fran Powers stands and surveys the sky, a skinny sacramental figure in the seventh phase of the sun, lone witness to the scores of seagulls that flutter down like the avenging hosts of the dead to squabble over the legacy of

Manny Hendershot.

* * *

At the stop sign south of the Nemmick farm Glen Haven Road slopes through cornfields and snarled lilac hedges to the secluded west shore of Skaneateles Lake. From this vantage point people walking at roadside can see almost the entire lake, including the northern end that takes the shape of a Native American princess's westward-facing profile, the 'beautiful maiden' named by the old Onandogan chief. The lake in high summer resembles a dark mirror sunk in a mold of dense greenery, its surface flecked with pleasure boats and shadows of slow-moving clouds. At the far end of Glen Haven Road the tree canopies grow into a woven corridor. Early in the morning and late in the afternoon the intersection at Lakeridge Lane and the unpaved road to Sevey's Boatyard becomes a thoroughfare for shy foxes, rabbits, wild turkeys, and nimble red-orange deer that bound out of the brambles, soundlessly strike the tarmac, and flag intruders with their white rumps. Past the garbage transfer station asphalt turns to gravel near a pasture, home to three droopy Appaloosas and a rusted front loader, two skeletal boat trailers, and a Tioga camper shell with a cracked rear window. A motion detector wired to a car battery triggers a clanking bell when a car or jogger passes, sending the dogs at Sevey's Welding Shop into howling hysterics.

As little girls Mandie and Rory Hendershot wander the back roads and get lost in the leafy, shadowy wonderland. They invent magical kingdoms and legends about Indian princesses and pirate gold. They scrape their knees, sink ankle-deep in mud in their new Thom McAns, and march through stinging nettles to bury dead chickadees in tissue paper, scrape moss from hollow trunks, and go on safaris for swallowtail caterpillars.

Then five years before Manny Hendershot dies the Lakeridge Cottage Association pools cash and trucks gravel in to cover the dirt roads. They post speed limit signs and station orange pylons at tricky doglegs. They install drainage culverts to stave off wash-outs. The day of Manny Hendershot's burial, the gravel road meandering to the cabin he built for his family makes a sanctuary of shaded confession for his two daughters, Mandie and Rory, who pause at the rusty cattle gate their father bolted together. Rory leans on the gate for support. Mandie tilts toward her sister to comfort her. Having finished her conversation with Rory, Mandie releases Rebecca Ruth's hand, and the excited girl scampers to a log, straddles it, and spurs it like a jockey. Back in the cabin Bonnimarie plays canasta with Autumn Teal and Trystan before enlisting their help with the ham sandwiches and German potato salad, mostly so Rory and Mandie can talk alone.

Side by side, the women look nothing like sisters. Rory, with the politician's smile, blond bangs, pinched nose and acidic Hendershot eyes. She looks unathletic, round-shouldered, and heavier-breasted standing next to Mandie's sturdy kickboxer frame, her toothy grin, mother dog eyes, and bouncy lava-red curls. At a distance from the sisters, Rebecca Ruth shrieks "whoa!" and "giddyup!" and spurs her pony log through the stretch toward an imaginary finish line.

"Husbands," Rory spurts, scooping tears from her eyes.

"They're not perfect."

Mandie pulls a sardonic Shirley Temple grin. "Unless it's Allan!"

With the tension vaporized they sigh and cry and trade shoulder-shaking hugs for the first time in years. At the mention of his name Allan materializes. Mandie spots him over her sister's shoulder and raises her hand, which sinks and freezes in a half wave. Sensing her sister's movement, Rory sniffles and steps out of the hug, turning to watch Allan storm up the rocky slope through a swirl of shadowy sunshine like the ghost of Manny Hendershot.

"Why!" he rages.

Mandie manages a breathy, "Allan."

She opens her arms to receive her husband and holds the pose, as if to applaud his final performance. He seizes her shoulders and shakes her hard enough to rattle the bewilderment from her face. Her arms stiffen and flail then she withers and hangs from him like a borrowed coat. Horrified, Rory throws herself between them, and Allan throttles both women in a violent dance.

"Stop it!" Rory screams. "Allan!"

"Why!"

On her horse log, Rebecca Ruth turns toward the struggle. Her father's face is a twitching red mask. Marionette strings jerk his arms and legs into grotesque seizures. Rory clamps her hands on Allan's wrists and tries to pry him off Mandie, but Allan whips his arm in a hard arc and sweeps her aside.

With a bellow he spins back, trying to regain his balance, and backhands Mandie with an open claw. The blow rocks Mandie's head back. She gapes open-jawed, like a baby bird straining for

God's medicine dropper, then crumples to the path, one limp arm over her head.

Rory cries out—"Mandie!"—and staggers to her sister's side. Rebecca Ruth screams for her daddy, and birds and squirrels flee through the trees, as if strafed by a low-flying jet, their alarmed flight rattling the air with cries of *don't wait, don't wait, don't wait!*

* * *

With the pace of lazy orienteers Mandie and Rory climb the gravel road toward the cattle gate. Little Rebecca Ruth toddles behind like a living reminder of their future. The sisters look as if they dread reaching the top, but they link arms and lean on each other and take turns leading the way to the higher ground of the main road. Mandie loops an arm around her older sister's waist. In doing so she hands her a piece of folded paper, this time not a burial shroud of sunflower-print tissue paper for a dead chickadee but a handwritten note—an example of a 'practice letter'—Mandie calls it, a therapeutic tool she has read about.

"Write something like this to Marshall and his kids," Mandie says, squeezing her sister's elbow. "Or Kevin, if there's unresolved issues there. Practice first. Then write a real one."

Rory knuckles away tears. Mascara skids blacken her cheeks. Mandie hugs her hard around the shoulder.

"They say it helps with anger management," she says. "Gets your feelings out. You don't even have to show it to them. I did this letter to Allan, with some made-up things, like I was in your situation. You could write your own."

At the top of the gravel drive the sisters turn and topple against the gate. Rebecca Ruth scrambles on a log and watches her mother hug her aunt. Then the husband Mandie waited so many years to find comes stalking up the road, a liberated slave glaring with eyes of white night from the front of his jacket, his heart the size of his fist.

* * *

Like a huge wayward seabird the Norwegian Princess plows a swath of salty foam from Houston to Cancun. A feverishly drunk woman sways on the stern deck at sunset. Her arm hooks through an orange life preserver, and her free hand grips a Corona, which she swings as if ringing a town crier's bell. The woman wears an ultramarine bikini top, pink rubber flip-flop sandals, a puka shell necklace, and a filmy tiger-stripe cover-up from the waist down. Bleary-eyed and cherry-nosed, she snuffles like a grade school girl and stares into the ship's wide wake. If she expects to tune her soul to the impressions of some cosmic revelation that will solve her problems, she receives nothing in return but a windy void of oceanic noise and a murderous sky mangled with clouds.

"God," she says.

She eyes the chain-link fence on the rear deck like an inmate resigned to everything but desperate speculation. Steel spiral staircases, painted white, ascend to the Lady Luck Casino and Pamper Me Spa. Cackling laughter from above punishes her ears, ringing like mockery. The frayed net on the basketball hoop flaps in gusts that buffet her face. A sun-bleached basketball with REC ROOM scrawled across it in black magic marker waits in a coil of nylon rope below the stairs. The woman sniffs and swipes the back of her wrist across her scorched eyes. The jubilant sounds of a shuffleboard game from the upper deck swirl around her head, and she spins away to soak her senses in the golden hum of alcohol and rough sea air—and finds the bottle in her hand empty—except for a thin halo of beer in the bottom, sparkling like the mellow sun of the tropics.

Even in her drunken state she sees the lie of her vacation. The telltale signs of fractured love and wasted life are etched in the fabric of the ship. The orange lifeboat losing paint. Ulcers of rust on the deck floor. Years of sun and wind have rendered the safety signs unreadable. Up close everything is a lie. She grips the handrail, feeling how easy it would be for her to vault over into the roaring surf of another world. The sun splinters the horizon, a distant torment behind a mob of gulls that churns like an exploded bale of unopened letters, rising and sinking over continents of stringy seaweed. Flying fish skip into the wind and glide for impossible distances before clipping the waves. The sight of the fish fills her with bitterness.

"How can you be both!" she demands. "Mom, lover, daughter! Can't be everything to everybody!"

Her daughters, ages three and one, have stayed in New York with her mother. Before her binge the woman dined on chateaubriand and chocolate mousse. She had a back-to-back pedicure and massage then overhauled her hairstyle in the on-board salon so that she now peers at the world through highlighted bangs. With her new look she returned to her cabin to seduce Kevin, her second husband, the precise moment she uncovered in one of the cabin drawers his business diary, open to a page where he had written that her explosive temper was officially too much for him, and he was, regrettably, going to seek a legal separation in the weeks following their trip.

Dizzy and weeping, she yanks her purse open and withdraws a Norwegian Cruise Lines notepad and pen. She scribbles a panicked appeal—*I don't know what to do oh God please I need help somebody my name's Rory*—shoves the scroll of paper into the Corona bottle, and plugs the neck with a champagne cork from dinner. With a hand on the rail she steadies herself and zones in on her target: the gaping sea. She whimpers and coils her body like a discus thrower then with an animal shriek launches the bottle over the rail. The force of the throw topples her back on her rump, where she shudders in a heap of sobs.

The glittering bottle sails like the purest of prayers, end-over-end, into the waves.

* * *

Fran Powers stows his sailboard in his boathouse and grunts up the stairs to his cabin. The staircase creaks, his knees creak, and in the leaf-filtered light his skin looks as pale as his bones. He sweeps a heap of old newspapers into the recycle bin and heats a can of pork and beans on the stove. Humming a nameless tune he peels two carrots and butters a slab of rye bread. Seated on his back deck he balances a paper plate on his lap, spoons beans into his mouth and chews, watching orchid-colored clouds collide like heavenly islands in the deepening sky. Chickadees and goldfinches bound into the air from springy branches. Geese flap across the lake at low altitudes. A dented pontoon boat towing a scuba buoy chugs past. The pilot, a beer-bellied man in a naval lieutenant's cap, waves, and Fran returns the salute. Somewhere to the south a stereo rolls out Led Zeppelin's 'All of My Love' then fizzles mid-song. For thirty minutes a black-headed gull zips back and forth over the water, its head angling left and right, as if run by some inner mechanism. Three times it knifes into the water, and every time it labors back into the air, a silver fish flops in its beak.

After locking up Fran loads two empty five-gallon gas cans and a generator in his truck bed. With Andy Griffith's 'I Love to Tell the Story' on his tape deck, he bumbles up the gravel road, past the Hendershot cabin—now unlit and locked and empty—and stops to padlock the gate. On his way back to his truck, he spies a corked bottle someone has tossed in the muddy, leaf-clogged ditch. He walks over and picks up the bottle and brings his face close to the glass. The Corona label is faded and worn. He turns the bottle slowly in his fingers, inches from his nose. His eyes widen at the sight of the note inside.

At the stop sign across from Bud Nemmick's farm he pulls off to watch three deer porpoise through the corn. He lets his truck idle on the shoulder and scuffs the heels of his boots across the gravel, tracking the boat lights of red and blue as they move like lost satellites over the leaden lake. Above the dark tree line a star presses a gem of luminescent gel through the membrane of violet sky.

At home, he enters through the garage, clomps through the kitchen, dumps his toolbox on the table, and shelves the canned pears and bran flakes he remembered to buy at the P&C. A framed picture of a chimpanzee clutching a boat racing trophy hangs on the wall next to a dandelion calendar with its May page still attached. Fran nibbles a Ritz cracker and peels away calendar pages until he reaches July, a picture of a cartoon tombstone holding a fishing rod in a rowboat.

"How was the funeral?"

Jeanie, his wife, is wedged in a scruffy blue corduroy armchair in the living room, watching television. On the screen a Latina woman in a flamboyant pink blouse and pistachio skirt stands next to a tumbling orb of numbered ping-pong balls.

"I'm Yo-*lahn*-da Vega!" the host calls.

"Fine," Fran says. He finds a glass in a cupboard and fills it with tap water. He swallows a gulp and stares at the calendar. "Sad."

"How was the dinner after?"

Fran sets the glass in the sink, folds his arms, and rests against the counter, his back to Jeanie.

"Didn't go."

Jeanie seizes the armrests and wrenches herself to her feet. In her poofy hippopotamus house slippers she shuffles into the kitchen. The glare from the television shines through her snapdragon-print housedress, and she waves her arms like a choir director escaped from an asylum. Wattles of flesh swing from her triceps. Her tinted hair shines like holy fire.

"You've known Manny Hendershot for thirty years!"

Fran strides out of the kitchen, massaging the back of his neck. He butts his body sideways through the screen door like a man shouldering out of a saloon.

"Didn't feel right," he calls back.

Jeanie limps to the kitchen table and rests her hands on it for support. She harumphs at the sight of her husband's junk, rolls her eyes to the ceiling, and slaps a thigh.

"I swear."

Like a disgruntled antique hunter she picks through the tools and parts, tossing aside spanners and crescent wrenches and cans of chain-saw lubricant, when her hand lands on the bottle. She squints at the note then lifts her head and stares at five watermelon kitchen towels hanging on shiny brass hooks above the stove, each one embroidered with her children's and grandchildren's names. She pops the cork out and shakes the note into her hand. She reads the note and aims a quizzical look out the door.

"Hm," she says.

Then she hitches herself and her second hip replacement across the room where for a moment she holds the bottle over the garbage can, as if waiting for it to fill with answers.

The Seal

Facing west from California's shores,
Inquiring, tireless, seeking what is yet unfound....
Now I face home again, very pleas'd and joyous,
(But where is what I started for so long ago?
And why is it yet unfound?)

—Whitman

Embarrassment of one another
And God
is Revelation's limit,
Aloud
Is nothing that is chief,
But still,
Divinity dwells under seal.

—Dickinson

I

AFTER A DELAY AT THE GATE Delta Flight 1708 rockets from the runway and banks north through the San Diego sky. The man from Idaho hunches in 14C, the aisle seat he requested. His chest heaves. Sweat burns the corner of his eye. He plucks an Ekco kitchen timer from his shirt pocket and sees that the LCD panel is cracked. 'Min' and 'Sec' have worn from their gray plastic buttons. The man's fingers quake as he sets the timer to one hour and forty-three minutes—the time that will elapse between takeoff and the moment the police will storm the security checkpoints in the Salt Lake City airport. The woman from New York, seated next to him, speaks out of the side of her mouth.

"Smash that damn thing, or I smash you."

The man gulps the knot in his throat. He squirms in his seat. "Time gets away," he says. "If you're not careful."

Their flight is full. Senior citizens in the fore cabin sag in billowy floral shirts. Trim businesswomen and men unfold laptops and laugh. The man from Idaho chews his lip and blinks at the blond stewardess with lavendar eye shadow, the Al Pacino-faced kid pumping his head to music, the gangly accountant headed to some fabulous drudgery somewhere between Anchorage and Buffalo—those, who along with him, make up this airborne carnival of souls trying to escape life sentences of professional and romantic routine. This the man sees with a kind of spiritual X-ray vision. Something supernatural, some visionary eye in the sky that fascinates and frightens him, has allowed him to peer into the secret life of things so that the passengers and crew look like transparent cocoons with throbbing pink centers of denial, bitterness, and hopeless vainglory. So how to survive? he thinks. Endure? Make your life a sacrifice? He sees a flash of the future, his life reverting to dreary episodes of daily failure, and then he sees himself plummeting, suddenly, in a screaming fireball of fledgling adulteries, doomed mergers, and summer internships.

"We could crash," he says, considering. "I could die."

"Talking to yourself," the woman from New York mutters. "Super."

The man drops the timer in his breast pocket and darkness blots his vision. His head wobbles like a gyroscope, and he sucks in air and snatches frantically at the armrest, shaking himself to his senses. With his other hand he feels his shirt pocket, fingering the kitchen timer like a desperate mystic reading the ridges on a prayer stone. His divine second sense dispatches visions but no prophecies: How will it end? Mid-air mechanical failure? Jail? Divorce court?

"Heard the latest?" the woman says. "Daddy talks to himself."

The man's eyelids flicker and a fairy mosquito buzzes into his left ear and out his right. The world below, so safely distant, resembles a sun-baked game board of toy office buildings and labyrinthine suburbs. Across the faultless blue sprawl of the ocean whitecaps drift toward shipyards and coastal condominiums. Seagulls bend slender wings, turning circles above naval destroyers. Highways loop like dirty shoelaces around the sparkling sapphire gems of swimming pools and the pure green patches of putting greens. The man exhales and tastes the salt of doubt in his mouth. The busy, sophisticated landscape below clashes with the somber picture of home in his mind: his farm house in St. Anthony; the May sky a charcoal smudge over the swollen Henry's Fork of the Snake River; scarlet willows scorched with frost on the muddy banks. He summons the standard slug of platitudes for why his move to Idaho was the smart thing to do: Clean water, low crime rate, no drugs, low cost of living!

The plane banks. The fuselage shudders and whines. A beam of sun blinds the man, and he knuckles his eyelids and blinks until the dramas on board assume a sharper focus. Across the aisle a Latino college student slides his Padres cap over his face and tips his head back. A Chinese girl waves a Point Loma Nazarene College banner and soft-shoes a Shamu doll across the lap of her skimpy tangerine skirt. A curly-headed grandmother in a tan silk blouse checks her lipstick in a hand mirror. The man cranes his neck, angling his head for a better view of the mirror. The grandmother's hand drops to the armrest, and the mirror shows the man his face. He yelps and claps a hand over his mouth. The woman from New York drives her elbow like a nightstick into his ribs.

"Trying to star on the news?" she says.

The man cradles his injured side and gapes at his evil twin in the hand mirror. His reflection makes Dorian Gray look like Don Juan. His spinach-leaf pattern golf shirt is unbuttoned to his navel. He narrows his eyes and fingers the yellow seahorse ric-rac that frolics down the seams of his tutti-frutti Bermuda shorts. With a cautious hand he probes his mess of mad scientist hair. His sunburned head glows like a chili pepper.

Why not bring a hat? the man chastises himself, as the plane levels off. Recklessly, he thinks of asking the woman from New York. As if reading his thoughts, the woman—brunette, his age, four months pregnant—sinks grappling hook fingernails into his forearm. Rather than hurt, the man feels aroused.

"You're squeezing those armrests like you're in the electric chair," the woman says through a clenched grin. Her claws withdraw. "Cute outfit. Who does your wardrobe?"

The man's jaw sets like a wolf trap. He stares with hooded eyes at the airsickness bag in the seat pocket. Against his will he risks a sideways glance at the woman and feels his temper cool at the sight of her contoured arms, her creamy ankles and pomegranate toenails. She wears a sleeveless orange sherbet blouse he's never seen before. Her sunglasses are propped on her head, and she sits in rigid defiance, as if the tension in her body is the only thing keeping the plane aloft.

"Tell me what's going on," she says. "Or I'm jumping out."

To the woman's left a three-year old redheaded girl sits in 14A, the window seat. The jet swings and levels again, and the woman pats the girl's knee. Since giving up a graduate assistantship in biology at Syracuse University, the woman has been assailed by a flock of delusions, the main one being that it was her spiritual calling to labor as a grossly overpaid consultant for a children's fashion magazine. For this trip she spent five hundred dollars on the redheaded girl's wardrobe.

The girl smiles out the window like a ventriloquist's dummy. Her shampooed hair in tight purple bows shines like heated copper, and her feet swing in maroon sneakers. Her expression reveals that she is daydreaming of sea-spangled manta rays, inflatable porpoises, and orangutans on tire swings. Flaky sunburn florets grace her freckled nose and pale shoulders. She wears a martial combination of lilac three-quarter length pants and a white T-shirt splashed with mauve daisies.

The woman from New York reaches over, loosens the girl's seatbelt, and with her palm irons the wrinkles from the girl's pant legs. The machinery in the plane's craw hoists up the landing gear, and the girl gives the woman a worried look, which the woman defuses with a maternal smile. The girl leans across the woman's lap.

"How much longer?" she asks the man.

"You have fun, Dilly?" he asks.

"Uh huh," she says, bobbing her head. "I like dolphins."

"Two hours on the plane. Four on the road. You can sleep in the car."

The woman expels a toxic sigh. The man zaps her sigh with a surge of brain waves. He knows her sighs mean she didn't want to go to California, that she thinks they should have flown to New York to help her mother, Sue Anne, care for her father, Terrell, who recently suffered a stroke. All this the man jettisons from his thoughts by sheer force of will, escaping into the noise of jet engines, the tangy memory of California flotsam and palm trees. Some reservoir of cosmic energy has siphoned into his heart the pluck of the world's most unlikely heroes—the brave little tailor, the one tin soldier—and he clings to this giddy boost of purpose in spite of the woman's efforts to demolish his spirit.

One great truth stands: He can't undo what he's done. This thought pumps a dizzy thrill through his glands. For better or worse he will live out the span of his life as demagogue and martyr, criminal and saint—and a born dreamer who imagines that the woman from New York and the redheaded girl have vanished, leaving him to sail solo around the globe, a rogue raptor with amethyst talons and wings of fluorescent fog, evolving with the tides and moon phases, breeding with thunderclouds and feeding on gamma rays, roving to wherever happiness howls in tribal ecstasy beyond the mountains, the moaning cities, the slick bloodline of sun.

Two rows of television screens pivot from the ceiling to run the local news, snapping the man's reverie.

"Hope the pilot's not watching, too," someone laughs.

On each little television Judy Hsu and Junior Ojeda of San Diego's Channel 8 News relate the morning's top story, which involves an as-of-yet unidentified man and the kidnapping of an abnormally small harbor seal named Otis. The newscast segues to drunken shots of a blue Accord in a sluggish police pursuit on a stretch of highway. A montage of amateur footage shows a crazed sunburned man lugging a blanket-wrapped seal across a parking lot. The cabin intercom fizzes, and the pilot's voice bumbles through static.

"Morning, folks. Welcome aboard Delta Flight 1708. Ah, we'll hit a cruising altitude, here in a bit, and the crew'll be coming around with drinks and munchies. And, ah, before you know it, we'll be back on the ground, so, we'll check back. Till then, enjoy the flight. Thanks for choosing Delta."

"Dude," the Padres fan says, pointing at a TV. "What's that guy's deal?"

The man from Idaho eyes the closest screen and simpers

like a flower child. He places a palm to his brow and feels the heat of a thousand deserts in his baked skin.

"Got me," he says.

The woman from New York tilts forward, squinting at a screen.

"Shhh!" she commands, even though the man hasn't spoken to her. Her forehead wrinkles. Her lips part. She watches with the intense focus of an anthropologist studying a fossil in a cave wall.

"Good God," she says.

The redheaded girl points at the seal heist. "Daddy," she says. "Who's that?"

Without looking at him the woman lays a hand on the man's wrist. Her touch drives a pang of divine longing through his body, a craving for storybook love and intimacy. He takes her hand tenderly. At his touch she throws him a wide-eyed look of revulsion and flings his hand away as if stabbed by a sea urchin.

The woman's brusque withdrawal plunges the man into black misery, and the last thing he thinks before she seizes his arm again—this time, in fury—is how supremely alone the fugitive on the news report must feel, how different his life must have been before the trouble started, and how exalted his state of panic must be with the savage clutch of time grappling for him even as he flies desperately to get away.

EARLY FRIDAY MORNING Phil Griffin minced like a big kid into the warm waters of Mission Bay. His jeans were rolled to his knees, his plaid flannel sleeves to his elbows. With the curiosity of a foreigner he collected rocks and lofted them into the deep. He stooped to inspect spears of driftwood and dainty crabs, as if scavenging through the shards of civilization. He burrowed his toes in silky sand, tangled his ankles in shackles of black seaweed. With both hands he scooped up clams that spurted cannonades of brine and snapped their shells shut, a defensive reaction, while natural, that struck him as rude. For half an hour he waded along the shoreline behind the Bahia Resort Hotel, lightheaded from the sun and free time, transported in the bliss of margarita breezes and unmoored clouds, skittish sandpipers and dive-bombing seagulls. On his way back to the hotel, he stopped and let out a gruff sigh.

"Idaho," he said.

Why live in Idaho? Because he grew up there? He side-armed a scallop shell across the shining water. With his hairy big toe he prodded up a scarred mussel, and with it, the answer. It was the same refrain, a doo-wop quartet crooning a tribute to conservative reason: cost of living, no drugs, no crime, clean water and air. Then why had conservative reason betrayed him?

From somewhere a car horn trumpeted. A bright pink dry-cleaning van was crossing a bridge, and he turned to watch it then scanned the bay, fists on hips. At the resort across the water snappy sailboats crowded a marina. Two jets stretched an X of white contrails across the sky. Already the sun was grilling the crown of his head, and he had to squint at the water. A squabbling sound announced the arrival of a navy of herring gulls paddling in a circle, twenty yards away.

Quickly he plunged his hand into the water and came up with a Coors Light can squashed into a disc. Like a submarine-style pitcher, he whipped the can at the gulls. The flock swept upward in a wheel that widened until the vortex of birds broke against the sky, hundreds of feet in the air. Phil watched without smiling.

"Idaho," he said. "Sounds like something you hide from your friends."

Back in the room he dried his feet with a fluffy beige towel. He rolled his pant legs down and stood at the kitchenette bar then pulled the fridge door open, poured a glass of orange juice, and sipped it, transfixed, as he gazed out the window. Each detail in the suite made him feel more alienated, more starved and restless. Brilliant jade carpet flowing wall-to-wall. Pygmy cacti on the coffee table of chiseled glass. In one corner a splendid philodendron looked ready to stumble out of its tub of glazed yellow clay. Above the television an airbrushed cormorant, as ethereal as a glider, swooped in a platinum frame, its wings trailing razor rainbows over a landscape of volcanic chrome. Against every wall a wicker sofa upholstered in tart magenta waited to receive the plush butts of the rich and bored.

Phil rapped his knuckles on the bar. "So. The vacation." He flipped out his thumb, then finger. "The marriage. The life."

He set his glass in the sink, crossed the living room, eased open the sliding glass door, and stepped onto the balcony. Across the bay a couple in shiny gold caps bobbed in a red paddleboat. A groundskeeper in a pith helmet buzzed by on a Snapper riding lawnmower, his walkie-talkie squawking Spanish. On the road that separated the hotel from the beach stray cars and gleaming motorbikes and VW vans were gathering like animals at a watering hole. A blond male bodybuilder in a hot pink thong rollerbladed up the sidewalk, slaloming through skateboarders and scooters and retirees in droopy sunhats. A white placard around the blader's neck fluttered like a tiny cape: *All Day Breakfast Bar $5.99!* Two clown-paint sunflowers, green and gold, grinned at Phil from the bronze bulbs of the man's buttocks.

Phil released a sardonic sigh and leaned on the railing. He thought of his father-in-law, who languished in New York, recovering from a stroke. How had Sonya's brothers, Christian and Blake, described the way he looked when they found him half-dressed on his bed at two in the morning? Ah, yes: 'like a tornado tried to strangle him with his pajamas.' Phil imagined the scene—the old man, wounded and bewildered, firing looks around the room like a senile bulldog on his first morning at the pound. Suddenly, Phil straightened.

A strange man stood below the balcony.

"Howdy," Phil said.

The man, a vagrant by all appearances, was camouflaged amid Areca palms and yuccas in a landscaped plot of cedar chips. He gazed up at Phil through half-open eyes, thumbs hooked in his belt loops. He looked like a roasted crack addict the grounds crew had stunned with a club and stationed there for decoration, a stoned but menacing *David.*

Phil coughed, looked away. "What's up?" he said, trying to laugh.

The man didn't flinch, so Phil, pretending to be unruffled, retreated through the sliding door and padded past the spare bedroom where he spied Delia, his daughter, still asleep in her collapsible Porta-Crib. In the master bedroom Sonya lay mummified in mango sheets. She was snoring with relish and bear hugging the body-length maternity pillow snaked between her thighs. Phil jostled her shoulder.

"Sunny!" he whispered. "Up, up, up!"

"Whuh?" Sonya groaned, rolling over. Dark hair netted her face. "Vay—kaysh—"

"There's—a guy. Stalking us—"

She blinked foggy eyes. "Stalking."

"Staring. From the balcony."

"Towel over his arm?" She levered herself to a sitting position. "Huevos rancheros on a silver platter?"

Phil's shoulders slumped. "No! Crazy, like—"

"Grapefruit," Sonya said. With one hand she massaged her lower back. "With the cherry. In the center. Pregnant lady's gonna eat right—"

"Like he wanted to kill me."

"Not if I beat him to it."

"Knock it off, awright? I'm trying—"

"You knock it off," Sonya said. She pried her leg into a half-lotus position, transferring the massage to her left foot. "I'm asking for room service, chop-chop. Honeydew spears, muesli, whatever. Pregnant lady needs vitamins. Since somebody forgot to pack my prenatals—"

"Sun," Phil said, waving his hands to stop traffic. "Some crackpot's casing the joint. I'm calling the police."

"What's he wearing?"

Phil beamed a glance out the doorway. "Why?"

Sonya stopped kneading her calf and eyed Phil up and down. "You can tell crazy people by their clothes," she said.

"T-shirt," Phil recited, searching the stucco ceiling. "Cutoffs, hemp sandals—"

"Hemp?"

"The kind Jesus wore in the Bible."

Sonya nodded, jaw cocked. "Now you've seen Jesus's sandals?"

"Long bongo drum," Phil said. He pointed his hand in pistol-shape at his armpit. "Under the arm."

Sonya closed her eyes and rolled her neck in exaggerated circles. "Caucasian? Latino?"

Phil watched her, one eyebrow raised. She peeped at him. He looked at the carpet.

"Sunburned," he said. He tapped his forehead. "One of those yellow Buddha smudges between the eyes."

"Speaking of sunburn," she said, reversing her head circles. "You out there without a hat? Your head'll get toasted. Sun's different down here. Thinner atmosphere."

Phil looked at the far wall and exhaled his words. "Yeah, heard it saps your brain in the morning."

Sonya bunched her lips in a critical kiss. She examined her husband until her eyelashes fluttered. Phil lowered his gaze into hers.

"Like he hadn't slept for days," he said, then inhaled a sharp sniff. "His hair was all matted and—"

"Ew! I'm taking a shower."

She hopped to her feet and strode for the door. Phil grabbed her bicep and spun her around.

"Wait! The shirt!"

"Ow!" she said, wrenching away.

"It said 'spiritual' something. Block letters—"

She cradled her arm and whisked a look of baffled outrage from Phil's feet to his face, a mother chimp shielding her young. "Some whack job," she said.

"Spiritual Warrior," Phil said. He tapped his pecs. "Spelled on his chest."

"Maybe he could teach you something. Move."

Sonya slipped her shiny apricot pajama bottoms to the floor and kicked her underwear into the corner. With a reckless sweep of her arm she pulled off her oversized Dole banana T-shirt and flung it into the hallway. Halfway to the bathroom, she snatched her bra from the floor, twirled it on her finger like a flapper's necklace, and snapped it slingshot-style at a tangle of coat hangers in the hall closet.

"Sunny," he said, following her. "Could you—"

"Take Dill to breakfast," she said. "Bring me something. You know what I like. Ouchihuahua! Next stop, Stretch Mark Central!"

From where Phil stood the morning light draped a soft gleam over Sonya's body. To him, she was today—as she was every day—Earth Mother Superior, the sexy fountainhead of every day's natural disaster. He had never kidded himself into believing she truly loved him. Maybe at first, but not now. Now she was a monument closed for despair, a booby-trapped valentine, a fleet of smiley-face warheads that could nuke the grandest good memory in an instant. There had been a time, in the early days of their dating, when she had seemed sincere in her praise of him, when words had risen from the wells of her honest desires, but now anything resembling a love note from Sonya always landed as a soggy newspaper of mere tolerance, three days late, at his feet. And there was no reason for him to believe things would change. Even in the dreamland of California, she—his wife—was a mystery. For longer than he could remember he had fought against admitting he had married and started a family with someone who offered him no emotional secrets, no sense of loyalty or friendship. But no matter how hard he tried to stoke a blaze of romance between them, every day ended in silent smoking surrender. At best, he and Sonya were business partners with shared living space and joint bank accounts. They were independent love brokers outsourcing each other's sexual parts when the occasion suited them.

"Who's gonna pay for this?" she said, speaking like a reporter into her hairbrush. She gaped at her bare thighs and winced. "Not me."

She stood at an angle, half addressing him and the full-length mirror in which she sized up her physique. Her skin glowed, darker and more luxurious than his pasty hide. She cupped her swollen belly then hefted her breasts. She rotated right, left, assessing the damage. During their first pregnancy, she had strutted around naked and watched him squirm. When it came to sex, she knew she was the cavalry officer chugging a canteen of water, and he was the Apache spy tied to a stake for weeks in the sun. She telegraphed the same notion night and day: Lookie, No Touchie. But the sight of her standing there, so unabashed and nude and ripe with motherly curves, flooded Phil's veins with confused desire.

"So what you want to do today?" he asked the floor.

"Something fun for your daughter."

"What about crazy guy?" He wobbled a thumb over his shoulder, glanced toward the bedroom.

"Mr. Soul Trooper?" Her eyes drilled the mirror. She yanked the brush through snarls of hair. "Probably the mayor with the key to the city. Agh! Look at that butt!"

She pivoted to view her backside in the mirror. "Can someone find that ass I had as an undergrad? Criminal. With some species," she said, turning clinical, "the rear end is what attracts a mate. Baboons—mandrills, for example—have florid hindquarters that swell up—"

Phil hovered closer. "Hindquarters?" he breathed.

"This motherhood racket. Your body takes a beating, and nobody tells you until—"

Phil circled his arms around her, his fingertips to her belly as if supporting a beach ball. He nuzzled his face in her neck.

"Dilly's asleep," he whispered. "There's the other, bedroom—"

She twitched and slammed her elbow into his gut, rocketing him backward.

"Phil!" she shrieked. With one hand she draped a towel fecklessly over her front. With the other she brandished her hairbrush, a voluptuous mama Ninja ready to disembowel her attacker. "What the hell could you possibly be doing?"

"Ow! You're beautiful! I'm—"

"I'm pregnant!" she rasped, beginning to weep.

With his fingertips Phil pressed invisible electrodes to his temples. "You're beautiful *and* pregnant."

Silence clawed the walls. Sonya worked her towel frantically, a starlet startled in the shower by paparazzi. She cinched it around her torso, tight under her arms. She brushed her hair in military chops, her mouth a taut line. She spoke to her reflection but addressed him.

"Phil—I'm, I'm serious. You need to control yourself. This is yet another—"

His hands formed a double-fisted rose under his chin. His eyebrows arched. "Another what?"

"Strike," she said. "It's been building up. You know it has, and I really can't—"

"What?"

"Go on, frankly." She dropped the brush on the counter, scrabbled in her make-up bag and found a squeeze bottle of amber soap. She turned on the faucet, shoveled water on her face, and worked up a mask of lather. Droplets of froth flew from her lips. "I don't want to say—but I—I have to draw the line somewhere. What I want to say is—"

"Should be interesting."

"—this little episode has brought me to this point, brought out the worst." She stopped lathering her face and searched the sink. "You should know how I feel. I'm—I want to tell you I'm not above leaving you—"

"Leaving me?" A laugh bubbled in his throat. "Again?"

"For Delia's sake. This one's sake. You didn't let me finish." She turned on the faucet and rinsed her hands. Foamy mascara rings blackened her eyes. The sudsy mask made her look comical and grotesque, a flustered kabuki actress in a stranger's dressing room. "I think they're entitled to loving parents. I wonder about you, Phil, seriously. I'm not overwrought with confidence in your—I mean, if you can't—"

"Loving!"

She bent over and worked palmfuls of water over her face, melting the mask. "If you'd—"

Phil propped a hand on his hip. "Hypocritical, don't you think? About as loving as a barracuda—"

"Phil, you wanted to have sex in the morning." She straightened and dabbed her eye with a washcloth. "I'm pregnant!"

"Sex during pregnancy is good. I read it somewhere."

"Where?" she said, swabbing her throat. "*Popular Mechanics*? Men's room wall?"

"The sexual response is good," he insisted. "Strengthens the uterus for delivery."

"Cassanova! Take me to bed with lines like that—"

A sneer warped his lip then vanished. "You're the one talking baboon butts and mating."

"Phil," she said, citing an invisible encyclopedia. "Most species would rather kill themselves than harm a mate or hurt offspring."

He widened his eyes, inclined his head. "Black widows? Praying mantis? Couple of cuddly homemakers."

Sonya rocked her head back in mock thoughtfulness. "I don't want this to sound cruel," she said. "But—look at yourself. You're—pitiful."

"Pitiful?" His tongue worked the inside of his cheek. He slid one hand up the door jamb and leaned against the other side, blocking the doorway.

She shrugged. "I don't know how else to put it," she said. "I don't want our kids to be negatively influenced—"

"By me?"

"You in your present state—"

He stepped forward. "Ah, better off with you, I suppose. Can't take your daughter on a walk without falling in the river—"

Sonya's body stiffened into a monolith of hate. She raised a magnetic finger to heaven. Her voice wavered like a bad recording. "We do not," she said, "talk about—"

"Pitiful?"

"We agreed," she said, wagging her head, "you wouldn't bring that up."

"That mirror'll show you pitiful."

"Stop it!"

Phil punched his chest. "You have to feel pity to see others don't have it!"

"Articulate this morning, Phil! And on vacation!"

In hot synchronicity they broke off, vibrating in wordless wrath. The harsh echo of their voices rang off the walls, blending with a third voice, a cry like the whine of a table saw, which grew louder and more insistent in the spare bedroom.

Sonya squeezed her eyes shut and groaned. She raised her face to the ceiling, arms flapped to her sides, awaiting teleportation. Phil held his hand like a visor over his eyes, his other hand clamped in his armpit. A puff of toilet paper tumbled from a vent under the sink and eddied in the instep of Sonya's foot.

"Take her," she said. She stanched sloppy sobs with the heel of her hand. "Get—go away—"

"We need to talk," Phil said.

She aimed bleary eyes at him. "We need to stop talking," she heaved. "You need to stop talking and take your daughter and get some breakfast *before I do something we'll all regret*—"

"Something else."

"Leave!"

"Why don't you?" he said, piloting his wooden body through the doorway. "It's what you do best."

At BJ's, the Bahia Resort's open-air café, Phil and Delia found the patio section stocked with drowsy grandparents, German tourists, and delinquent surfer kids who pretended not to know their affluent, puffy-faced parents. Phil led his daughter past the 'Please Seat Yourself' sign to a table next to a bubbling marble fountain. The fountain's centerpiece, a buxom mermaid in a scallop-shell bikini top, spouted water into a lagoon of shimmering pennies. Mariner figures in various postures of dejected despondence rimmed the lagoon. From hidden speakers candied saxophone and piano muzak—'Take a Look at Me Now'—troubled the drone of conversations. Phil hoisted Delia up and plomped her on a chair.

"Hungry, Dill?" he said.

"Yummy!" she cheered.

To stave off the guilt he was feeling, Phil splurged. He bought Delia a triple stack of strawberry 'Smiley the Whale' pancakes, bacon, and orange juice. She ate eagerly, grinning at him through a whipped cream Van Dyke beard, wielding her fork like a miniature Henry VIII. Phil simmered over a penitent's repast of black coffee, grapefruit, and whole wheat English muffins.

"Boo," he said between bites.

"Yummy in my tummy!" Delia sang, clapping her hands.

After ten minutes Phil flagged a muscular waiter whose blond mane was bundled in a green bandanna.

"Suite eighteen," Phil said. "For my wife. Kiwi fruit, strawberries, yogurt, bagels."

"Absolutely," the waiter said, away with the order.

As Phil made goofy faces at his daughter and daubed the corners of her mouth with a monogrammed BJ's napkin, he marked the movements of the deranged drifter who loitered in the parking lot. The man—Phil was convinced by now—was stalking him and his family. Why, he had no idea. But from his table Phil could see the man clearly: a scrawny street freak pacing like an arthritic panther, turning the same triangular lap from fire hydrant to towering coconut palm to silver Mercedes. With his thumb the man rapped a ritualistic rhythm on a beat-up tambourin slung like a bazooka under his arm. Every so often he stopped his march, glared, and shook the exotic instrument in Phil's direction. Despite the distance Phil could see the phrase 'Spiritual Warrior' emblazoned across the man's T-shirt.

"Daddy?" Delia said. She was staring at him. Concern grooved her forehead. She held her fork aloft, a syrupy sponge of sliced pancake skewered on the tines. Whipped cream dribbled down her shirt.

Phil snatched a napkin. "Sweetie," he said. "What happened?"

"I'm messy."

"You're cute," he said, wiping her hands. "And you know what? We might see some baboons today—"

"Yay!"

"—if we haven't seen some already."

He wadded the sticky napkin and bounce-passed it into a

water glass, where it bloated like a jellyfish. When he looked back toward the parking lot, the homeless man was gone. He turned to Delia and rested his chin in his hands.

"Stay close, Dill," he said. He smiled into her eyes until she blurred in his. "Stay young as long as you can."

***

Neither Sonya nor Phil could remember when he started calling her 'Sunny.' But the nickname stuck from the time they found their bodies jostled together in a mob of tanked frat brothers and sorority sisters at Syracuse University's Gamma Phi Beta house during Nik and the Nice Guys' third encore of 'Twist and Shout.' That night in early May, Sonya, on a tip from one of her lab students, crashed Gamma Phi's end-of-the-semester 'Yard O' Cloth' party. She wore a fuchsia paisley bikini under a pleated hip-length toga, a yellow jump rope looped around her waist. At the last minute she added butternut platform heels with criss-cross ties that snaked up her slinky calves. A tiara of plastic pineapple leaves crowned the ensemble, which said, 'Beach Goddess: Brainy and Greek.'

Phil wore royal blue deck sandals and a pair of polyester golf pants from The Salvation Army. A Hawaiian Punch straw hat slanted across his forehead at a rakish angle, and a chartreuse toy seahorse circled his waist. Before the party he hacked the pants into a pair of castaway shorts whose ketchup-and-mustard plaid, once he made his entrance, only enhanced the drug trips savored by the hooded undergrads who crouched like The Three Wise Monkeys against Gamma Phi's mold-marbled walls.

Halfway into the room Phil sailed ten bucks into the cooler marked 'Refreshment Fund' then stripped off his seahorse and elbowed his way to the poker tables through throngs of scantily-clad, rubber-jointed tributes to 'The Pony' and 'The Twist.' Gamma Phi's signature gold corduroy Hide-A-Bed had been banished to the front lawn where it soaked in a filmy drizzle. Nik and the Nice Guys, in nothing but boxer shorts, channeled the Woodstock zeitgeist and jammed to the point of hemorrhaging. They played on a dais of cinderblocks and plywood pallets under the framed 1874 dedicatory plaque, which jiggled on its nail as if it might crash to the ground.

Sonya and Phil stood elbow-to-elbow and listened to the band until a cross-current of bodies toppled them into two empty chairs at a card table.

"We'll just sit here!" she laughed.

"Sounds good!" he said.

"I'm Sonya."

"Phil," he said, plucking the last beer from an ice bucket. "Nice to meet you, Sunny."

"Sonya," she said, then shrugged. "Or Sunny."

Phil tried not to show it, but Sonya's beauty immobilized him. She gave off a streamlined splendor, a force not lavish or slit-your-throat sexual, but a velvet voltage that made him swallow. She, too, noticed his charm. His figure was plain but chiseled—dimpled chin, pebble-gray eyes, thin waist and Tour de France shoulders and arms. His dull blond hair had thinned, but he had grown his sideburns and brushed the rest back with gel so he resembled one of the Beach Boys from the 70's. Sonya was so engrossed in her new love target she found herself only mildly irked when his wristwatch alarm beeped, and he covered it with a hand.

"Gotta check some investments," he said over the noise. "Later."

They fell into conversation the way people slump into comfortable chairs. Phil remembered how hard it was to look a woman over without showing it. His gaze roved over Sonya's features as he babbled about his upbringing in Weiser, Idaho. He jabbed his half-empty Bud Light at the space between them and talked about his days as captain of the Wolverine football team; the foreman's job he got bored with at his dad's lumber yard; his BA at Boise State in mass communications; and the sense of Rocky Mountain wanderlust that landed him in the MBA program at the Whitman School of Management. All the while, The Nice Guys' steroid-throttled version of 'Do You Love Me?' passed through Sonya like a lullaby. She smiled territorially and thumbed a Lucky Horseshoe Zippo lighter someone left on the table. Little flames of gold danced The Watusi in her eyes.

The more Sonya gabbed, the more animated she grew. She catalogued the Braddock clan: Christian and Blake, older brothers, lacrosse fanatics; her mother, Sue; her father, Terrell, a nearly retired United Airlines mechanic. The band dropped power chords like depth charges into 'Rollin' on the River,' and she plotted her hopes of doing post-doc work in a dozy coastal hamlet in northern California or Mexico. She could see herself, she told Phil—poking flirtatiously at his hands across the table—bounding through sea-spray in a speedboat, racing harbor seal pods, shooting reels of film for documentaries.

"Wouldn't shave my legs for weeks!" she cackled like an

auk. "Have to live like a seal to study seals."

It was this last reference—to seals—that would keep Phil in a walking trance for the rest of their lives together. He tried to classify Sonya's eyes, the way they probed him as if assessing a mate or food source. A steady power smoldered in them, dark and remote, but with a tender, soaring plaintiveness. It would be an image he would never shake. Sonya: his seal. So stark was this first impression—along with her dusky shoulders, dark waterfall of hair, and muscular wriggling way of walking—that during their later years, in the moonlit wash of their bedroom, Phil often saw himself barking in the middle of a troubled ocean as he and his mate bounded belly-to-belly from their mattress through metallic fleets of mackerel, bucking turrets of foamy surf, kicking laundry and utility bills to the floor as they cried out with pleasure, straining toward a shore they never seemed to reach.

The year after they met, they married. Neither was the kind to 'bop and drop,' they confided. The raw heat between them, which sparked a dozen picnics-turned-breathless-romps in the woods around Green Lakes and Verona Beach, still drew them toward respectability and higher commitment. Their choice to trade vows—though they never disclosed this—was also tied to their ability to count back four generations and find men and women who married, had children, settled down, and worked toward blemish-free if not unremarkable deaths. In some zone of speechlessness beneath the skin, they simply felt it would have been unnatural to swap their middle-class pedigrees for a more Bohemian fling.

Sonya, the more scientific and logical of the two, was drawn to

Phil's business sense, the kaleidoscopic flair of his entrepreneurial spirit.

"Be my own boss," he told her over lunch at Friendly's. Strawberry milkshake lipstick dribbled from his lips. He smooched the air. "More flexible. For us—the kids."

Phil, the right-brained Capricorn who lived for the next twenty-four hours, was hooked on the clockwork of Sonya's mind. Even the simplest gesture from her, a slow head turn or sudden wave to someone across the street, struck him as something untamed and glorious, as shapely and inscrutable as the receding horizon. She was a jaw-dropper—he knew this, everyone did—but over time he came to regard her as a trick equation whose solution would always be zero. Her ultraviolet beauty, the thrumming dynamo of her intellect. All of it mesmerized and confounded him. On their honeymoon, he slouched naked on the loveseat in their Cape Cod bed and breakfast suite and sawed a vertical line with his hand in the air, dissecting her dimensions. She laughed at his antics, nude in the alkaline light, the Atlantic breeze parting lace drapes behind her.

"Everything put together okay?" she said.

"Like a Rorshach inkblot," he told her, squinting. "Cuter. But symmetrical. How's that possible?"

They settled in St. Anthony, Idaho. At first Sonya didn't agree to the move, but she warmed to her husband's sales pitch about the clean water and air, the low cost of living, the absence of crime and drugs. They chose St. Anthony by tacking a map of Idaho over a dartboard in a Gart Sporting Goods in DeWitt after stopping for dinner at Ground Round to celebrate the completion of Phil's degree. Phil's shamrock dart arched through the air and stuck in the Kootenai River before dropping like a zapped mosquito to the floor. Sonya's cupid dart whizzed to the eastern part of the state and speared St. Anthony dead center.

"Must be providence," she said.

"We'll find out," he said.

That summer they tossed their belongings in a Ryder truck and drove west. As they lumbered through North Platte, Phil slumped over the steering wheel and rattled the grogginess from his head. He steered through swarming waves of hail, awed by the swordplay of prairie lightning, the pewter thunderheads that dragged their bombed hulls over miles of grassland and sodden beef cattle. At dusk, as they crossed the Continental Divide in Wyoming, Sonya yawned and peeled her face from Phil's shoulder, where she had been snoring. Yellow bug blood greased the windshield. A dirty white butterfly wing clung to a wiper blade, vibrating in the wind. Sonya blinked at the caravan of trucks and cars towing long shadows down the tar-veined highway.

"I'm thinking we should go with a ranch-house motif," she said. She squirted pink lotion on her hands and worked her palms together, squinting at distant plateaus. "There's baby clothes, too. The color schemes. Can you fingerpaint?"

Phil sniffed the scent of cherries and almonds and pressed the heel of his hand into his eye. He glanced sideways. A wadded Burger King napkin clung to the back of Sonya's head like a snowy burr.

"Can learn," he said.

They moved into a refurbished two-story house, No. 139 on St. Anthony's historic Main Street, east of Bridge Street, one block from Clyde Keefer Memorial Park. New black roof tile and spiffy vanilla siding made the whole place look like a giant birthday package garnished with sparkling rain gutters. A new brick walk and flowerbeds swerved up to kiss the front porch. Three prim gables rose from the roof, each with a window and forest green shutters. The previous owner, a quarter horse trainer named Bob Wilkes, had bolted a weatherproofed deck to the east face. Scraggly lilac hedges bordered the back yard, which ranged like unsettled prairie into an abandoned horse pasture.

"Perfect," Sonya remarked, as she unpacked a box. With a gold flannel cloth she swabbed a green quartz lamp shaped like a helix of surfacing sea turtles. "For the Shetland pony our daughter will get for Christmas."

Phil dumped an army surplus bag of sports gear on the living room floor. From the pile he plucked his old red and white Wolverine Baseball cap and screwed it on his head. He whistled through his teeth and worked his hand into the third baseman's mitt that helped him lose the state championship to the Salmon River Savages—a Bill Buckner dribbler through his legs, winning run on third, final score 3-2. He smacked his fist in the glove pocket.

"Daughter?" he said.

Their house sat on a bluff overlooking the Henry's Fork of the Snake River, which turned brassy in the glare of late spring. The river paralleled the highway, and in her private moments—as Phil worked to stake out his business—Sonya sat on a cushioned seat of walnut trim and green baize in the large bay window and watched semi trucks and lame pickups roll in and out of her life. She watched the river slink its sluggish muddy brown phase through crumpled barns and uprooted wire fences until it flooded pastures of speckled ponies. When the water turned glassy and swift, it crashed over lichen-scabbed boulders and churned around sandy gray shoals of cattails and crimson willows. She watched the river and wondered where she was going.

Online, and with a quarterly catalog printed at the Arnold Press in Rigby, Phil sold the latest in compact corporate electronics, as well as accessories. He christened his home-based operation Tronix Northwest. Sonya was quick to nix his plans for a blinking neon sign in their front yard. At home Phil wrangled the books and promo while pushing the inventory out of a warehouse in Idaho Falls.

Occasionally Phil's self-propelled work docket and handyman exploits sank him to his knees—literally. Late one Tuesday afternoon, Sonya, arms laden with a tower of folded lavender towels, passed Phil's office nook and found him asleep in the act of kneeling and staining the replica Susan B. Anthony nursing rocker she'd had custom-made and shipped from New York. Like a drugged confessor, Phil swayed and snored, his hand clutching a paint brush glued to the chair's slats.

"Honey?" Sonya said. "Everything okay?"

Phil snorted and convulsed. "Haw, huh? Hi."

"Gonna need more room when the baby comes," she said.

"When's that?" he called as she disappeared down the hallway.

During their second summer in St. Anthony, as an offering to the local fertility gods, Phil rolled up his sleeves and hammered a cement-floored workspace on the back of the house. The addition's north wall was a large screen window that could be boarded up during winter and propped open in summer. With an electric drill and coffee can of nuts and bolts, Phil racked his new office walls with plywood shelves from floor to ceiling. He hung portraits of Rockefeller, Hershey, Heinz, and Firestone over his computer desk and files.

At first nobody noticed the Griffins. Bob Wilkes had been a successful horse trainer and livestock man. So the town had grown used to his refurbished house perched at the pinnacle of Main Street, shining like a Delphic temple in the rusty sunlight. But soon, especially after Phil bought a zippy midnight-blue BMW and the Griffins still hadn't been spotted in a single St. Anthony church, locals began to grumble and snoop like trolls tumbling out of the undergrowth on market day. *The Standard Journal* sent Kelly Fullmer, one of their delivery boys, to invite the Griffins to subscribe. Lemke Storrs, withered septuagenarian president of the B. P. O. E., paid a visit one Thursday evening 'to say howdy.' Lem thumbed the bill of his Wilco Foods cap and rested a manure-stained snakeskin boot on the front porch. A toothpick flickered across his bottom lip, and the crowns in his tobacco-stained grin flashed like crushed beer cans.

"Food drives," he said. "White elephant auctions. Bottomless cups of coffee on bingo night."

Sonya materialized behind her bewildered husband—her index finger plugged in *1001 Fabulous Baby Names*—and watched Storrs amble like the aged offspring of Louis L'Amour down the driveway.

"Best people on earth," she said.

So their first five years elapsed, and the Griffins settled into success but stuck out in St. Anthony. They had no friends; they belonged to no local clubs; they simply paid taxes, sent Christmas cards to their families, made money, and sucked up scenery and space. Phil chased his goals along a dotted yellow line down the highway in his head, beside which he imagined a fluorescent red score clock ticking away years, months, days, hours, minutes, and seconds beyond which lay—what?

At night he dreamed the same dream in which he held hands with Sonya, and like twitterpated teens, they scampered after a trail of gold paint footprints left by steer wrestlers and garage mechanics. The footprints spattered over a porcelain sidewalk that began at their porch and bounded past amusement parks and garbage dumps to the coast, where it rained broken tiles on a yelping riot of cliff-bound seals. The gold foot prints never dropped off the sidewalk's edge but soared over the ocean beyond the horizon. He and Sonya always plunged over the final ridge, throbbing like lemmings into the pounding surf.

As if to confirm Phil's dark dreams, Sonya began to obsess over feelings that she wasn't 'getting anywhere.' She calibrated her ovulation cycles with an hourglass of rainbow sand that would appear in her head as she and Phil drove through bison herds in Yellowstone, or as they hugged and kissed in a hot-air balloon basket or screamed in a glider that sailed over the Tetons from Driggs to Jackson. Once they took the day off—as they often did because they could—drove to Teton Village, and boarded a tram packed with affluent jet setters. The gondola swayed on its cable up the mountainside toward Rendezvous Peak, and they spotted swift pika in the cleft rocks and moose and black bear in the pine and aspen trees. Through the creaking quiet of the car, an exotic brew of accents murmured: Chicago,

Bombay, Antwerp.

"Pretty scenery," Sonya said, hands rammed in her pockets. Phil grinned and peered at her through bird-watching binoculars.

"Stunning," he said.

Lifted higher and higher, Sonya counted the years and realized she could have knocked out her doctorate if she had stayed at Syracuse. She could have written a book about elk parasites in the Wyoming-Idaho bioregion. Could have raced porpoises in The Mediterranean. Could have wrangled macaque monkeys on Mauritius and chatted about volcano worship in a lilting French patois with mossy-headed Hindus. Could have *had a baby*. And while no one could have traced it to a single source in St. Anthony, the ebb and flow of lunch counter gossip at Jill's Place Family Restaurant revealed that most people viewed the Griffin house in the same way unemployed kooks regard crop circles. If it hadn't been for Sonya's most public mental breakdown, things might have continued that way for years, perhaps until the Griffins had died, perhaps until St. Anthony had wheeled away in the wind like a tumbleweed— the people outside the upscale house aching to know what was going on inside, and the people on the inside struggling not to drag each other down in their new town.

"We don't know anybody!" Sonya cried one night, slashing a pair of knitting needles like a switchblade through the azure glow of the CBS Friday Night Movie. With a jockey's urgency she drove her Susan B. Anthony rocker and held aloft a snarl of coral yarn. Phil lowered his newspaper, examined his wife's handiwork.

"Pretty starfish," he said, raising the newspaper.

"It's a bootie," she huffed.

The newspaper rattled. "Pretty bootie."

To stave off the rising tide of domestic strife, Phil reached out. Not knowing what else to do, he called the guidance counselor at South Fremont High School and asked for two or three dependable teens looking for after-school work. The counselor, a Notre Dame alum named Greg Ainsworth, referred Phil to two Hispanic youths—a girl named Rabeena, and a fifteen-year old named Donny, a Speedy Gonzalez look-alike with a yellow elfin grin.

Rabeena was heavy for a girl of sixteen. She wore pricey Fila athletic shoes and Redwings hockey jerseys and primped her frizzy bangs into a gravity-defying tribute to hairspray. Spangly skull rings adorned her fingers, and silver teddy bear earrings dangled from her floppy lobes. No matter the time of day, her lips were dyed—with blood, Phil suspected—a bright purple rimmed in black. Whenever she spoke to Phil her eyelashes fluttered, and she would look at the floor, out a window, or up the wall as if tracking the path of a jumping spider.

Donny reeked of cigarettes. His Oakland A's cap jutted sideways like a bent propeller. He always wore new jeans and baseball jerseys two sizes too large, and his boxer shorts peeked above his beltline and cast a polka-dot grin to rearward wherever he shambled.

The first day the teenagers rang the doorbell, Sonya opened the door, saw Rabeena planted on the porch like a man-eating shrub, and bolted for the bedroom. In the hall she collided with Phil, who was emerging from the bathroom.

"Gangsters!" she whispered, untangling herself from his

arms. "Outside!"

Phil shouldered past her. "They're from the school!"

When he opened the door Rabeena was tramping down the front walk, and Donny was standing in her place, grinning like a leprechaun assassin.

"Mr. Griffin?" he said, staring at Phil's belt buckle. "They told us to come here."

At first Phil gave the teens rudimentary tasks: inventory, filing. Later, as his trust expanded, he parceled out some low-level marketing and sales report work to them.

As a result of this civic outreach the Griffins became instant celebrities. Everywhere they went, strangers bombarded them with gratitude. After Rabeena and Donny had been working for two months, Sonya fueled up at Mutt's Fried Chicken & Gas, and Sheri Clabber, the stout curly-haired girl at the counter, followed her out, her hand raised to shade her eyes from the sun that reddened the squid-shaped birthmark on her neck.

"It's great what you're doing," Sheri said. "With them kids."

Mayor Walt Frieberg sent the Griffins a personal letter of appreciation, and as far away as Sugar City, in Schofield's Foods, a Norwegian-looking woman named Norda let Sonya jump ahead of her in the line because, as Sonya overheard Norda telling the woman behind her, "People oughta notice what they did."

To the Griffins it was people being people. The larger issues remained: the growth of their business, the tightrope act of their childless marriage. What Greg Ainsworth had failed to tell Phil, however, was that Rabeena and Donny were enrolled at South Fremont High School but also being processed at the State of Idaho Juvenile Corrections Center west of the school, three miles from the sand dunes.

Rabeena was forever insisting she had been booked for assault but not 'with no deadly weapon.' Donny flashed his quivery muskrat grin and stared ahead when anyone brought up the basement meth lab in which he had been collared and cuffed. He said nothing when people described the incident as they'd heard it—how the cops had grabbed his ankles and yanked him back through the window, how Donny had fought like a terrified chipmunk. Not to mention the busted pellet gun, the one his cousin had fashioned into a fake Glock pistol, and the way Donny had tried to hurl it into a screen of cottonwoods but instead had flung it back and bopped the nearest approaching deputy on the nose.

Delia Amelia Griffin was born in December. The shock of circus-clown hair that sprouted from her head set Phil on his heels. From her first day on earth Delia confirmed all the stereotypes about ginger babies, proving to be fresh and feisty, always kicking and whining. In the Fremont County Regional Medical Center Sonya sipped watery pink lemonade from a navy blue insulated mug and when two nurses with Mötley Crüe hair appeared in green parakeet scrubs to ask if Sonya wanted to hold the baby, she waved them away.

"When we have a name," Sonya said. The nurses blinked in unison and padded with their pink bundle back to the nursery.

Phil crashed at home on the couch for the afternoon and returned to the hospital with cinnamon chrysanthemums and a Mylar smiley-face balloon. He sat at Sonya's bedside and

254 Matthew James Babcock

pretended through his weary smile that he didn't see a black hollowness bleed into the heart-tenderizing eyes he adored. Like a climber with altitude sickness, Sonya wrapped her knees in a blackberry Fremont County RMC blanket and watched reels of interior design shows. Phil stroked his knuckles across her cheek and pulled the name 'Delia' from an obscure drawer in his mind, suggesting it between commercials.

"Pretty," she said with a sour smile, elbowing him out of the way of the television. "Like leaves and rain and flowers. Like New York."

Given Sonya's demeanor, Phil thought it unwise to reveal that the name came from the insane American woman who traveled to England to dig up Shakespeare's body. It was, he was going to tell her before he thought better of it, the only thing he retained from the English classes Boise State had forced him to take. Instead he let his wife mingle thoughts of their daughter with dew-lipped tulips, jamborees of cardinals, family junkets to Lake George, and the sweet-sap bliss of childhood innocence.

The deeper Sonya sank into the doldrums, the tighter Phil strapped on his happy clown mask, throwing his energy into an act of 'We've got it together!' When the head nurse, Cynthia Blacker, ushered him to the side of the fruit punch fountain in the hospital cafeteria and disclosed in hushed tones that Sonya hadn't asked to hold Delia, he smiled.

"Not once," she told Phil, balancing tater tots and a chicken burger on a red tray and flapping batwing eyelashes. Phil dunked a mini corn dog in pleated cup of mustard and popped it in his mouth.

"We're aware," he said.

On leaving the hospital Phil kept the doctors' firm-lipped caveats about postpartum depression packed in a mental box, tagged and dated for future analysis. He was too loopy with the sumptuousness of daddyhood to let it trouble him to the point of taking action. Somewhere in the leaky cellar of his soul, he understood that doing something would mean admitting there was a problem. Instead, as Delia grew to toddler age, he worked longer hours, bought her more stuffed toy porcupines and giraffes, paid Sonya more compliments about her looks and refinements, and spent more time rolling around with his new she-cub on the living room rug, drooling and snuffling like a rough-and-tumble papa timber wolf.

Until Sonya started to break things.

The television went first. On a clear-skied Thursday afternoon after Labor Day, having driven with Sonya and Delia to Sheep Falls to toss stale bread to trout, Phil returned home with some Mutt's Fried Chicken and found his sheetrock hammer lodged in the television screen, as if a contractor had used it to practice his tomahawk-throwing act.

Phil stood in the living room, gold bags of chicken dripping from both hands. He looked from the totaled television to objects in the room: a fascicle of Indian paintbrush in a Kerr jar on the windowsill, a mess of crayons and coloring books on the coffee table. The hammer looked like a pickaxe stuck in a dartboard of smashed glass. Had Delia tried to kill a bug on the screen? He muttered a 'hmm' and entered the kitchen.

"Sun?" he called. "What's up?"

He found his long-legged, stormy-eyed wife in a pea-green rollneck sweater, jeans, and burgundy sandals seated at the table.

Delia was perched in her high chair. Sonya had squirreled Delia's firecracker hair into a sassy spout and strapped her *cap-à-pie* in crimson and plaid. Delia's face was smeared with applesauce, and she giggled and pattered like a bongo player in the tray's sticky mess. Sonya sat close by, a vacant smile on her face, washcloth in hand. Phil took a step and an applesauce bomb splotched the floor. Sonya dabbed it with her cloth. With a finger she swiped a fleck of applesauce from her jeans and popped it in her mouth. On seeing Phil, she flashed a bitter smile that flattened to a smirk.

"Daddy!" Delia cheered.

"The TV," Phil said. He lowered lunch onto the bar. "What—"

"It's old," Sonya said, beaming at Delia. "We need a new one."

"Old, sure. But—"

"It didn't go with the house."

Phil touched his thumbs and forefingers to his belt like a gunfighter making sure he was armed. His palms turned outward. "Go?"

"With our arrangement." Sonya swept her hand in an arc, game show attendant-style. She gave Delia a crinkled-faced grin and jabbed her nose as if pushing a button. "Boop!"

"Go," he said.

"It didn't."

The wedding china went next. In late May, after returning from an inventory trip to Idaho Falls, Phil walked through the kitchen door with three tickets to the circus—The Jordan Company, which at the moment was using two elephants to hoist its strawberry-banana big top at the county fairgrounds—to find Delia plopped on the floor amid twelve explosions of ceramic dishware.

Phil stood with his hand on the doorknob. In the center of the wreck his two-year old daughter sat and grinned like an impish guru, a gold-rimmed dagger of Lenox china squeezed in her perfect hand.

Phil found Sonya in the living room. She was rocking back and forth, legs crossed, in her Susan B. Anthony chair, half-smiling like a Charlie Manson groupie.

"The china?" he ventured.

She stopped rocking. "I don't need it anymore," she said. Phil knelt by her side. His fingertips stroked the armrest.

"Need it?"

"It's—material."

"Material, okay. But our—"

"It's a hassle to pack everywhere we go," she said, looking him in the face. Phil looked at the floor then into her eyes.

"We've moved once."

"I know."

"You know." Phil stood and took a step toward the kitchen, pointing. A house sparrow flailed against the dirty living room window then vaporized in a swelling of sun. "Can't Dilly—can't she cut herself?"

Sonya resumed rocking. "China's not glass," she said. She plucked a tuft of lint from her sleeve and flicked it away. "The edges. She's okay."

"So—I should help clean up?"

"Soon," she said.

"Good," he said. He pulled a broom and dustpan from the hall closet and entered the kitchen. "When you're ready, I'll—"

"I'll let you know."

Days before Delia's third birthday the microwave sailed through the kitchen window and landed like a smoking satellite in the snow under the lilac hedges. While breaking ice on the driveway Phil noticed someone had used a crowbar to gouge the garage door's crème exterior. In a desperate effort to show loyalty he marched inside and found Sonya ironing Delia's underwear. He stamped snow from his boots on the doormat.

"I think Donny or Rabeena may have vandalized our garage," he said.

"Oh, ho no," Sonya laughed, as if addressing a cute but stupid child. She set the iron on the ironing board, and it shot out a squeal of steam. She eyed the frilly bluebird undies in her hands for wrinkles. "Honey, that was *me*."

Afraid things might get worse, Phil retreated. Instead of confronting Sonya about her outbursts he cajoled her, let her 'de-stress.' After all, he lectured himself, as he rapped at his workstation computer late into the night, it was hard for a woman to do what she had done for him and their daughter. To surrender everything—promising education, career, familiar surroundings—took sacrifice and selfless purpose. Maybe, he told himself, as he watched the winter dawn spread rashes of rosy light across the dead flies on his office windowsill, this was her way of dealing with the ball and chain of motherhood.

Sonya's calm-faced craziness milked Phil's sense of failure but at the same time stroked the fiber of narcissism that had wormed through his heart since childhood. So even when he returned from manning his 'Entrepreneurs in Fremont County' booth at the St. Anthony 4th of July Bazaar and Cattle Auction, arms loaded with sacks of Red Devil Lady Fingers and Black Cat Chinese Pagodas—and found Sonya in the driveway, his ball-ping hammer like a medieval mace in her hand—he listened to her story, strolled into the house, shut himself in the bathroom, and told himself in the mirror that maybe his BMW *did* need new headlights, maybe the hail-sized dings in the hood *did* make his car look less pretentious, and maybe re-doing the paint job *would* help him appreciate her more.

In August things turned dark. On a placid Friday morning, windless and dry, Phil awoke and dressed early.

"Inventory in Idaho Falls," he said, tightening his favorite candy-stripe tie. "How about dinner at Big Jud's when I get back? My treat."

Sonya lay in bed and stared at the ceiling. She nodded and smiled. "Good," she announced to the world. "Delia loves walks."

After a poached egg breakfast, Phil rose from the kitchen table and kissed them both. The screen door slammed behind him as he jumped from the porch to the walkway.

"We'll see you later!" he called over his shoulder.

"We'll see!" she answered.

Sonya's reply—echo? mimicry? threat?—replayed on auto loop in Phil's head as he sweated and shook and backed out of the driveway. He waved to his wife and daughter, teeth chattering, and they waved back from the living room window, Sonya in her filmy orchid nightgown, Delia blowing dramatic kisses. And all he could think about doing, as he motored away, was calling his old English professor at Boise State to ask about the day he snorted and peeled his face from his desk for the last five minutes of something his professor was calling 'seven types of ambiguity.'

Sonya watched Phil's car until it was out of sight. Then she returned to the kitchen and cooked two poached eggs, one for herself and one for Delia. While they ate, she and Delia imitated robin calls and tried to find animal shapes in the clouds that moved like smoke signals across the skylight.

"How about a walk?" Sonya said, bouncing her eyebrows.

"Walk, yay!" Delia sang. She clapped her hands and nearly fell off her barstool. "Birdies, animals! Can we swing, Mommy?"

"Some of us might swing."

Sonya dressed Delia in a marshmallow T-shirt, baby blue windbreaker, jeans embroidered with glitzy butterflies, and pink sneakers. She twined Delia's hair into French braids with primrose ribbons. She dressed herself in three-quarter length jeans, white cross trainers, red plaid shirt, and red windbreaker. Before heading out she snugged her hair in a pert ponytail. With Delia in her banana stroller, Sonya headed west down Main Street into the summer scent of ripe pastures and fragrant alfalfa.

Despite the warm air the leaves on the maples along Main Street burned yellow-orange at the fringes. As they walked, Delia called out with girlish glee, announcing each lucky pebble and Marlboro pack in the gutter. At Bridge Street two squirrels scampered up a poplar trunk in a skittery game of tag. Sonya struggled but soon had the name.

"*Sciurus carolinensis*," she pronounced.

North on Bridge Street they passed the decayed Fisher Insurance building, home of Tissues with Issues Massage. In front of Sassy's Floral a stray Pomeranian in a camouflage collar sniffed at them and pranced away. At the old Silver Horseshoe Lounge, Sonya stopped, cupped her hands around her eyes, and peered through the large front window. Long cracks forked like tributaries across the glass, patched with yellowed packing tape. The lounge's insides had been gutted. Sheetrock dust powdered the concrete floor. Multi-colored wires hung like useless veins from ceiling sockets. In a far corner two crusty jugs of rubber cement sat under a stepladder spattered in cornflower paint.

Not seeing any ghosts of fox-trotters or jitterbuggers, Sonya stepped back and checked her reflection in the cracked glass. She sucked in her cheeks. She stood like a ballerina in fifth position, then like a 1960's catalog model, one ankle angled in front, a hand propped on her hip. She popped her bosom forward, buttocks back, twisted and checked her profile. Traffic streamed behind: an Exxon tanker that shook the earth, a lime-green Baja-style Volkswagen bug, a Dodge pickup hauling big wooden spools. The Dodge driver, a bearded grunt with Popeye forearms, rolled down the window and let fly a piercing wolf whistle.

"Woo hoo!"

Sonya pirouetted and curtsied to her admirer.

"Mom, you're funny!" Delia laughed. She made her reflection dance, waggling her arms and legs like a spastic marionette. "I want out!"

"And we're off," Sonya said. As she strode away, the panes of flawed glass broke her departing reflection into a woman cut in pieces, a free-floating head, one arm swinging, legs strutting behind a stroller propelled by motherless hands.

At the Roxy Theatre Sonya and Delia bumped across the street. In plump licorice letters the Roxy's marquee announced the

South Fremont Junior Miss Pageant would be staged there in four
weeks. They walked two blocks south past the hardware store,
and west again to the courthouse, whose salmon bricks and
columns and white trim made it look like a cake designed by an
architect. After standing and rehearsing The Pledge of Allegiance
they backtracked to the main intersection then south down
Bridge Street where the Shell station's sign read, 'Summer Fun
Is On The Run.'

"Got that right," Sonya said, wiping her forehead.

They traversed river and highway on the overpass, and Delia's
face turned solemn at the roar of water and big rigs below. On the
other side Sonya strode past Mutt's Fried Chicken & Gas and The
Bottle Stop Liquor Store. She leaned forward and grunted as she
jumped Delia over the railroad tracks between the teetering
cathedral-like towers of the Trost Feed 'n' Seed grain silos.

On First East Street, the banged-up garages at Parker's
Machine and Welding gaped like train tunnels. An orange dune
buggy sat on the oil-stained driveway like a huge crab, and Davis
Parker, in tattered overalls, wiped his meaty face and flipped his
tinted face shield down. A blue flame popped out of his torch's
nose, and he returned to welding the buggy's frame. Davis's
son, Kelly, with his back to the greasy black hunk of a tractor
engine, crouched on a cinderblock in slashed jeans and a
sleeveless pink Big Johnson T-shirt. He chugged Coke and
gnawed a chicken leg, doing his best John Cougar Mellencamp
doing his best James Dean.

Sonya pushed Delia past five ruined tree houses, a skinny
Irish setter staked in a grassless lot, and a dirt bike course of sun-
baked jumps and banked turns cut with deep ruts. Corroded oil

drums and gas cans clustered like outdated ordnance around every garden shed, and at No. 844, a dark brown wood-tiled hut stuccoed with river rock, they halted.

"Look," Sonya said, pointing. "Where's Goldilocks? Hansel and Gretel?"

Delia blinked and looked around. The tiny dwelling, no bigger than a trapper's cabin, sat shrouded in young poplars and giant blue spruce on the bank of a grassy creek that ran through a concrete culvert under the street. Marigolds withered in the window boxes and hanging baskets under the slanted eaves. A cartoonish array of wood saws and fly rods and baskets decorated the little house's north side.

"My tummy!" Delia said. She grabbed the sides of the stroller and shook her body. "Out! I want out!"

Sonya spun a one eighty and half-jogged, half-marched back across the overpass, past Jill's Place. In the restaurant's big window the usual brunch bunch, a line of slack denim backsides and mangled straw hats, crouched at the counter like satisfied monkeys on a limb. Offroad again, Sonya maneuvered into Clyde Keefer Park, where she sat on a picnic bench and unbuckled Delia. Delia scampered toward the swings, arms raised like a religious lunatic.

"Go high!" she shrieked.

In effect Sonya completed the shape of a crucifix on her walk. She had noted this to Phil after one of her first strolls outside—how someone could walk the entire town of St. Anthony and trace the shape of a cross, a remark that had stolen three nights of sleep from him.

Sonja sat and smiled. She thought of how interesting it was

that the park she was resting in was actually an island of volcanic rock in the middle of the Henry's Fork of the Snake River. What geological forces had brought her on this migration?

A custom car horn beeped 'Shave and a Haircut,' and a Rocky Mountain Power utility truck rumbled across the bridge and rolled down the onramp. In the entry to Neil's and Joe's Tire Store stood an old man in cowboy boots and a shimmery royal blue jacket, his snowy hair scooped in a pompadour. He lit a cigarette and flicked the match into the wind. Sonya tried to imagine what the town of St. Anthony had looked like fifty years ago, thousands of years ago, with no people, just trumpeter swans and wildcats and mother eagles posing in dead trees, scanning the water for chubby trout. The merry-go-round, the picnic shelters and kiddie frontier fort, the Sherman tank corked with concrete and the baby-faced WWI 'doughboy' statue with his shrapnel helmet and puttees—they had all come later and one day would be gone. What had always existed was this island, the howl of the river, along with the rasp of sawgrass, the screams of raptors, the pillowy waves of dandelion paratroopers riding the silky afternoon. But soon, perhaps sooner than anyone thought possible, the old mill wheel of the earth, the mortar and pestle of windy rain and gravity, would grind the truck stops and gift shops and Sonya and Phil and their generations to powder, scattering the seeds of their bones over the watersheds of the world and washing them to the sea.

"Mommy!"

Sonya scanned the park and saw Delia hooting like a chimpanzee. Her small body was tangled in a horsey swing custom-made from a snow tire. Delia yanked the reins and throttled her body back and forth like a maniac jockey, failing to move her mount an inch. Frustrated, she jumped off and flung herself stomach-style on one of the other swings.

"Higher!" she called. "Push me higher!"

Sonya and Phil had promised each other to stay alert with Delia in the park, given the deadly current, the craggy falls, the lack of safety fences on the riverbank. So it was strange, even to Sonya, that with no feelings of hypocrisy she rose and walked to the river's edge, her blood a torrent of glacial runoff, the tears on her face a fire of communion.

A woman named Breanne Nordfelt saw her go in. Breanne, an anorexic single mother of two boys—Chase and Conner, who were attending Choo-Choo Childcare—was watching Sonya and Delia outside Jill's Place Family Restaurant in her icing-stained frock and acid-wash jeans. She was enjoying her morning smoke break in the rusty porch swing on the grassy hill overlooking the park. Breanne's former live-in lover, Chad Meyer, a landscaper and AC/DC aficionado, had ditched her on a bright Tuesday morning, sold his assets, and absconded to Fair Oaks, California, with a busty maple-eyed Mickelsen's Hardware salesgirl named Riki Clegg, all to the tune of 'The Jack.' Meyer left his biological sons to fate and Breanne with a hundred deadweight of victim's mentality, which is why she simply smoked and watched the redheaded girl's mother until the mother crossed her arms like an Egyptian mummy and hopped feet-first into the rushing rapids.

Then Breanne squealed, flicked her cigarette into the grass, rushed inside Jill's Place, and called 911. Two police cruisers and the Fremont County sheriff arrived with an ambulance and—using yellow ropes, orange flotation vests, and a human chain—

fished Sonya from the river on the west side of the bridge.

On the weedy riverbank Breanne gave a statement. She folded her arms across her bony chest and shivered, her Ramen-noodle hair, freckled skin, and chipmunk teeth making her look like a lost schoolgirl.

"Just jumped in," she told the officer. "From the park."

Thirty yards away, surrounded by officers on the rocks, a sopping wet Sonya wobbled to her feet, a rescue blanket wrapped around her shoulders.

"My daughter's at the park," she spluttered as two EMT's assisted her into the ambulance. "Please!"

The sheriff drove to the park and spotted Delia. Two Jill's Place cooks in aprons and hairnets, Mona Gibbons and Sue 'Gimp' Gonzalez, were pushing Delia back and forth on the swings and singing 'The Wheels on the Bus.' The sheriff stepped out of his car and lumbered down the hill.

"Morning, Tommy," Mona called.

"Ladies," the sheriff said. Then to Delia, "We got your mommy!" He dropped into a catcher's stance with an "ooph!" and clapped his hands and opened his arms like the grandpa of five that he was. Delia ran to him. "Let's get this little missy home."

The sheriff shuttled Delia to the hospital in his cruiser. On the way he let her trigger the siren and lights. After a routine exam for both Sonya and Delia, the hospital called Phil on his cell phone after Sonya gave them the number. As soon as word reached him Phil cut his inventory trip short and zoomed back from Idaho Falls. As he pulled up to the emergency room exit bay, Sonya hunched her shoulders and waved an apology. Delia capered like an organ-grinder monkey.

"Hop in, Dill," Phil said. Sonya inclined toward the open window. Phil looked up at her. "How are things?" he said.

"Fine," she said. "Considering."

Reports were filed. The newspaper called. But what Sonya never told anyone went like this: At the rocky ledge she turned to make sure Delia was okay then stepped into the watery scream of eons to embrace the call of God. Her foot snapped a rung of air, and she plunged into cheering bubbles. The craggy cold shrank her soul to a blue cinder. Her lungs throbbed for air as she thrashed and wheeled over swaying weeds and muddy troves of motor oil cans. The river jostled her and jetted her along, sucking all light and marrow from the universe. In the strongest current she went limp and trusted her webbed toes, the promise of a new home. Eighteen-wheelers sailed through murky sky with giant tubes of concrete chained to their backs. She screamed, and water filled her mouth, when she saw her husband and daughter frozen in a wall of mud with trilobites and sawfish bones. Her fingernails clawed trenches in pebbly silt, and her arms and legs and hindquarters—so slender and sleek for a mother of her age and education—channeled the power of the water and turned her ravenous and alert until she was rocketing through the waves in slick arcs and cutbacks after squiggly food sources to ease her animal hunger. Only when she was bawling for air did she break the surface and gulp oxygen, jubilant, alive, barking for someone to save her, for everyone to leave her alone. Hands scrabbled to pin down her neck and haunches. They wanted her spread-eagled to bludgeon her brains out with axe handles. Pikes gouged her ribs, and grappling hooks tore blubber from her bones. It was her hide they wanted, to jail her and make her a circus freak, a stuffed trophy. Against the attack she slapped and slashed and roared, butting savagely at her oppressors and flashing bloody fangs, crying out for her mate. The longer she fought, the more her lungs spouted sorrow as they dragged her body over boulders.

"You okay?" the voices called. "Here! Throw it!"

She was shoved back and held to the ground. She stared, exhausted, into the mustache-and-sunglasses scowl of an EMT in a brown, gold-trimmed Fremont County Search & Rescue cap. She gasped, gave one last struggle, then sank to the mossy riverbank. Rolled on her side, she belched black mud, and nobody, especially not her captors, saw her spirit drain from her bones, a ribbon of noble blood flowing to the ocean.

Then she was sitting at home in a bathrobe at the kitchen table, cupping a mug of anise seed tea, and beholding a man she vaguely recognized as her husband, Phil. As the two adults faced off Delia played on the living room rug with a bucket of giant Legos. After a monster silence, Phil spoke.

"I want to know what's going on."

"Going on?" she asked. Phil stared at her, eyes filmy.

He pointed out the window. "That woman from the restaurant said you jumped in after—"

"Slipped," Sonya said. She pressed the mug to her lips and sipped. "No juicy gossip on the town docket, I guess." Phil's chin jutted out and in.

"And, and the sheriff said you were babbling—"

"Latin would sound like babbling to Wyatt Earp."

"—about the ocean, the sea—"

Sonya scowled. "What sea?"

Phil jumped to his feet and threw his hands to the ceiling. "How the hell do I know! Pick one!"

"Keep your voice down!" Sonya hunched her body over the mug. "Delia's gonna—"

"I don't care!" he hissed. He drummed his fist on the table. The ceramic beluga whale centerpiece rattled.

"Phil, I think—"

"I'm through! Hear me?"

She braced her head in her hands. "Kinda hard not to."

"The whole town sees my wife abandon her daughter in the park, at the river—"

"I didn't abandon her!"

"—try to drown herself on the five o'clock news—"

She widened her eyes. "I was swimming for my life! Ever try it with clothes on?"

Phil swirled his hands around his head. "The whole town's talking," he said. "I've started some business around here."

"Good."

"Now they're talking about my nutcase wife, the loonies who moved in next door."

"I fell," Sonya said. She turned her face and palms skyward. "I don't know—maybe I tapped into a primal urge, you know, pulling me to the water? Like Kennedy said, we all go back to the sea."

"Kennedys," Phil scoffed, checking her expression. "Perverts. Irish drunks."

"Phil," she said after a pause. "This is really hard on me—"

"You?"

She scooted her chair around to face him. "What I mean is here I am. I almost died today. Now, how's a girl supposed to feel? I almost died, and you're ranting! Now, what goes on in my mind—"

"I'd love to know—"

"Stop, alright? You're banging overtime with the cruelty hammer, don't you think?"

Phil looked at her. "Cruelty hammer?"

"What I'm saying is—right now?—you should be folding me in your arms and telling me with kisses and tears you're glad I'm alive."

Phil sagged against the bar. "I am glad, Sun," he said. "And Delia, too."

"But you're not. Otherwise—"

"I am! It's just a shock, and there've been other—"

"What I mean is you're not showing me, Phil. I want you to hold me, and you're not. You're shouting, lecturing. So over there."

"Sorry," he exhaled. He ran a hand over his crown. "I know you've had an ordeal."

"I haven't felt that way," she said, looking upward. "Closer. For a while. It's not the same. Not since we moved here from New York and my family—"

Phil stiffened. "You don't like it here."

Sonya put her fists to her ears. "No," she said. "I do."

"All I've put together, built up—"

"I do, yes! It's just hard for a woman to pack up and leave her family."

Phil tilted forward and slapped his chest. "I'm your family. We are! You make it sound like a concentration camp."

"Phil—"

He gestured violently around the room, showcasing ghost merchandise. "I'd be happy with what I've done."

"I am," she said, shoulders slumping. "Delia is. It's just—"

"Clean air, water. No drugs, no crime, cost of living—"

"I know."

"—a crack local first response unit—"

"Enough."

Phil tapped the table. "Then? Answers."

"About?"

"Why you'd try to drown yourself," he blurted.

"Never again!" she snapped. Then she relaxed, channeling a casual personality. "Besides, all that drowning yourself stuff is a lie."

"Is it?" he said. He twiddled his lower lip with his thumb, staring at her.

She nodded. "Ophelia? Virginia Woolf? Your body's survival mechanisms won't allow it."

"Mm."

"Like tickling yourself," she said. "Sneezing with your eyes open." She rose and swiped crumbs off the table into her cupped hand. "Some things your body won't let you do."

"That so?"

"We're all hardwired with built-in safety settings."

"I want you to take counseling," he said.

She forced a quick smile. "Okay."

"Okay?"

"I'm fine—with it."

He breathed in and out. "You want to call, or should I?"

"Give me a few days," she said, smoothing the wrinkles from

her robe. "A girl likes to shop around."

Then Delia was standing like an emissary of hope in the doorway to the kitchen, a horrendous red, yellow, and blue Franken-Lego thingie in her fist.

"Look," Delia piped. She waved her cubist nightmare. "I made it."

"Oo, honey," Sonya cooed. She approached Delia and squatted down. "Can I see?"

Delia grapevined one leg behind the other and dipped her head in a shy nod. "I made it," she said.

With amplified awe Sonya took the Lego enigma from her daughter and examined it with clownish pride. The sculpture was grotesque in its dimensions, barbed and lopsided, some warped and ghastly intestinal blockage Picasso's cat might have coughed up on the carpet.

"Pretty, Dill," Phil said.

"Absolutely gorgeous, baby," Sonya said. "What is it?"

Delia grinned. "Mommy," she said.

"That's Mommy?" Phil said. He checked Sonya's reaction. "Where's Daddy?"

"Here," Delia said, doddering into the living room.

They followed her and found a heap of Legos scattered on the floor.

"Where?" Phil asked.

"There!" Delia said. She laughed and pointed at the jumbled piles.

"Got that right," Phil said. "Been working too hard."

At that moment the kitchen timer in Phil's shirt pocket started beeping. He blushed and poked his finger in and snapped it off.

"When you gonna trash that?" Sonya said.

Phil pulled the timer out and waved it like a magic key. "Keeps me on schedule."

"It's annoying," Sonya said. She propped her hands on her hips. "Fifteen minutes for love? Check! Ten minutes of quality time? Check!"

"I'm my own boss," he said stalking across the living room. "If I don't—you know, watch it—bye, bye mortgage—"

With her finger Sonya slashed a check mark in the air. "Five minutes of tenderness? Done!"

He stood in the hall doorway and turned to face her. "Some days, you're lucky to get five."

She stooped to gather Delia's shoes and socks. "Five's all you need if you use it."

For Halloween Delia went as a monarch butterfly princess. With their daughter swinging between them the Griffins scoured every leaf-speckled street in St. Anthony for the goody mother lode. In passing, they caught winks and smiles from strangers chaperoning green-faced ghouls in pajamas, frowzy Sleeping Beauties in cowboy boots, and the odd sucker-wielding baby Mephistopheles in a stroller. When they dumped Delia's pillowcase of treats on the living room floor, they found handwritten notes mixed in with the Tootsie Rolls and Neopolitan Coconut Sundaes and Idaho Spud bars. Some of the messages were knotted in rainbow yarn, others sealed with 'God Is Love' stickers: 'Hang In There,' 'Motherhood Is a Noble Calling,' and 'Keep Your Head Above Water (Just

Kidding! Nice To See You're Doing So Well!).'

Early in November the high school Youth for Life group showed up to rake and winterize the Griffins' lawn. Plastic-wrapped paper plates of pecan rolls and snickerdoodles appeared on the Griffin porch after sundown. A gang of gum-smacking cheerleaders dropped by on Tuesdays and Thursdays to tend Delia so Sonya could get out of the house. By Thanksgiving, Sonya had started weekly counseling sessions with Rita Cosworth, MSW, in Sugar City.

In many ways counseling gave Sonya what she needed. Rita was sixty-three, a spectacled and frumpy throwback from the days of Dobie Gillis. She ran her practice at home, and she always wore something argyle with a nylon skirt, scruffy pantyhose, and one thick-soled shoe that failed to hide her Long John Silver limp. She had two adult sons in the army and a truck-driving, elk-hunting ex-husband in his grave in Tetonia. But she was patient and pleasant, and Sonya liked her. For the most part the sessions went well, with Sonya spilling out her split-level desires and Rita nodding, smiling benignly, and jotting notes on a yellow pad.

The upshot of Sonya's therapy was that Rita, being a woman, sympathized with Sonya's plight. Rita was awed by Sonya's intelligence, rationale, and academic feats. Often Rita would abandon pad and pencil and walk with Sonya to Judy's Bakery for coffee and huckleberry Danish. On the way they would swap stories about children, careers, survival strategies, and 'making it all work.' More often than not Phil's workaholic lifestyle was stirred into the mix of the conversation. Both women gestured toward it as 'part of the problem.'

This female kinship lifted Sonya once a week when she

knew her session was coming. Then a six-day smog of wordless tension would descend on the Griffin home and dare anyone to dispel it. From Phil's perspective Sonya switched from shades of blue to lightning bipolar, at least at the outset. She withdrew from him during the day and then at night, draped in transparent tigerlily negligee, would burst from the bathroom closet, pin him to the bed, and devour him body and soul. Mornings after these bouts of sexual blitzkrieg, Phil, stunned but satiated, would pad into the kitchen in his T-shirt and striped pajama bottoms, circle his arms around Sonya, and purr notes of blissful rapture in her ear. At his touch Sonya would weep and spring back like an electrocuted cat, leaving him burned and bewildered. Two weeks after New Year's Eve (which involved imported champagne, chocolate truffles, a chinchilla shoulder wrap, and a nude *pas de deux* to *Boléro*), Phil's efforts to hold out and hope for the best were rewarded with a yellow sticky note from Sonya on the fridge: 'Gone. Needed a Break.'

Phil stood at the bar, the note searing his fingertips. In peach porcupine slippers and Strawberry Shortcake pajamas Delia shuffled in and stood behind him, her red hair tousled from sleep, a stretched Gund polar bear in her fist. She twined an arm around his knee.

"Where's Mommy?" she asked.

"Gone for a little while, honey," Phil said. He stared out the window at the boy scouts shoveling snow from his driveway.

"Where?" Delia said. Her face shriveled in a panicked whine. "I want her! I want her now!"

Phil kneeled down, looked in her eyes. He cupped her cheek. "Me too, sweetie."

Phil guessed Sonya had gone to stay with her parents in Rochester. But he didn't call. Instead, he filled the time by working longer hours. He launched some overseas sales reconnaissance, spotted buffleheads on the river through the living room window, and learned how to build a better Lincoln Log tower with Delia. After two weeks of forced single parenthood he bought Delia some cotton candy from the Kiwanis fundraiser stand at the Co-op and drove to Bob Wilkes's ranch east of town to inquire about the price of a Shetland pony. On returning home he galloped with Delia piggyback through the kitchen door, set down the 3D globe puzzle he bought her at Porter's Books, and found that the phone was ringing. He whinnied, plopped Delia down, and picked up the receiver.

"Hi," Sonya said.

"Dilly!" Phil said. "It's Mom! Wanna talk to her? Honey, where have—"

"Talk!" Delia pleaded, bouncing for the phone. "I want to!"

"Phil," Sonya cut in. "Look, I—"

Phil rested a hand on Delia. Delia clamped a boa-constrictor hug on his leg. "Sun, hey, what's—Dilly, shh, just a second!—what's the matter, dear? Where are you?"

The sound of Sonya's breath tunneled into Phil's ear. It made him think of coyotes scavenging through sagebrush, a sky of falling stars over a ghost town.

"Sunny?" he prodded.

"I'm here," she sniffled.

"Why are you crying? Why haven't—"

"I'm at my parents."

Phil pressed his lips together. "Yeah."

"I'm—Phil? I'm pregnant."

His eyelids fluttered, and he blew out a laugh. "Wonderful, Sun! That's so—"

She ejected a sob then sucked in air. "No," she said. "It's not. It's—"

Phil looked down at Delia and searched the ground around her feet. He pressed the phone to his jaw. "Not wonderful? I'm happy for us. Dilly will have a playmate, a little brother."

"You're not listening!" Sonya cried. "You're not—what I'm feeling right now! I've got—"

"Go ahead. It's just—"

"—bearing down like a world of weight. I should have known before—I'm not making sense, am I?—before I got into—I can't come back."

"Can't come back?" Phil's skeleton went slack. Delia's hug tightened. He rubbed a soothing circle over her shoulder. "Why, what—"

"Phil, I think it's better."

His eyes darted around the kitchen. "Are we talking long-term here?"

"Don't know."

"You don't know," he said. Fury thickened in his throat.

"No, and I'd appreciate it—"

He stopped the circle motion and held Delia's arm as if to show her to the world. "Well, I've got a helpless three-year old here who'd like to know—"

"She'll be fine."

"She asks about you every day, and I—"

"You've done great."

"This," Phil said, clenching his teeth, "is crazy."

"I'm not crazy."

Phil pressed a palm to his ear then cupped his chin, fingernails hooked over his bottom teeth. "Gonna put number two up for adoption?" he said. "Abortion?"

"Phil!"

"Picnic basket on a doorstep?" He walked a hop-along circle, hand aloft. Delia whimpered and rode the carousel horse of his leg. "This is my kid, too, you know. I've got some chromosomes in there. Where are your mom and dad in all this?"

"They say they support me."

"Gotta back the ones you birth, huh?"

"Would you like to talk to them?"

"No, this is all us."

"And Delia—"

"Right," he said, stroking Delia's curls. "The Dillybobber."

"And the new one, the little one."

"So should I call?" Phil said. Tears stung his nostrils. Delia's hug cinched a tourniquet above his kneecap. He started to pry her off, scanning the air for answers. "Or should—"

"Don't, um—let's not. For now."

"God," he muttered.

"I wasn't listening to myself," she snuffled. "My nature."

Phil felt his finger being squeezed. "Nature?"

"I'm choosing now," Sonya said. "I should have listened to myself, I wasn't cut out for this."

"I wasn't cut out," Phil said. He bent over as if setting

down a heavy suitcase. "But I'm here."

"That's *your* nature," she said. "Speaking to *you*. You should give praise, be glad you found it. I—I can't talk, Phil. There's things—I gotta go. I'll—bye. "

Phil swallowed and licked his dry lips. "Bye," he croaked, then set the phone on the hook.

Delia crow-hopped in a circle. "Mommy!" she squealed. "I want to talk! I want—"

"I know, Dilly," Phil said. He scooped her up and shook a giggle into her tummy. "But Mommy had to go, and Silly Dilly needs to take a bath! Silly Dilly's a dirty little pilly!"

So Phil waltzed his daughter off to her bubble bath, dredging up funny face after funny face from the black bog of despair in which he sank toward total collapse. After tucking Delia in bed, he watched television in the moon-glazed living room for two hours, a CNN special report on Venezuelan oil and the financial market in Hong Kong. Then he clicked the TV off and padded into the kitchen. There, he picked up the phone, coiled his body back, and shattered the receiver across the fridge with a swing that would have shamed Hank Aaron.

Phil floated from January to March. He repaired the phone but didn't call. He was afraid of a reactor core meltdown, of having to face something he might have done or not done. With work and winter sledding trips with Delia, Phil distracted himself into believing he and Sonya weren't finished even though, as far as the town of St. Anthony could tell, they were.

To survive Phil shifted his work hours to earlier in the

morning so he could read, feed, and play with Delia. He maintained naptimes—for both of them. He limited Delia's TV time and kept her mind and hands stimulated with trips to the public library. They toured the fish hatcheries, Camas National Wildlife Refuge, Mesa Falls, and the Teton Dam site. Crafting excuses for her mother's absence became tough, however, and soon Delia's expression stopped swooping into wild rapture each time he said that her mommy was making monkey tree houses in Jamaica, shopping for a lifetime supply of cherry marshmallow ice cream, or pinning stars to the sky.

In the meantime nothing could stop St. Anthony's crusades of kindness. The Ladies' Bingo League brought cowboy chili and cornbread over on Wednesday nights after games. Kyle Wanamaker, the Griffins' next-door neighbor, trudged up Phil's driveway one morning after a blizzard and pushed an old snow blower into Phil's garage, calling back over his shoulder that he 'had two already anyways.' Choo-Choo Childcare in St. Anthony and Starbrite Academy in Sugar City offered to take Delia on at half-tuition for starters, but Phil turned them down, indicating that he and his daughter were 'managing.'

They weren't. Phil's first quarter earnings dropped by eighteen percent. Delia slipped into pools of moodiness for hours, and crusty bowls of Cheerios crowded the kitchen table. Damp land mines of dirty clothes stayed in the laundry room for weeks and cycled out one outfit at a time. The vacuum cleaner sat in the hallway where it conked out, its cord snaking into Phil's room like the tail of an extinct reptile. It became harder for Phil to read a Sesame Street ABC's book with Delia on his lap while he juggled a shipment of cell phones to Abilene, Texas, on his computer.

At first he took her with him on his bi-monthly drives to the warehouse in Idaho Falls. But she either fell asleep in the car or, once inside, scampered into the path of a forklift. So he was forced to halt his 'Daddy Day Trips' and get a babysitter.

To top things off, certain items—hardware, CD's, loose change, and steak knives—began to disappear from the house. Right off, he suspected Donny and Rabeena and began to padlock the one access door from the house to the workroom, after which the thefts stopped.

The morning after the padlocking Phil sat at his work desk, chewing a piece of Quench gum, thinking. Then he picked up the phone and, instead of packing Donny and Rabeena off to their P. O., gave them a five-dollar raise, which had a stunning effect on their work ethic. They showed up early, worked late. They offered to take out the trash, babysit Delia, do the dishes. Not wanting to douse their fire for housework, Phil sicced them— always supervised—on the shopping, laundry, and housecleaning. So in a sense, when Sonya showed up on April Fool's Day with her manicured fingers slinging a black-and-gold travel valise and her belly blooming like a spring tulip under a tan suede Lord and Taylor jacket and pink silk chemise, the house had returned to the way it was before she left.

After re-arranging the furniture for three hours, she slept for two days.

Her slinky queen-of-the-night hair was gone. She'd chopped it into perky swoops that brushed her shoulders. By the third day Delia was leaping and shrieking with joy around her mother, running up with the pictures of farm animals she'd drawn, books from the library, stories of car trips with Phil. Over the next week, as he helped Sonya with her jacket and opened the door for her, Phil struggled to control his trembling jaw and hands. He couldn't help staring at the mound of her belly, the way she eased into a straddle-style sitting position on the couch, her eyes wide with overblown zeal as she listened to Delia's mile-a-minute travelogues.

As Delia and Sonya traded catch-up stories, Phil hung back and monitored his wife's face for a trace of psychological change, all the while trying to calm the tremors of hope in his throat. When his wife and daughter talked he perched on their rose-patterned re-upholstered ottoman, listening to the chatter but thinking of the helpless life in Sonya's womb and how at that moment his offspring swam—scared and alone—in a lagoon of translucent unknowns. He ached to promise his unborn kit that everything would be fine when he couldn't promise even himself that.

Sonya talked about visiting the Syracuse campus. As if cataloging priceless relics, she described her old study carrel in the Bird Library, the gnarled network of vines on the Lyman Cornelius Smith College of Applied Science. With the wild gestures and forced grin of a suicidal clown, she told Delia about how she slept in her old bed at Grandma and Grandpa's house. She chatted about dolls and old books, trips to see former professors, lecture halls, her walks around campus.

Phil listened with strained patience. He tried not to think of how she hadn't offered him any affection since arriving home— no kiss, no hug. He was further rocked off his foundation when, after putting Delia to bed, he mustered the courage to try some humor.

"This April Fool's?" he asked. "You staying?"

Sonya sat on the couch, smiled like a mannequin, and folded her hands as if talking to Delia. "We'll have to see, now, won't we?"

That night, when Phil retired to bed, Sonya didn't follow. At first she slept on the couch in the living room, a patchwork denim quilt from the St. Anthony Sisters of Mercy Society draped over her. Eventually Phil persuaded her to bed so he could take the couch, a swap she accepted with a sisterly smile.

With sleeping arrangements behind them they entered a tolerable but tense daily routine. To tip the scales Phil invited Rita Cosworth over for tea and blueberry muffins. The reunion shot genuine glee into Sonya's frozen features. By the end of April, with Rita dropping by twice a week, it appeared to Phil that the ice cobra around Sonya's soul was thawing. All the same, dreams from their former life resurfaced. At night—once he was allowed back in bed—Phil positioned himself like a curled armadillo as far away from her as possible, and rocked himself into an open-eyed trance, thinking of Sonya, his lost seal, pregnant with their terrified pup, who, as far as he could tell, didn't have a chance of survival.

When he did drift into an exhausted half-sleep at around two in the morning, his many mind screens would unfold the same horrors, nightmares of Promethean proportions that swept in like bombing raids. In one of the worst scenes, Sonya bounded into the raging Atlantic surf, leaving him to bawl a bellyful of agony from a barnacle-encrusted ledge of flint. From his razor-edged rock he bellowed over the crash of the waves, a choked plea for pity, calling for his lost young, his deranged mate. At the end a murderous crescendo of killer whales stormed the rainy beaches at dusk, seizing his pink baby in their jaws. With spasms of cruel delight they shook the calf to a bloody rag on the shore. Each morning, after three hours of torpor, Phil would rise and stand in his room, his body a useless bag. Swaying in the swell of dawn, he would think of the baby while watching his sleeping wife, whom he felt he would never touch again without being savaged.

Then Terrell Braddock suffered a stroke. First week in May, Phil returned home from Murdock Travel—a breezy smile on his face and a Bahia Resort Hotel information packet in his hand—to find Sonya weeping on the phone to Sue Anne, her mother, and a teary-eyed, raw-nosed Delia scooted into a corner of the kitchen, her blanket scrunched to her chin.

"Completely changed," Sonya said, hanging up the phone. "He's fine, healthwise. Doctors are baffled."

"Changed?" Phil said.

"Mom says everything's backward," she began. She made soft karate chops in the air, sucked in a cry. "It's not his health, just logic. Today? She caught him reading a book upside down. She turned the book right side up. Know what he said?"

Phil's eyes dodged left and right. "No."

"He said, 'No thanks, Sue. I can read it better this way.'"

"Weird."

"Sad," she continued. "He signs his name upside down. In cursive! Mom held a mirror to a check after he signed it. The signature was perfect! Just backward. And he never remembers to pay bills."

Phil pried open the packet and removed a bundle of brochures. "Definitely not your dad."

Sonya flung her arms out. "Airline mechanic! Live and die by the punch clock. They went to the bank, and he remembered his PIN number and how to put his card in the ATM. But he couldn't remember how to use the keypad."

Phil eyed a glossy brochure with dolphins on the front. "Whoa," he said.

Sonya stepped up to him. He folded the brochure, looked in her eyes. "Get this," she said. "The other day? You know he gets up at, what, four in the morning? Now he sleeps 'til nine! Mom can't shake him out of bed."

"Impossible."

She slapped her hip. "On weekdays!" She walked to the sink, turned on the spigot, and washed her hands, speaking to Phil but looking out the window at the budding lilac hedge. "He's really messy. He used to be so neat. Leaves drawers open, clothes on the floor, things like that. He tried to put his shoes on before his pants. It took him an hour to figure it out."

Phil folded his arms and thought about it. "That is—I don't know."

"Listen to this," she said. The energy in her voice withered to pain. "He, uh—he's wearing flashier clothes. Bright colors. You know he was so conservative in his dress? Grays? Tweeds?"

Phil pulled a bar stool out and sat down. "That's his thing."

"Mom found him walking around the house in her pink silk nightgown, her peacock pajama bottoms, and a string of pearls!"

Phil puckered his lips and blinked. "Isn't that a song?"

Sonya dried her hands with a towel and shook her head. "He

said he liked the colors better."

Phil shrugged and smiled. "Maybe he just needed some spicing up."

"Phil."

"Nothing wrong with a little color."

"He watches TV all day."

Phil tapped the brochure on the bar. "Wasn't he—I don't know—outdoorsy? Liked a hammer in his hand?"

"Never watched TV."

Phil put a brochure corner between his lips. "How's your mom?"

Sonya placed her hands on the sink and leaned forward like a gymnast testing the apparatus. "They're starting therapy. Imagine having to watch your spouse walk around in a nightie?"

Phil ran his fingertips over the bar. "Might be nice. Otherwise, he's okay?"

"Everything checked out at the emergency room. Just his reasoning's off."

"But he's breathing and everything."

"Fine," she said, staring at the floor. "Other than that."

"Then maybe," Phil said, seductively waving the brochure in front of his face like a hundred dollar bill, "a little trip to California is what we need! Little cheering up? Dill, you want to fly on a plane and go swimming and see animals?"

"Animals!" Delia cheered. She scampered over and hugged his leg. "I like swimming!"

Mouth agape, Sonya glared at Phil. "Excuse me?"

"It'll be good," Phil said, swinging Delia in his arms. "For us. Wanna get away?"

She blinked. "Phil, he's just had a stroke."

"Otherwise he's fine, you said—"

"A stroke!" she wailed. She slapped her knee, each word a two-ton tear. "My dad has just had *a stroke*, and all you can think about is flying off to California when—"

Delia slid down Phil's trunk and hid behind him. "He's gonna be fine, Sun. You just have to—"

"He's my father!" she roared. She wagged her hand like a broadsword. "You have no respect or interest at all for family. I just told Mom we were on our way to New York."

"Whoa!" Phil said, hands up. "I've had these plans made for weeks, and Delia—"

"Change the tickets! Dammit, you can be so self-centered! Don't you care about family? Or is the almighty dollar—"

"I work for all of us!" Phil said. He jabbed a finger in his sternum. "If you think it's easy to sit back there in that *cave*, slaving into the night, then you're more than a little off the mark! By the way, I do care about family! We're your family! When does anyone realize that or give a damn about me!"

With one accord they stopped and listened to the tortured howl that was drilling the ceiling. Like a stunned dance duo they rotated their gazes, looking for the baby cougar that had crawled into the kitchen. Delia sat hunched in a corner, shaking and screaming. She brandished her fists, clawed at the flesh of her reddened cheeks. She cried as if trying to expel her soul from her lungs. Then she bolted across the room. To Phil's surprise she didn't charge him or Sonya but half-hopped, half-ran like a drunken lemur to the door, where with her back to it, she sank to her haunches in a one-girl huddle of sobs. There she wailed loud and long, tears streaming from her eyes.

Later, when Delia's shrieks ebbed to snuffles, Phil and Sonya crept in from the living room and tried to approach her. Each time, she flamed to life and launched a flurry of kung fu strikes and floppy kicks that forced them to retreat. When the light in the house failed and darkness filled the kitchen, Sonya and Phil, dressed for bed, peeked in and saw their daughter sleeping, curled like a dormouse on her blanket in front of the back door, sucking her fingers and guarding the only exit from her heart.

The next week, the Griffins locked the house, left the key with Rita Cosworth's college-age niece, and boarded a Delta Airlines jet bound for San Diego.

After breakfast Phil paid the bill and led Delia out of BJ's. To kill time they walked over to watch the seals in the Bahia Resort's landscaped 'seal park,' a hasty assembly of wood and tile walkways that meandered through shattered shrubs and starved palm trees. The seals sunned themselves on slanted boulders in a sunken concrete pen built to keep seals in and people out, Phil observed, and did the world's worst job of mimicking a seal's natural habitat. The sculpted shape of the enclosure—the contoured walls and conspicuous lack of flat surfaces and sharp corners—was meant to communicate a feeling of wild boundlessness but looked more like a child's clay model abandoned in the rain. Delia pointed and squealed and ran to the pen and hoisted her body onto the wobbly guard rail.

"Seals, Daddy!" she called. "There they are!"

Phil jogged forward and pinched the back of her shirt. "Easy, baby."

Roused by the noise, the seals gaped about like drugged senior citizens. A translucent scum of mucus glazed their black, depthless eyes. On their stone lounges they sprawled, bloated and distended, as if any movement more taxing than a whisker twitch would spark an infarction. Their patchy coats were as shabby as throw rugs. Phil leaned over the railing, his arm around Delia's waist.

"They can't swim in there," he said. "Seal Sing Sing."

The seals regarded Delia and Phil, wrinkled their noses, and slumped on the boulders.

Soon, Sonya appeared in a wide-brimmed straw sunhat with a pastel-striped band and bow anchored under her chin. Apart from the sunhat, her body and soul were snapped together in tennis-lawn white: white shoes, white shorts, white sleeveless top. Large sunglasses masked her puffy eyes, and as she assumed a post alongside her husband without saying a word, she watched Delia and the seals with analytical ardor, alternating her aura back and forth between Jackie Onassis to Audrey Hepburn.

"You all right?" Phil said, addressing the sun.

"No," she said. "How's Delia?"

"We ate. You get breakfast?"

Her chin tensed. "Yes," she said. "Thank you."

"You're welcome," Phil said, turning to read from a plaque on the railing. "Look at these guys. This little one with the collar is named Otis."

Sonya cocked her head. "Looks like a baby."

"Don't think so," Phil said. "Environment stunted his growth, maybe. Small enough to pick up and take home."

"They weigh hundreds of pounds."

"Hm," Phil said, eyes narrowed at the plaque. "Says here, 'The marine mammals in this facility are refugees from the sea.' Huh, how they figure that? Anyway, 'Every year, hundreds of orphaned, weak, sick, and dying marine mammals beach or strand themselves along the coast.' How does a sea lion strand itself? Well, "These mammals were found stranded on coastal beaches and were rescued and rehabilitated through the California Marine Mammal Stranding Network (CMMSN).' Geewillikers, there's a network, AA for seals. What if they were resting and didn't want to be rescued? Now they're stuck here thanks to these misguided do-gooders. So, 'The Bahia Resort Hotel provides these mammals with a state-of-the-art facility, which includes clean filtered salt water'—The Pacific's filtered?—'fresh fish, vitamin and mineral supplementation'—found, naturally, like Flintstones chewables, in the wild—'veterinary care, and husbandry.' I am all for the husbandry, of course, but I'm a little irked that massage and exfoliation aren't part of the package. Says, 'The normal social behavior of these mammals is generally quiet and wary of others—like some people I know, or *unlike* some people I know. 'Adults are usually solitary and rarely interact with others other than to mate.' *That* would suck! Also, 'These mammals show aggression by growling and waving threateningly with their fore flippers. Another aggressive behavior is head thrusting—the sharp, rapid extension and retraction of the neck.' Head games and emotional manipulation have been observed in some of the less-advanced species presumed to be extinct. But, "These are wild and unpredictable mammals, and at no time should you reach or lean into or over the exhibit,' nor should you get emotionally involved or, worst of all, actually breed with one. And can't miss the last bit—'Do not feed these mammals. These mammals can bite.' For sure! 'These mammals are here for your viewing pleasure.' I can't believe these are real sea lions!"

"*Phoca vitulina*," Sonya pronounced.

"Fawka who?"

"Harbor seal," she said. "Carnivorous marine mammal. Native to frigid and temperate zones. Not the monk seal, though. She's tropical. Three families. True seals, walrus, and eared seals, your fur seals and sea lions. These guys were hunted for their hides. Pelagic sealers almost wiped them out. A treaty around, uh, 1911—England, Japan, Russia—stopped the craziness. Another treaty made the Pribilof Islands a sanctuary, so they got up to a couple million over time. Some kind of law protects most seals now. Hotels and animal parks still kill them this way, though, for money-mongering, buffet-gorked, out-of-towners who try to buy each other's love. This is what makes me ashamed to be human. Makes you wonder who the animals are. These guys should be free to swim and kill crabs and find happiness. If I could, I'd get them out of here right now and count my life worth living. By the way, where are we going? I'd like some quality time with Delia."

The kitchen timer in Phil's pocket beeped. He snapped it off.

"Sea World," he said. "Open in fifteen minutes."

"Gonna trash that thing," she said, stomping away.

As they drove their rented blue Accord out of the parking lot, Phil thought he saw a flash of movement in the rearview mirror, a quick blur that looked like a sunburned man in trashy cutoffs slinging his drum over his shoulder and hoisting a leg over the seal park rail as if to climb in without being noticed.

At Sea World the mid-morning sun hammered the pavement. Sonya kept her sunhat on and smeared gobs of sunscreen on Delia's nose, cheeks, and tender shoulders.

"Want some for your head?" she asked Phil, holding up the tube.

Phil objected with a smirk.

At the seal show Delia clapped and laughed at the gags and stunts, especially at the otter that hobbled upright in a *Pagliacci* clown suit and the grumpy walrus that spurted water at the crowd.

For a while Phil was able to enjoy himself as he watched his daughter celebrate life as a kid. But he thought he was going insane when the crowd stood to leave and a haggard-looking man in cutoff jeans, sandals, and white 'Spiritual Warrior' T-shirt strolled onto the stage and collected metal fish buckets. Before exiting stage left the man held up a rubbery mackerel for Phil and slapped his hands together like flippers.

Phil blinked at the stage, but the man had disappeared. So Phil rubbed his eyes and scanned the emptying stadium but could only make out bundles of balloons, sun umbrellas, and hundreds of people streaming out in clothes of summery peach, aquamarine, and violet. But no rogue homeless guy. Before long Delia was tugging his hand and Sonya was yanking his elbow.

"Daddy, go!" Delia commanded.

Sonya cupped a dollop of sunscreen in her hand. "What are you gawking at?" she said. "You really should put this on. You're looking red."

Before Phil could describe what he'd seen, Sonya took Delia's hand and shoved him past a trio of chattering Japanese grandmothers in sailor hats.

From the twenty-first row at the killer whale show, Phil thought he saw the same oddly dressed vagrant join the kids who volunteered to give the whale's trainer signals in the 'splash zone.' After the killer whales exploded into the air and soaked everyone, it appeared to Phil that the homeless man, who was still dripping wet, turned to him and repeated the whale signals, as if trying to put Phil under a long-distance spell.

At the dolphin show the Spiritual Warrior patrolled the stadium aisles, singing Steve Miller songs, hawking racks of blue-green dolphin visors and neon red starfish pinwheels. He wore a rainbow octopus beanie with a twirling propeller. But when Phil shook his head and took a second look, the man had vanished.

At lunch the Griffins found a table under a large blue and white umbrella. They dined silently on coral reef corn dogs, seahorse tater tots, lemonade, and 'Squid Sherbet.' The hot pink plastic spoon Phil used to eat was temperature sensitive. Each time he speared it into the lump of orange sherbet, the tip changed to lavender. After holding it in his mouth, it changed, like a mood ring, to holistic pink. He ate slowly, a look of haggard paranoia on his face, but he tried to cover with sarcasm.

"Squid Sherbet," he said, smacking his lips and twiddling the stumpy spoon in his fingers. "Which marketing genius dreamed that up?"

"Delia liked hers," Sonya said.

From behind Phil a park worker in a tubby foam-rubber killer whale suit toddled over and tickled Delia. The whale wrapped her in its flexible fins and gave her a hug. Delia shrieked with delight.

"Easy," Phil told the person in the suit.

"Cute, huh?" Sonya said.

Phil stared into the screen recessed in the whale's throat. "Unless Shamu's a baby-snatcher wanted in a few gulfs."

A muffled grunt sounded within the whale suit. The worker released Delia, propped flippers on hips, and uttered an indignant, "Tsk, tsk, tsk!"

Sonya glared at Phil, Phil shrugged back, and the whale waddled a hundred yards off toward the entry gates, looking back dejectedly. Then to Phil's astonishment the worker unzipped the suit, stepped out in cutoffs and 'Spiritual Warrior' T-shirt, and shook his skinny drum in Phil's direction as if summoning voodoo hail.

Phil seized the table. It shook in his hands and sent his Squid Sherbet cup clattering to the ground. Delia scrambled on a chair, clapped her hands on his neck, and sang whale songs in his ear.

"Sunny?" Phil wheezed.

Sonya scraped her spoon in her sherbet cup. "Yeah?"

Phil pushed out two ragged breaths. "I think I'm going crazy."

"So I'm not the only one?"

"Serious," he said, eyes flitting sideways. "I mean—don't look behind you—*don't look!*—that whale that was here? I think I know the guy inside."

"So the secrets come out—"

"Not *know*," Phil said. He held his hands like bookends. "But, okay—remember that guy this morning, stalking us?"

Sonya shaded her eyes with her hand and leaned forward.

"Holy Roller Padre?"

"Spiritual Warrior," Phil said. He made a corridor with his hands and looked through them at Sonya. "I'm—I'm seeing him."

"Should we tell Dill her daddy likes men on vacation, or wait?"

Phil smacked the table top. "Not seeing! Seeing. Everywhere."

"Let's go!" Delia sang. She yanked Phil's shirt to emphasize each word. "Let's go see!"

"For how long?" Sonya asked. "Dilly, shh! Leave Daddy alone." She reached over and held Delia's wrist until Delia stopped pulling. She examined Phil's creased eyes and fried head. "You've gotten too much sun."

Phil spoke through the portal of his hands. "Since we got here. At the hotel, while we were eating. From the balcony, like I told you. He's been at all the shows. In the seal pen, hotel, and I swear he was in that whale suit. I think I'm losing it because I keep seeing him when I don't want to, seeing him, just seeing—"

She took his hand. He stopped shaking. He whimpered and turned away so Delia wouldn't see him.

"Phil, just—calm down."

"I—don't know," he said, heaving kept-in cries. "I—don't, don't—there's been so many—"

"What was it?" Sonya said. She stroked his knuckles and forearms. "Spiritual Guide?"

"Warrior."

"Warrior!" Delia exulted, clapping her hands. "I see him!"

Sonya searched Phil's eyes. "Sign from God?" she said, releasing a deflated laugh. She smiled at Delia, whose face was lacquered in Squid Sherbet. "Looked for a couple in my day. Maybe you're one of the lucky ones."

"Doesn't feel like luck," Phil panted.

On Saturday they visited the San Diego Zoo where Phil's tailspin into a parallel dimension accelerated. At the front entrance, where crowds thickened, Phil again spotted the Spiritual Warrior still wearing his signature shirt and cutoffs, but now equipped with headphones and doing a subdued Riverdance. In between dance steps he twirled a litter stick like a cane and speared trash and popped it into the open end of his tambourin.

Outwardly Phil played the good father and husband, but inside he was tripping to the point of total mind warp. There was no explanation for the freakish beatnik and his disturbing ubiquity, and yet, the more frequently Phil saw the Spiritual Warrior, the less he resisted, the more he began to accept the otherworldly man's existence as normal, even predestined. Soon, in fact, Phil started to feel a warm peacefulness in the man's company, a glow like menthol in his chest. He couldn't explain it, but he found himself unable to beat back a strong feeling of brotherhood toward the haggard stranger, as if he felt driven to speak with him.

At the Snake Snack Shack Phil sat with Sonya and presented turquoise cotton candy and popcorn to Delia. He set out little white cups of ketchup and mustard, unwrapped a corn dog, took a bite and chewed and watched the Warrior help a toddler sit astride a fiberglass grizzly bear, at which time he received a jolt of pure revelation. Sitting there with his wife and daughter, Phil understood, even if they didn't, that the strange man was somehow a semblance of his inner spiritual identity, his alter ego, his Ghost of Christmas Forever, and he was there as a messenger, sent to reunite Phil with his true self, to bring him enlightenment and alignment if he could only make contact.

"My twin," Phil said. He held his half-eaten corndog to his mouth as if speaking into a mustard-dipped microphone.

"Might win what?" Sonya said.

"Nothing," Phil said, smiling at a Chinese man puttering past in a motorized wheelchair. The wheelchair scattered sparrows from a greasy puddle. "Thinking out loud."

In the Ituri Forest attraction Phil held hands with Sonya and Delia, and they strolled along powdery dirt paths through the steamy jungle ambience of bamboo and tambourine doves. On the way he stopped to watch the Spiritual Warrior—now dressed in green zookeeper's coveralls—loft cabbages, shotput-style, into the cavernous pink mouth of a hippo. At the Polar Bear Plunge Delia traded antics through the glass with the cubs, Kalluk and Tatqiq, while the adults, Chinook and Shikari, paddled through the scummy water and batted around pale blue basketballs and bright orange buckets. On a bench nearby the Spiritual Warrior chomped on a razzleberry sno cone and like a frat buddy toasted Phil with it when Phil glanced back.

The longer Phil straddled the fence of sanity, the more he began to accept the truth: he was a chosen vessel. Given his long-term struggle at home, he concluded, God had sent him a coveted second birth. Heaven had endowed him with a supernal vision no one else in the world possessed. Was it a reward, he wondered, for passing some kind of test?

So when the Spiritual Warrior swung from the orangutan tires, turned triple backflips in the air, and high-fived Chi Chi, the alpha male, Phil laughed and pointed with Sonya and Delia and the rest of the crowd. As they left the zoo that evening on the Skyfari Aerial Tram, Phil nodded and grinned at the Warrior, who, like a pygmy chimp, hung from the cable nearest their chair and scratched his armpit, dangling fifty feet above ground. Sonya, noticing the sunfire glazing Phil's sculpted features, took his arm, scooted closer, and nuzzled her breast against his ribs. She twined her fingers in his hair.

"Why the smile?"

"Happy to be with my family," he said.

"This is fun!" Delia chirped, bouncing in her seat.

At the Skyfari terminus the Spiritual Warrior, assisted by two bored young women in staff uniforms, opened the door to help the Griffins disembark. As the Warrior escorted them through the turnstiles, he gave Phil the 'thumbs up' and a soft slug in the shoulder.

Sunday morning at Legoland, the day before the Griffins flew home, the Warrior spoke to Phil. Previous to that moment, the Griffins bobbed down the Fairy Tale Brook, where Phil watched the Spiritual Warrior sneeze and demolish the Little Pigs' houses. Then they rode up and down the Kid Power Towers, one of which the Warrior suspended, à la Atlas, on his shoulders. Later, as they watched Delia putter around the Junior Driving School course, Phil glanced over and saw the Warrior materialize next to him. The Warrior was slouched against the fence, forearms draped over the top, thumbing oil-smudged puffs of marbled cotton candy into his mouth. With the Warrior on his left and

Sonya on his right, Phil watched Delia and a gaggle of kids rumble past in blocky racecars. The Warrior grinned like every kid's uncle lollygagging around the little league diamond.

"Dude," the Warrior said, licking his fingers. "Head's a tad red. Hightailin' down the carcinogenic freeway. Check it out to avoid major damage."

"My head's red?" Phil said.

"A little," Sonya said. She stroked his pate. "Cute, but red. Sunscreen's in my bag."

The Warrior's skin was reddish-brown, like old saddlebags. Golden hairs glowed on his monkey knuckles. Years of wind and grit and body oil had sculpted his hair into a spiky bush. His eyes were sea-salt blue, shriveled in their sockets. With restless energy, he looked back, not at Phil, but through him, from the crystal tempest of another universe, a stoned sunshine junkie one fairy-dusted fandango from the next free-love apocalypse. Holes peppered his T-shirt, as if a meteor shower had shotgunned him and left him standing. The 'Spiritual Warrior' letters on his shirt had faded from licorice black to koala gray, and his sandals were woven from rope. His cutoffs hung on his hips like sun-stiffened laundry, with dark blue pentagons in place of the missing back pockets. His tambourin was long and slim, a glossy amber-colored wood, slung over his shoulder like a rocket launcher on a frayed rope. Scarlet bands of faceless aborigines and prancing elk circled the drum, arms and antlers raised in orgasmic ecstasy. The Warrior stared at Phil like a crack addict. Phil smelled on the Warrior's breath a thousand tropical spices. From the Warrior blew the aromatic history of ocean currents, the smoke of planetary collisions, the breath of the laughing owl. Between his eyes, like a lone galaxy, glowed a daub of mustard ochre.

"Cute kid," the Warrior said. He flipped a cotton candy sprig in his mouth and nodded at Delia as she tooted past in her blue Lego racecar. "We gotta talk."

"Talk?" Phil asked.

"We have been talking, Phil," Sonya said, smiling at the kiddie drivers. "Delia's having fun. And I'm—I don't know—seeing things differently? Maybe this is all we needed."

"Seal park, dude," the Warrior said, ambling off. He tossed his cotton candy bag in a trash barrel, behind his back, like a Harlem Globetrotter. "As in, back at the hotel tonight. Kosher?"

"Seal park," Phil echoed, watching the Warrior saunter away.

"Didn't we do Sea World?" Sonya asked. "I'm game, if you want to go back. Keep the troops happy. Aren't we going home tomorrow?"

Later that night in their room at the Bahia, Phil lay on his back in bed, listening to Sonya snore, watching shadows squirm on the ceiling. When the digital clock on the nightstand changed from 2:01 to 2:02, he slid out of bed, put on his jeans and plaid shirt, slipped out the door, and crossed the parking lot to the seal park outside BJ's Café. The night was warm, but his teeth chattered.

"Stupid," he said. "Stupid, stupid, stupid."

The parking lot was full of gleaming cars, but no people. He crossed the asphalt on scarecrow legs, listening to the sparse traffic coast along Mission Bay Drive. From a distance he could see both sternwheeler boats, the William D. Evans and Bahia

Belle, moored at the hotel pier, and what looked like watery gold dust and a million waterlilies of fire floating on the black bay— the reflection of stars, neon signs, and streetlights. The tempo of his breathing matched the swelling surf, which sounded like the hungry sighs of a slumbering beast.

At the seal park Phil found the Spiritual Warrior in lotus position on a boulder next to Otis. He was resting a benevolent hand on the seal's neck and chanting a dirge in a sibilant falsetto, swaying his shoulders. Incense smoke rose from a coconut half shell on his crossed ankles, and as Phil neared, the Warrior levitated to a standing position and wiped his hands on the back of his cutoffs and flashed the peace sign.

"Mazal tov, goombah," the Warrior said. "Ready to rock?"

"Wh-who are you?" Phil said. "What are—"

The Warrior put his palms out. "Ho!" he said. "Me steer, you ride shotgun. Awright, big dog?"

"Okay," Phil said.

"Good, dandy, peachy." The Warrior held up a reporter's invisible pad and pen. "Sun can fry your brain like an egg. That happenin' to you?"

"Don't know," Phil blurted. His body sagged, and he gulped in spasms. "I—don't know! I don't even know-oh, if you're re-ee-eal! "

"What is real?" the Warrior mused, stroking his stubbly chin. "Can we really call anything real? Are you real?"

"Real sad!" Phil blubbered.

"Is the ocean real? The beach, the stars?"

"Yes," Phil sniffed.

"Is tonight real?" the Warrior said. He turned slowly,

theatrically, like a sales agent gesturing at the features of a luxury home. "The hotel? The sky? Are we really talking out here on this real night on a real planet of real people in real trouble?"

"I, uh—"

The Warrior waved to the seals. "Otis?" he said. "Are you real?"

Otis grunted.

"Am I real?" the Warrior said.

Phil coughed. "How can I—"

"Amigo," the Warrior butted in. "Listen, and I'm serious. I'm as real as your sorrow."

At this Phil sank into a fit of rhythmic weeping that went on for a full minute before weakening to soft hiccups. The Warrior monitored his watchless wrist, eyes half open, bottom lip protruding.

"When you're ready," he said.

Phil raised his tear-smoked face. "Ready?"

The Warrior smacked his forehead with his palm. "For the love of—do I have to spell it out for ya? Dude, 'ready' means ready to talk! Spill mongo guts! Ain't no psychotherapist, but I got ears, dig? C'mon, spud boy, let 'er rip. Alcoholic mom? Dad beat ya? Scope this. Ever since that boneless prom night, it's been a downer—"

"Sonya," Phil ventured.

"Wife troubles," the Warrior said. "Continue."

"She's, she's," Phil said. "She's gonna leave me. I know it! And—what?—I'm powerless! To stop her, you know? And that makes me feel—what?—like I've built up this, this life, and she wants to leave me for it? I'm out for love and understanding, and she says *I'm* not understanding. Says she's doing all these crazy things because of me. And Delia's seeing it all. Who knows how it's affected her! And the baby. That—life—screwed up because of us! But I refuse to be those guys on the talk shows! I won't—"

"Rambling," the Warrior said, picking his teeth. "But this is good stuff. What is it, really, with Sonya?"

"She's so withdrawn. I can't—"

"Sorry for butting in, Cap'n Domestic. Look where you moved her! Jeez, Louise! Anybody'd go stir crazy in that compost pile you call a town."

"It's not that bad."

The Warrior made notes on an invisible pad, flipping pages. "You work too much to notice anything in her life. Not to mention that Shirley Temple redhead you got."

"Better than living in California," Phil said, drumming up gumption.

The Warrior propped a pair of spectacles on his nose and examined his non-existent notes. "Not saying much," he snorted.

"Clean water," Phil rattled. "Clean air, no crime, no drugs—"

The Warrior cooled Phil with a twenty-four karat stare. "Grizzly Adams," he said. "You're just killing yourself more slowly. Take Otis, here."

Phil hugged himself. "Otis?"

At the mention of his name Otis the seal farted and raised his head. He cast a heavy-lidded glance at Phil then with a husky croak plopped his head down. The brass nametag on his collar chimed a fairy-wand note against the rock.

"Behold," the Warrior said. "The evil ravages of contentment. I give him a year. Two, tops."

Phil leaned on the railing and squinted at the seal. "Meaning what?"

"You're just like him, Dr. Weisenheimer."

"The seal?"

"Bingo, Billy Bob. You got it too easy."

"Easy?"

The Warrior jumped up like a Methodist preacher, hand raised in the metal horns sign.

"Aye, aye!" he sang. "He sits there, waiting for the next bucket 'o fish to slam him in the mug! Baby, waitin' your whole life like that—it's dinner bell and death knell. Don't blow brain cells asking for whom the bell tolls, dude. It tolls for you freakin' know who! Otis? He don't swim for chow. He takes it on the rocks and leaves the rest. No starving kids in China on the conscience of this crawdad connoisseur! Check it out, Skippy. Nature's first law is pain and hunger. It's a bunch of bunk to try and change the laws. But we never learn. These activists, these seal advocates? They're spoon-feedin' Otis some killer medicine. We gotta get more laid back with death. Long time back—in the seal crèche, the sunflower patch, the firestarter's cave—the world crouched at death's feet for the sermon of the day. Now? We squander everything—we're obsessed!—stretchin' our lives like Silly Putty. It's spiritual anorexia! We spread ourselves, maestro, way too thin. See any drive to survive in Otis's eyes? Zilch, dude. Bupkiss. He's a zombie. Like you're a zombie. Self-taught and sleepwalkin' to your grave, shmendrik. I'm telling you, look in those seal eyes, and you see your own, dog. You're hanging on the same rack of problems. You're like—what's the best way to put it?—seal brothers. Sealed brothers. Catchin' the same wave to a swan song nobody—hear me? nobody!—will hang around for. Check it out. You built the palace that's your prison. And nobody forced you! These so-called seal saviors raised the sanctuary that made Otis a slave. He was powerless to stop it 'cause he lacked a voice. Way I see it, it's simple. The seal! You, the old lady, your girl, that little *in vivo* babykins? The rub, freakazoid, is to fix the seal. What was hidden, you'll reveal. Every glitch in the universe—tsunamis, fights over parking spaces, every senator turned pedophile—is restored in the paradox of the seal. And you! Selah! Lone soul pilgrim! Astral Achilles! You'll tilt the planet back on keel, when you fix the seal. It'll feel—real! When you fix the seal! No big deal. When you fix the seal! Your soul's big meal! The heart's jig and reel! High on zeal, cut me a peel of what the devil tried to steal and watch hell squeal! When you fix the seal, fix the seal, when you fix the seal—"

The Spiritual Warrior snapped his fingers and jigged in feverish rapture, punctuating each beat of his manifesto with a thwhack on his drum.

"The seal," Phil said.

The Warrior sashayed off with slow snakehips into the darkness, weaving through parked cars. "Amen, dude," he said. "And don't eat veal."

"Seal," Phil whispered to the night.

Then, in that one word, Phil Griffin discovered the answer, standing there, gazing at Otis's roly-poly body. All around the planet, stars bloomed like cosmic roses, and he heard violins and carillons, the creaking bones of icebergs. Kettle drums in canyons rolled as the heavens unzipped and the silent moon rained storms of pure reason.

He smiled at the night sky. "That's it!"

It was a strange sensation—receiving a revelation. The mint-flavored snow of truth baptized his taste buds, and atoms massaged his mind. Wind currents hummed like symphonies, and with each breath he veered out of body and his eyesight telescoped out to behold square-dancing satellites and Ferris wheel galaxies passing through one another undamaged. It was as if God—as a prelude to Phil's birth—had removed a shard of Phil's spirit then snapped it into a soul cavity Phil had never known was there. All the dark notions he had nurtured as 'truth' crackled to cinders in his veins, and steam hissed from his pores, blanketing his skin in a balm of lava-ice. He shivered from sole to crown, and his vision sharpened, summoning landscapes of unbroken beach and pristine tundra to his mind where they assembled like primeval maps. He spread his arms and looked around for someone to tell, but he was alone. It was better that way, he realized, perhaps decreed to be so. His course was clear before him, and it would be best to run it alone, as God's secret agent.

"The seal."

He giggled and clapped as he said it. The answer was, as the Spiritual Warrior said, to fix the seal. If he did—though he didn't understand how—everything else in his life would be made right. He didn't grasp all the connections, but he sensed the essence of the cure, tasted its eucalyptus lozenge on his tongue. Somehow, saving Otis's life would nudge a tectonic keystone into place and the sprung cogs in the cosmos, everything out-of-whack in creation, would rumble into order. And he, Phil Griffin, would act as prime mover of the miracle.

"Well, let's do it!" he said.

With the bounce of a springbok he vaulted over the railing into the seal park and leaped awkwardly to the boulder next to Otis. An intoxicating surge of power, but also a greater infusion of humility and gentleness, flooded his bones. Sensing the animal's apprehension, Phil knelt and stroked Otis's patchy hide. To Phil's surprise Otis didn't feel slimy but smooth, like a dog.

"Hey, boy. Ready to ride?"

At Phil's touch Otis didn't bite, as Phil expected he might, but ejected a snotty sneeze. Through Otis's trunk rolled a low contented rumble, a chugging of blood that made Phil feel as if he were resting his hand on the hood of an idling Volkswagen. The contact shot a prickly charge beneath Phil's skin. His nerves warmed like a network of glowing wires, a million celestial pathways channeling wild brotherhood between man and beast comrade. Then he locked his hands around Otis's porky trunk and, with a groan, hoisted him upward.

"It's what Sonya wanted, buddy," he said, grimacing. "She'd have done it herself. You heard her."

Otis balanced on Phil's shoulder like a sack of meal. Though surprising, and seemingly superhuman, Phil's feat matched stories he had heard about adrenalin-pumped people lifting overturned cars and toppled pine trees to save foster children and pets trapped underneath. With one arm he steadied Otis, and with his free hand, he grabbed the railing and pulled himself out.

"Alley oop!" he huffed. "Hang tight!"

With his mind clearer than the lucid sky, with arms and legs burning spaceship fuel, he jogged his little seal across the parking lot, the tag on Otis's collar tinkling like a sleigh bell. On reaching the car Phil wrapped Otis in an emergency blanket, stowed him in the trunk and drove off. Lily Mendez, the night manager, who had been watching the whole time from the front desk, scribbled the car's plate number and called the police.

Phil drove without a target, trusting he would find it. He exited the Bahia's parking lot and pulled a dangerous U-turn in the intersection between the Belmont Park roller coaster and Roberto's Tacos, then he followed his nose to I-5 and headed north. From an old data chip in his brain, Missing Persons' 'Destination Unknown' played and then fizzled out. Freewheeling up the highway on a monorail of ultraviolet energy, he felt invincible. It was more than strength or power but a heavenly guarantee he'd never felt before, a sureness in his pulse, the belief that time and space had evaporated, replaced by divine instinct. Soon, though, the foamy rash of dawn was soaking the sky over the endless developed hills and apartment buildings and offices, and he was awakened to the reality that he and Otis were speeding to nowhere.

"So?" he asked the air. "Talk to me."

He gripped the steering wheel and listened for a guiding voice, but nothing came. Knuckling tears from his eyes, he swerved around cars and SUVs, around Doritos vans and Red Baron delivery trucks and grimy semi-trucks piloted by sleepy, bearded Southerners in baseball caps. He was scared, but he was convinced he would discover his goal if he pushed forward, if he obeyed the holy tremors in his spine, the star fire telegrams sending shock waves to his senses.

"Seriously. What do I do?"

As if in reply, the answer snapped into his brain. It was so simple he laughed out loud: he would return Otis to the sea. It was possible, he reasoned, as he changed lanes in thickening traffic, that he might be jailed. He might die attempting what heaven had called him to do. But to drink from the pearl-lipped chalice of self-sacrifice, if only once, would be worth the risk. If he was arrested, if he died, if he met public shame—Sonya would remember his last act as one not of capitalistic lust but of selfless altruism, a deed of eternal kindness offered to a creature more helpless than himself. He glanced into his rabid eyes in the rearview mirror. His head was slick with sweat. He pumped his fist.

"Greater love hath no man!" he shouted. "Or seal!"

This alone, he told himself, as he absent-mindedly signaled to leave I-5 at the La Jolla exit, would show Sonya he was more than a patriarchal, money-mongering workaholic. In one stroke, his feat of natural piety would fix the planet's crippled spin and heal his wife's wounds. How simple for love to beget love! How wonderful, in a single morning, to pave his children a legacy that would surpass the last crash of time's irrevocable gong!

The speeding swarm of police cruisers behind him didn't surprise him, the mournful chorus of sirens, the twirling lights and racks of shotguns. On spying the first cruiser, he understood that the police were part of the grand design, another piece in the unfolding puzzle. He expected them to follow him, and so he didn't exceed the speed limit or make desperate moves. By the time he exited the interstate—passing a Schwann's Ice Cream van and a rig hauling two backhoes—five patrol cars had bunched behind him in a flashing blue-and-red wedge.

"Not packin', boys," he said, waving one empty palm then

the other.

A thick-necked blond officer wearing aviator sunglasses pulled alongside to get a visual on the latest wacko to storm San Diego. The officer, seeing Phil wasn't armed, jerked his index finger toward the highway shoulder. Phil smiled and waved but didn't accelerate. The officer gritted his teeth and shook his head and eased his cruiser back into formation. Phil rolled his eyes in mock annoyance.

"No reason to get testy."

He couldn't remember a time when he'd felt more calm. It didn't bother him that cops were tailing him, that he didn't know how he would get close enough to the sea to free Otis. The unknowns pacified him. As he drove, he tried to kick the plug out of his reason. Instead of clinging to what he knew, he surrendered to the benevolent tune of mystical notes guiding his movements. He felt so sure of himself, so confident in the source of his quest, that he believed he could close his eyes and speed through every intersection without injuring as much as an ant on the pavement.

In La Jolla, thanks to a grandmother bulldogging an aluminum walker across a crosswalk and a malfunctioning barrier gate arm, he ditched the cops long enough—yet another sign of providence!—to nip into a parking space between two furniture vans with snoozing drivers. When the police screamed by, he zipped out and buzzed back and forth through the upscale houses, apartments, and businesses. He veered down Torrey Pines Road, up Girard Avenue. He flew past rollerbladers in Spandex shorts and knee pads, women sipping espresso, men yawning at newspapers. He passed an art gallery with a maroon awning, and as he shot by, heads snapped in his direction and a tiny Jack Russell in a teal doggie vest bolted from the gallery doorway after a Siamese cat. All along the car-lined streets, Phil could hear the police hounding him, searching him out, their sirens shredding the peaceful morning with a melancholy wail.

At the end of a T-junction Phil turned left on Coast Boulevard and discovered he had stumbled onto the La Jolla Ecological Preserve, which struck him as serendipitous and prophetic. He drummed his fist on the dashboard.

"Eureka!"

At the sight of the sea he slammed on the brakes, and the car lurched onto the curb. He slapped his thigh with satisfaction and yanked on the parking brake then shouldered open the door and jumped out, leaving the key in the ignition because— as he saw with sudden clarity—his would be a one-way trip.

He circled to the back of the car and popped the trunk, and there was Otis like a big stolen cigar. On seeing Phil, Otis let out a garbled roar. His black eyes rolled and his pink mouth gaped, yellow fangs gleaming, whiskers bristling. Phil tossed aside a tire iron.

"It's all right, boy," he said. "You're going home."

Otis belched a chain-smoker's protest. He moaned and brandished a foreflipper.

"Not gonna hurt you," Phil cooed. He petted the spooked mammal's side. "I know it's scary. Today's our day."

Smooching and oinking soothingly, Phil peeled off the blanket and hefted Otis onto his shoulder. He bounded down the sidewalk with phenomenal spring in his knees, like a marine carrying a wounded buddy. The La Jolla preserve's waxed cars and greenery and potted plants dazzled his eyes. He had never seen so many exotic torch-colored flowers, fulsome green palms, and elaborate fronds, so many high balconies and luxurious cars and upscale open-air restaurants. It was all so new to him—the hues and aromas of the California coast, this supercharged feeling of courage, of righteousness turned into action. The burden he carried didn't stop him from busting out a song.

"Oh, when the seals go marchin' in!"

Down in the cove, snorkelers and scuba divers surfaced, lifted their masks, and blinked. On pale sand, at the foot of a concrete staircase, Tropicana Suntan Lotion was setting up umbrellas and tripods for a photo shoot. Three lanky models lounged in bright white robes and canvas folding chairs. Two models and one of the producers, a gray-haired man in a bleached cap and denim shirt, looked up as Phil chugged past.

In the grassy park area a few street people sprawled on benches and shooed seagulls from burger wrappers and popcorn bags. Joggers and rollerbladers swerved around Phil, headphones pumping Tupac and Mozart. At the retaining wall a student in an SDSU T-shirt was handing out free antacid samples. Phil snatched one from the bewildered student and called "Thanks!" as he hustled by. On an immaculate bed of white vapor, the sun floated over the sea, hazy wings of ruby and gold waiting to take its newest convert—Phil Griffin—to his final home on the morning of his rebirth.

"Whatcha you doing?" somebody called. "Look out!"

The sheer size of the sea staggered Phil. On both sides of the rising sun huge cumulus clouds bulged like mountains of magic over the water, and ships and catamarans lay scattered across the limitless blue. Brown pelicans, gulls, and terns glided through the air without flapping their wings. Angels, Phil thought, hitching Otis's body higher on his shoulder.

Phil ignored the shouts, but the voices turned hostile once he mounted the stone barrier and lugged Otis to the other side. Carefully, he picked his way over the rocks to a point beyond the cove where the sea lapped a bony ledge of mossy, barnacle-crusted stone. Phil moved closer to the waves, and the shouts escalated to riot volume, mixed with police sirens and radio dispatches and screeching tires.

"So beautiful," he panted, staring at the sea. "Why would they keep you from this?"

On the rocky jetty Phil was surrounded by ocean. She had taken him in her bountiful arms, and she was ready to receive his final leap into her womb, back to where Kennedy said Phil and his family would return with the rest of humanity. On this last precipice, he couldn't help feeling a twinge of tragedy. He had rushed through the moment without savoring it, without making a record of his journey. He would have to trust that future generations would appreciate his sacrifice. He felt like a parent who wakes up to find himself in his late sixties with no real memories. The salty wind slashed through his clothing, and he shivered, shifting Otis on his aching shoulder.

"Getting heavy, pal."

Closer to the churning tide, he startled a ten-year old girl in a daisy-patterned bikini and terry wrap. The girl whirled, stared into the faces of the tottering half-man, half-seal mutant, dropped her driftwood collection, and screamed. Otis roared with fright and wrenched his body back and forth. The crowd hurled jeers and protests.

"Freeze!" a cop's voice commanded. "Step away from the girl! Put the seal down!"

Phil turned. All along the reef's barrier, people of all breeds formed a chorus of rage. He reeled at the size of the mob, all ready to ram his head on a pike. He saw bums in tattered Padres caps and trench coats, joggers in shorts, women in bikini tops and towels, retirees in sunglasses and droopy sunhats, children with balloons, Great Danes and Cairn Terriers gnashing Frisbees in their teeth—all threatening him with violent gestures and hateful slurs, as if he were a Christian about to be hacked to pieces in The Colosseum.

"Don't panic, kid," Phil whispered. "We got this."

A dozen squad cars flanked the bloodthirsty crowd, parked at hasty angles, doors flung open, lights twirling like disco balls. A few cops in uniform were vaulting over the barrier and picking their way down the treacherous rocks toward Phil, Otis, and the girl. The cop who had shouted—an African-American officer with dreadlocks and a bodybuilder's chest—stood twenty feet from Phil, straddling a crevice in the slippery rock. He aimed his firearm at Phil.

"Howdy," Phil said. "Be with you in a minute."

Sweat poured from Phil's face. His thighs trembled. The superman steroids had fled his system, and Otis's weight now threatened to shatter his shoulder blades. Phil nodded for the girl to move away. Quaking with terror, the girl crossed the rocks to her mother, a woman in a navy shirt and white pants, who embraced her and wept.

Martyr for an unknown cause, Phil surveyed the scene. He

sucked in all his strength and delivered his manifesto.

"I'm returning this seal to his home!" he declared, unable to hide the shudder in his chest. "Because—he's tired of living a pointless, unnatural existence. And so am I!"

The crowd quieted. The cops stopped their advance. A Channel Eight news reporter's syncopated spiel rose over the crash of the surf and the creaking cry of gulls.

Straining like a deadlifter, Phil set Otis down.

"Swim, boy," he urged.

Gently, he rolled Otis into the water.

"Swim, Otis. You're home! You're free!"

At the moment Phil shoved Otis into the tide a wave sloshed over the stony lip of land and bore the seal aloft on the foam. The undertow drew Otis's sausage body into the deep. The crowd murmured. The television reporter's voice grew louder.

But fear smote Phil's chest, and he staggered to his knees, as he watched Otis, who instead of diving and barrel-rolling like a veteran, started to sink like a sodden loveseat. The little seal flailed and flapped and bawled a strangled plea for help. Everyone, including Phil, gaped at the impossible: Otis was drowning.

"You're killin' the seal!" the dreadlock cop shouted, holstering his gun. "He ain't used to it!"

Out of the crowd a search and rescue crew deployed over the wall, armed with life preservers and coils of fluorescent rope. Unable to be restrained, the rabble surged over the wall and streamed down behind the rescue workers and policeman in a human rockslide of hate.

"Otis!" Phil screamed, hands to his head. "Swim, boy! You gotta—don't do this to me, Otis!"

Without thinking Phil whipped off his jeans and shoes and hove his body into the sea. Instantly, his scrotum jumped into a square knot and all his delusions about the Pacific being a dreamy tropical Jacuzzi were replaced with the truth: the sea was a frigid killing machine. He floundered and spluttered and fought to remain afloat.

"Otis!" he called. "Here!"

On shore, Armageddon had reached its apex. The rocks resounded with news dispatches, shouts through bullhorns, and calls for unnatural acts of cruelty to be performed on Phil's children. Closing his ears to the clamor Phil thrashed through the malicious undertow to reach Otis. With his last stroke he hooked his fingers through the seal's collar. At Phil's touch Otis gave an apprehensive bark. Phil could read the seal's name stamped in ornate letters on the brass nametag.

"C'mon, boy," he coughed, gulping salt water. "For me, Otis. I don't have anything left."

Otis blinked and snorted like a motorcycle kick start.

"Try, boy," Phil coaxed. "Work those flippers. I'm going—"

What happened next drew conflicting reports. To Phil, what occurred in the miracle of the mad tides was hard to believe but as real as the saline bite of death. At Phil's first pronouncement of faith, Otis wiggled his fore and hind flippers. The little seal struggled valiantly to keep his head above water, and Phil, with his fingers snagged in Otis's collar, paddled his free arm and legs. Fighting to live, they spouted water and blasted air from their mouths as if clearing blowholes. Like a synchronized swimming duo of Siamese twins, they windmilled into the waves, flapping and thrashing and paddling away from the squash racquets and

Styrofoam takeaway boxes of Eggs Benedict lobbed by the barbaric mobs, until they were safely bobbing through strong swells, propelled by the sum of their pure wills.

At the point they disappeared from the crowd's view Phil was transformed. Just as his strength failed and he dipped beneath the surface, Otis, from regions unknown, summoned a jolt of youthful fuel, and the years of pampering slipped from his sleek trunk, changing him from waterlogged pimento loaf to ballistic missile. He heaved his body forward, his rear flippers rotoring like outboard props. Sensing the awakening, Phil gripped Otis's collar.

"There it is!" he whooped. "Otis, baby!"

Spurred on by Phil's praise, Otis torpedoed ahead, seal and man powering forward like tiger shark and remora. They dipped and dove, lighter than sunlight on spray. It felt impossible, but Phil didn't question the seal's strength. They merely swam and dipped and motored through the waves. To where, Phil didn't know. Home, heaven, death—it didn't matter. With the slap of salt water in his face Phil felt like Poseidon on a hydroplaning catamaran of dolphins bound for the far shore of paradise.

Phil marveled at his ability to hold his breath. Like mermaid sisters on a wild weekend he and Otis cycled at incredible depths below the surface. They chased snapper and tuna, spiraled through schools of silvertail and sunfish, and as they strove on, Phil grew tireless instead of weak. He siphoned energy from the raw embrace of the ocean, the immense blue goddess he hailed as the bringer of life and fortune. He glimpsed a trail of iridescent mirages—Sonya, Delia, and his unborn child—backstroking after him like a trio of puffins. Toward the end of their swim,

Phil gave up trying to paddle and relaxed his free arm against his side. He clapped his feet together and undulated his body like a muscular fluke. He couldn't tell where or how long they swam, only that he and his seal co-captain coursed through a living watercolor of beautiful hallucinations, whale sharks, loggerhead sea turtle convoys, and sea palaces of coral.

Only when he felt the gritty suck of wet sand beneath his fingertips did Phil realize he had never worried about drowning. Too soon, he found himself sprawled on sandy earth, wishing his journey hadn't ended, wondering if it had happened at all. He awoke face down in a tide pool, his nose and mouth snuffling the hearty stink of fish bones and kelp. Crabs and sandpipers tickled his arms.

"God," he breathed. "Let me stay here forever."

Gradually he became aware of a solar glare pulsing on the other side of his eyelids. Despite the pink light's throbbing warmth, he felt reluctant to open his eyes. In the attitude of a delivered Jonah, he rose to his knees and raised his face and arms to the sounds of this coastal afterworld. His soaked plaid shirt and boxer shorts cloaked him in a chilly second skin. The blind posture he struck gave him the look of a zealot waiting to catch a basket of life-giving blossoms from a friendly deity. He listened for the voice of God. A seagull gave a laughing cry.

Smiling, Phil opened his eyes.

He was kneeling on an empty beach, a long narrow arc of rocky sand and flattened beds of pitted pinkish-gray stone. The blue Accord idled on a street that crested a modest bluff, some fifty yards above, alongside a gravelly park with a barbecue pit, blue-lidded garbage cans, molded concrete benches, and dense shrubs with red flowers. The car's passenger side door hung open, inviting him to nirvana. Upscale bungalows and vacation homes, some with mission-style orange clay roof tiles, topped the bluffs overlooking the beach. Shaggy-headed palm trees reached toward the pure sky, their elegant trunks rising like ropes from the baskets of snake charmers.

The Spiritual Warrior towered over Phil, a whiskery grin on his face. The Warrior's palm was extended, offering Phil something—a shard of starfish candy, a pearl capsule. Phil followed the line of the Warrior's gesture and saw that he was pointing to a motley lump of leisure clothes in the sand: sandals, a wacky golf shirt, and discount-rack Bermuda shorts. Phil's heart throbbed when he saw his benefactor beaming before him, welcoming him to the summer of his transcendence.

Phil threw his hands skyward.

"The kid's reborn!" he cried. "Boom, baby!"

The Warrior frowned. "What have you done?"

Phil pointed across his body to the sea. "The seal! He's better! He's home!"

"You broke the law, dude."

Phil swiped sand from his lower lip. "What law?"

"You stole," the Warrior said. He flicked his tambourin with his middle finger—*pong*—as if killing a bug. "You kidnapped Otis. Endangered innocent lives."

"Hey, hey, hey," Phil broke in. He rose to his feet. "I fixed the seal. Like you said."

"If anything," the Warrior said, "you broke the seal, shattered it."

"Shattered? What—"

"You kidnapped Otis."

Phil shaded his eyes and searched the waves. "I saved his seal butt. He swims! He frolics in the ocean! He's chowin' Lobster Thermidor right now!"

The Warrior shook his head.

"Phildo," he intoned, fingertips together in pagoda shape. "The seal keeps the universe together, twirls dudes and dames in the eternal tango. Binds sea to shore, keeps the stars huggin' the sky, Mama Yin kissin' Papa Yang. True, it's gone by other names, over the centuries. But nomenclature isn't primo right now in your situation, compadre. Busting the law, kidnapping Otis, that means you broke the seal, the glue between Magna Mater and King Kronos. If you, if anyone, does anything to disrupt the seal, we're—we'll, it's bad, man. That's all I'm saying."

"Bad?" Phil rasped.

The Warrior held his thumb up like a German counting. "God's gift," he said, "is the power to act, not to be acted on. People, animals—we have to account for our choices, hermano. Otherwise, the planets throw an axle. When you seal-napped Otis, you screwed with the choices of the people who put him there, and Otis's choice to cave to their intervention B.S. It's all about consequankies, kapellmeister. Coulda told you if you'd waited. But you went and twanked the universe's flow of events. Basically, you're in cosmic doo-doo, dude. Not to mention a wanted man."

Phil clawed his sunburned skull. "The hell you talking about!"

"The seal, like I said, is—"

"Can the mumbo jumbo, ya beach freak!" Phil shouted. "I

thought you were my friend, my kindred fairy guardian—"

"Just a guy doin' the right thing," the Warrior said. "Unlike you. Seal klepto on a So-Cal Bonny and Clyde."

"You *told* me to help Otis, to return him—"

"I told you to fix the seal," the Warrior said, glancing toward the sound of police sirens. "You misunderstood."

Phil advanced. "You won't misunderstand if I snap your spine."

"That'd heal the karma of the universe," the Warrior said. "Better yet, be an oil executive. Asphyxiate a few albatrosses. You'll be pleased to know, Chico, in our case the student has most definitely not become the master."

"Who are you?" Phil asked. "What's with the smudge on your forehead? Hare Krishna? Tantric?"

"Something on my face?" the Warrior said. He probed a forefinger on his forehead.

"There," Phil said. "Between the eyes."

"Mustard," the Warrior said. He licked his finger and removed the yellow dot. "Had a corn dog. Musta scratched myself. Left a smudge."

Phil stared, listening to the sirens.

"Anyhoo," the Warrior said, wiping his palms on his butt. "You got potential, so I brought your car back. Saved you a few bucks and a law suit there. Change of clothes, too, so they won't recognize you. If you hustle your Idaho keister, you could make your flight. Oh, almost forgot. Catch!"

With the fluid sidearm motion of a seasoned Frisbee slinger, the Warrior tossed something to Phil. The white plastic rectangle spun through the air. Phil's hand shot out, and the Ekco kitchen timer landed in his hand with a clack and a bleep.

Phil stared at his timer with dumb pathos, as if cradling an injured pelican chick.

"Been clinging to it for a while," the Warrior said. "Why break precedent?"

Without waiting for further madness, Phil stripped and changed into the clothes the Warrior had brought. He scrambled up a whitewashed switchback staircase to his rental car and dumped his soggy underwear and shirt in a garbage can. The golf shirt and Bermuda shorts felt stiff on his body, as if starched in sea water. Before jumping in the car, Phil danced a jig to shake sand from his hair. Seatbelted behind the wheel, he dropped the timer in his shirt pocket.

Directionless at first, Phil followed his internal compass—and a few road signs—down La Jolla Bouelvard to Mission Boulevard, through the long stretch of stuccoed villas and strip malls and putty-colored office blocks and surf shacks. Swarmed on all sides by buzzing traffic, he retrieved his cell phone from the glove compartment, called Sonya, and asked her to get ready to leave. At the Bahia she met him in the parking lot below the stairs to their suite. Her bags were packed, her face locked in a scowl. Delia, primped and poised in purple, waved at him.

"You're acting weird," she said. "Where've you been?"

"Needed some 'me' time," he answered, swallowing panic. "Last look at the sea."

She vetted his kooky beachcomber's getup.

"In the car," she ordered.

"Yes, ma'am."

"I dare you to make us miss our flight."

At the Bahia's reservation counter, Lily Mendez framed her buoyant breasts in her arms and propped her upper half on the counter. She smiled at Officer David Powell, leaned toward him, and showcased her right dimple.

Officer Powell removed his mirrored sunglasses and rested an elbow on the counter. He grinned but felt self-conscious because of his red hair, freckles, and hammy schoolboy's face. There was something—he didn't know what—in the eyes of the girl at the counter, something untamed and adventurous, something soft and brown and mammalian that he could fall for in an instant.

Lily, noting the misty look in his eyes, laughed and tossed her hair, smacked her cinnamon gum. Officer Powell echoed her laughter to break the tension. He flashed an energetic grin and drove his leather gloves into the palm of his hand.

"So this guy," he said, bouncing on his toes. "He's no trouble?"

Lily wagged her curly mane. "Some loony," she said. She toyed with the zipper pendant on the neck of her uniform. "He's taken cars."

Officer Powell widened his eyes. "Grand theft auto?"

"Joyrides," Lily said, crinkling her eyes. "He brings them back. He likes the seals. Especially the little one. My friend, DeeDee, in La Jolla? He shows up and hangs around her clothing flea market. She takes the pricey stuff inside and puts old things out for him."

III

THE MAN FROM NEW YORK sits in a walnut rocking chair. He wears a filmy silk scarf the color of honeydew melon, pink marabou negligee, and licorice vinyl heels. He is entering his sixth hour of *I Love Lucy* and *My Three Sons* re-runs on the TV Land Channel. His beefsteak face, creased from age and hard labor, stares at the screen, his eyes as changeless as a week of cloud cover.

He sits in the living room he framed with his own hands. The mantelpiece is made of sculpted oak, and the fireplace and chimney are solid brick. A cast-iron chandelier hangs from the low, old-world beam ceiling. Pictures of his sons and daughter and grandchildren adorn the paneled walls, together with insignia patches and hats from his navy days. A black and white photo from his time as a Boston College defensive end sits on a shelf above the television. Hillocks of dirty laundry litter the floor around the rocker, as do rolls of stamps and perforated stubs from unpaid bills. Near his feet sit two unwashed cereal bowls, each with a sugar-encrusted spoon.

He rocks and stares like a sailor waiting for a trawler to plow into port. Then, goaded by a neural twitch, he points the remote at the television and changes the channel to CNN. The story that's running is about a sunburned tourist who abducted a seal in California. The man from New York watches the screen, which shows a man from Idaho being headlocked and grappled to the ground by police in the Salt Lake airport. Police restrain the tackled man's pregnant wife and redheaded daughter, who weep at the sight of the cuffed man.

The man from New York stops rocking.

He squints at the screen. As he looks on, the story cuts to a jumble of amateur footage that shows the man from Idaho lugging a puny seal across a parking lot, then more shots of the man forcing the seal to swim in the ocean while squads of police descend and incensed crowds lob cinderblock chunks and rollerblades. The CNN reporter, a black man in a green plaid shirt and strawberry tie, says the hotel that owned the seal dropped the charges since the seal was returned unharmed. Luckily, the reporter adds, it was a California Marine Mammal Stranding Network volunteer on twenty-four hour watch who found the exhausted animal on the shore near La Jolla Hermosa Park. The camera cuts to a shot of a knobby towhead named Norman 'Vybe' Huka. Huka's black pink-paneled wetsuit is unzipped to his navel. His sunburned face is freckled and peeling, and his chapped lips are cracked and bleeding. With a hand he sweeps a fringe of braided rope-like bangs from his eyes and aims his finger at the sea.

"He was on his flippers," Huka says. "Barking. Like a trainer was tossing him a fish. But nobody was there."

"Salt Lake authorities who made the arrest," the CNN reporter concludes, "were informed of the hotel's decision and let the man go."

The man from New York blinks at the television. The news story has something to do with him, he feels, but his mind bumbles through boundless fog. He holds two visions in his mind—a bowl of Cheerios and sliced bananas, and the absurd picture of a sunburned man trying to teach a seal to swim. The longer he thinks about the man and the seal, the more topsy-turvy the world seems, as if his rocking chair rests on the ceiling. Then with the force of complete awakening, he feels a massive clearing of soul, an inner wave that rushes his chest, and an audible pop in the back of his skull. He looks around, eyes lucid and hungry, searching. He sits up, shocked to find himself in the living room he's been meaning to spackle and shellac since Tuesday.

He clicks off the television and wonders about what he's been watching and why he's been watching it at all with the lawn unfertilized, the bird feeder in disrepair, and the garden in need of tilling and composting. Like a mental patient reviving in a lab of horrors, he surveys the laundry, the bills, the cereal bowls and—as if besieged by alien spiders—rises and tears the negligee from his body. He puts his weight on a stiletto heel and sprains his ankle.

"Sue Anne!" he bellows, limping in an angry circle. Like a cross-dressing drill sergeant, he storms half-naked into the kitchen. "What the hell we doin' inside on a day like this? Why'm I in this fairy-ass underwear of yours? How come the bills aren't paid?"

The man from Idaho drives from Salt Lake City to St. Anthony in silence, past opaque reservoirs and wrinkled brown farmland, past sturdy peaks and plateaus of dark green scrub brush, past the steaming dairy plants and ugly little trailers crowded around rust-dappled Volkswagen vans and Camaro chassis. Sober black cattle with white faces stand in sloping corrals of dark earth, and badgerweed dusts the sagebrush-covered hills like pollen. The woman from New York and the redheaded girl sleep, slumped against the windows. Past Tremonton, the man considers calling Rita Cosworth, MSW, for a little chat, but he shakes off the notion as extreme.

At home he puts his daughter to bed and stays up past midnight. He stares, half-smiling, at the woman from New York, who blinks and returns his stare, her gaze drifting from warily focused to thoughtfully distant. At the kitchen table they sit and tilt from side to side, trying to see each other over the 'Welcome Back!' centerpiece bowl of pineapples and papayas wrapped in crackly pink cellophane that the local girl scout troop left on their doorstep. The man opens his mouth. His brow bunches, and he sits back, unable to look her in the eye. He taps his finger like a blunt drill on the table top.

"How," he says, "do you get so obsessed with time you never take any?"

"Profound," she says. "For somebody so cute and crazy."

"Let's drop the 'crazy.'"

Her face creases into a sob. She pronounces her daughter's name and rubs her growing belly. The man moves to her, hands out to steady her shoulders. She brings the heel of her hand to her forehead and whimpers.

"Forgive me?" she says.

"For?"

"Well," she says, wiping tears from her face and examining her glistening fingertips. "Not trusting my instincts for one."

He lowers his chin until it rests on her head. "So, for being human?"

The next day, with the woman and girl on a homecoming walk through the streets of St. Anthony, the man from Idaho succumbs to a surge of civic goodwill and strolls off to welcome the new family that has moved into the trailer park at the end of Main Street. Outside the last trailer on the lot—a battered avocado single-wide with mangled TV antennae, rickety unstained porch, sunflower windmills, and lawn flamingoes—the man rounds an open Ryder truck and rusty gold El Camino packed with laundry, televisions, and open bags of chili lime pork rinds. Behind the Ryder truck the man discovers Rabeena and Donny. They are gabbing with several young Hispanic men and women decked out in neck chains and basketball jerseys and red bandannas. On seeing the man approach, Donny turns and smiles. He jerks his thumb at St. Anthony's newest crew and announces that they've escaped the hell of L. A. and hired on the day shift at the Sun-Glo potato plant.

"Mr. Griffin!" Donny says, grinning like a weasel. "You ever want some stuff—you know, these guys?—they get it for you! Fast!"

On the way back the man halts near a screen of riverside reeds. From his pocket he produces an Ecko kitchen timer. He juggles it a few times thoughtfully in his hand then like a man skipping a rock slings it toward the water. The timer whizzes through the air, tilting to one side, and clips a stone, exploding across the swift current like the pieces of an impossible puzzle.

At the bottom of the driveway to his home the man collects the mail. He enters his house, whistling a sea chanty. In the kitchen he slits open two envelopes: a water boil advisory from the city council and a bulletin outlining the recent property tax increase in Fremont County.

He reads the news—and smiles.

More books from
Harvard Square Editions

People and Peppers, Kelvin Christopher James

Gates of Eden, Charles Degelman

Love's Affliction, Fidelis Mkparu

Transoceanic Lights, S. Li

Close, Erika Raskin

Anomie, Jeff Lockwood

Living Treasures, Yang Huang

Leaving Kent State, Sabrina Fedel

Dark Lady of Hollywood, Diane Haithman

How Fast Can You Run, Harriet Levin Millan

A Cat Came Back, Simone Martel

Nature's Confession, J.L. Morin

No Worse Sin, Kyla Bennett

Stained, Abda Khan

Dear Reader, we would love to hear your thoughts
on our books. If you enjoyed this book,
please leave a review!